FITZGERALD

CHET POWELL

Cover Photo: The elaborate four-story, 150-room, Lee-Grant Hotel in Fitzgerald, was the largest wooden structure in Georgia at the turn of the twentieth century. It was named for Generals Robert E. Lee and Ulysses S. Grant, the leaders of the Confederate and Union armies, respectively, during the Civil War. This photo, courtesy of Georgia Archives, Vanishing Georgia Collection, was taken after its completion in 1898.

Rear cover photo of Chet Powell by Stephanie McDaniel.

DEDICATION

For my mother, Georgia Powell, on her birthday.

CONTENTS

Acknowledgments   i

1   A Wakeup Call   1

2   Of Chickens and Men   23

3   Shacktown   45

4   The Blue and The Gray Area   57

5   A Midnight Rendezvous   80

6   Robert Francis Carroll   99

7   Where's Lenny   120

8   Isabella Ruth Jackson   136

9   Family Reunion   156

10   Looking for Laura Lenu   172

11   The Death of John Tucker   189

12   Evergreen Cemetery   205

13   Planes: Real and Imagined   218

14   Chasing Jeff   236

15   The Return of Billy Bob McCoy   256

16   Carroll in Wonderland   275

17   The Missing Man   300

18   Carroll in Wonderland, Part 2   313

19   Epilogue   343

ACKNOWLEDGMENTS

Completing Fitzgerald, my first novel, would not have been possible without the assistance of Lennis Johnson Powell, whom I coaxed, cajoled and finally hoodwinked out of retirement to act as my editor.

1

A Wakeup Call

Robert Carroll opened his eyes at precisely 5:00 a.m. just as he did every morning. There was no alarm clock or wake-up call. He simply woke up. It had not always been this way. The conversion from being forced awake by an alarm clock to not requiring one had begun nearly three decades earlier, when he was still a beat cop with the Indianapolis Police Department.

It was not something he had intended, this preprogrammed ability to arise at the same time day after day. It had evolved out of repetition and had occurred so naturally that he could not even say when he became aware of the change. It was now just the initial first step of his daily routine: step one, wake up. Step two, actually getting up, was a bit harder. And of course, he naturally proceeded from there: Step three, go to the bathroom, and so on and so forth. It is the same process billions of people around the world go through every morning, sans alarm clocks.

Step four for Carroll required making the long trek to the kitchen. The aroma wafting down the hall coaxed him forward with the promise of a reward at the end of his journey: There will be coffee.

He reached over his recliner and picked up the remote, pressing *TV*, as he passed through the den. The wall-mounted LED flat screen was as reluctant to wake up as he had been. It finally yawned and slowly opened its giant single eye. He selected *Favorites* from the menu, then *WTHR* the local NBC affiliate, from the list of channels.

He entered the kitchen and retrieved his coffee cup from the rack in the sink, placing it and the TV remote on the counter. WTHR Eyewitness News Sunrise, anchor, Bruce Kopp's familiar voice was still going over the latest news headlines as Carroll removed the pot from the commercial Bunn coffee maker and poured his first cup of coffee.

"In our top story," Kopp continued, "an Indianapolis police officer is in critical condition after being dragged by a robbery suspect's vehicle. One suspect is dead, and another suspect is in custody."

Carroll quickly replaced the pot in the coffeemaker, grabbed his cup and the remote and hurried back into the den. News video showed police vehicles, lights flashing, parked in front of a Get It 'N Go package store as uniformed officers and detectives, several of whom Carroll knew personally, could be seen outside as well as through the windows of the store.

Bruce Kopp continued to report over the footage;

"At 11:33 p.m. last night, police officers responded to a silent alarm, indicating a possible armed robbery in progress at the Get It N' Go package store on Massachusetts Avenue. Two suspects exited the store as officers arrived and attempted to flee in a van. One officer was struck by the van and dragged nearly 100 feet. Two other police officers fired their weapons, striking the driver, causing him to lose control of the vehicle."

The news video switched to show a gray Ford van that had crashed into a utility pole, surrounded by crime scene tape, as Kopp concluded, "The van crashed into a utility pole a block away from the store. The second suspect was not injured and surrendered to police. Indy PD has not released the name of the deceased suspect or the officer, who remains in critical condition. We'll be following this story and will provide updates on the condition of the officer. In other news, the EPD has released a report after..."

It was doubtful that Carroll knew the injured patrolman, but that didn't lessen his concern over the officer's condition. After all, they were all part of the same family. He tossed the remote onto the recliner as he returned to his bathroom, sipping his coffee along the way. He had robotically completed several more steps of his morning routine when he realized he had been standing at the sink in front of the mirror, staring at himself. He was face-to-face and less than two feet away – from a stranger.

He studied the face, his face. The eyes were cold, devoid of emotion. It would have been better to have seen anger in them, or fear, or anything that would indicate that the person standing before him had the capacity to feel. Carroll could always figure out how to deal with someone after determining his emotional state. The man in the mirror had been acting more like a robot than a person. How does one reason with a robot?

The hot water caused a mist to fill the room. The silence was suddenly broken by a loud liquid, *plop*! He glanced down to where the sound originated. There, in the sink, amid the half-filled bowl of water, was a dark dot. There was another plop as a second dot fell upon the first. They merged together, then dissolved, turning the water red. When Carroll looked back up he realized he had a cut on his right cheek. A thin trail of blood ran down to his chin where it was gathering, sagging lower, preparing for another drop.

He could not help but follow its progress as the blood drop gained mass and stretched longer, until the weight ripped it from his chin and sent it plunging into the water below.

Carroll put down his razor and, using the edge of his hand like a windshield wiper, gave the mirror a couple of swipes, an effort done as much to wipe away his own image as well as the moisture. He leaned forward and inspected the cut on his cheek. It was still seeping blood. He picked up the washcloth and wiped the remaining shaving cream from his face. He tore a tiny piece of toilet paper from the roll on the wall, touched the paper to his tongue and applied it to the cut on his cheek. It stuck there, like a tiny white tick, growing fatter as it fed on his blood.

Recently, he had increasingly become aware that he was no longer the person whom his colleagues once described as coolheaded under pressure and fun to be around. He had known it for some time but had brushed it aside. It was time to acknowledge it as fact. The solution was simple: Robert Carroll needed a break. But he was a hardcore workaholic, adept at making excuses for the manifested symptoms of his disease: the constant fatigue, his short attention span, and his even shorter temper.

He did not agree with those who say that most people are usually unaware that they have addictions. Whether it is to alcohol, drugs, or whatever, they know it, and he knew it, too. But knowing that you have a problem and doing something about it is not as easy as one might think.

People usually have to get to a certain low point, he knew whether it is by experiencing some traumatic event or by someone pushing them and forcing them to the realization, before they will admit to their specific problem. Fortunately, Carroll had arrived at that place on his own without either happening. Or, at least that's how he saw it.

The truth was that everyone – his family, his friends and, most of all, his secretary, Suzi, had been telling him the same thing for months:

"You need a break, Bob!"

Well, maybe not necessarily a break, he thought, as he buttoned up his shirt, more like a change in the routine. After all, he had been doing the same thing, following the exact same schedule, almost every day, including weekends, for nearly five months. It was an investigation involving corporate theft and, from a business perspective, the case was a gold mine. He would make more money on this one case than with everything that he had done over the last year combined.

Besides the tedious daily schedule, the other problem he had with the case was that it was not exactly his most challenging. In fact, it was the opposite. It was easy, too easy – even demeaning to a certain degree, for an experienced investigator, especially one of his caliber.

How easy had it been? Well, for starters, he had had the name of his main suspect within the first five minutes of meeting with his new client, Linder Technologies. He even had gotten a good idea of how the theft was taking place. It probably had helped that the good folks at Linder had furnished him with most of this information.

It really was not unusual for a company to name a suspect in a theft case. Most of them had systems in place to track inventory, so they obviously had an idea as to when and where the theft took place. And Linder's system was even more advanced. It tracked their products during every phase, from development through production, quality control, storage and, of course, shipping.

As their name implies, Linder Technologies is in the computer business. They manufacture satellite tracking technology. So, when they discovered what appeared to be corporate espionage, something that could break their company, they reacted immediately and began a search for a capable and reputable private investigator. That road led straight to Robert Carroll. When he was initially considering taking the case his secretary, Suzi, had asked him what was being stolen.

"Their LDC-26," Carroll answered.

"Their *what*?"

"It's like a microchip or something," he explained.

When Suzi kept staring at him blankly, he added, "Okay, you know how when you're using your GPS on your phone and the little car or arrow moves down the correct street or highway as you do?"

She nodded.

"Well, it has something to do with that."

"Oh! Wow!" she replied, dramatically over-acting with false excitement. Then, in typical Suzi fashion, she had placed the tip of her forefinger against her cheek and in a loud, obnoxious, operatic voice, she sang, "Borrrring!"

Her response was part of an ongoing joke the two of them shared.

Suzi had been with him since he started his business as a private investigator, three years earlier. Actually, they had worked together even before that. She was the secretary for Carroll and another detective when he was still a detective with the Indianapolis Police Department. The fact that Suzi was able to handle all of the work from the two investigators proved just how good she was at her job, something that she never let them forget. It was also something she still regularly reminded Carroll of when she thought he got too cocky. Suzi's retirement had happened to coincide with Carroll's. The question of who his office manager should be was a no-brainer for him, and she had immediately accepted his offer when he started Carroll Investigative Services.

She was an integral part of his operation and deserved much of the credit for the fact that CIS was so successful from the start, and Robert Carroll rewarded her well for it — both in salary and with frequent bonuses from bigger cases.

Their ongoing joke had to do with their proclivity for old TV variety shows. Both were particularly nostalgic for programs like The Carol Burnett Show, The Sonny & Cher Comedy Hour, Rowan & Martin's Laugh-In and The Smothers Brothers Comedy Hour. It was not unusual for Carroll and Suzi to converse or respond to each other as a character from one of those shows if there were no guests or clients in the office. Suzi's imitation of Laugh-In regular, Jo Anne Worley's, "Boring!" had turned out to be terribly prophetic with the Linder case taking the better part of five monotonous months to complete. It was Carroll's job to provide absolute proof, not only of the theft, but enough evidence for an airtight case that would result in a conviction in court. Monotonous had turned into excruciating over that time. With the investigative work now having been completed, he would be spending the next two weeks working closely with the district attorney's office to prepare the case and turn over the evidence.

Carroll always enjoyed this part of the process, even the long boring investigations. It meant the case was over for the most part. It also gave him the opportunity to work with many of the same prosecutors from his former job. After all, he was still basically doing the same thing, with two big differences: He chose the cases that he wanted to work on now instead of having to take whatever was assigned to him, and he got paid a hell of a lot better as private investigator.

As he opened the door to his closet, Carroll realized there was yet another advantage to being a private investigator: He could dress however he wished. Although he had not worn the navy blue uniform of an Indy police officer as a detective, Carroll's detective attire had been a uniform of sorts. Most of the other male detectives dressed similarly: A white or light blue dress shirt, a tie, khakis and a jacket — usually navy. He remembered thinking he should have bought stock in Levi's because so many of the detectives sported Dockers.

A two-tiered rotatable necktie hanger was mounted on the backside of the closet door, centered near the top. The only time he wore a tie nowadays was when he had to appear in court and when he had to meet prospective clients, as he would do later today. He scanned over the ties as he tucked in the forest green shirt that he had selected the night before. He picked out two that matched the shirt and returned to the bathroom to make the final selection. Standing in front of the same mirror where he had had his earlier revelation, he alternately held each tie up in front of him.

It was a meaningless procedure as he already knew which one went better with the shirt and jacket. It was something done out of habit, just part of his routine. There was that word again – routine. Carroll hated the word. Routine was a cop's worst enemy. He could cite two dozen examples of officers who were either killed or seriously wounded because they got careless and let their guard down. *We thought it was just another routine call* was a phrase Carroll had heard all too often.

He continued to study his reflection; however, he did so with a more retrospective eye on this second go-around. Before him stood a middle-aged white male. Other than being a bit taller than most men of his age, everything else about him was typical, right down to the receding hairline and slight potbelly. Where he had seen a stranger less than an hour before, Carroll now saw something worse. He had become something he had hoped never to be. He was *average*.

And, as if being average was not bad enough, he was also the classic stereotype of a retired cop: Carroll was twice divorced. His only friends were cops and all of them were still at Indy PD, which left him as a bit of a loner out here in the world. Carroll had never been a heavy drinker; however, he seemed to be spending more and more of his evenings lately on bar stools rather than on his couch at home. And there was one more thing: What was the most typical stereotype of all for an old ex-cop? He was a private investigator, a PI. Carroll looked up to see that he was frowning. Actually, it was more of a scowl. That's it, he thought. It all changes today, starting right now!

He exited the bathroom and tossed the ties in the general direction of the bed as he headed for the bedroom door. Neither reached the intended goal; both ties landed on the floor. Carroll hesitated and even took a step forward to pick them up, but his mind was set. He wheeled around and headed for the kitchen, uncharacteristically leaving them on the floor.

Back in the kitchen, he rinsed out his cup and placed it in the sink. Carroll pulled the pot from coffee maker and emptied it into his larger travel mug. He patted his shirt pocket, checking for his glasses, and then his front left pants pocket, for his cell phone, before walking through the utility room to the garage door.

The three-car garage was a quarter the size of the house. Carroll had purchased the property six years before. He was still married at the time. He and his wife had carefully planned the house together. In retrospect, he thought it was a last-ditch effort to save their troubled marriage. If they had been younger they might have considered having another child, but that was not an option. So, they had built a home instead.

It actually had been kind of exciting. They had found a perfect spot: Waterfront property on west side of the Morse Reservoir in Noblesville, a small community just 23 miles northeast of downtown Indianapolis. They had selected an architect and designed the 3,800 square-foot home together. Then came the frightening part. They had searched for a reputable contractor who would build their new dream home. Friends and family related personal horror stories of their own dealings with contractors.

Carroll recalled seeing the comedian, Gallagher, perform once in Indy. A one-liner from the melon-basher came to mind; "Where do contractors go when their jobs are half-done?" Carroll had been a nervous wreck during the construction. He had kept waiting for the inevitable, but the entire process went smoothly from planning to completion, and their home was finished three weeks ahead of schedule.

Their baby had arrived, but it did not help. Their relationship had continued to deteriorate over the previous year, and they had separated the month before it was finished. Carroll's ex took a job in Chicago. She never set foot in the completed home. The subsequent divorce went even faster and smoother than building the house. Carroll still was not sure if that was a good or a bad thing.

Even though there was no logical reason for it, from the time he had received the keys to the house, Carroll always parked his Land Rover in the third space, the one farthest from the kitchen door. They had agreed it was to be his spot. His wife would have parked in the first, closest to the house. The middle was to have been for visitors, like when the children or other family or friends came and stayed over. The mostly empty garage amplified the sound of his footsteps, echoing them as if he were in a huge, underground cavern. It sounded even more lonely. He climbed in and started the vehicle, then touched the button to open the garage door. The sun had just peaked above the tree line as he backed out and left his home on Oak Cove Lane.

Carroll's house was only six miles from downtown Noblesville, but he had to drive southeast long the reservoir and then across it before going through his little town and starting the longer trek to Indianapolis. He turned left onto Oakbay Drive, then took another left onto Carrigan Road. He instinctively donned his sunglasses and flipped the sun visor down as he approached the long curve that would take him due east across the bridge, directly into the rising sun. "East-bankers" loved to boast about their sunsets, but Carroll was more of a morning person. Not that he did not appreciate and enjoy a beautiful sunset. He did. In fact, he would sometimes drive across the bridge just to watch one. However, Carroll equated sunsets with endings: The end of the day, or even, the end of life.

Besides end, the only other words he associated with sunset were night and dark, both depressing as far as he was concerned. However, a sunrise brought a plethora of words to mind; the dawn of a new day. A new beginning. A sunrise is hope. As if to emphasize his point, the morning light suddenly burst through his windshield as he came out of the curve and onto the bridge. It reflected brilliantly, like millions of diamonds, off of the water. He raised his left hand, both to shield his eyes and to readjust the visor. Fortunately, the eastern portion of his morning commute was brief. He turned right onto Hague Road, which put him southbound with the sun on his left. He swiveled the visor again.

The Carrolls had chosen Noblesville as the location to build their new home for three reasons, the most obvious two being the beautiful waterfront property and close proximity to Indy. The third was the community itself. They loved it – she, for its authenticity and quaintness, with its boutiques, eateries and antique shops, and he, for the town's historical aspects. A confirmed history buff, Carroll had discovered that many of those boutiques, eateries and antique shops that his wife loved so much were housed in structures dating from the 19th century. Although Noblesville was incorporated in 1851, it had actually begun in 1802 when a trapper and scout named, William Conner, established what most believe was the first permanent trading post in Indiana on the east bank of the White River. Others arrived, settling around him, and by 1823, he had laid out what would become downtown Noblesville. The city limits eventually stretched across the river as the town grew, but the heart of Noblesville remains on the east bank where the trading post had been located.

Coming into town on Logan Street, Carroll could see the Hamilton County Governmental and Judicial Center on the east bank of the White River even before he crossed the bridge. The JC, as the cops and attorneys call it, is a massive modern structure, occupying an entire city block. It houses the superior courtrooms as well as other county offices.

Following the same route he took every day, Carroll turned right on 8th Street, which took him between the JC and his two favorite buildings in town; the Old Hamilton County Sheriff's Residence and Jail, and the Hamilton County Courthouse, on his left. Carroll liked the contrast between the modern JC and the two historic buildings. The Sheriff's Residence and Jail and Hamilton County Courthouse were both built during the period when French architecture was sweeping the globe, the former being completed in 1876 and the latter, four years later. Both were constructed primarily of red brick with lots of white trim and topped with the four-sided mansard roofs. Both structures sport bell towers, but the one on the courthouse is two stories high and is adorned with a massive four-faced clock.

Carroll continued through town on Conner Street and made his usual stop at the Hardees drive-thru before departing for Indianapolis.

So, now here he was, southbound on I-69, amid rush hour traffic, headed to his office in downtown Indianapolis on Tuesday morning after the long President's Day weekend, and despite the traffic and unseasonably colder weather that had blown in overnight, Robert Carroll felt better than he had in months. He had only one appointment scheduled for the entire day. It was to meet with an elderly couple who were trying to locate their missing grandson. Surprisingly, he found that he was seriously considering canceling the appointment. Or, after further thought, it might be better to go through with the meeting and then politely turn them down with a plausible excuse and take a vacation instead.

A vacation.

Just the fact that he was even considering the idea was a huge step forward for him. He tried to remember when he had last taken an actual vacation. The trip to San Francisco in 2007? No, that was actually to attend a conference, although he had managed to get out to Alcatraz while he was there. There had been no way that he would have left San Francisco without a visit to the infamous prison that had been featured in so many stories and movies.

What about Dallas in 2005? Nope. After thinking about it, he remembered that wasn't really a vacation either. It was a trip to locate a potential witness in a homicide case; however, he did spend an afternoon at Dealey Plaza, the location where John F. Kennedy was shot on November 22, 1963. Carroll was only five years old when that happened. It was one of his earliest memories. He had been in the living room playing with his toy soldiers on the floor while his mother was sitting on the couch, folding clothes as she watched one of her soaps on television. A special news report interrupted the program.

He remembered how his mother had gasped, that she had dropped the clothes basket, how his father had come running into the house shortly after, and how, from that moment on, for the rest of the week, his family sat in their living room, glued to the ongoing news coverage surrounding the murder of the president. It had been the same for millions of other families across America. The entire country had watched as events unfolded over the next several days. They were watching when the announcement was made officially confirming the president's death. They were watching when a little skinny man, identified as Lee Harvey Oswald, was brought into the Dallas police station.

They were watching when the president's body was unloaded from the plane after it arrived back in Washington.

They were watching when Jack Ruby shot Oswald. They were watching when President John F. Kennedy's flag-draped casket was placed on a caisson and as the procession made its way down Pennsylvania Avenue for the president's final trip from the White House to the Capitol. Even today, half a century later, Robert Carroll can still close his eyes and clearly hear the sounds: The military drum corps' cadence beat out on 24 drums, their bright hand-painted national arms and emblems covered by black crepe, which muffled the sound, the combined clacking of the hooves of the six grey horses pulling the caisson and, at least for Carroll, the even sadder clippity-clops of Black Jack, the solitary black riderless horse, that followed it.

In 2005, being in the actual place where the assassination occurred was surreal, partly because at least in Carroll's opinion, serious mistakes were made during the investigation. Although he never agreed with any of the numerous conspiracy theories that had popped up over the decades, he did believe that the botched handling of the case was the major reason why so many people had doubts about Oswald being the lone gunman and why many still believe that other conspirators were involved.

As far as Carroll was concerned, any case with still unanswered questions meant that it wasn't closed. With so many questions still out there swirling around the Kennedy assassination, his visit to Dealey Plaza was like being at the scene of a still unsolved crime. As crazy as it sounded, Carroll really believed that one of the reasons that he was so successful as an investigator, both in law enforcement and as a PI, was because he saw how those unanswered questions about the Kennedy assassination still affected him and so many other Americans half a century later. Granted, his cases were not comparable to one involving the murder of a president, but he treated them as if they were. From those involving petty thefts to major heists, or from simple assaults to homicides, Carroll was meticulous about all of his cases. He had already established a reputation as an effective investigator during his law enforcement career, and that reputation had continued to grow with every case that he solved as a PI. There was always a line of prospective clients waiting.

He suddenly slapped his hand to his forehead.

"2004!" he said out loud.

That was it. It was the summer of 2004. That was his last real vacation. He had rented a big house right on the beach on Saint George Island in Florida. That really was a fantastic trip! The whole family was there. They had spent the entire week. And not just his wife and kids, his in-laws had driven up from a retirement community near Ocala, and his son had brought his family, including Carroll's two granddaughters.

They had swum and surfed, fished from the pier, hunted for seashells and sand dollars and seen wild dolphins swimming just offshore. Carroll finished reading the book that he had brought with him and was even able to start and finish another.

Then, on their last night there, they walked up on a sea turtle laying eggs during a midnight walk on the beach. Not just any old sea turtle. It was a leatherback, the largest turtle species on earth. It was like seeing a live dinosaur.

"The damn thing was half the size of a Volkswagen!" Carroll would say when relating he experience to others. He had equated it with seeing a living dinosaur.

He remembered thinking they would make the family beach trip an annual thing. He had decided that they would have to rent a larger house next year because he wanted to invite more of the family. Then, life happened. He got divorced again. His son got a big promotion, which meant that he was transferred even farther away. And of course there was also Carroll's own work. He was always working. But, something different was happening today. He usually felt anxious at the end of a case and remained so until he started another, but he didn't feel that way at all today. Instead of anxious, he felt unburdened.

He had reached a turning point. If there had been such a thing as Workaholics Anonymous he would have gone to a meeting, stood up and loudly proclaimed; "Hi, I'm Bob and I'm a workaholic."

"Hi, Bob," they would have responded.

He would have been assigned a sponsor, someone to call when he felt the overwhelming urge to work when he needed rest.

"Don't do it Bob," they would say. "You're strong! Pick up a book instead!"

The stories from other WA members would have helped to encourage him to stay the course;

"I had Colts tickets last Saturday," said another member, "but something just kept bugging me about work and I finally realized what it was. I had misfiled a folder alphabetically by the first name instead of the last name. So I lied to my friends and said that my grandmother died and I ended up driving back to the office. And after I fixed the mistake I was afraid there might be more, so I rechecked all of the files. I was there all night! I'm so ashamed!"

He caught a glimpse of himself in the rearview mirror as he changed lanes. The guy now looking back at him was smiling. This was not the same man than he had seen in his bathroom mirror a couple of hours ago. This was the Robert Carroll that people knew and respected.

Not wanting to take a chance on accidentally hearing any depressing news to ruin his good mood, he reached over and double-tapped the 3 on the console, which instantly changed the radio station from 93.1, *Indy's News Center*, to 99.5, WZPL, *Indy's Hit Music Station*.

The choice to bypass his normal classic oldies station was deliberate. Just as he did not want to hear any depressing news, he did not want to take a chance on hearing an old song that reminded him of a breakup or brought back an old memory about something he regretted, that he obviously could never go back and correct. No chance of that now. He wasn't sure if they still used the term, but Carroll called 99.5 a pop station.

He glanced over at the display on the console which showed the title of the song that was playing. It streamed from right to left;

---*Can't* ---*Feel* ---*My* ---*Face.*

Carroll chuckled. He would have to try and hear that whole song later. A catchy tune with a nice beat followed it. He looked at the display again;

--- *Fight Song* ---*Rachel Platten.*

Never heard of her, he thought, but then again, he doubted that he would know any of the other artists either. Still, he liked what he was hearing so far,

This is my fight song. Take back my life song!

He was definitely on to something new this morning. He bumped up the volume three levels.

I'll play my fight song – and I don't really care if nobody else believes – cause I've still got a lot of fight left in me!

An incoming cell phone call interrupted his personal pep rally. Feeling irritated, he frowned as he checked the display. It was Suzi calling from the office. He pressed the button to answer the call, which automatically muted the radio.

"Morn'n Suzi," he said.

"A gracious good morning. Have I reached the party to whom I am speaking?" came a constricted high-pitched nasally voice on the other end.

Carroll's frown immediately reverted to a smile. How could he be irritated when Suzi was doing her version of Lily Tomlin's *Ernestine*, the operator from the telephone company? Suzi was obviously still on her Laugh-In binge.

He played along;

"I'm sorry. I thought you were my secretary."

Still in character, Suzi continued;

"Here at the Phone Company we handle 84 billion calls a year, serving everyone from presidents and kings to the scum of the earth."

There was a loud snort over the phone before she continued;

"We realize that ever so often you can't get an operator, or for no apparent reason your phone goes out of order, or perhaps you're charged for a call you didn't make – *We don't care!*"

Suzi was in rare form this morning. Her Ernestine was spot on and she wasn't finished;

"You see, our system consists of a multibillion dollar matrix of space-age technology that is so sophisticated, even we can't handle it. But that's your problem, isn't it? Next time you complain about your phone service, why don't you try using two Dixie cups with a string! We don't care! We don't have to. *We're the Phone Company!*"

He was about to respond when he heard a click. Suzi had hung up. He was still laughing when the phone rang again. He answered without looking at the console;

"Morn'n Suzi."

"What the hell boss?" responded his secretary, "I've been trying to call you for ten minutes!"

"Yeah, sorry. The damn phone company called again."

"Oh! I hate it when that happens! They are so annoying!" she said convincingly.

"Tell me about it!"

"Anyway, your eleven o'clock is here."

Carroll checked the clock, "But, it's not even nine yet."

All business now, Suzi replied, "I know. They said they left early because of rush hour traffic."

Carroll wasn't ready for work yet. He still wanted to cut up, "Jeez, when did they leave their house, yesterday?"

He thought that would have at least produced a little chuckle from her, but Suzi's tone became even more serious.

"Listen, I don't know how I screwed this up, but this is not a missing person case."

She paused for a second, as if she wasn't sure how to continue. Carroll heard her take a breath, before she gave him the worst of it;

"Their grandson was murdered, in December. And boss, it's still unsolved."

At first, Robert Carroll wasn't sure if he had heard his secretary correctly. Suzi never made mistakes, but this was a big one. Missing person cases were a big part of what had helped to build his business, but they required a lot of hard work. That is why he was already considering turning this one down. Unsolved homicides were obviously a whole new ballgame. They could break you, both physically and mentally. This was a real game-changer.

13

In Carroll's mind, it would be like someone informing you that you have got to run another marathon while you are still lying on the ground, puking your guts up after you have barely managed to crawl across the finish line of the marathon you just completed instead of going from a stressful case to a vacation.

"You there, boss?" Suzi inquired.

Even over the phone he could tell that she felt terrible. Suzi was punishing herself enough. He would not add to it.

"Yeah yeah, sorry. Look, don't worry about it. I'm almost there."

"Okay," replied Suzi. "Coffee's hot."

"Sounds good. Thanks."

Carroll pushed the button to end the call. The radio automatically came back on, but he reached over and turned it off completely. Suzi's news had automatically sent him back into work mode. He tried to recall the facts behind this scheduled meeting. He remembered that it was an elderly couple, but he had been too wrapped up in the final details of the Linder case to pay attention to information from a case that he hadn't even taken on yet.

He checked the traffic flow as he approached Indy and decided to take an alternate route into the city. One advantage to having been a cop was that he had learned his way around the streets and alleys of the city. Taking local streets, he made his way through Oakhill, Reagan Park and emerged at Old Northside, just above his office.

The city's downtown district had undergone a massive overhaul, sparking a revival in the mid-1990s, including the construction of the large Circle Centre Mall. Indy received another huge upgrade in preparation for Super Bowl XLVI in 2012 with numerous improvements to infrastructure and landscaping projects. The combined efforts had been quite effective. Downtown Indianapolis had been transformed. It was now an ideal spot for visitors to find a little bit of everything.

He continued down Pennsylvania Street and turned left onto East Wabash. There was a small parking lot about halfway down the block. He pulled into the empty space marked, CIS Employee Parking Only. Carroll reached over and picked up his cell phone and newspaper from the passenger seat. He grabbed the door handle with his left hand, but he hesitated before leaving the vehicle. He was trying to prepare himself for the short walk from the Rover to the back door of the building that housed his office.

Carroll had watched the local weather report at home while drinking his first cup of coffee as he did every morning. A cold front had swept through overnight. The wind chill was well below zero and still dropping.

Having entered his Rover in the garage at home, he hadn't yet faced the bitter cold. This would be it.

One would think he would be accustomed to Indiana's winter conditions after having lived there for most of his adult life, but he was not. Carroll had been born in Virginia, but his family had moved to Indianapolis over the summer between his freshman and sophomore year in high school. He had never adapted to the cold weather. Carroll loved his city dearly, but he hated the Indy winters.

He hesitated with his hand on the door handle as he surveyed Talbott Street. They called it a street. It might have been one once, but Talbott today was more of an alley, so narrow that it was designated for one-way traffic only. Carroll had long before arrived at the conclusion that the Talbott street had been constructed as part of an elaborate conspiracy.

He had revealed this information to Suzi over coffee one morning.

"It's a perfect wind tunnel," he explained, "designed and constructed for one sole purpose, to torture me."

"First, *you don't build an alley*," Suzi had reasoned.

"I know you don't normally build an alley," he retorted, "That's the brilliant part of their plan! It's what they *want* you to think!"

He continued to explain;

"The truth is that their main objective was to create a giant wind tunnel. The buildings are inconsequential, a byproduct of the wind tunnel design."

"Which brings me to my second point," Suzi interjected, "You do realize that most of these buildings were constructed before you were even born right?"

"So it's a long-term conspiracy," he said, without missing a beat.

Like their running gags about old TV shows, the wind tunnel conspiracy thing was just another way of having fun and keeping things light. They had milked the topic for weeks.

When he finally got up enough courage, Carroll took a deep breath and exited the Rover. He cautiously looked around. At first he was pleasantly surprised. While it was definitely colder, it wasn't nearly as bad as he had feared. The morning sun was peeking over the buildings into the alley and the clear blue sky and bright sunlight appeared more like spring, not winter. He pressed the button on his key and listened for the familiar chirp-chirp indicating the alarm was activated as he started toward the door to his office.

He heard it first, the sound that he was all too familiar with, like the whistling noise from a horror movie. Then, he saw it, coming straight toward him, in the form of a tidal wave of flying newspapers, napkins, paper cups and other debris.

Carroll reached up and tugged his collar tight, turned his body sideways to brace himself and tilted his head forward just as it hit him. He might as well have been tossed into the White River.

He tried to yell, "Holy shi...," but the icy wind tore the words from his lips and froze them in midair, where they met an instantaneous icy death. He leaned forward and made his way toward the door, knowing that he looked like someone doing a bad impression of a mime in the wind.

Suzi was waiting, cup of coffee in hand, as he entered the hallway.

"A bit nippy this morning?" she teased.

"Quick, call 911," he said. "I'm pretty sure I've been stabbed."

She shook her head as she handed him a file;

"Toughen up, cowboy!"

Carroll weighed the file in his hand. It seemed unusually thin. He opened it to find it contained only one item, the CIS Client Information Form which Suzi always compiled prior to the initial interview of prospective new clients. She normally included everything she could find about the case— police reports, statements, newspaper accounts and any other relevant material, but there was nothing else.

"That's it?" he asked.

Suzi nodded, "Yep, and sorry about the..."

"Don't worry about it," he interrupted, waiving it off, "I'll take it out of your Linder bonus."

"The hell you will!" she popped back.

Suzi did feel badly about the missing person goof, but her mistakes were so rare that she could not even think of another one. She was not being arrogant, just honest. Her boss had told her, twice now, not to worry about it and she was taking him literally. She was already moving on.

"You want me to tell you about the times that I covered your ass and fixed your screw-ups?"

"No thank you," Carroll replied with a grin, as he walked into the conference room.

He walked over to the wall and flipped a switch. There was a low hum as a projection screen retracted toward the ceiling, revealing a large two-way mirror between the conference room and lobby. He sipped his coffee as he stood, watching the elderly couple waiting there.

Thomas and Mary McDowell did their best to calm their nerves as they sat, waiting. They should have been used to it by now. Their grandson had been killed more than two months ago and the police still had no suspects. Just last week they had decided to hire a private investigator. They had been searching to find the right one and had narrowed it down to three choices, one of which was Carroll Investigative Services.

Not knowing that Carroll was among their final three choices, a family member who is a police officer, suggested Robert Carroll. That was the deciding factor. They had immediately called his office and booked an appointment with Suzi.

The McDowells obviously had no idea that it was just lucky timing on their part that Carroll was finishing up the tedious Linder case. They were also lucky in another respect, that Suzi had made her rare mistake of labeling it as a missing person case. Carroll would have immediately referred them to someone else if he had known it was an unsolved homicide. But they were here now and he decided to go ahead with the meeting, although he still intended to refer them to someone else.

Carroll watched the couple through the mirror as they occupied their time by doing the things that people normally do when they're in waiting rooms. Mrs. McDowell fumbled through the contents of her purse, rearranging items into zippered compartments and removing trash, consisting of chewing gum foil, cough drop wrappers, lipstick kissed napkins, overused nail files and bits of paper.

Her husband was flipping through the magazines as if he were trying to find something interesting to read, but Carroll could see that he was even more fidgety than his wife. While she could at least appear to remain calm and occupied, Mr. McDowell's nerves were shot. He was leafing through the magazines so fast that he couldn't have possibly even seen the covers. He might as well have been shuffling cards.

Carroll watched them intently for several minutes. Having completed the pre-spring cleaning of her pocketbook, Mrs. McDowell now held a Ladies Home Journal. Her blank stare indicated that she was not really reading the article. Or, perhaps she was reading it, but her mind was so preoccupied and full of other thoughts that it simply could not process anymore.

Carroll flipped the switch to lower the screen and then touched another one on the opposite wall turning on the lights before leaving the conference room. He entered the lobby and greeted his prospective clients.

"Good morning Mr. and Mrs. McDowell. I'm Robert Carroll." They both stood as he entered.

"Good morning Mr. Carroll," said Mrs. McDowell.

He shook their hands. First, with Mr. McDowell, who had a surprisingly firm handshake for his age, and then his wife's.

"Looks like Suzi has taken care of you. Would you like more coffee, or perhaps something else?"

"No, we're fine, Thank you very much," Mrs. McDowell responded. Her husband simply shook his head.

"Why don't we step into the conference room?" Carroll suggested, as he opened and held the hall door.

He ushered the McDowells through the first door on the right, into the same room from where he had observed them moments before. The McDowells took the two chairs near the end, closest to the door. Instead of sitting opposite from them and completely across the table, Carroll pulled one of the chairs over and sat, catty-cornered, closer to them. It was just another thing that he had learned how to do over the years to make potential clients feel more comfortable, like it was not so formal.

"We're sorry for being so early," Mrs. McDowell apologized, "but as I told your secretary, we didn't want to take a chance on being late because of traffic."

"It's not a problem at all," Carroll responded. "In fact, it will probably help me get started on schedule today. Although, I doubt that will actually last very long," he added with a smile.

"Yes, I'm sure you're very busy," she replied. "We checked around and were told that you were the man that could help us."

"I'm curious, how did you find me? Did you just Google private investigators?"

She chuckled, "I'm not much good on computers. It was my nephew, my sister's son, Fred Thomas, who told me about you. He's on the police department. Do you know him?"

"I do," he nodded. "Freddie is a great example of why they say, Indy's Finest."

Carroll was not just being cordial; he honestly meant it. He maintained his smile, but he felt a bit queasy. He was in serious trouble. Carroll still planned to weasel out of the case, but he was already feeling sympathetic toward the elderly couple. It had begun as he watched them in the lobby. Now, finding that they had been referred by a fellow officer put him in a tight spot. Freddie Thomas was not just any officer. He was an old-school beat cop, the kind of policeman who knew everything about everyone on his beat, the kind of cop who was even respected by the gangs. Freddie had helped Carroll out when he was still a detective at Indy PD and had even assisted him several times since. Freddie was also part of a group that Carroll still got together with socially on occasion. He suddenly found himself wishing that Workaholics Anonymous was real.

"I understand that this is about your grandson. Can you tell me a little bit about him?" Carroll inquired.

"We're very proud of him," Mrs. McDowell said with a beaming smile, "He overcame a lot to get to where he is today... or, where he was, when..."

She wiped away tears as her composure broke for the first time.

It was only then that her husband spoke for the first time.

"You see Mr. Carroll, his parents, our son and daughter-in-law, were killed in a traffic accident when Thomas was eight years old. We've had him ever since."

"I'm sorry to hear that," Carroll responded.

He had wondered why the grandparents and not the parents of a man murdered in his youth were the ones looking into the matter.

"I lost my father in accident, too," he told them. "I was 18 when it happened."

"Well then, you have an idea of what Thomas was going through, but imagine if it had been both of your parents and, instead of twenty years old, you were only eight."

Carroll acknowledged with a nod.

Thomas McDowell continued, "That was 17 years ago," shaking his head in disbelief. He added, "Sometimes it feels like it was 17 minutes ago."

"I thought losing my son and daughter-in-law was bad, but at least that was an accident," added Mrs. McDowell.

She looked straight into Robert Carroll's eyes as she continued, "But, to know that he was murdered? That someone intentionally took his life? Why, that's just too much Mr. Carroll!"

Carroll could only nod again.

"We did the best we could. Thomas never got into any trouble and he was a straight-A student," she added.

Carroll shifted forward in his seat and addressed Mr. McDowell. "I understand that going over the details is not a pleasant, but I have to know as much about your grandson and the case as possible. You've said, Thomas, so he's named after you?"

"Me and his daddy. I'm senior. He was the third." The elder Thomas suddenly hung his head, realizing what he had said.

Carroll had seen that reaction before. It was the same thing that had upset his Mrs. McDowell earlier. It was those little things that can break you after suddenly losing a loved one. Like using the word, was, instead of, is. It is an unconscious acknowledgement that you're moving ahead without them.

It was now Mrs. McDowell's turn to take over while her husband composed himself.

"We brought as much information as we have," she said. "The police department sent us a report."

She handed Robert Carroll an envelope.

"There's really not much information there, but there is also an article from the newspaper."

Carroll scanned the first page.

"I'm not familiar with Fitzgerald," he admitted with a wrinkled brow. "What part of the state is that in?" he asked.

"It's in Ben Hill County," replied Thomas McDowell.

Carroll scratched his head.

"Are you sure?" he asked. "I've worked all over the state. I've been to all 92 counties at one time or another and there is no Ben Hill County."

Mr. McDowell leaned over the table and pointed to the form;

"It's right there on the paperwork Mr. Carroll."

Carroll looked at the Incident Report, the standard form that any police department would have filed when it initially opened a case. He checked the date and time, but he stopped abruptly when he saw the location. He checked it again.

"This happened in *Georgia?*"

The McDowells both nodded.

"Yes sir, Fitzgerald, in Ben Hill County, Georgia," Mr. McDowell confirmed.

Carroll was stunned. He read through the incident report for a few minutes, before he continued, "I'm sorry Mr. and Mrs. McDowell, but I can't take this case. I'm not licensed as a private investigator in Georgia."

The elderly couple did not respond. They turned and looked at each other. Mr. McDowell hung his head again. It was a look of total rejection, but his wife was not giving up.

"Please Mr. Carroll! Can't you just go down there and see what you can find out?" she asked. "Do you have to have a license for that?"

"It's not that simple," he began to explain. "If this were a missing persons case or something like that I could probably get away with it, but this is a —"

Carroll caught himself. It was bad enough that he was turning them down. There was no reason to add to their grief by using a word like homicide or murder.

"— much more complicated case," he concluded. "And besides that, there is a time factor involved here. I just finished a very big corporate case and I'll be working with the district attorney's office for the next two or three weeks."

Carroll was attempting to extricate himself as gracefully as possible. He was telling the McDowells the truth when he added;

"And after that I'll be testifying in yet another trial. It would be next month before I could even consider going to Georgia. They'll probably have the case solved by then anyway."

He felt like he had successfully made his point. While he truly sympathized with the elderly couple, he just didn't see how he could work it out. Mrs. McDowell stood up from her chair, walked around her husband's, and took Robert Carroll's right hand in both of hers as she got down on her knees in front of him.

"Please Mr. Carroll. Help us," she begged. "We don't know what else to do."

"Mrs. McDowell, please get up."

He was the one who was pleading now. He knew that he had about five seconds before he would have to start wiping his own tears. He helped her back to her seat and then returned to his own. He reread the police report, the coroner's death certificate and skimmed through the newspaper article. He looked back over at the McDowells. Thomas had not moved and was still sitting with his head bowed. He had given up. Carroll looked over to see that Mary McDowell was looking him straight in the eye. It was more than he could take.

"I'll tell you what," he said, caving in. "Why don't you leave the file with me? Let me look at it and if there hasn't been any progress by the time I've finished with the DA on the Linder case and the trial, then I'll consider taking it further."

Thomas McDowell raised his head and looked at Carroll. He wanted to be sure that he had heard him correctly. It was the first time that someone had given them something positive to hope for since their grandson's death.

His wife smiled, "Bless you Mr. Carroll!"

"You understand, I'm not making any promises," he cautioned, "I'm just going to do some research."

Both nodded, but their faces were beaming. He asked them several more questions about their grandson. They did not know why he went to Georgia. In fact, they did not even know that he was there until he called them the day before his death. According to the elder McDowells, there was no indication that their grandson was having a problem. He reportedly acted completely normal and told them that he was working on a project.

"What kind of project?" Carroll asked.

"We don't know," she shrugged, "He was always doing research on one thing or another."

After asking every question he could think of, he reiterated that he was not obligating himself to the case. Still smiling, the McDowells agreed, fully accepting his condition. He escorted them to the door where they thanked him again before departing.

Carroll reentered the hallway and headed for Suzi's office. Their normal procedure during the interviews of potential new clients was for him to meet with the prospects in the conference room while Suzi watched and listened in on a monitor. They would then confer and compare notes.

Suzi looked up as he entered the room. Her eyes were red.

"I am so sorry!" she sputtered. "I don't know what to say. First, I screwed up with the missing person thing, and then, *Georgia*? How the hell did I miss that?"

Carroll waived his hand dismissively;

"I told you twice already, don't worry about it. They'll probably have it solved by the time that I'm through preparing the Linder case with the DA anyway."

Suzi nodded, "Is there anything I should do in the meantime?"

"Yeah, you can start by contacting Jerry Hall in Atlanta. Tell him about the McDowells coming to see us and find out if they have any leads at all."

"And if there aren't any by the time that you finish with the DA on the Linder case and the court after?" she asked.

"Well – then it looks like I'll be going to Georgia."

2

Of Chickens and Men

Robert Carroll was off on his time estimate of working with the DA on the Linder Technologies case. It took three weeks, not two, before they were satisfied with the results. He spent the following week and a half sitting alone in a small room, sequestered, waiting to testify in another, older, case.

As he had promised the McDowells, he had made some inquiries into their grandson's murder investigation during that time. Even though he was not licensed in Georgia, Carroll had established a number of law enforcement contacts there when he had been a detective with the Indianapolis Police Department. Most of those contacts were in Atlanta.

Besides being a major city, Atlanta had two interstate highways running directly through downtown. I-75, stretching from Canada to South Florida, is the one of the longest and busiest interstates in the entire country. I-20 runs east and west, originating in Florence, South Carolina, on the Atlantic coast, where it connects to I-95, and terminates at Kent, Texas, where it merges with I-10. Considering the fact that Hartsfield-Jackson Atlanta International Airport is the world's busiest, and it is easy to see why Atlanta is described as the transportation center of the southeastern United States.

What does any of this have to do with his law enforcement contacts? Well, it means that tens of thousands of people come through Atlanta, Georgia every single day. Unfortunately, some of them are criminals who either choose to stay or get stuck there for one reason or another. Carroll had tracked at least two dozen suspects from Indianapolis to Atlanta over the years. A quarter of those were murder suspects.

In fact, his very last homicide case with Indianapolis PD had led him to the capital of the Peach State. It had taken nearly a month of investigation and surveillance, working together with Atlanta PD and the Georgia Bureau of Investigation, but they finally ended up getting their guy, William Poole. Subsequently convicted of murdering three people, he will spend the rest of his life behind bars.

One of Carroll's oldest friends was a guy by the name of, Jerry Hall. Jerry was an ex-Indy cop turned FBI agent. Like Carroll, Jerry was old-school LE. They always enjoyed working together and it paid off. They developed a chemistry. Some of the biggest cases that either of them had were when they worked as partners. The FBI had bounced Jerry across America, from city to city after he joined the Bureau, before he finally settled in the Atlanta office.

When the FBI later indicted Joseph "Little Joey" Serico, they tried unsuccessfully to turn him as a CW, a cooperative witness, which is what the bureau calls informants. They worked on Serico for months, offering deals, but Joey wouldn't budge. It was Jerry who had suggested that they should fly Carroll down to Atlanta from Indianapolis to talk to Little Joey. Hall knew Serico was from Indy and that Carroll had known him for more than 20 years. He also knew that his friend was one of the few cops that Serico respected and, more importantly, trusted.

Carroll and Serico had first met when he was just a street punk, a gangster wannabe, and Carroll was still a uniformed beat cop. Carroll had tried to steer young Joey in the right direction, but everybody said he was wasting his time; Little Joey was too far gone. Even though he knew it was probably true, Carroll never gave up. He always tried to help Joey whenever he could. By the time he was in his early twenties, Little Joey had his fingers into all kinds of illegal activity: Gambling, extortion and money laundering, to name a few. Joey would steal in a heartbeat, but he had never even been accused of doing anything violent.

So, when Robert got a call from Jerry Hall asking him to come to Atlanta, he did not even have to think about it. And because of Carroll's subsequent involvement, Little Joey Serico turned and became the government's star witness. When word got out that Serico had flipped, it started a chain reaction. Other key players and codefendants in the criminal conspiracy who had been offered deals began accepting them, but most had waited too long and the offers were rescinded. Or, if they did take a deal, it wasn't as good for them as the original offer. Joey Serico was the only one who got lucky. And it was all because of Robert Carroll — something that Serico would never forget.

There was only one other place in Georgia where Carroll had good law enforcement contacts. Brunswick is a relatively small town in Glynn County on Georgia's Atlantic coast. It is located halfway between Savannah and Jacksonville, Florida. After the United States entered World War II in 1941, military training sites sprang up all across America. The coastal location was perfect for the Navy and Glynco Naval Air Station was established there. When the base closed in the early 1970s, the part with the runways and hangers evolved into the Brunswick Golden Isles Airport.

The rest of the base would eventually become one of the most elite law enforcement training facilities in the world. Today, Glynco is the headquarters of the U.S. Department of Homeland Security's four Federal Law Enforcement Training Centers. Besides serving more than 90 federal agencies, Glynco also trains local and state law enforcement officers from all over the country.

Carroll had been to Brunswick several times for a wide range of training courses, including Forensic Techniques in Crime Scene Investigations, Covert Electronic Surveillance, Advanced Interviewing for Law Enforcement Investigators and Protective Service Operations, among others. There was another bonus. Glynco is only a few miles from Jekyll Island and St. Simons Island, so free time could be spent at the beaches. Carroll had learned to watch out for course announcements so he could quickly grab the primo courses at the best times. The spring and summer were obviously the best times to go, but it was also a great way to escape the harsh Indiana winters for a week or two.

One of Carroll's favorite trips to Glynco came after he was assigned to a statewide task force in Indiana. He was told that because much of Indiana was rural and "since you're a city boy," they would be sending him to the Federal Law Enforcement Training Center's All Terrain Vehicle Training Program. The result was several days of riding four-wheelers and spending the rest of his time at the beach.

"It's a tough life, but somebody has to do it," he taunted Suzi from his cell phone.

Carroll didn't know any of the GBI agents or other police investigators in the Fitzgerald area so he made inquiries through his Atlanta friends. They reported that nothing had changed in the McDowell case. There were no leads. Carroll expected the McDowells to take the news badly; however, they remained composed as he informed them of his findings and they were thrilled when he told them that he planned to fly down to Georgia the following week. He reminded them that he was not licensed there and he was simply going down to take a look around.

"You understand, I'm not making any promises," Carroll reminded them. "And I'm not charging you for this. If –" he stressed the word twice, "If I come up with anything, then we'll talk about expense reimbursement."

Thomas and Mary McDowell were at a loss for words. The fact that he was willing to go at all was already enough for them. They had skimped and saved money and were even preparing to get a second mortgage on their home to furnish Carroll with funds to cover his expenses, but that would not be necessary now, at least not for the moment.

Carroll watched the flickering lights of Indianapolis fade away as the Delta MD-80 banked around and headed south. From his experience on previous flights to Atlanta, he knew it would take slightly more than 90 minutes to get there. During those trips, Carroll had discovered that, with one exception, likely due to inclement weather or a change in wind direction, incoming flights to Atlanta's Hartsfield-Jackson International Airport always arrived from the east.

The flights from Indianapolis came into Georgia on a southeastern direction toward Savannah and then banked around to the right. The final approach to Hartsfield involved crossing low over Interstates 75 and 85 to the runways on the west side. This usually afforded a great view of Atlanta's skyline. He had mentioned it to Suzi once during a conversation, describing the view in detail, especially how the sunlight had reflected off of the gold dome of Georgia's State Capitol.

Carroll was overly sentimental about things like that. There was something about seeing America from high up above that appealed to him deeply. Whether it was a small town or a major city, farm fields or a mountain range, the Atlantic or Pacific Ocean, he appreciated that he was enjoying a view that many people never got to see. Suzi jokingly called him "hokey." However, even after making that little remark, she proved to be just as "hokey" as he was, because, for every Atlanta-bound flight since, she had always booked him in a window seat on the right side of the aircraft.

With a successful business, Carroll was also lucky enough that he could afford first class seats if he wanted but, unless he had pressing work to do, he would say something to Suzi like, "Put me in the can with the other sardines." He would usually read or just enjoy the view during the flight. To his surprise, he also found that more often than not, he enjoyed meeting whoever happened to seated next to him.

Carroll had met many interesting people that way. For instance, during his first year in business he had begun chatting with the man seated next to him on a return flight back home. They had started on current news events and had eventually moved on to other topics. After talking for the better part of an hour, the other passenger, a guy by the name of Brenton, mentioned that he was flying to Indianapolis on business. Their company had just merged with another and some questionable practices had been occurring. Brenton's job was to look into the situation and, if necessary, to locate and hire a private investigator.

By the time that they landed Carroll felt sure that he would be considered if Brenton had to hire a PI. Because he already had his Rover at the airport, Carroll offered to give him a ride to his hotel. After all, it was more convenient and cheaper than hailing a cab. Brenton quickly accepted.

They were about halfway to the hotel when Brenton asked, "So, where is your office in relation to the hotel?"

Knowing that his reservation was at the Omni Severin and assuming that Brenton didn't want him to go out of the way, Carroll assured him, "It's not a problem at all. I'm just a few blocks from you."

"No, I was just thinking, why don't we just go straight to your office and sign a contract?" Brenton suggested. "That is, if you've got the time. From what I already know, I'm sure we're going to need to hire someone and it seems that you and I already have the preliminary stuff out of the way."

"Sounds good," Carroll agreed.

That chance meeting resulted in an efficient and thorough investigation for his new client, Sindt, Inc. And, because Sindt was just getting established in the Indianapolis area and would periodically need more of this type work, Brenton had called Carroll a couple of weeks later to arrange a long-term contract, naming CIS as their official investigative provider, not just in Indianapolis, but for the entire state of Indiana. Later, after learning that Carroll was also licensed as a private investigator in the neighboring states of Ohio and Illinois, Brenton modified the contract to include those states.

More recently, after doing a CIS account update, Suzi tossed a question to her boss: "How much do you think Sindt has brought in?"

"What do you mean?" Carroll responded. "Didn't you get the expense and time logs?"

"No, I'm not talking about their last case. I meant, all together."

"Seriously? I have no idea."

"Guess," she said.

Carroll hated guessing games. He was about to tell Suzi to just go ahead and give him a total, but she shot him one of her, Do it now!, looks. He grinned and did some quick calculating in his head.

"Okay, I'd say around – 80?"

"Nope. Do you want to guess again?" she asked, although she already knew the answer.

It was Carroll's turn to communicate nonverbally. One look confirmed that he did not want to try to guess again.

"You're no fun!" she said. "Our total receipts from Sindt, Inc. total out at $118,365.42."

"Seriously?" asked Carroll, truly shocked at the amount.

"Yep! Not bad, huh? All because you flew coach that day."

"It's Karma," he said matter-of-factly.

"Yeah, right," replied Suzi, but she knew he meant it.

In Carroll's mind, his offer to give Brenton a lift, made spontaneously, out of courtesy and without any other motive, was rewarded with instant Karma.

"Maybe you should fly only coach on jam-packed planes from now on? You know, where you can talk to a lot of people at once?" she had suggested sarcastically.

"Maybe you should kiss my ass?" he popped back.

Suzi promptly got up, walked over and gave him a peck on his cheek. "Done!" she smirked.

However, this morning, after boarding his Delta flight to Atlanta, Carroll found he had no immediate neighbor. The fact that it was 5:30 a.m. probably had something to do with that. He preferred early morning flights for trips of two hours or less. It got him out of Indianapolis before rush hour and usually put him in his destination city just as rush hour was ending. And, of course, there was always the view. Thanks to the under-booked flight, soon after the lights of his city were behind him, he was able to scoot across the aisle to the port side to enjoy a beautiful sunrise.

Carroll found he was getting apprehensive as he got closer to Georgia. With the exception of his Glynco trips, which were themselves confined to a small area, he had never been outside of the greater Atlanta area. This would be a first, traveling to rural Georgia to look into a case –and he wasn't even licensed in the state.

Carroll could have used Delta's smaller regional carrier, ExpressJet, to fly to Albany, roughly an hour from Fitzgerald, but he opted instead to rent a car at Hartsfield and make the two and a half hour drive down. It was actually still rush hour when his flight touched down, but Carroll would be driving southbound, away from Atlanta, so he was not too concerned. Depending on the amount of traffic, stops for fuel and restroom breaks, he calculated that he should arrive by noon.

He decided to start by meeting with Ben Walden, the reporter who had written the news story the McDowells included in the information furnished during their initial meeting. Previous experience had taught Carroll that newspaper reporters could be valuable assets. While their TV counterparts jammed as many stories as possible into a news segment, print reporters were usually able to take the time to dig deeper. That also included vetting facts and sources. He considered journalistic integrity a valuable tool in his line of work.

Carroll had telephoned Walden the day before, explaining that he was "doing some research on a project" and offered to buy him lunch. Although he didn't come right out and say so, Carroll tried to give the vague impression that he was a fellow writer. His intention was to meet the reporter and size him up before revealing why he was really there.

After picking up the keys for his rental at the Hertz counter, he called Walden again, but got his voicemail instead.

He left a message; "Good morning Ben. Bob Carroll here. I just wanted to let you know that I'm leaving Atlanta now and I'll be there by lunch. Let me know if something's come up. Otherwise, I'll see you in a couple of hours. Thanks."

Carroll exited the terminal and took the short walk to his rental, a Ford Escape. He usually didn't have much of a preference when it came to rental cars. He normally let Suzi decide on the vehicle, but he had been more specific for this particular trip. It was embarrassing to admit it, but he was nervous. He was venturing into unfamiliar territory, the rural South.

Suzi had not helped matters much. She had said things like:

"Is this anywhere close to where Deliverance was filmed?" adding with a long drawl, "cause you got a *real* purty mouth!"

Or, she would also give him pointers:

"For God's sake, don't say, yous guys, or, you all. It's ya'll. And use fix'n as much as you can."

"Fixing?" Carroll asked.

"No! Not *fix–ing*," she said, overemphasizing the correct pronunciation of the word.

He tried again, "Fixing."

Shaking her head emphatically, Suzi explained:

"Jesus! Do you want to get yourself killed? Because, if you go down there talking like that that's exactly what's going to happen. And I'm too old and set in my ways to train a new boss," she added matter-of-factly.

"Well, help me then!" Carroll pleaded.

Suzi had been on a roll that morning and he played along.

She repeated it again, even more slowly:

"Fix–n. You've got to drop the I-N-G, or, at least the G. Just chop that son of a bitch off! Fix–N. Now, you try it."

"Fix'n," Carroll repeated successfully. "Now, what am I fix'n?"

"Every damn thing!" she yelled. "I'm fix'n to watch TV. I'm fix'n to go to the store. I'm fix'n to wash my hands. I'm fix'n to eat supper – and be damn sure to say supper, instead of dinner."

Carroll's grin widened with each example, but Suzi was not finished:

"I'm fix'n to go hunt'n. Remember, chop that off that G! I'm fix'n to go to the store. I'm fix'n to go to the bathroom. I'm fix'n to take a shi– " Suzi stopped abruptly, her eyes wide.

Carroll turned around to see his two o'clock appointment, two business representatives from Linder, standing in the doorway. He did not miss a beat.

"Good morning, gentlemen," he said, "Suzi was just fix'n me a cup of coffee. How do you like yours?"

It had taken a full 30 minutes for Suzi's face to change from bright red back to its normal color.

Later, as they were making final preparations for his trip to Georgia, Carroll had asked, "Can you rent me a truck?"

Suzi looked confused, asking, "You mean like a U-Haul or Ryder?"

"No. A pickup truck. Like a Dodge Ram or a Ford F-something."

"A Ford *F-something*? Jesus, you really need to get out of the city more. *Please* don't say, Ford F-something, in Georgia!" she warned him.

Suzi checked with two rental companies and reported back, "They don't do trucks."

"Well, just do whatever you can. I'll be conspicuous enough without driving up in an obvious rental car."

Now, as he stood there, looking at his rental vehicle, he realized he had made a big mistake. The Ford Escape was a mid-sized SUV that looked like it had just been driven off the lot. And, to top it off, it was bright red. It stood out like a sore thumb.

Carroll actually enjoyed the drive from Atlanta to Fitzgerald. Traffic was amazingly light so he was making good time. He wondered if this were normal for a weekday. He also enjoyed the scenery. He was slightly surprised to find that the urban sprawl did not extend as far on Atlanta's south side as he had expected. It was not long before structures bordering I-75 were replaced by trees. He noticed another transformation south of Macon as the trees were being replaced by fields, some with tractors plowing and some with cattle.

He pulled into a parking space in front of the Fitzgerald Observer at 11:22 a.m.. He was ahead of schedule. He was exiting the vehicle when a young man walked out of the building and walked straight up to him.

"Hi, Bob," he said, extending his hand. "I'm Ben Walden."

"Morn'n Ben," Carroll responded, remembering to drop the G as he accepted the handshake. "How did you know it was me?"

"Well, I got your message and figured you were due about now, and–," Walden gestured toward the bright red Ford Escape, "here you are."

"Yeah, I know," Carroll sighed. "I wanted a truck."

Walden grinned.

"I thought we might walk to lunch. It's only a couple of blocks down the street. After the flight and driving all morning I figured you might want to stretch your legs a bit."

"Yeah, that'd be great," he replied, stretching his arms his and arching his back on cue.

The two men started down the sidewalk. They made small talk for a few minutes before Carroll explained that he was there as a friend of the grandparents of Thomas McDowell, the murder victim in one of Walden's newspaper reports.

"So, you're a friend of McDowell's grandparents, huh?" Walden asked.

"Yeah, I used to work with his dad." To take the edge off the lie Carroll added a bit of truth, "His dad's name was Thomas too, Thomas McDowell, Jr."

"Oh?" Walden raised his eyebrows, "Was he also a cop? Or does he work with you as a PI?"

Carroll winced. *I haven't been in town five minutes and I'm already busted!* he thought. The two men stopped walking.

Ben Walden looked Robert Carroll straight in the eye, and said, "Look, I may just be a reporter in a little hick town to you, but I'm not stupid. You're an ex-cop, and from what I gather, now, a pretty damn good private detective."

Walden seemed more perturbed that Carroll was treating him like a yokel than anything else. Carroll knew he had made a huge mistake. He should have been honest with Walden from the start. He had to try to repair the damage.

"I'm sorry about that, Ben," he said. Deciding to lay it all on the line, he added, "Look, like I told the McDowells, I'm not licensed in Georgia, but I promised them I would come down here and look around. We haven't signed a contract and they haven't paid me any money. I'm just trying to keep a low profile before I decide how – or even if, I'll proceed on this."

The reporter's expression remained stoic as he removed his glasses with his right hand and a small soft cloth from his shirt pocket with his left. Carroll felt relieved when Walden finally released him from his stare and lowered his eyes, focusing them on his glasses as he slowly wiped the lenses. Walden returned the cloth to his pocket and glasses to their nose perch as he responded, "I can understand that, Bob. I'll be glad to help you out any way I can. I just expect you to be straight up with me from now on."

Carroll realized that he had been holding his breath. He fought the temptation to gulp the air as if he had just emerged from underwater.

"Thanks. I really appreciate it," he said. "I didn't mean to offend you. As an ex-detective who's worked my fair share of homicides, I know that nothing ticks local cops off more than an outsider coming in to meddle in their murder investigation. I'm just trying to stay under the radar."

"I understand," Walden assured him. "I do think you'll find out more that way. Nobody knows why you're really here, but if you're gonna be in town for more than a day you're going to be noticed, so we'll just say that you're here to work with me as a publisher. Just don't put me in a legal bind."

Carroll thanked Walden again. The two men shook hands again, sealing their new understanding, before resuming their walk.

31

"I guess I just felt sorry for them," Carroll admitted, thinking about the McDowells.

"Yeah, me too. I never met them in person, but I interviewed them over the phone for a follow-up article. They seem like good folks. Like I said, whatever I can do."

Walden had one more stipulation. It was actually a request: "If you do solve his thing, then I want to be able to publish the story as an exclusive."

"You're making a big assumption there – that I'll be able to solve it."

Walden grinned, "Like I said, I did some digging, and – based on your previous record, I'll give you a 50/50 chance."

"I think that even a 50/50 is being overly generous, but you've got a deal."

"I've been on top of this story since they found the body," Ben said. "I would love to see it solved. A murder isn't good for a small town and an unsolved murder really makes people nervous. So, what do you want to know?"

"Well, let's start with the basics. What about overall crime? Robberies, burglaries?"

Walden shrugged, "Sure, we have some, but I've done news stories on Fitzgerald's crime rate before. On average, we actually have far fewer than most communities comparable to ours."

"What about homicides?"

"A murder here is even rarer. And I can't even remember one that's gone unsolved for more than a month or two."

As an experienced investigator, Carroll knew most homicides are crimes of passion – the result of an argument or somebody's girlfriend, boyfriend, wife or husband getting caught running around, so they are usually easily and quickly solved. To have a crime of this nature, a true murder-mystery, in Fitzgerald, was obviously very rare.

According to Walden, the general consensus of the local citizenry as well as law enforcement was that the perpetrator was most likely a drifter who was passing through and was probably long gone. He asked Ben a few more questions, but Carroll had done his homework, too, having researched the FBI's crime statistics on Fitzgerald and Ben Hill County before he left Indianapolis. He already knew the answers to his questions. He wanted to see if Walden's responses were genuine. They were.

Ben momentarily veered off the main subject just after they crossed a street. He began to tell Carroll something about the building they were passing. At that moment, a large chicken suddenly emerged from under the shrubbery near Carroll's leg. It happened so quickly that he did not even have time to jump before the bird gave his right foot a peck and then casually strolled away in the opposite direction.

Walden was still talking, but Carroll's brain wasn't processing the words. He was looking back at the chicken as it occasionally stopped to peck at objects on the sidewalk.

The sound of Walden's voice brought Carroll back.

"...oldest and continuously owned family business in town."

"Sorry, Ben, what was that again?"

Ben gestured toward the building. "The Standard Supply Company. It's one of the oldest buildings in Fitzgerald, probably even in the whole state," he explained.

Carroll stopped and looked up at the structure. He checked to be sure it was safe, then left the sidewalk and took a few steps into the street to get a better overall view. It was not a tall building. The front resembled an old Spanish mission. It had a brick parapet and a large archway around the entrance.

"So, when was it built?" he asked.

"In 1897, and it's also the oldest continuously owned family business in town."

Carroll was beginning to appreciate his good fortune. After catching him in a lie during their introduction, Ben Walden could have easily walked away from him. He could not have blamed Walden if he had, but here he was, still walking with him instead. It told Carroll two things: Ben was more concerned about his community than his own personal feelings; and, he obviously was not someone who reacted without thinking first. Walden had apparently analyzed Carroll's rationale, understood it, and, more importantly, agreed with it.

There was another bonus. Like Carroll, Ben appeared to be a history buff. Carroll was about to ask him a question, when another chicken, a *different* chicken, came walking up beside them. Ben was now talking about something else, but Carroll could not keep his eyes off the chicken.

It wasn't like he had never seen a chicken. Of course he had. Lots of people had them in rural Indiana too, but they were usually in pens or around homes out in the country. Fitzgerald was not Atlanta or Indianapolis, but it was a decent-sized town and this was the second chicken Carroll had seen within less than two blocks.

Actually, if you want to get technical, the first one was a hen. This one was a rooster. And what a rooster, Carroll thought. He had to admit that it was the most handsome rooster that he had ever seen. Its colors were varied and brilliant. Struggling for a relative comparison, he thought it was like looking across a lake to see the trees of October reflected in the water.

On second thought, he realized that analogy didn't do this rooster justice. Such a comparison would be an insult to such a magnificent bird, Carroll concluded.

There were more colors on this rooster than he had ever seen in any fall foliage. The neck and back feathers were multiple shades of red, from a deep blood-red to rusty, golden, orange and variations between.

It had a white tuft on the lower back and from there the feathers turned a metallic-green, then a darker forest green, and —finally, very long dark, almost black tail feathers. The breast was a glossy, bluish-green mixed with dark red, maroon and orange, all topped by a vivid scarlet-red comb and lappets.

Carroll chuckled to himself, realizing he had mentally waxed rhapsodic — about a rooster. By this point Ben's voice was merely noise, distorted into Charlie Brown's teacher-speak as he continued;

Wah wah waah wah. Waaah wah wah.

Carroll was not even pretending to pay attention at this point. Finally, unable to resist any longer, he interrupted Walden, "Sorry, Ben, but, is this normal?"

Walden stopped, looked around and then leaned back and looked up at the sky, musing, "Yeah, I'd say so, for this time of year, the first day of spring. Although, today's actually a bit cooler than it was during the first of the week."

Realizing he and Walden were discussing apples and oranges, Carroll explained, "No, not the weather. *That*," he said, pointing at the chicken. "Is that normal?"

The rooster stopped and looked up at Walden, as if it were also waiting for an answer.

"Oh, that? Yeah, that's very normal here," Ben chuckled. "It's actually a failed government experiment."

"Yeah, right." Carroll didn't get the joke, but he laughed anyway. It seemed to be the courteous thing to do.

"Seriously, I'm not kidding," Ben added, as he began to walk toward the restaurant again. He took several steps before realizing Carroll was not with him. He turned around to find Carroll still standing by the rooster, staring at Walden with an incredulous look. Obviously, Carroll was not buying it.

"It's actually a pretty amazing story," Walden said, shooting Carroll an inquisitive, shall-I-continue? – look.

Carroll felt as if he were being set up for a joke. He was beginning to wonder if Suzi had not somehow arranged it, but he could not resist. He had to know more about the chickens. He nodded, "Okay, I'm hooked. Reel me in."

Ben proceeded to give Carroll what he considered his "chicken talk," something he had done for many others. According to Walden, it started in the late 1940s with Gardiner Bump, a wildlife biologist who specialized in ornithology.

"First, you've got to understand what had happened to wild birds in America by that time," Walden explained, continuing, "From the last part of the 19th century to the late 1920s Americans were literally slaughtering birds by the millions. And it wasn't just hunting them for food, although that was a part of it."

They resumed their stroll, with Walden closest to the street, Carroll walking the middle and the rooster tagging along on his right.

"The big fashion craze for ladies was bird feathers," Ben continued, "feathers in hats, on headbands and even on their dresses. I mean, if it had feathers, it was a game bird whether you could eat the damn thing or not, and it was probably going to end up being worn by a lady somewhere. In fact, more herons, egrets, storks and cranes were killed during that time than in any other part of world history."

Walden glanced over to make sure that Carroll was still with him, in step as well as with the conversation. Satisfied that Carroll was with him in both senses, Ben continued, "So, we're whacking out birds left and right and then along comes the Great Depression and people start relying on them even more for food, which makes sense, because people have to eat, right?"

Carroll nodded. He was surprised that Ben knew so much on the subject and also surprised at himself. Merely curious at first, Carroll was now seriously interested in the topic. And apparently, he thought, with amusement, so was the rooster. It continued to walk with them.

Ben related how, after World War II ended, America's massive, nationwide period of growth in housing and industry also negatively impacted bird species in the United States.

"So now we're throwing up factories, apartments and suburbs all over the damn place and we've added yet another thing to kill birds, habitat destruction, to the equation. Get the picture?"

Carroll nodded again.

"This was a very serious issue at the time, both environmentally and economically," said Ben, "Some nongame species were nearing extinction due to both the fashion thing and habitat destruction, and game birds were just as endangered in some areas because they had also been hunted for food. Do you know what an ivory-billed woodpecker is?"

"Well, I'm assuming it's a woodpecker with an ivory-colored bill, but that would be a guess on my part," Carroll replied.

Walden laughed, "So you are a real detective, huh?"

Carroll shrugged his shoulders as Ben continued, "You haven't seen one because they're probably extinct. Every few years somebody claims to have spotted one, but it's all bullshit – either a misidentification or, more likely, an attempt to get attention. Ornithologists go crazy whenever there's a reported sighting, but there's never a decent photo, or video, or a recording of the call.

That's what was happening to tons of bird species in America at that time. Some pulled through; some didn't."

"And some people believe that humans can't have an impact on nature," said Carroll, shaking his head in disgust.

The rooster clucked in agreement as Walden proceeded;

"So along comes Gardiner Bump. He made a proposal to Georgia's Department of Natural Resources to introduce this bird, the red jungle fowl, as a wild game bird, kind of like quail and pheasants."

Ben stopped again. They had arrived at The Sportsman, their destination for lunch. He opened and held the door for Carroll, while using his foot to block the rooster's path. There was no need. The rooster, well aware of the etiquette for a proper rooster, was not about to violate it. He seemed to value his reputation in the community.

"Hey, Ben," a waitress greeted as they walked in. "Just cleaned your booth."

"Thanks, Becky," he said.

Some locals stopped Ben to remark about an item in the newspaper. Becky led Carroll to the last booth on the right where she placed a menu on the table. He went ahead and took a seat at the booth and began reevaluating Walden's chicken lesson while he waited. Ben's explanation sounded plausible. The government had been notorious for accidentally introducing invasive species of plants and animals through misguided programs. Carroll was well aware that kudzu had been introduced that way. The fast-growing, viney plant has since completely taken over parts of the South since its introduction in the late 1800s.

With this in mind, he thought it was not farfetched to see how Gardiner Bump managed to convince both the U.S. Fish and Wildlife Service and the Georgia DNR that the Burmese red jungle fowl was going to be the solution to Georgia's depleted wild game bird population. Bump had predicted that the new hunting craze for the imported chickens would take the heat off of America's native wild birds. Walden quickly joined Carroll at the booth and proceeded to sum up the outcome of his story.

"So, in the mid-60s they released thousands of these Burmese chickens around the local rivers for hunters," Ben explained.

"There were hunters alright," he laughed. "Bobcats, raccoons, red and gray foxes. We still had a few eastern cougars roaming around back then, too. Most of the chickens were wiped out within the very first year."

Walden said the only chickens that survived were those that stayed close to communities and farms. For some odd reason, he added, Fitzgerald had ended up with a sizable population that has continued to thrive. Some people liked the chickens and wanted them to stay, while others consider them a nuisance.

The tension concerning the fate of the chickens grew and created quite a rift in the community.

"It all came to a head about ten years ago after the formation of the FCCWCD," Walden said.

He paused and looked at Carroll. Ben was keeping a straight face, but his eyes were smiling. He was holding back. It was obvious that he was clearly waiting for Carroll to ask the question.

"Okay, I'll bite," Carroll relented. "What's the FCCWCD?"

"What?" Walden asked, pretending not to hear him.

"What is the FCCWCD?" Carroll repeated with a grin.

"Oh, that. It's the Fitzgerald Citizens Committee for Wild Chicken Deportation," Walden sputtered, barely getting it out.

"The *what?*"

Carroll was wondering once again if this was an elaborate joke.

Walden couldn't answer. He was laughing so hard that he had tears running down his cheeks. He finally managed to regain enough composure to repeat it again.

"The Fitzgerald Citizens Committee for Wild Chicken Deportation."

"You've gotta be shitting me!"

Walden could not speak. He simply shook his head.

"I'm dead serious," he said, after he was able to catch his breath. "It divided the whole town."

Carroll could not help it. He had to say it himself.

"The Fitzgerald Citizens Committee for Wild Chicken Deportation," he repeated slowly.

Hearing Carroll say the words out loud caused Ben Walden to literally collapse into hysterical laughter. He was lying on the booth's bench seat as Becky returned with the menus. ·

"Hey, Ben, you wanna check for gum stuck under the table while you're down there?" she asked.

Becky's comment sent the two of them further over the edge.

They recovered enough to place their orders and then got down to business while they awaited their food. Carroll casually glanced around to confirm that no one was sitting within hearing distance. Seeing that the only other customers were nearer the entrance, he leaned forward, putting his forearms on the table.

"So let's just say, what if?" he asked Walden. "What if Thomas McDowell wasn't killed by a drifter? Who would you suspect?"

Ben shook his head, "I can't even imagine anyone local doing this, Bob. Like I told you, I want this thing solved as much as you do, probably more, but I just don't see it being a local person."

"There's got to be somebody," Carroll pressed him. "Who is it? If you've thought about this as much as I think you have, then you've come up with at least one name, maybe more."

Walden started to speak, but hesitated. Carroll could see that he had struck a nerve. Ben had someone in mind.

Carroll prodded him again:

"It doesn't mean that he's an official suspect. It's just you and me talking here. Give me just one name."

Walden took a breath.

"Come on, Ben." Carroll coaxed him.

"Billy Bob McCoy," Walden said, sighing as if the name had literally been ripped from him.

Carroll knew it had been a tough decision for Ben to divulge it, but he could not help but smile at the name.

"Seriously?" he asked. "Billy Bob?"

Walden grinned. He had known Carroll would enjoy the whole Southern yokel thing about the name.

"Don't forget the McCoy part," he added. "I mean, what's more Southern than having the same last name as one side of the oldest and deadliest family feuds in history?"

Carroll's look became serious, "So tell me about him."

"He's a real hothead. He's also the biggest racist in the county."

There it was. Hearing Walden utter those words, Carroll now understood that Ben's hesitancy was not just about mentioning a name. It was evident that there was so much more involved with this particular name. If this turned out to be a race-related murder, a hate crime, it would rip the community apart. And if McCoy was wrongly accused and word got out that it was Walden who had first named him it would also ruin Ben's credibility as a journalist and his career would be over.

Carroll's experience and training, however, required that he consider every possibility during an investigation, so, when he had met the McDowells on that first day and discovered that their grandson, an African-American, had been murdered in the rural south, he had added hate crime to his list of possible motives. He had not been jumping to a conclusion; he had simply been doing his job.

During their second meeting, Thomas Sr. had admitted that he had wondered if his grandson could have gotten into a racial confrontation and responded without thinking. According to the elder McDowell, Tommy – as his grandfather called him – was more knowledgeable about history than most people of his age, but he still worried that his grandson was naïve about lingering racial prejudice in some areas of the south.

The fact that Ben used the words hothead and racist in his first comment to describe Billy Bob McCoy showed that Walden had also considered the possibility of a hate crime. Carroll's ears perked up when Ben stated that McCoy was not from Fitzgerald. In fact, he had moved to town only just two months prior to McDowell's death.

Billy Bob operated a garage on the outskirts of town. Together, Walden and Carroll came up with a believable story – that Carroll was a publisher and was in Fitzgerald to help Walden with some newspaper business. The excuse to visit McCoy's garage was the only part that wasn't a fabrication. On the way from Atlanta, the car in front of Carroll had suddenly swerved to miss a huge piece of a blown truck tire on I-75. That car was able to avoid it, but Carroll saw it too late. Corralled by a motorhome on his left and a tractor-trailer on his right, he had no option but to plow right over it, bouncing dangerously close to both the truck and motorhome.

He had immediately pulled off of the interstate to inspect the damage. Miraculously, he saw none. Now, however, Carroll would tell McCoy that he just wanted to be sure nothing underneath the vehicle was damaged or leaking. Walden suggested that they should go in his vehicle and claim they happened to be passing by. Doing it this way would allow Carroll to meet Billy Bob briefly, while giving him an excuse to return with the Escape after he had done some background work.

They finished their meal and quickly walked back to Walden's office to get Carroll's vehicle. He saw two more chickens on the way back. Ben was parked in the lot behind the newspaper office, so they cut through the alley. Carroll observed several parked cars as they emerged into the parking area, but Walden walked past them to the truck that was parked next to the street.

Carroll chuckled to himself when he saw the Ford logo on the grill of the truck and the F 150 on the fender.

"So how do you like your Ford?" he asked.

"Love it!" Walden replied.

"Yeah, the F-150 is a good damn truck!" he agreed, trying to sound like he knew what he was talking about and thinking that he would have to tell Suzi about this later.

Billy Bob McCoy's garage was located in an old gas station on the north side of town. Carroll surveyed the area as they drove up. The building itself was typical of service stations constructed during the 1950s and 60s. You could barely make out the word, GULF, on the old faded round sign next to the street. The two gas pumps remained, also bearing the faded GULF logo, but it was clear they had not been used in years. The pumps were covered by a shelter that was supported by two poles. A Rebel flag flew from one and the old Georgia state flag – the one that displayed the

Confederate emblem – flew from the other. Carroll guessed that the station had probably closed when the Gulf Oil Corporation was bought out by Chevron and, later, British Petroleum in the mid-80s.

Billy Bob McCoy was in the "pit," underneath a car in the garage when they parked. He climbed out as they exited Ben's truck. Carroll sized him up as they walked over. McCoy was not really short, but he was a bit below the average height of most men of his age. At six feet, two inches, Thomas McDowell's height was above average and he was also heavier than McCoy. Unless he had surprised him from behind or unless Billy Bob was a lot tougher than he appeared to be, Carroll did not see how McCoy could have killed McDowell without a prolonged fight that would have attracted attention from the other hotel guests or people in the general area.

McCoy squinted as he stepped into the sunlight.

Walden made the introductions:

"Hey, Billy Bob. This is Bob Carroll."

"How ya do'n, Bob," McCoy said, as they shook hands.

Carroll felt something smushy and looked down at the grease on his hand.

"Aw shit! Sorry about that!" said McCoy, but he was laughing.

Billy Bob turned back toward the garage and shouted, "Hey Lenny! Bring me a gob of Go-Jo and a rag!"

There was no answer, but Carroll could tell that Lenny, whoever he was, was complying by the sounds coming from the garage. He heard the squeak of a door, the snap of a lid being removed, and then the door being reclosed. Lenny emerged, gob in one hand and a red shop rag in the other. Carroll had met some pretty big guys in his day. He had always considered a guy, appropriately called, Mike the Tank, the biggest person he had ever met personally, but he changed his mind when Lenny walked out of the garage door.

If Mike was a tank, Sauls was a mountain, Carroll thought. There was no other way to describe him. He was at least six-five, maybe taller, with a massive torso and huge arms. And his size was not due to body fat. Sauls was all muscle. He did not appear to be a bodybuilder. He was like one of those big guys you read about in a fable, like the legendary John Henry.

He was bald even though he appeared to be only in his early thirties. Carroll suddenly had a strange feeling. He was not sure how or where it had occurred, but he thought that he might have met or seen Lenny Sauls somewhere in the past.

Lenny walked over and started to hand the towel to Billy Bob. "Not me, dumbass!" McCoy yelled. "Give it to Mr. Carroll!"

Sauls plopped the glob of Go-Jo on Carroll's hands as he handed him the towel with his other hand..

McCoy shook his head in disbelief;

"You are one simple son of a bitch, Lenny! The man's gotta clean his hands *before* you give him the damn towel."

Carroll rubbed his hands briskly, instantly producing the distinct oily odor that he remembered from his Uncle Jack's garage during his youth. Lenny stood waiting, like an attendant in the bathroom of an upscale gentlemen's club, holding the towel for the guests.

Carroll was doing his best to work out why Lenny looked so familiar as Ben explained the situation about the rental vehicle to Billy Bob. Carroll studied Sauls intently as he took the towel from him and wiped his hands, but he just could not make the connection.

Could Sauls have been to Indianapolis? Was it possible that he knew Thomas McDowell before the murder? A break this quick in a case was rare, but it was not unprecedented. Carroll's heart rate increased. He was trying to remember if he had ever arrested anyone by that name or if the name had ever popped up as a witness or suspect in a case. What was it about this guy? Carroll asked himself. I feel like he I've been déjà voodooed by a witch doctor.

When he looked back over at McCoy, he saw that Billy Bob was grinning from ear to ear. Obviously, he had been watching Carroll's reaction to seeing Lenny for the first time. Billy Bob looked as if he were waiting for Carroll to say something.

"Well?" said McCoy, raising his eyebrows.

"Well, what?" asked Carroll.

He was still mentally going through old case files.

McCoy could not wait any longer:

"Don't he look just like him? He can sound like him, too!"

Carroll was lost, but then he saw that Ben was also smiling.

McCoy snapped his finger to get Lenny's attention:

"Hey, Lenny. Do one."

"Aw, come on Billy Bob! I don't feel like it."

It was the first time Carroll had heard Lenny speak. His voice didn't match his size. He sounded like a kid who did not want to go to school.

"Go ahead on and do it!" McCoy ordered.

"I don't want to," Sauls whined.

"I don't give a shit. Do it anyway," Billy Bob commanded.

"I don't feel like it," Lenny whimpered.

McCoy's demeanor changed so quickly it was as if someone had flipped a switch, changing his personality. He spun around and yelled, "I said *do it* — you son of a bitch! Before I come over there and stomp your stupid ass!"

Carroll expected Lenny Sauls to bolt over and squash Billy Bob McCoy like the lowly bug he obviously was, but it did not happen. Instead, Lenny stood up, raised his hands and curled his fingers as if he were holding onto something in front of him, and then said, "I helped Del's mouse become a circus mouse. He gonna live in a mouse city. Down in Florida."

Billy Bob yelled his approval and slapped his own knee.

"Do another one!" he shouted.

Without hesitation this time, Lenny said, "You know; I fell asleep this afternoon and had me a dream. I dreamed about Del's mouse."

McCoy howled and banged the side of the old gas pump. Ben was laughing, too. It suddenly made sense to Carroll. He knew where he had seen Lenny. Actually, he had not. They had never met before, but Sauls was the spitting image of Michael Clarke Duncan, the actor who played John Coffey in The Green Mile, except that Lenny was white.

It was so obvious that Carroll silently berated himself for not seeing it immediately. I'm an idiot he thought. He had to admit that Lenny's John Coffey impression was absolutely perfect. He even sounded like John Coffey. Carroll imagined the two of them had re-watched the movie many times and supposed McCoy had coached Sauls on the impersonation. He looked over at Walden and McCoy again. Both were rolling with laughter. Lenny was into it now. He needed no further encouragement. Their laughter was all the motivation he needed.

"Boss Percy bad. He mean! He stepped on Del's mouse. I took it back though."

It was too much even for Robert Carroll. Unable to resist the urge, he began to laugh along as Sauls, fueled now by the attention, continued his one-act show with one line after another.

"I helped it. Didn't I help it?"

"I just took it back, is all."

"Awful tired now, boss. Dog tired."

"Please boss, don't put that thing over my face. Don't put me in the dark. I's afraid of the dark!"

McCoy walked over and slapped Robert Carroll on the shoulder.

"Don't he sound just like that nigger?"

Carroll felt a twinge at hearing the word, but he responded, "Yep, he's pretty good."

Billy Bob shook his head in bewilderment, asking, "Pretty good?"

McCoy obviously took Carroll's mild response as a personal critique of his coaching ability with his large pet.

"Pretty good?" he repeated. "Shit! I swear, I could get me a can of black spray paint, strip his fat ass down, paint him black and make me a fortune lett'n people get their picture taken with the nigger from The Green Mile!"

Carroll winced again. Beyond the twinge, he started to get another feeling, the kind he always got when he was onto something important about a case. He watched as Sauls walked over and prepared to take a seat on a folding metal chair.

Carroll half expected the chair to get up and run away in fear of being crushed to death by the massive buttocks descending upon it.

McCoy jumped up and ran over to Sauls just as he plopped down on the creaking chair. Billy Bob grabbed Lenny in a headlock from behind as he hollered, "Del ain't the onliest one to have a circus mouse. I got my own circus mouse! And he sure is one big ole sumbitch!"

Sauls was trying to reach around to pull McCoy off, but Billy Bob was dodging and jumping around, making it difficult for Lenny to latch on to him. Walden and Carroll watched with growing apprehension as the scene continued.

Lenny flailed his arms wildly in an attempt to grab McCoy as Billy Bob continued to hold him in a headlock, whooping and shouting obscenities the entire time. But Sauls finally had enough. He stood up, taking Billy Bob with him as if he were no heavier or bothersome than a gnat. Unable to get his hands on McCoy, Lenny began to whirl around as McCoy's taunting continued, "Hey, look at me! I'm on the Fat Ass Ride at the County Fair!"

Billy Bob's whooping quickly changed to yells of fear as Sauls spun faster and faster. By the time he decided to let go, McCoy did not dare. It would have indeed been like jumping off of a ride at the fair while it ran at full-speed. The centrifugal force finally made the decision for him. Billy Bob's grasp was ripped from Sauls and he went flying through the air. He landed at least ten feet away, knocking over a stack of old tires. He was lucky. Two feet either way to the left or right, and he would have hit sharp tools on one side or a farm plow on the other.

Damn shame, Carroll thought. That could've solved a lot of problems.

McCoy stood up, but he was apparently groggy. He immediately fell backward onto the tires again. Lenny quickly ran over to help him. Carroll thought that it was genuine concern on Lenny's part but, as absurd as it sounded, he also wondered if part of Sauls' response was not motivated by fear. McCoy was obviously a dangerous man. It was entirely possible that Lenny didn't want to be on his bad side.

"You okay, Billy Bob?" Lenny asked.

"Why, hell yeah! It'll take more than you to hurt me!"

McCoy talked tough, but Carroll observed that he was still relying on Lenny to hold him up. His "why, hell yeah" response had been directed toward Walden, not Lenny, who had asked the question. Clearly McCoy was still disoriented. This gave Carroll something to smile about.

He looked over at Ben. It was time to go. In an unspoken agreement, they waited around a few minutes: First, to make sure that Billy Bob was physically okay, but also to be sure that he did not shoot Lenny or kill him with a tire tool. Walden and Carroll had started walking back toward the truck when Billy Bob yelled, "Just bring that Escape around here when you get time, Bob, and I'll take a look at it."

"Thanks, Billy Bob. I appreciate it," Carroll responded, waving to him. "I'll have it here first thing in the morning."

Even with the truck windows closed, Carroll waited until they were half a block away before he spoke.

"Holy shit, Ben!"

"Yeah, I know. That damn guy's a powder keg and he's gonna blow one day."

"Or maybe he already did," Carroll suggested, thinking of Thomas McDowell.

Ben shrugged, "That's why I told you about him. I knew he had a mouth on him. But, hell, Bob, I've never seen him go off like that before."

"And what about Lenny Sauls?" Carroll asked. "Jesus! He could kill a man with his pinky finger."

Walden disagreed about Sauls.

"Billy Bob might have it in him, but not Lenny."

Carroll was still replaying the whole thing in his head.

"From what I saw back there, Sauls is just as capable of killing a man as Billy Bob McCoy."

"Yeah, sure he is – if he's being hurt, in self defense, but he doesn't have, what they call, malice in his heart," Ben insisted. "Lenny, well, he's like Lennie in John Steinbeck's Of Mice and Men. He would never intentionally hurt anyone."

When Carroll did not immediately respond, Walden added, "And seriously, Bob, you've got to admit that what happened to that McDowell kid was as intentional as you can get. That was no accident."

"You've got that right," Carroll agreed, remembering the details from the incident report.

"So what's the plan?" Walden asked.

"I'll take the Escape over there in the morning and spend some time with Billy Bob while he looks at it. If I'm lucky I'll have a chance to poke around while he's under the car."

Walden looked concerned.

"Do you think that's a good idea?" he asked with a frown. "I mean, what if he catches you snooping around? You better be careful with Billy Bob."

"Gee, you think so?" Carroll laughed, but then he saw the serious look on Walden's face.

He popped him on the shoulder,

"Don't worry about me, Ben. This ain't my first rodeo."

3

Shacktown

Robert Carroll had been in Fitzgerald for less than half the day, but those few hours had proven to be amazingly productive. He had met Ben Walden, someone whom he determined to be an asset for the investigation, and – oddly enough, even though they had just met, an ally and possibly, even, a friend. More importantly, Carroll had also found two people who could have been capable of committing the murder. He hesitated to use the word, suspects, but as he told Suzi when he felt that he was on to something, his Spidey senses were definitely tingling.

Even a blind man could see that Billy Bob McCoy was potentially a dangerous and violent person. Carroll thought back to his earlier question: Did Billy Bob surprise Thomas McDowell from behind? He stood by his initial assessment – that if McCoy were the killer and if he had acted on his own, he had to have ambushed McDowell. Otherwise, he thought it would have been one hell of a fight and it definitely would have attracted attention. He made a mental note to look for any indication that McCoy might have been in the military which would have given him combat training.

And what about Lenny Sauls? Again, there was no doubt that Sauls had the physical strength to accomplish the task of killing a person. He didn't even need a knife. Lenny could have done it with his bare hands, but Carroll also agreed with Walden's assessment. Sauls might be as big as a bear, but he was a Teddy Bear, not a grizzly.

He recalled Lenny's Green Mile performance. Billy Bob had manipulated him as easily as if Lenny were a marionette and McCoy the puppeteer. Could Billy Bob have encouraged Lenny to perform other acts? Did he have enough influence and power over him to make him commit murder? Carroll's thought process was interrupted as Ben stopped the truck abruptly.

"Sorry about that, Bob," Walden apologized, pointing toward the front of the truck.

There, crossing the street in front of them, was a large hen, followed by four tiny chicks. Other vehicles had also stopped to allow the feathered family to safely cross the street.

Carroll grinned as he looked over at Walden.

"Welcome to Fitzgerald," Ben said, shaking his head.

The chickens reached the opposite side. Ben took his foot off the brake to proceed, but just as the vehicles began to move again, someone shouted from another car. They screeched to a halt as one tiny little yellow chick, which had been left behind, came scurrying across the street to catch up with his mother and siblings.

Walden shook his head again, appearing slightly embarrassed.

"We'll get there," he said. "Eventually."

"No problem," Carroll replied, "There's actually something about that that I like."

"About what? Chickens crossing the road?"

"Well, yeah," he admitted. "I like that people stop for them."

He was being honest. He appreciated that the other motorists were giving the hen and chicks the same deference they would have afforded a human family.

Carroll suddenly slapped the dashboard, exclaiming, "Jesus Ben! You're a reporter! You've got an opportunity here to do something that millions and millions of people had been trying to do for years."

He stopped talking, waiting for Walden to pick up on it, but it was Ben's turn to be confused. He had no idea what Carroll was talking about; however, he was intrigued. He was always looking for an interesting topic to write about, and if Bob was right he might even gain some national attention.

Carroll waited, like a patient fisherman, but Ben still did not bite. He decided to jiggle the bait.

"Wouldn't that be something?" he wondered aloud. "To answer a question that mankind has been asking for decades, but no one has ever been able to solve it?"

He stopped again.

Ben could not stand it any longer;

"And the question is?"

Carroll looked around to be sure no one was close, as if he were about to reveal a secret. He leaned toward Walden and said in a hushed voice, "Why did the chicken cross the road?"

"You son of a bitch!" Ben snapped. He had fallen for it, hook, line and sinker.

"I mean, how many chickens are there in Fitzgerald?" Carroll asked. "Hundreds? Thousands? All that you have to do is find *one*, just *one*, that will talk on the record – or should I say cluck on the record?"

"Very damn funny!" Ben retorted.

"Think of it! You could win a Pulitzer! You just need to find one talking chicken! Hell, screw the Pulitzer. They'll give you a Nobel Prize!"

Carroll was now laughing even more hysterically than Walden had in The Sportsman.

"You know, you really are a bastard." Walden said, shaking his head. They were finally able to continue south on Lee street. Carroll was still grinning as he looked out the window. He had been too preoccupied with his thoughts about McCoy and Sauls to notice the scenery earlier, but he began to pay attention to the homes they were passing. They reminded him of the historical homes back in Noblesville, both in style and in age.

"Hey, Ben, how old are these houses?" Carroll inquired.

"Well, some are as old as the town itself."

"And how old is that?" he asked, because Walden hadn't exactly answered his question.

"Jeez, Bob, what did you find out about Fitzgerald?"

"What do you mean?"

Ben laughed, "Let me guess. You researched the homicide, but nothing further, right?

"Well, yeah. I'm down here investigating a murder, Ben. I'm not a tourist, but you piqued my interest when you showed me the Standard Supply Company building."

"So you don't know anything about the history of the town itself? Walden asked.

"Again, I think you're giving me more credit than I deserve as an investigator."

Ben appeared to be genuinely surprised as he stopped the Ford pickup again, this time pulling over to the curb.

"Holy cow! I can't believe this. So, you don't know about the historical connection between Fitzgerald, Georgia and Indianapolis, the city where you're from?"

Carroll simply shook his head. He had almost asked, what connection? He was glad that he had not. Walden said something else, but he did not hear what it was. He was too busy trying to count up the number of times that he had made himself look foolish since his arrival in Fitzgerald.

"Bob?" Ben was staring at him with a smile.

"No. I have no idea," he reluctantly admitted.

He had to laugh along with Walden. Once again, he thought, I'm busted. Once again, I am looking like a complete idiot. What was it, five or six times now?

"I just assumed, with your being from Indianapolis, and on top of that, a hotshot detective, that you actually knew this already."

"Jesus Ben! You're killing me here! Get on with it!"

Carroll was serious. Walden's toying around was almost painful. There was obviously some kind of connection between the little South Georgia town and the northern city where Carroll had spent his career, but he had no idea what it was.

Ben was still grinning. His procrastination was payback for his new friend's, why did the chicken cross the road, joke.

"Ever hear of a guy named Philander H. Fitzgerald?" he asked.

"Jeez n' crackers! There you go with the damn questions again! Hell no! But, like your damn question about the pearl-billed woodpecker, it's not that difficult to figure out. I'm assuming that Philander Fitzgerald is the guy the town is named after, but that's just a guess on my part."

"Well, you got that partly right," Ben informed him. "The town is named after him."

"What do you mean partly right? I said that the town was named after him, so I got the whole thing right."

"No, you said the town was named after Philander Fitzgerald, but you got the first part wrong. You said a pearl-billed woodpecker. It was an ivory-billed woodpecker. There's no such damn thing as a pearl-billed woodpecker," Walden chuckled.

Ben was really enjoying himself now.

"You know; you're really starting to piss me off," Carroll warned, but his grin indicated otherwise.

"Philander Fitzgerald was an attorney in Indianapolis," Ben explained. "He was also the publisher of The American Tribune. At one time, it supposedly had the largest circulation in the nation. Around the early 1890s he came up with the idea to find a place down south where people could retire and escape the brutal winters."

"So, Fitzgerald was started as like a 19th century Sun City," said Carroll. "That means that even soldiers from the Union army could have possibly moved down here after the Civil War."

"Not possibly," Walden responded.

He watched and waited for Carroll to get the full import of that statement. It was obvious that, like him, Bob had a deep interest in American history.

"So, you're saying that there were – for sure – veterans of the Union Army that moved here just a few years after the Civil War?"

"Yes, but you're still not getting it. And by the way, they called it the War Between the States, or, the War of Northern Aggression, not the Civil War. You might want to remember that around town," he joked.

It was not clear which of the two of them was enjoying the conversation more. Whether it was about chickens, old buildings, or the people who founded the town, Ben Walden obviously enjoyed talking about the history of his community. He had quickly determined that Robert Carroll was a decent guy but, as the day had progressed, he found that he liked him even more. He had been able to find out much more about Carroll than he had admitted to him earlier.

Walden had discovered that Carroll was widely respected as one of the best investigators, in or out of law enforcement, and not just in the city of Indianapolis, but in the entire state of Indiana. The fact that he was human and made mistakes and, especially, that he had a sense of humor about it, only added to his appeal.

Carroll had a similar view of Ben Walden. He realized he luckily had found a teammate on his quest for the truth in the murder of Thomas McDowell. And, finding that Ben had the same sense of humor took some of the tension away. As one might expect, homicide investigations have a natural tendency to depress one after a short time. Walden was unknowingly doing what Suzi had done back in Indianapolis; providing comic relief.

Carroll also appreciated the fact that, like him, Walden loved history. Ben could not have possibly picked a more interested listener for his lesson as he continued:

"Philander Fitzgerald was too young to fight in the war, but he did serve in the Union Army, as a drummer boy. Then, after the war, he went to school and became an attorney, a very successful attorney. And, like I said, he published The American Tribune, which was more like a magazine. Do you know why The Tribune had such a big circulation?"

Walden did not wait for an answer.

"Because the vast majority of its readers were Union Army veterans. It was actually called The Veteran's Review when Fitzgerald first purchased it. He changed the name to the American Tribune later."

As Ben explained it, a large part of Fitzgerald's law practice in Indiana involved representing Union veterans and their widows. He had been appointed by Indiana Governor James Williams to file and settle claims resulting from the loss of property during the Civil War. In addition to settling hundreds and hundreds of claims in this capacity, Fitzgerald also began to assist veterans with other legal matters. As he got to know more and more of the veterans and their families personally, he began to try and think of other ways to assist them.

Carroll sat like a student as Walden began making the final connection between Indianapolis and the little town where he now sat in a Ford F150 pickup.

"In the early 1890s, America was hit with its first real national depression. And on top of that, a large part of the Midwest underwent a prolonged drought. It was devastating to families all across the Midwest and a national appeal for help went out to other states."

A car pulled up and stopped beside them, momentarily interrupting Walden. Thinking the other driver probably wanted to ask for directions, he reached for the button to lower the driver's window, but then he noticed a rooster crossing in front of them. It was as if the chickens were in competition with the town's history and they were determined to get top billing, or at least, equal time.

Walden's knowledge of the town's early history should not have been surprising to Carroll. After all, Ben was the main reporter for their only newspaper. So it would stand to reason that he would know more about the town than the average person. According to Walden, Philander Fitzgerald had been toying around with his idea about a retirement community for some time. He even had a specific demographic in mind. Although no one was excluded, Fitzgerald proposed to build a retirement community specifically for Union veterans and their families.

The thing that had finally spurred Fitzgerald to act on his idea was the response to that appeal for assistance for those poor, suffering people in the Midwest. The citizens of Georgia sent help in the form of food, shipping beef, pork, and other supplies by the trainloads. In fact, Georgians sent more than any other state – so much that it was eventually distributed in three states, Illinois, Indiana and Iowa.

When Philander Fitzgerald saw that kind of support coming from Georgia he realized that his dream was achievable. He contacted William Northern, the governor of Georgia, explaining what he hoped to accomplish. Governor Northern was more than supportive. He invited Fitzgerald to bring a delegation to Georgia and even accompanied them on a tour of some possible locations around the state. Walden paused.

The next part of the story made Walden a bit uncomfortable, but it was historical fact and, therefore, should not be left out.

"So, when Fitzgerald and his delegation got to Georgia they found there was some public property that had been abandoned by the Creek Indians that was available down in South Central Georgia."

Ben grimaced, adding, "Abandoned, my ass."

Carroll understood. Here was yet another area where he and Walden obviously agreed. Both felt that the historical record of the government's treatment of Native Americans had been purposely hidden. One such atrocity was how the Cherokee, Creek and Seminoles tribes, were forced out of Georgia, to walk more than 1,000 miles to the newly established "Indian territory" in present-day Oklahoma. The estimate was that approximately 8,500 died along the way, but historians now say that number was grossly conservative and that the accurate number was probably double that, possibly even as high as 20,000. Walden ranted briefly on the subject before returning to the main topic.

"Philander Fitzgerald started the American Tribune Soldiers Colony for the sole purpose of selling stock at $10 a share. That's how he hoped to be able make the initial purchase of the 50,000 acres."

Walden explained that the means of funding having been decided, the next task was to get the veterans and their families to participate. This obviously meant contacting tens of thousands of veterans over the northern states at a time when there was no radio, television or other modern forms of mass communication. Fortunately, Fitzgerald already had the perfect tool to spread the word. Readers of The American Tribune, were mostly Union veterans, the very people he was trying to reach. Stories were written and ads were placed. The response was immediate. It was so overwhelming and stock sold so quickly that Fitzgerald realized they would need another 50,000 acres.

An initial crew of builders and surveyors consisting of 462 men and 72 teams of horses arrived in Georgia in 1895 to begin surveying and clearing the land for eventual settlement. However, eventual turned out to be immediate as eager settlers began arriving literally right behind them.

"Can you imagine that?" Ben asked, smiling and shaking his head. "It was almost like those places out West that you read about. Like Deadwood, where people just kept piling in. There were 2,500 people here by the end of the summer! That's why they first called the place Shacktown, because people arrived so fast that the town was mostly tents, lean-tos and covered wagons."

It was chaos, but it was organized chaos, and it was brief. The preplanning for the community had been done so meticulously that all they had to do to correct the overcrowding problem and prevent a full-scale disaster was to speed up the building process.

"What street are we on?" Walden asked rhetorically.

Carroll looked over his shoulder toward the intersection and answered, "Lee Street."

"Right," Ben nodded, "The plan was for the town to be laid out on a giant perfect square. The streets were to be named after Northern generals, starting with Grant and then Sherman, Sheridan, Thomas, Logan, Mead, Hooker and so on, but then Confederate veterans also began to settle in Shacktown. So they modified their plan and made a decision to name streets on the west side of town, where we are now, after Southern generals. Lee Street, closest to the square was named for the Commander of the Confederacy, and then you have Johnston, Jackson, Longstreet, Gordon, Bragg and Hill."

"So, the streets on the east side of town are named after Northern generals," Carroll concluded.

"Correct," said Ben, "and the four streets bordering the original square are named after Northern and Southern battleships – the Roanoke, Monitor, Merrimac and Sultana."

"This is really amazing stuff, Ben!"

Carroll had completely forgotten about why he was in Fitzgerald. He thought about the first residents of the community. Collectively, they probably fought in every major battle of the Civil War. He had been to many of those battlefields and memorials over the years, including Gettysburg. Being at that place, where Union and Confederate soldiers had slaughtered each other for three long days in July of 1863, where Lincoln had delivered his most famous speech, and seeing the rows and rows of graves had overwhelmed Carroll. It was even more emotional for him than it had been when he was at Arlington National Cemetery. The death of an American soldier resulting from a battle halfway around the world is easier to rationalize as necessary than killing your fellow countrymen in the fields of Pennsylvania. That gave Carroll another thought.

"What about Fitzgerald's cemetery, Ben?"

"It's on the southeast side of town."

"Are there any historic graves there?"

"Are you kidding? Of course there are. There's a whole separate section where Confederate and Union veterans are buried side by side."

Carroll suddenly felt guilty for enjoying himself so much. As a Civil War buff, he felt fortunate to be in Fitzgerald, but he was there because two people back in Indianapolis were still grieving over the loss of their murdered grandson. As much as he enjoyed Walden's educational jaunts, he realized they were distracting him from the case. Just as he was about to refocus the conversation on the McDowell case, Ben sidetracked him again.

"What do you think the name of the cemetery is?" he asked.

Carroll shrugged his shoulders in an attempt to appear disinterested and return to the reason for his visit. It did not work.

"Take a guess," Walden prodded.

Carroll thought about it. If the name of the cemetery was related to the Civil War, it probably would have been named for some place where many soldiers from both sides perished.

He went with his first instinct.

"Evergreen?" he guessed.

Walden raised his eyebrows, "So maybe you are a real detective, after all."

Carroll shrugged again, this time because he felt the question had been too easy. Even an amateur historian would have known the name of the cemetery at Gettysburg. Evergreen Cemetery predated the battles by a decade. Carroll thought that if he was anything beyond being a cop, he was definitely an amateur historian.

He remembered his initial question that had prompted Ben's impromptu history lesson, "How old are these houses?" They were still parked at the same location on Lee Street and Carroll looked at the homes around him once again, now realizing that men who actually fought in the Civil War had lived out the rest of their lives in these homes, far from the old battlefields.

"I don't get it, Ben," Carroll confessed. "Why haven't I ever heard of Fitzgerald before? I mean, this is part of history, and not only that, it's an interesting part of history."

"Yeah, I think so. There've been some attempts to promote it nationally, but it never got it off the ground. I've always wondered what would've happened if Fitzgerald had been mentioned on PBS's documentary, The Civil War."

"I met him once." Carroll remarked absentmindedly.

"Met who?" Ben asked.

"Ken Burns. It was at a fund-raising event for Indiana Public Broadcasting. It was several years ago and only briefly, but he was a pretty nice guy — even posed for a picture with me."

"Really? That's pretty cool! Too bad the timing wasn't better. Like, if you had already been here before Ken Burns finished making The Civil War, you could've mentio—" Ben stopped midsentence, realizing the insensitivity of his remark.

"Damn, I'm sorry Bob," he said, genuinely ashamed of himself.

"Don't worry about it," Carroll replied. "I understand. To tell you the truth, I've been feeling pretty guilty myself for enjoying the trip. You're really going to have to give me a guided tour before I leave town."

"I'll be glad to. Nice to see that someone else appreciates it."

"Now, why don't we get back to work?" Carroll suggested.

"Right," replied Ben, as he started the truck and pulled back into traffic.

It was only a couple of miles to the location where Thomas McDowell's body had been found. He had been staying at the Ridgeway Hotel on the south side of town. With a couple of exceptions, most of Fitzgerald's hotels and restaurants were located within the same general area. There were also several car dealerships, a Wal-Mart, a couple of grocery stores and other businesses typical of most any town in most any state.

Ben pulled into the parking lot of a grocery store. The plan was to walk over to the hotel so as not to attract unwanted attention. Carroll was about to exit the vehicle, but Ben hit the door locks to stop him.

"Hold on for a second," he said.

Walden reached around behind him into a bag in the club-cab. He pulled out a folder and handed it to his passenger. Carroll opened it and looked at the first page. It was labeled, Incident Report. He leafed through the contents until he saw another envelope marked, Crime Scene Photos.

Carroll's eyes widened; "Holy shit, Ben! Is this the case file?"

"It's actually a copy of the case file but, unless they've added something within the last day or two, it's current. Like I said, I checked you out.

When I found out that you were a PI from Indianapolis, I put two and two together. I figure if you can help us solve this, then, I'm all in."

"Thanks," said Carroll, as he continued to look through the file.

In addition to the initial incident report, there were statements from witnesses, hotel records, notes from police officers and investigators and, most importantly, the photos of the crime scene. Carroll was not sure if he should ask Ben how he obtained the file. If it was not legal, then he certainly did not want to know any more details. He instinctively sat up and looked around to be sure no one was able to see what he was holding.

"Don't worry," Walden laughed. "I know what you're thinking. It's all legal. It was furnished to me as a reporter by a reliable source in law enforcement, so I didn't do anything illegal or unethical to obtain it."

Carroll felt relieved. Here he was, an unlicensed private investigator from Indianapolis, nosing around an unsolved murder investigation in Georgia. As long as he did not break any local or state laws or interfere with the case, it probably was not that big of a deal. As a detective with Indianapolis PD he had occasionally dealt with PIs from other states who were working in Indiana where they were not licensed. Most law enforcement officials looked the other way.

Returning his attention to the case file, Carroll pulled out the envelope containing the crime scene photos. He would read the documents later, but he wanted to view the photos in the privacy of the truck because they were going to the crime scene where McDowell's body was recovered. Copied or not, the last thing that he wanted was to be seen standing there holding the case file of an unsolved murder.

Carroll first read the report from the crime scene photographer. It was detailed and thorough. He then studied each photo individually, sometimes rotating it in his hand, or flipping back to a previous photo before continuing. Carroll was impressed. The work was as good has anything he had seen at Indy PD. He had initially been concerned when he learned the murder had taken place in a small rural Georgia town. He had worried about shoddy investigative work, but his fears were unfounded. From what he had seen in the file so far, it appeared that they were doing everything that could and should be done to solve the crime. Carroll replaced the contents in the file and handed it back to Walden.

"Ready?" Ben asked.

"Yep, let's go."

They exited the truck and walked across from the grocery store to the parking area for commercial trucks behind the Ridgeway Hotel next door. Nearly three months had passed since the murder. There were no longer any visible signs of what had occurred near the large dumpster there.

There were no chalk lines, no crime scene tape, numbered markers, blood or any other evidence to indicate someone had been brutally murdered there, but Carroll knew exactly where to go.

Walden watched as Carroll moved from place to place, standing in the same locations where the photographer had stood, mentally recalling the details of each photo, sometimes stepping back to a previous spot. He then walked over to the Ridgeway hotel and took the exterior stairs to the second floor. Carroll stood at the railing in front of the doorway to room 237. The person who had made the gruesome discovery and made the initial 911 call was a lady named Doris Tucker.

Lugging her suitcase, she had stepped out of 237 at 7:20 that morning and looked down to see Thomas McDowell's body lying on the opposite side of the parking lot. Her scream had awakened other hotel guests. She dropped her suitcase, which popped open –spilling the contents everywhere and ran back into the room to call 911. The crime scene photos included shots of her suitcase lying on the walkway and shots of McDowell's body from her point of view before it was removed.

One of people who heard Mrs. Tucker's scream happened to be a doctor. He immediately ran to McDowell in an attempt to render aide, only to discover that he had probably been dead for several hours. The Fitzgerald Police Department and Ben Hill County Sheriff's Department had responded promptly. In fact, it was impressive. A patrol car had arrived in less than a minute, 49 seconds to be exact. Carroll left the balcony and returned to join Ben near the dumpster.

Walden gave him a moment before he asked;

"Any thoughts?"

"Tons, but unfortunately, they all end with a question mark."

"Yeah, me too."

"What are the chances of me being able to sleep with this file tonight?"

"No Problem," Ben replied, "Like I said, whatever I can do to help."

Carroll turned around several times to look back at the crime scene as they walked back to Walden's truck. As they were backing out of the parking space, he asked Ben to circle the hotel parking lot so he could see it from a driver's point of view since one of the other witnesses had driven in that morning.

Neither man spoke on the way back to town. The joking was over for the day. It was well after 5:00 p.m. when they arrived back at Ben's office. His coworkers had already gone for the day and there were no other vehicles out front except Robert Carroll's rental, the red Ford Escape. It stood out like a neon sign. It would have been funny any other time, but Carroll was too preoccupied to notice.

"It's dinnertime," Walden said. "You already bought lunch. I'll cover it. How about it?"

Carroll sighed, "I appreciate it, Ben, but I'm pretty beat. I was up at 3:00 a.m. this morning. You know, the whole, be at the airport one hour early, thing. How about breakfast instead?"

"Yeah, sure. Sorry, I forgot about that. I'll give you a buzz in the AM."

Carroll extended his right hand; "I've gotta tell you Ben, except for this last hour, it was a helluva day!"

"Same here," Ben replied as the two men shook hands.

"What's that saying? Sometimes you got to laugh to keep from crying, right?" Walden added.

"So they say," replied Carroll. "Thanks!"

Walden waved, "See ya in the morn'n, buddy."

Carroll had just started the Escape when Ben tooted his horn.

"Hey, dipshit!" Walden shouted from his window.

Carroll turned around to see Ben holding up the case file.

"Forget something? Or do you have some kind of photographic memory, Mr. Super Detective?"

Carroll palmed his forehead and walked back over to the truck.

"You said dinnertime," he remarked as he took the file.

"What?"

"You said dinnertime. I thought ya'll called it supper down here."

"We do. I was trying to sound sophisticated. I wanted to impress the big shot Yankee detective."

Carroll lifted his middle finger.

"Right back at you, asshole!" Walden shouted, returning the gesture as he peeled out of the parking lot.

4

The Blue and The Gray Area

Like anyone who find themselves waking up in a unfamiliar environments, Carroll was momentarily confused when he opened his eyes. But then he heard it, the sound that reminded him exactly where he was – a rooster crowed in the distance.

He grinned. "Welcome to Fitzgerald," he said out loud.

With the town obviously having no rush hour and most businesses not opening until nine or ten, there was certainly no need for him to be up before daybreak. But that is the downside of having an internal clock, you could not turn it off. The upside was that he could quietly take a look around.

Carroll had purposely booked a room at the Ridgeway Hotel, the same place McDowell had stayed and where he had died. In fact, when he had checked in on the previous afternoon, Carroll had told the clerk at the desk that he would like a room on the far side if possible because he sometimes had to sleep during the day due to his schedule.

In truth, he had wanted to be able to walk out of his room at roughly the same time that Doris Tucker had on the morning that she had discovered the body. He took it as a positive sign when the clerk handed him the card key in the tiny envelope with the number 237 written on it.

Carroll was up to step four of his morning routine, drinking his first cup of coffee, when he heard the unmistakable sound of the trash truck coming into the parking area behind the hotel.

In reviewing the case file, he had discovered that Jason Reynolds, the driver of Granger's truck, had emptied the dumpster before Mrs. Tucker had made her gruesome discovery. According to his statement, Reynolds told investigators that he had performed his daily task between 5:15 and 5:40, but when questioned, he reported that he had not seen anything unusual on that particular morning.

Carroll opened the door and stepped out onto the balcony. He watched as the massive gray truck came lumbering around the corner like a giant Tyrannosaurus rex. It crept toward its unsuspecting prey, seizing it in its powerful jaws and tossing it high above its head. The poor victim hung there, helpless, as the T. rex shook it violently, forcing it to regurgitate the contents from its belly. It was over in less than a minute. Hungry for more, the T. rex dropped the metal carcass and left in search of more. Carroll checked his watch. It was 5:31.

He stood at the railing on the balcony, surveying the area. He frowned. It did not make sense. A street light on a pole less than thirty feet from the dumpster left no doubt in his mind; had Carroll been standing there three months earlier, he definitely would have seen the body of Thomas McDowell lying below him, just a few feet away.

As the driver of the truck, Jason Reynolds had been closer to the body than any other person, yet he claimed that he did not see it. The time of death was undisputed. The coroner had estimated it to be between midnight and 2. A hotel employee had taken trash to the dumpster around 12:30, narrowing the time of death to a window of an hour and a half. Was Reynolds lying? And, if so, why?

Carroll walked over to his rental and put his cup of coffee on the roof of the Escape while he opened the door. The sound of another door closing made him turn around. He watched as a young family of four lugged their suitcases out and proceeded to their car. They were obviously on a trip and must have still had quite some distance to go to be leaving this early with small children, he thought.

The little girl, no more than two or three years old and still wearing her onesie, looked like she was still asleep as she followed her mother like a tiny zombie. Dad loaded the luggage while the mother cleaned out the car, putting empty cups and containers from various fast food restaurants into the trash bag that she had brought from the hotel room. Their son, who was older than his little sister, probably around seven or eight, helped his mother. They finished tidying up the car and the mother instructed the boy to dispose of the trash bag.

Pointing at the dumpster, she asked;

"Do you think you can reach it?"

"I can do it!" the boy said, confidently grabbing the bag.

His little sister, now finally awake, asked, "Can I help?"

"Donnie, let Sherry help you," his mom instructed.

"Okay."

They both knew that Sherry's "helping" consisted only of walking along beside her big brother holding onto the bag as he actually carried it, but it made her feel like she was contributing, so everyone played along. The mother stood smiling and dutifully watched her two children as they headed for the dumpster just a few yards away. Carroll reached up and retrieved his coffee mug from the roof of the rental car. The action produced the tiniest sound that probably would not have been heard during the normal activity of the day, but it caught the mother's attention.

She noticed the man standing by the Ford Escape for the first time. Upon seeing Carroll, her smile evaporated as she went into mother mode, analyzing the stranger standing before her. Her smile returned after she concluded that, like her own family, the stranger was likely going on a trip and was merely leaving early.

"Good morning," Carroll greeted, toasting her with his coffee mug.

"Good morning," she replied, returning his toast with her cup.

The woman's husband, also seeing Carroll for the first time, threw a "morn'n," and a nod toward Carroll. It was both a greeting and a friendly warning. He was basically saying I see you there, watching my family.

Bam!

All three adults jumped as Donnie dropped the lid back on the dumpster. Carroll almost dropped his coffee. The little girl began running back toward her mother.

"I'm gonna beat you!" she yelled at her brother.

"No, you're not!" he shouted back.

The two children raced back to the car, with her big brother clearly letting his little sister barely edge him out to win the race.

"I beat you. I beat you," she sang, taunting him.

"Dang! I'll beat you next time," said Donnie, sounding seriously distressed, but determined.

Carroll waved as the family climbed into the vehicle.

"Have a safe trip!" he said.

"You too," said the mother, "Nice to meet you."

Carroll nodded and raised his cup again. He watched as they drove away. "Nice to meet you." Isn't that strange, he thought. They had spoken, what was it? Five words? Six or seven at the most. And it was not as if were close enough to call it a meeting. They practically had to shout to hear each other, yet there had been some type of connection. And it was a pleasant one, a nice way to start the morning.

What they did not know was that the entire time Carroll was watching those two children he had been thinking, what if? What if they had been here three months earlier? What if those two beautiful children had carried the trash to the dumpster? From what he now knew about the crime scene, those children would have been the first ones to discover the body of Thomas McDowell. That is what Carroll was thinking as he had watched the children as they had walked toward the dumpster.

He could imagine it – with the little boy more than likely being the first to see the body of a man, covered with stab wounds and surrounded by blood. Recalling the protective, big-brotherly way he had treated his little sister earlier, Carroll could see the little boy grabbing his sister and turning her away to keep her from seeing the carnage.

Or, it might have frightened him so badly that he froze, which would have allowed the little sister to observe the scene. He imagined how traumatic it would have been for two children of their ages. Seeing something like that will stay with one for a lifetime. It is bad enough for an adult to have to deal with. The thought of the children seeing such a gruesome sight disturbed Carroll.

The parents would have blamed themselves:

"I shouldn't have let them go over there alone."

"I should have walked with them."

"I should have made them stay at the car and carried it myself."

As he watched the family drive away Carroll thought it was all about timing. Yes, there had been an interval of several months, but it was still about timing, and that young family was lucky, even though they would never know it.

Carroll circled the back side of the hotel in the Ford Escape. He left the parking lot, taking a right onto U.S. highway 319, then turned immediately into the Flash Foods store, looped around the gas pumps and returned back to the hotel parking lot, driving in from the entrance on the opposite side just as he had watched the trash truck do a few moments before.

He pulled the car straight up to the dumpster as if his rental was the giant trash truck. As he sat there in the Escape with the grill almost touching the dumpster, Carroll's suspicion was confirmed. Sitting in the driver's seat, parked where he was at that moment, there was no doubt in his mind that he would have been able to see McDowell's body if he had been sitting there three months before. Could Jason Reynolds, the driver of the truck, have been involved? Or, maybe he did see the body and was just afraid to tell the truth for some reason.

Carroll cautiously looked around to be sure no one was watching before he exited the vehicle. Everyone who worked at the surrounding businesses knew what had happened there. They also knew that it was still unsolved, that a murderer was still on the loose. All it would take to send people into panic mode would be for someone to see him standing there before daylight staring at the crime scene.

He could imagine someone calling 911 screaming, "There's an SUV parked at the dumpster where that guy was killed and a strange man is standing there staring at the exact place where he died!"

Carroll had been impressed with the speedy response of local law enforcement. He guessed that if someone had seen him this morning, they were probably making a call like that right then. He expected the responding officers would probably be professional, but, then again, every police department, large or small, has at least one rookie goofball who probably should not be wearing a badge and with his luck, that's the one that would respond this morning.

Carroll looked around, half expecting to see flashing blue lights. He chuckled, knowing that he had actually made himself nervous. Not wanting to push his luck, he started back toward his vehicle. Suddenly, there was a commotion from directly above his head; limbs cracked as leaves and twigs began falling on him. There was a terrifying scream, and he saw a shadow move as he looked up.

Carroll instinctively dropped to the ground, reached down and yanked the Glock 27 from his leg holster. He had done his research before coming to Georgia, ensuring that his concealed carry permit was valid here. The biggest obstacle was the extra time and effort that was required to follow the airline's protocol to disassemble it and send it through in a secured manner.

Unlike some people, who griped about the stringent Transportation Security Administration at airports, Carroll understood that we are living in a different world, one that most other countries around the globe have been living in for decades. There was no doubt in his mind that these stricter security requirements, even though there had been some well-publicized glitches, had likely prevented other terrorist attacks.

Now, as he lay there on the ground, waiting to defend himself against whomever was pouncing from above, he was glad that he had the training and capability to do whatever was required. He cautiously looked around for any sign of danger, but there was none. In fact, there was no sound at all. The noise had subsided as suddenly as it had started.

Then he saw something falling from the area above him where the sound had originated. It was small and dark, either brown or reddish colored. It fell slowly, wafting from side to side, like a feather, landing inches from his nose. It was a feather.

"Welcome to Fitzgerald," he said for the second time this morning. Still lying on his belly, he gave a puff and watched as the feather danced away. He stood up and looked around, as one does after stumbling over a nonexistent something on a sidewalk, to see how many people were laughing. Thankfully, there was no one else around.

Carroll picked up an aluminum beer can and tossed it into the tree. Not one, but two chickens emerged, squawking and clucking as they dropped down to the ground.

"Wake up!" he said. "It's sunrise. Or, is that just for roosters?"

The chickens proceeded to the area around the dumpster and began pecking away, clucking between pecks. Carroll suspected they were making fun of him. He completed the trip to his SUV and cranked up the vehicle. He was backing away from the dumpster when he stopped again. Carroll looked back up at the tree limb from where he sat, and then pulled the Escape right up to the dumpster again and looked up. He hadn't noticed it earlier, but the limb was from a huge magnolia tree. The trunk of the tree was located at least 20 feet away. Two limbs nearest the dumpster had been trimmed, obviously to accommodate the dumping process.

"Well I'll be damned," he said, shaking his head.

The driver of the trash truck had been telling the truth he suddenly realized. The driver's seat of the big truck would have been at least three to four feet higher than the Escape's, which would have meant the driver's view to the crime scene would have been partially obscured. It was good to confirm it, and Carroll knew that he had to give credit to the two chickens for their assistance. He checked the time again. It was now just after six.

Carroll put the SUV into reverse, turned around and pulled into the parking lot of the grocery store located on the north side of the hotel, the same place he and Ben had parked the previous day. As expected, he saw the Sunbeam delivery truck parked on the south side of the store.

His plan was simple: Knowing the store didn't open until 7, he would pull into a close, but inconspicuous, parking space, near the delivery truck and then catch the deliveryman in an accidental encounter and strike up a conversation from there. He found the perfect parking spot and then sat and waited.

Carroll glanced over at the delivery truck so familiar to millions of Americans, with its overall blue color wrapped with the yellow rectangle and the iconic "Little Miss Sunbeam," the little blonde-haired girl, taking a bite of toast on each side. As he looked at the logo on the truck, Carroll realized that he probably knew more about that little girl and the woman who originally painted her than most people. Just as he was finding out more about this small little town in South Georgia because of his work on a case, he had discovered some interesting facts about Little Miss Sunbeam in much the same way.

It had started as a simple missing person case for someone named Barbara Segner. Through subsequent research he had found an Ellen Barbara Segner that he thought could be the person that he was looking for, but there were several problems. The first was that Ellen Segner was deceased. She had died of natural causes in 2001. This would obviously have ended the case if he could prove that it was the same person.

That is where the second problem came in. Ellen was apparently a very private person. Carroll could not seem to find her date of birth, something that he normally had no problem doing, and without a date of birth or death certificate, he could not confirm if they were in fact the same person. What he did find out about Ellen Segner was that she was very famous – for an unknown person. It would probably be difficult to find an American that had not seen and loved her work through her two most well known works.

Ellen Segner was the artist who painted the image that so many of us are familiar with, that little yellow-haired girl in the blue dress that we call Little Miss Sunbeam. Segner was also the illustrator for many popular children's books, including the Dick and Jane series. Her work also appeared in national magazines such as Glamour and Look. And, Carroll mused, partly because of her illustrations in Girl Scout guide books, countless numbers of young girls had learned to be:

Honest and Fair, Friendly and Helpful, Considerate and Caring, Courageous and Strong, and Responsible for what I say and do... And to respect myself and others, respect authority, use resources wisely, make the world a better place, and be a sister to every Girl Scout.

During his quest to verify Segner's identity, Carroll had come across the story of how she had found the real Little Miss Sunbeam. Well, sort of.

In 1942, Segner was commissioned by Quality Bakers of America to create a marketing symbol using a "young child." Such a vague description allowed Ellen unlimited creativity and she began to look for her muse. This apparently proved more difficult than she expected. Feeling frustrated, the story goes, she stepped out of her Greenwich Village studio one day to take a break. She walked down the street to Washington Square Park where she plopped down on a bench. She saw a young, blonde headed girl playing nearby, so she took out her sketch pad and went to work. It was one of those things that was just meant to happen. She was so preoccupied with her sketching that when she looked back up a few minutes later, the little girl had completely disappeared. Segner jumped up and began frantically searching the park, looking like a mother who had lost her own child, but it was all in vain. The little girl was gone.

We will never know who the real Little Miss Sunbeam was. The little girl who later got the credit as the original Little Miss Sunbeam and became famous was five year old Patty Michaels, a child model. Not only was she naturally beautiful, she had a personality to match her looks. Michaels was also truly multitalented. She was an excellent performer. She could dance and sing, which landed her the role of Louisa von Trapp in the original Broadway production of Rodgers & Hammerstein's The Sound of Music.

Because of her success in such a huge production, she soon found herself on most of the top TV variety programs of the day, Jackie Gleason, Garry Moore, Sid Caesar. She was also a regular on Sing Along With Mitch, the hugely popular program hosted by Mitch Miller, the big Columbia executive.

That led to a recording contract. Some of her records, like "Mrs. Johnny" and "They're Dancing Now" sold well, but like a lot of other recording artists of the time she eventually faded into relative obscurity.

Most people today would not know her name even though they still see her face as a young girl daily.

Carroll was later able to get his hands on Ellen Segner's death certificate. In an unusual twist, the certificate still contained no information about Ellen's exact birthday. He later learned that she had actually destroyed her birth records intentionally to "maintain her privacy."

There was still enough other information on the death certificate to determine that she was not the person he was looking for. It took another long month of tracking leads before he finally located the right Barbara Segner. It turned out that she was never really missing at all.

It was something that he should have half expected. He had seen similar cases before, people who were not really missing but were actually escaping. What were they escaping from? Bad relationships, work they hated, the memories of the past – whatever. Missing person cases were monotonous. Few were really very challenging and it was the lowest paying gig on his scale.

The Barbara Segner case had ended the same way. She was fine and unhurt. In fact, she had accomplished her goal. She was happily remarried and had two children. In the end, to keep from revealing her whereabouts, Carroll had returned the money to his clients, her distant cousins who were trying to find her. After locating Segner and talking to her, Carroll determined her relatives were simply trying to find a way to finagle her out of money that she had legally inherited, money that they neither deserved nor were entitled to.

He had to laugh about it now. He had wasted three months on a missing person case where the person was not missing, a case where he didn't make one red cent. The only good thing to come from it was that he had a really cool story to tell at cocktail parties – that is, if he went to them.

Carroll looked up just as the Sunbeam driver came walking out of the grocery store, headed back toward his truck pushing a cart of empty containers.

Carroll got out and started toward the store.

"Morn'n," he said as he walked past the deliveryman.

Suzi would have been proud of how he had dropped the G like a bad habit, but he was beginning to think that he was losing his touch – for a moment. However, the deliveryman returned his greeting and added, "They're not open yet. Don't open until seven."

"Okay, thanks," Carroll replied.

The timing was perfect. It allowed Carroll to turn around as if he were returning to his own vehicle, which momentarily put them walking side by side, and it appeared to be completely coincidental.

"I'll just wait in the car," he said.

Then Carroll tossed out the hook with the bait on it. Pointing back toward the dumpster near the hotel, he added, "Although, I may move and park on the other side."

The deliveryman stopped and turned toward him. Carroll's bait was being nibbled. He just needed to jiggle it a bit.

"After what happened over there I get a little nervous here at night," Carroll added.

"Tell me about it," the deliveryman replied. "I was jittery for two months. I thought about moving to the other side too, but that's where Little Debbie parks so I just stuck with my own spot."

"I'll bet that it was pretty tense right after it happened, huh? Carroll inquired.

"You have no idea! I still get chills every time I think about it."

Carroll shook his head, "I can't even imagine seeing something like that,"

"Oh, I didn't see it," the bread man responded.

He looked up at the moonless sky and added, "I thank God every day that I didn't see it. I don't think I could live with those kinds of images floating around in my head."

He had no way of knowing that the person he was talking to had seen hundreds and hundreds of those images over the decades. He was right. They never go away.

Carroll nodded and extended his right arm as he introduced himself, "Bob."

The two men shook hands.

"Name's Todd. Nice to meet you, Bob."

Carroll already knew his first name. He knew his last name, too – and whole lot more, but he continued to play the role.

"I just wish they would solve the damn thing," said Carroll.

"Me too, but I don't think they ever will. I believe whoever did it is long gone. That's pretty much what everybody in the store thinks, too."

"I hope that's right," Carroll agreed. "Still, not knowing is the hardest part."

"Yeah, all of us delivery guys have an agreement to look after each other. As much as we like to joke and pick on one another inside the store, there's none of that, sneaking up and scaring the hell out of each other crap, out here in the parking lot."

"I heard that," said Carroll. "A guy could get hurt playing around like that now."

"You ain't kidding! I damn near killed a chicken with a loaf of bread during that first week."

Carroll smiled. He could relate. The ninja-chickens in the magnolia by the dumpster had no idea how close they had come to death. The thought amused Carroll. He did his best to stifle a laugh, but he was having difficulty holding it back.

"Seriously? You threw a loaf of bread at a chicken?"

"I shit you not!" Todd swore. "Damn thing came out from under the truck in the dark and bumped my leg. I thought someone was try'n to grab me, so I used the only weapon I had, a loaf of Sunbeam."

That was it. Carroll could not hold back any longer. He managed to blurt out another question, "Did you actually hit it?"

"Hell yeah! Knocked that little bastard halfway across the parking lot!"

Carroll was snorting by this point and Todd joined in. The two men leaned against the truck, laughing and looking like drunks who would topple over without the aid of Little Miss Sunbeam.

"Little son of a bitch was lucky that I grabbed a Lite Wheat. If it'd been a loaf of Giant, there'd be one less rooster in Fitzgerald."

Carroll collapsed to his knees. Todd leaned over and rubbed his now aching belly. They eventually calmed down and talked for a few more minutes before shaking hands again. Todd had to resume his deliveries and Carroll, seeing that the store was now open, went inside, to keep up appearances.

It was a quarter after seven. Carroll hurriedly returned to the hotel. He reentered room 237, closed the door and stood there, watching the second hand on his watch. He waited less than a minute before he promptly stepped back onto the balcony at 7:20.

He had hoped to see something new by looking at the crime scene at the exact same time and from the same angle that Doris Tucker had, but he was not that lucky. There was nothing. His cell phone rang. He checked the display.

"Morn'n, Ben."

"Hey, Bob. I know that we ate there for lunch yesterday, but you can't beat breakfast at The Sportsman."

"Sounds good to me," Carroll replied. "Are you already out and about?"

"Oh, hell yeah. I've got a paper to put together."

"Okay, I'm on my way."

It took Carroll less than five minutes to drive to The Sportsman. Walden was pulling up at the same time. He grabbed the USA Today before getting out. The two men walked into the restaurant together and went straight to be Ben's booth. Carroll put his keys, cell phone and the paper on the table next to the wall.

Ben looked at the USA Today and grinned;

"What's that for? You got some fresh fish to wrap?"

"I wish! I can't even remember the last time I went fishing."

"I'll have you in a boat by the end of the week," Ben replied confidently.

"Man, that would be nice!"

Walden added, "So hold onto that USA Today for the fish and I'll give you a real newspaper after we put ours together today.

"It's a deal."

Becky started toward their table with menus in her right hand, but when she saw Ben, she suddenly held up her left hand, snapped her fingers spun around and walked back into the kitchen like she had forgotten something. She returned momentarily with a small saucer plate and placed it on the table in front of Ben. He looked at Carroll and shrugged his shoulders. The plate was apparently not part of Walden's normal morning routine.

"And just what is this for?" Ben asked Becky.

She reached into her apron and dropped a butter knife on the plate, saying, "I just figured I'd get a jumpstart, 'cause if you act like you usually do, you'll be lying on the bench in a few minutes. You might as well help me out while you're down there and scrape off gum."

Walden wet his finger on his tongue, then reached up and marked an imaginary tally board in the air.

"Score one for Becky!" he said.

Between his earlier discussion with Todd and the way his day was beginning with Walden at The Sportsman, Carroll was in a pretty good mood. He did not know how the rest of the day would go, but he felt that he was lucky to start it on a light note. It did not take long for Becky's foresight to pay off. After Carroll related the story about the ninja chickens in the tree and Todd's story about the loaf of bread, Walden was in the same shape he had been in the day before as he rolled and laughed on the booth seat. Carroll was almost as bad.

"Aren't you two supposed to be in your Pre-K class?" Becky asked as she walked by.

By including Carroll in her verbal jab she had unknowingly made him feel like he was now part of the community, if not the town, at least inside of The Sportsman's walls. Carroll and Walden both had a busy day ahead. Ben had a newspaper to put together and Carroll was going to proceed with their plan from the day before. He would be taking the Escape to Billy Bob's garage.

He also hoped to try and get in a bit of sightseeing. After finding out that he was truly interested in the town's history, Walden had given him a folder containing some material from the Fitzgerald-Ben Hill County Chamber of Commerce. Carroll had briefly glanced through it, inventorying the contents. There was a glossy magazine promoting the town, a city map, a little booklet entitled Architectural Treasures Tour, and three pamphlets,

Evergreen Cemetery Tour Map and Guide, The Unique Story of a Unique City and one for something that Carroll was really looking forward to seeing, "The Blue & Gray Museum."

Upon seeing the pamphlet for the museum, Carroll realized that his perception of that short phrase the Blue and the Gray had changed forever, at least in his own mind. Whenever he had heard it before, it had conjured up images of divisiveness that led to conflict, battle, destruction and death. Now, after visiting Fitzgerald and learning about its history, he could also associate the phrase the Blue and the Gray with harmony and community.

Carroll told Ben about his discovery after the episode with the chickens by the dumpster – about Jason Reynolds's statement when he said that he had not see anything that morning. Carroll explained that it did not make a difference in a car or even in the SUV, but if one were sitting just a few feet higher, like in the seat of a big truck, his vision would have been obscured by the tree limb.

"Reynolds was telling the truth," Carroll said. "He was just a few feet away from a body, but he never even knew it."

Carroll told Ben that he also believed Todd Sellers was being truthful, although he did not have anything as substantial as a tree limb as proof. What he did have was something almost as reliable. He had honed his cop instincts over the years to the point where he was rarely mistaken when he followed them. Those instincts told him the bread man was being truthful.

Walden was impressed. He had occasionally poked fun at his new friend, joking about his detective skills, but he was beginning to appreciate that the process was more nuanced. True, the ultimate goal was to identify the suspect, but Walden was learning that eliminating potential suspects was also important.

He liked that something as crazy as ninja chickens in a tree had enabled Carroll to clear one man's name from the list. Ben also agreed with him on Todd Sellers. He had not mentioned it before, but Todd was a close personal friend.

"I've known Todd since high school. He's talked to me about that day," said Ben. "I believe him. He doesn't talk about it much, but it really bothers him."

Becky brought out their orders. Walden did a double-take when he saw his friend's plate.

"Damn, son!" he exclaimed, "Why don't you have some grits?"

"Thank you! I believe I will!"

Carroll already had some grits. In fact, he had a double order. He had discovered grits during his first trip to Georgia and had added them to his breakfast menu on every trip since. One of his Glynco training sessions had provided him with another amazing revelation – grits were also regularly served with fish. And not just grits – cheese grits!

They continued to discuss the case as they ate. Carroll had spent hours going over and over the file during the night. He stood by his initial assessment – that the law enforcement investigators had done a good job with the little evidence they had. There were no witnesses. The murder weapon, a large knife, was never recovered. Other than the victim's, there was no DNA evidence, fingerprints or anything else that would give them a suspect. All that was known is that McDowell was stabbed to death.

Because his wallet was missing, the motive for the murder appeared to be one of the oldest in existence, robbery. But, as Carroll and Walden had also agreed, they still had to include hate crime as a possibility, especially after seeing Billy Bob's less-than-playful romp with Lenny Sauls at McCoy's Auto Repair on the previous day.

McCoy's was Carroll's intended destination as soon as they finished their meals. Unfortunately, Walden had to be at his office. If it had been another day or, if Carroll would wait a few hours, Ben could go with him.

"A couple of hours won't make a big difference," Walden reasoned, "Why not wait?"

He clearly did not like the idea of Carroll going alone.

"I told him I would be there the first this morning, remember?" Carroll explained. "You've gotta build trust with a guy like McCoy. Don't worry, Ben. I know what I'm doing."

After assuring Walden that he would call as soon as he left the garage, Carroll proceeded to McCoy's Auto Repair. Billy Bob was talking to an older man as Carroll pulled in. They were standing by the man's truck. The hood was up and they had their elbows on the fender looking at the engine. Carroll parked on the side and spoke as he walked up.

"Morn'n, Billy Bob." Looking at the elderly man he repeated, "Morn'n."

The other man nodded and returned the greeting.

"Hey, Bob, I'll be with ya in a bit," McCoy said.

Carroll looked around, but Lenny Sauls was nowhere in sight. At first he was disappointed, but Carroll decided it was actually a good thing. It gave him a chance to look around while Billy Bob was preoccupied with the other customer. Not wanting to appear too anxious or nosy, he lingered around the outside for a few minutes before walking through the open door into the office. Using his peripheral vision, he watched for a reaction from McCoy. Apparently, he either did not see Carroll or did not care.

Billy Bob's office was typical of what Carroll expected it to be – filthy and disorganized. There were seven calendars on the walls, all featuring scantily clad or completely nude women. Of the seven, only one was for the current year. The rest spanned years from the 70s to the present. There were also lots of posters on the walls, also with women on them, featuring auto parts or racing.

There were auto parts lying everywhere, some in boxes and some in pieces. There was a desk, but it appeared that its usefulness was limited to being just another place to stack items. Carroll was beginning to doubt that Billy Bob could read or write anyway, so why would he need to use the desktop? All of the drawers were either open or partially open. The paperwork looked old and yellow, and there was what appeared to be either a bird or rat nest in one.

A peek out the window made him feel better. Billy Bob had his back turned to the office and was focused on the man's engine. Even if he had turned around, the old posters, flyers and amount of filth on the window would have likely prevented McCoy from seeing exactly what Carroll was doing inside.

Still using his peripheral vision to keep one eye on Billy Bob, he quickly searched the office, rifling through everything he could find. Carroll knew it was a long shot, so he was not surprised when he came up empty-handed. There was nothing to implicate Billy Bob for anything other than being the typical redneck male of his age. He closed the last drawer just as McCoy finished with the old man and started toward the office. Carroll was standing at one of the calendars, flipping through the months as Billy Bob walked in.

"Hope you ain't plan'n noth'n using that calendar. It's an old one," he informed Carroll. "They were up when I bought the place and damn if I'm gonna take'em down," McCoy explained.

"Hell, I don't blame you. Those are some beautiful women."

He turned around to see McCoy staring at him with a smirk. He was not sure if Billy Bob thought he was that stupid or if he was taunting him again. He suspected the latter. Carroll could not put his finger on it, but there was something about McCoy that just did not feel right.

Billy Bob pointed to the NASCAR clock on the wall;

"I've got a lady that'll be here in a few minutes for an oil change. You wanna pull yours in right quick? I'm gonna put it on the lift 'stead of using the pit, so I can see better under there."

"Sure thing."

Carroll jumped into the Escape and followed Billy Bob's hand signals as he guided him onto the lift. As soon as he was out of the vehicle, McCoy pulled a lever. There was a loud hiss of pressure as the massive hydraulic column began to rise slowly. As it struggled to make the lift, it groaned like an old out-of-shape weight lifter, trying to relive his glory days.

Carroll squatted down and cocked his head sideways, trying to get a view as it rose. He was not just doing it for show. He half expected to see some damage. The low hum of the lift changed to a higher whine as the old athlete proudly reached his intended goal.

Carroll ducked his head and started to step under, but Billy Bob threw out his arm like a railroad crossing barricade.

"Hold on there, cowboy!" he warned. "That damn lift is as old as this station. Safety first, right?"

McCoy turned the lever, locking it into position.

"Hand me them 4X4's, Bob," he said. "One-at-a time."

Carroll was puzzled, but he did as instructed, retrieving four identical pieces of lumber from the floor. McCoy took them and placed them lengthwise under the frame of the lift, jamming one under each tire, like columns supporting a roof. They were about five feet in length and fit perfectly under the frame. It was obvious that he had cut them specifically for that purpose. Billy Bob gave each one a shake, testing to be sure they were all snug. Satisfied, he turned around to find Carroll eying the columns suspiciously. McCoy grinned.

"Yeah, I know," he acknowledged, "They might not hold it, but they'll at least slow the son of a bitch down until I get my thin ass out from under it," he said, going under it with no hesitation.

Carroll simply nodded. He had changed his mind about joining Billy Bob underneath the vehicle. McCoy spent several minutes going back and forth and up and down the length of the SUV before he came out.

"You're good to go Bob. I don't see no damage at all," he reported.

Billy Bob walked from column to column, giving each a kick at the base to knock them down and another to slide them further away from the lift.

"That's good to know," Carroll replied, feeling relieved. "What do I owe you?"

"Let's see," McCoy pondered, as he lowered the SUV.

"Let's call it $36.95 for labor."

Carroll reached for his wallet.

"Damn, son! I was just kid'n! I only pulled a damn lever and squinted at some dirt. You gonna pay me for that?"

"Well, hell, Billy Bob," Carroll said seriously, "you risked your life going under there."

"You got that shit right!" he laughed.

"So where's Lenny today?"

"Oh, that big dumbass don't usually show up 'til mid-morn'n or after lunch."

"It scared the hell out of me when he threw you yesterday," Carroll admitted.

"Scared you? You weren't the one fly'n through the air wonder'n if you're fix'n to be part of a plow or landing with a shovel stuck up your ass!"

Carroll could not help but laugh.

"He didn't mean it though," McCoy quickly added.

Carroll decided to play it out.

"I don't know, Billy Bob. Lenny looks pretty dangerous to me. I'd sure hate to be on the receiving end if he ever really did get mad."

"That bastard's as strong as an ox," McCoy confirmed. "Those 4X4's that I was using in there? I seen him break one with his bare hands one time. No shit!"

"I don't doubt that one bit. So, is he related to you?"

"Hell no!" Billy Bob shot back defensively. "This place used to belong to his uncle. He played here as a kid and he worked here for his uncle when he got bigger. Me, I ain't from around here."

It was an opening for Carroll.

"You're not? Where are you from?"

"Texas."

"Whereabouts in Texas?"

McCoy shot Carroll a look, "Jesus, Bob! You write'n a damn book? Cause if ya are – then, as the say'n goes – leave that damn chapter out!"

"Didn't mean noth'n by it, Billy Bob. I've been there a few times and I was just curious."

Billy Bob walked up behind Carroll, grabbed him by the shoulders and shook him roughly.

"I was just mess'n with you, Bob! You gotta learn to light'n up, dude!"

A blue car pulled in and Billy Bob walked out to meet it, giving Carroll a pop on the back of the head as he walked away. McCoy's words might have suggested playfulness, but his actions did not. He was sending a message. Carroll would have the marks on his shoulders and a sore head to prove it. Another car pulled in behind the first, and after speaking to McCoy, the lady who had driven the first car, climbed into the passenger seat of the other car and rode away.

Billy Bob walked back in, saying, "That's my oil change. Wanna get your hands dirty, Bob? How 'bout taking this one for me?"

Carroll was attempting to stutter a response when McCoy added, "I'm just shit'n you, Bob! But, how about watch'n the store for a sec while I get my coveralls on?"

"Sure, no problem."

McCoy went into the bathroom and emerged in a few minutes wearing a pair of the dirtiest, oiliest coveralls that Carroll had ever seen.

"Hey Bob, can you drive up on the rack for me?"

"Sure, I'd be glad to."

"You sure are one cooperative son of a bitch!" he chuckled.

"I do what I can."

"You'd make a damn good wife," McCoy shot back in a voice that Carroll could only characterize as mocking.

He looked up to find Billy Bob staring at him intently. It was obvious that he was suspicious. There was something unusual about McCoy, but

Carroll could not quite put his finger on it. Not wanting to push it further, he climbed into the rental, backed it from the rack and parked it out of the way. Billy Bob tossed him the keys to the customer's car and then guided him onto the rack just as he had done earlier.

Carroll walked back into the office to retrieve his cell phone and was about to say goodbye when he noticed McCoy's blue jeans hanging on a peg in the bathroom. He realized that instead of putting the coveralls over his clothes, Billy Bob had actually removed his jeans and hung them up. The only reason the car had to be on the lift rails was so it was aligned properly for the oil change. Instead of raising the car up as he had done with the Escape, McCoy took the steps down into the pit underneath the vehicle. It was perfect.

Jesus! Carroll thought. Could I be that lucky? If Billy Bob had raised the car up instead it would have been too risky to do what he was about to attempt.

As soon as McCoy climbed into the hole, Carroll slipped into the bathroom. With one eye on the door and listening for any noise indicating that Billy Bob was coming back, he reached around and felt the back of the blue jeans. He couldn't believe it. Sure enough, there was Billy Bob McCoy's wallet. He flipped it open, removed his driver's license and copied the license number and birthday. Carroll quickly checked the wallet for anything else that might be useful. He found two credit cards, which was something that really surprised him. He wrote down the information from the cards and then found another bonus, McCoy's Social Security card. He replaced everything exactly as he found it, being sure that everything was not only in its proper place, but was also facing in the same position that it had been.

"Hey, Billy Bob, I'm gonna cut out!" he shouted.

"Okay, later dude!"

"Thanks a lot for the help!" Carroll said as he left, but Billy Bob didn't hear him. He had turned up the volume on the sound system and Lynyrd Skynyrd's Sweet Home Alabama was blasting away.

Carroll did not care about a response anyway. His only focus was to get down the street and out of sight, where he could call Suzi to give her the information about Billy Bob to run a background check. He was looking for a parking lot or place to pull over to call Suzi when he had a second stroke of good luck. He saw the unmistakable huge profile of Lenny Sauls walking down the sidewalk. But, Sauls was headed in the opposite direction, away from Billy Bob's Garage. Carroll pulled up to the curb and tooted his horn.

"Hey, Lenny!" he shouted, waving.

Lenny squinted against the sun to see who was hollering at him. He smiled and waved back as his eyes focused.

"Hey, Mr. Carroll!"

He kept walking and Carroll pulled closer, driving along with him.

"Where you going?"

Sauls pointed south to where most of the fast-food restaurants were located, "To get breakfast."

"Hop in and I'll give you a ride."

"Okay!" he replied gratefully.

Carroll stopped the vehicle, pressed the button to unlock the passenger door. Lenny tried to get into the passenger side, but the seat was too close. He looked at the front of the seat and was reaching around for a handle so he could release it and push the seat back.

"It's electric," Carroll informed him. "Push that little button there and the seat will move."

Lenny pressed the button. There was a humming sound as the seat began to move backwards. Sauls grinned like a two year-old child that had just accomplished some task that would have been a minor effort for anyone over the age of three.

"Seatbelt," Carroll reminded Lenny as he got situated in his seat. Sauls dutifully buckled his seat belt and looked around at the interior of the vehicle.

"Wow! This is nice ain't it?"

Carroll had to admit that it was pretty nice. The interior of the Escape was similar to his Range Rover Evoque. The six-speed automatic stick shift was on the console, but instead of being located back between the seats as it is in most vehicles, it was situated farther forward and at an angle, just under the controls for the heat and air conditioner. He also liked the fact that most of the gauges were in fact, actual gauges, and not idiot lights. There was; however, a lot of new technology on the dash: GPS, fuel economy, weather information about the exterior, comfort level indicators for the interior, and so forth. In short, there were a lot of buttons and knobs. Carroll thought he had just lucked out, but he would later learn that Suzi had researched the rentals to find something as close to his personal vehicle as possible.

Lenny Sauls was thrilled.

"It's like an airplane!" he exclaimed.

"Yeah, it is nice."

"It's better than nice! It's like an airplane!"

Carroll pulled back into traffic and proceeded south on Main Street. He had driven barely half a block when the street forked and Main became a one-way designated only for southbound traffic. Once again Carroll realized just how lucky he was. If Lenny had been just a little farther ahead he might have missed him due to the one way street.

"So where you feel like eating?" Carroll asked.

"I like McDonald's."

"Then McDonald's it is."

Sauls grinned contentedly and then asked in a timid voice,

"Can we turn on the radio?"

"Sure. What kind of music do you like?"

"All kinds. I don't care what kind. I just like music."

Carroll smiled. He knew he was about to blow Lenny's mind. Being careful that Sauls did not see, he touched a button on the steering wheel. Then, without touching any other buttons or controls, he commanded in a clear voice, "Mobile apps ... Pandora."

Lenny's eyes widened and his mouth literally dropped open.

Carroll gave another verbal command, "Listen to Beatles Radio."

The sound system immediately erupted with the Beatles'; *Yellow Submarine.*

"Ha ha ha!" Sauls began laughing and clapping his hands as if he had just seen an amazing magic trick.

Carroll was surprised to find that Lenny knew the words. Well, sort of. Actually, he knew the chorus. He began to clap along, having difficulty keeping in time with the beat, as he sang;

"We all live in a yellow submarine, a yellow submarine, a yellow submarine. We all live in a yellow submarine, a yellow submarine, a yellow submarine!"

As it ended, Carroll asked Lenny how he would rate the song.

"Is it a good song?" he asked Lenny, holding his right hand in a thumbs up position.

"Or is it a bad song?" he asked, flipping his thumb downward.

Lenny extended his arm and gave Carroll a thumbs up.

"No, not to me, to the radio."

Sauls reached forward, literally touching his thumbs up against the console. Carroll had to force himself to remain composed and not laugh. Poor Lenny, he thought.

"No, say it," he told Sauls, mouthing the words, thumbs up, so Lenny could do it.

Lenny looked at Carroll, then back at the console and nodded, finally understanding. He leaned as far forward and as close to the console as the seatbelt and his massive frame would permit.

He shouted, "THUMBS UP!"

The system immediately acknowledged his rating, giving it a thumbs up approval. Lenny was ecstatic. He actually squealed in such a high pitch that it hurt Carroll's ears. They arrived at McDonald's and Carroll began turning into a parking spot. Lenny was visibly disappointed.

"Can we go through the drive-thru?" he asked.

"Sure, we can do that."

Lenny grinned broadly and began to rock back and forth in anticipation. Carroll lowered the driver's window as he pulled up to the speaker.

"Welcome to McDonald's. How may I help you today?" came a young female voice.

"Hey, Can you give us just a sec, please?" Carroll requested.

"Sure! Just go ahead when you're ready," She replied.

He turned to Sauls, "What do you want, Lenny?"

"Can I order?"

Carroll grinned and nodded.

Lenny leaned forward again, this time toward Carroll as the drive-thru speaker was on his side. Sauls yelled at the speaker, "TWO, TWO, TWO AND TWO!"

Carroll reached up and cupped his right ear, the one that was directly in the line of fire and was receiving the most damage. He was about to intercede and assist Lenny with his order. Besides having a problem with the level of his voice, it was apparent to Carroll that Lenny had no idea what he was doing with the numbers. Carroll was not sure if Sauls wanted the number two breakfast meal from the menu, or if he wanted two of an item and was just trying to make sure that they understood by repeating it.

He started to speak, but then the female voice crackled back over the speaker, "Okay, that's two steak, egg & cheese McMuffins, two sausage, two Cinnamon Melts and two cokes. Anything else, Lenny?"

"NO! NUTH'N ELSE! THAT'S ALL! WE DON'T WANT NUTH'N ELSE! THAT'S ALL!" he shouted back.

It was clear the concept of modern audio technology was alien to Sauls. In his mind, if he could not actually see the person he was talking to then he had to shout to be sure that they could hear him.

"Okay, I'll be happy to serve you at the window."

Carroll became a bit worried as he reviewed the order in his head. That was an awful lot of food. Lenny apparently thought that Carroll's appetite was as big as his own. Carroll knew he couldn't possibly keep up with Sauls when it came to eating, but it quickly became evident that he wouldn't have to do that.

A look of concern suddenly came over Lenny's face as he asked, "Wait, don't you want nuth'n?"

"No thanks. I already had breakfast," Carroll replied, no longer able to keep from chuckling.

As much as Carroll liked his rental vehicle, it lacked one important feature that he really would have liked to have been able to use at that moment, the ability to stream a live video of Lenny Sauls placing his order at the McDonald's drive-thru to Suzi back in Indianapolis. Just the thought of her watching from her desk got him tickled again as they pulled up to the drive-thru window where a young girl waited.

"Hey, Lenny!" she yelled, completely ignoring Carroll.

"Hey, Sheila! I'm at the drive-thru!"

"I know! I see you! I don't think I've ever seen you at the drive-thru before!"

Carroll was trying to figure out if Sheila was playing along because she was aware of Lenny's personal challenges or if she had some issues of her own, when, in an attempt to look into the Escape, she climbed halfway through the drive-thru window and leaned into Carroll's, forcing him to melt back into the seat.

"You've really got a nice car!" she said, again addressing Lenny and ignoring the man that she had just brushed up against.

"I ain't got no car. Ain't got no truck neither," Sauls patiently explained to the poor, misinformed Sheila.

"It's his," Lenny said, pointing at Carroll.

It was suddenly obvious to Carroll that Sheila was not playing along as he had first suspected. She simply appeared to be immature.

"We thought it was almost time for you." she answered, still paying no attention to the driver whom she knew only as, his.

"Here's your order," she said, reaching in front of his's face to Lenny's. "Thank you, Lenny. See ya later!"

"BYE, SHEILA!" he screamed, back on speaker volume.

Carroll made a right at the next traffic light and then a left into the Wal-Mart parking lot. He pulled into a spot and left the vehicle and the radio running. Lenny pulled out one of the containers, removed one of the steak, egg and cheese muffins, stuffed the entire thing into his mouth, chewed twice and swallowed. Carroll quickly turned his head away and looked out the driver's window as he wiped his eyes.

"Hey, Lenny, how did you meet Billy Bob?" he asked.

"Oh, he bought Uncle Jack's gas station," Sauls responded as he crumpled up an empty container.

Paul McCartney sang Let It Be over the radio.

"Do you like Billy Bob?"

"Yeah, but not when he gets really really really mean."

"Like when he was choking you the other day?"

"Naw, that was just play'n. I'm talking about when he's mean to other people," he said as he removed the lid of one of the Cokes.

"What other people?"

Sauls gulped several ounces of Coke and burped, "Well, he don't like niggers none."

Carroll nodded, and said, "Yeah, I figured that out. Did you ever see him hurt anybody?"

"He took me with him and James one time and…"

Lenny interrupted himself, suddenly shouting at the console to rate *Let It Be*;

"THUMBS UP!"

He woofed down a sausage muffin and a Cinnamon Melt back-to-back in the same manner as he had destroyed the McMuffin. Then he wiped his mouth with his sleeve even though he had at least ten napkins in his lap. The Beatles' *All You Need Is Love* began playing on Pandora.

"Who's James and what did y'all do?" Carroll prompted him.

"All I know is, James. He ain't from here. He came to go with Billy Bob to find a nigger that Billy Bob was supposed to beat up."

"Did y'all find him?"

Sauls took another swig of Coke and nodded;

"Uh huh"

A chill ran through Carroll's body as he asked Lenny,

"And what happened then?"

"Billy Bob beat him up pretty good."

"Was this the guy that they found dead at the hotel?"

"No, this weren't the same one that got kilt. This was a different nigger. It was right after Billy Bob moved here."

"So this was a different guy. Who was he? What was his name?"

Lenny reached up and rubbed his now wrinkled forehead. He was confused.

"The nigger that Billy Bob beat or James?"

"The guy who Billy Bob beat up. What was his name?"

"I don't know his name none. All I know is James."

Lenny seemed unable to comprehend the severity of the situation. He continued to eat and hum along with the radio as he attempted to answer Carroll's questions.

"Did you and the other guy – James – did you help, too?"

"No, we just watched. It was just Billy Bob that done the beat'n. James just did his phone."

"What do you mean, did his phone, Lenny?" Carroll quizzed him.

"THUMBS UP!" Sauls yelled as *All You Need is Love* ended.

"Did he take photos or video?" asked Carroll.

"He did a movie of it on his phone, cause we watched it later."

"He has done that kind of stuff on other times?"

"Uh huh," Lenny nodded. "But he told me that I couldn't go with him no more so that's the only time that I seen him do it."

Robert Carroll was not smiling any more. Here he was, talking about a vicious, racially motivated hate crime with a simple-minded man who probably had an IQ equal to that of a small child. And all to a soundtrack of

All You Need Is Love. He did not want to overdo it with Lenny Sauls so he let him finish his meal without having to answer any more questions.

Lenny ate happily, throwing in ratings between gulps of food and Coke. Carroll was not sure if Lenny really liked all of the songs enough to rate them thumbs up as he did or if he was just so kindhearted that he didn't want to hurt Pandora's feelings. He suspected it was the latter. He did have one more objective to accomplish before he dropped Lenny off.

"Hey, Lenny, do you want to drive?"

Sauls was in the process of eating another McMuffin, but he stopped just before stuffing it into his mouth. Carroll suspected that food did not usually get a second chance when it was that close to Lenny's mouth. He looked momentarily stunned.

"Can I?" he finally asked.

"Well, do you know how?"

"Oh, yeah! My Uncle Jack taught me how when I was just eleven." he said proudly.

"Do you have a driver's license?" Carroll asked.

Lenny looked dejected.

"No, I just got a ID card" he said sadly.

"That might work. Let me see it."

Carroll watched as Sauls pulled out his wallet. It appeared to hold only a single ten dollar bill. The windowed place where a person would normally keep a driver's license was empty. Lenny unsnapped the tiny photo compartment, fished out the card and handed it to him. He knew better, but Carroll pretended to examine the card for any official driver's license information as he made a mental note of Lenny's birthday.

He frowned and shook his head, pointing at the top of the card, "Aw, that's too bad. See, it says right there, Georgia Voter ID Card. You can't drive with this."

"Yeah, I know," Sauls pouted.

"Well, I tell you what, I'll get you on another day and we'll find a big parking lot where you can drive okay?"

Lenny perked up, "Okay! Deal!"

He asked if Carroll could take him to Billy Bob's garage, but Carroll wanted to keep McCoy from getting too suspicious. He made up an excuse about having to see Ben Walden and told Lenny that he could drop him downtown. It was just a few blocks from McCoy's shop. Carroll waited until Sauls rounded the corner before he made the block and headed for the hotel where he could sort out his notes and call Suzi. He now had the birthdays for both McCoy and Sauls. He also had Billy Bob's social security number. He had hit the jackpot.

5

A Midnight Rendezvous

Carroll returned to the Ridgeway as fast as possible without breaking any traffic laws. The last thing he needed right now was to get noticed by local law enforcement. He parked close to the exterior stairway and took the stairs, two at a time, to the second floor. He was dialing his office with one hand and using the keycard to unlock the hotel room with the other. The phone rang twice, "Carroll Investigative Services, this is Deborah. How may I help you?"

"I'm sorry. Who is this?"

"This is Deborah. How may I help you, sir?"

"Where is Suzi?" he asked.

"I'm sorry, Suzi is unavailable. May I help you with something?"

Trying to remain calm, he said, "Well, yeah. This is Robert Carroll. What's going on at my office?"

"Oh! I apologize, Mr. Carroll. I don't know your voice yet, but don't worry, I'm a quick study!"

He took a deep breath. He did not want to over react and take out his frustration on someone who was just was trying to do her best. Suzi had obviously made the decision to hire her, and the young lady on the other end of the line was actually quite professional. Her tone of voice was nice and her phone etiquette was impressive, especially considering that she realized it was her new boss whom she was talking to for the very first time and that he was not pleased at being surprised.

"Don't worry about not recognizing my voice, Deborah. After all, we haven't even met yet. I just need to know where Suzi is."

"I understand Mr. Carroll. She took some time off. Trust me, I'm fully capable of handling things until she returns. She made sure that I was up to speed on everything."

"Some time off? Why didn't she call me? Was she in an accident? Is she okay?"

"Yes sir, she's fine. In fact, she called less than 30 minutes ago to be sure everything was going okay. She even asked if you had called yet. She just said that since you were taking a vacation, she was going to do the same. "

"A *vacation*?" he repeated, getting more upset. "I'm not on a vacation. I'm out of state, but it isn't really a vacation."

"She didn't go into the details of what you were doing."

"Okay, fine. Don't worry about it. I'll just call her cell phone. You're doing an excellent job. You have my number. Call me if you have any problems."

He was about to touch the "End Call" button when Deborah stopped him, "Wait! You can't call her Mr. Carroll."

"And why is that?"

"Because when she called, she said that she would probably only have a signal for a few more minutes because they were getting too far out."

"Too far out?"

"Yes, sir – on the ship."

Carroll was speechless.

Unlike himself, Suzi was a Hoosier, "bred, born and raised," as she had often said. Moreover, she was also an alumna of Indiana University. Carroll would not have been as concerned if it had been summertime. Yes, he would have still been irritated, but not concerned.

He knew Suzi enjoyed going out on Lake Michigan. She made the trip as often as she could. It was only 185 miles to Chicago, a drive that normally took just over an hour and a half. Or, if you didn't feel like driving yourself, you could take Amtrak and read a book or just relax.

Of course, a shuttle flight was even quicker. You basically buckled your seat belt, took off, unbuckled briefly, rebuckled and then landed. The Indy-Chicago shuttle was the flight that he used the most and Carroll gave Suzi free access to the CIS account. It was the time of year that worried him.

As much as she liked to joke around and appear like a goofball, Suzi was highly intelligent. She had graduated with honors from IU's Kelley School of Business, the B School, as she and her fellow classmates called it. Suzi would never go out on a boat on Lake Michigan in February under hazardous conditions. There was only one explanation for what was happening. He had to be dreaming.

He looked across the hotel room at the dressing mirror on the far wall expecting to see a reflection of himself, head down, eyes closed, seated in the chair at the little workstation by the front window. He hoped he was not drooling. But, there he was, Robert Carroll, staring back with a look of dazed confusion. As much as he hated to upset Deborah, his new – he wasn't sure what to call her, receptionist? He would have to worry about her job title later. If she got upset then he could also correct that later but, right now, he had to know more details.

"Deborah, I know that Suzi would never go out on Lake Michigan in February."

"Lake Michigan?" she responded. "Mr. Carroll, she's not on Lake Michigan. She's on a Caribbean cruise."

"What? Seriously?"

"Well, yes sir. I just assumed you knew that."

He didn't need to look in the mirror to know his face was turning red. He could feel it. He took another deep breath and counted to ten before he spoke again, "Listen Deborah; tell me exactly what she said."

"I already did, Mr. Carroll. She wanted to be sure everything was going okay and she asked if you had called yet."

Deborah's voice had become shaky and he heard her sniffle.

"I'm not upset with you at all. In fact, it appears that you are doing an outstanding job. Now, I want to know *exactly* what Suzi said when she hired you, before she left."

"She said that you had just finished a pretty long case and that you were taking some time off and that you were going to Georgia. Then she said that since it was between cases and everything was caught up that she was going to take a vacation, too."

Carroll had managed to calm himself down, but this was not like Suzi at all.

"Okay good. Did she say anything else?" he managed.

"Yes, sir. She said that you told her it was 50 degrees warmer down there so she was going south until she could go naked." Deborah chuckled, and then began laughing. Her laugh sounded strangely familiar.

"Oh – my – God!" came Suzi's voice, practically yelling at him, "*Please* tell me that you were just playing along. *Please* tell me that a couple of days in Georgia didn't drop your IQ into the single digits! *Please* – tell me that I don't work for a complete idiot!"

He knew that he would never hear the end of this one. Suzi had really gotten him good this time.

"Well, not a complete idiot, but apparently, I'm pretty close," he admitted. "So who is she?"

"You're kidding! She?" Suzi erupted into more laughter.

Carroll listened as she completely lost control, now realizing that he had been talking to his secretary all along. He looked back over at the mirror. He could not count the times that he had felt like an idiot over the last two days. Now he had the opportunity to see if he looked like one. He nodded to his reflection, Yep, there I am! Carroll leaned back in the chair waiting for Suzi to finish enjoying herself. It was the least that he could do. She had earned it.

Suzi had continued to run his office like a finely tuned machine while he had been down in Georgia enjoying the warmer weather. And again, as much as he hated to admit it and as guilty as it made him feel, it had been more fun than work. The Georgia trip was perfect. He had made a new friend in Ben Walden and the historical aspects had been an added bonus. He wasn't just blowing smoke when he told Ben that he intended to return to Fitzgerald at some point, just to enjoy and explore the history of the community.

Now, as he listened to Suzi's cackling and snorting, which, by the way, was completely different from the snorting in her Ernestine impression, he came to appreciate the last two days for what they had provided him, a reminder that he could actually still enjoy doing his job. He felt like the guy that got slapped in those old Skin Bracer TV commercials. "Thanks! I needed that!" he thought.

Carroll heard a crash and a loud THUD over the phone.

"Are you OK?" he asked.

"Yeah, I just fell off my chair!" Suzi sputtered.

"I'll call you back in five minutes," he said.

"Better make it thirty," she managed, before breaking back into hysterical laughter and snorts.

He gave her the full thirty minutes and then some, before calling back. She answered with,

"Okay, I'm good to go now."

"How many people have you already told since we hung up?"

"Nobody yet," she replied. "It took the whole thirty minutes for me to get myself back together. I'll start telling people after we're finished. I can't wait to call the guys downtown. Maybe I'll go down there so I can tell them in person."

She was talking about the detectives and cops back at their old office at Indianapolis PD. He knew that she was serious. She would probably drive straight over as soon as they hung up. He still could not believe it. In an effort to assist with investigations and obtain information, Suzi often posed a business secretary, travel agent, hotel clerk, telemarketer or a host of other characters over the telephone in an effort to obtain information.

"I thought I knew all your voices?" he said.

"Are you kidding? I haven't even scratched the surface!"

Her tone had changed and she was back in business mode now.

"Ready?" he asked.

"Shoot."

"First one is Lenny Dewayne Sauls. That's Lenny with a Y and Dewayne is D-E-W-A-Y-N-E. Sauls is common spelling. He's a white male, about six -five, around 275 to 300 with a D.O.B of March 12th, 87. Got it?"

"Yep, Big S.O.B, huh?"

"You have no idea. Number two, ready?"

"Duh!"

He smiled, both at her *duh* and also knowing what her response would be to what was coming.

"Second one is Billy Bob McCoy..."

Suzi snorted again.

"Now you're just making shit up," she laughed.

"Hand to God," he said.

"I love it! Go on."

"White male, double average, DOB is June 12th of 84."

The double average simply meant that his height and weight were typical of an adult male, typical being 5'7" to six feet in height and from 175 to 195 pounds.

"Got it. Anything else?"

"Nope"

"Well I have. In fact two things. First, the McDowells called. They wanted to know if you had found out anything, but they also said that they have some new information. I told them that I would call them back after I talked to you."

"That's interesting," said Carroll. "The other thing?"

Suzi hesitated, "I know you just got down there, but Jay Stewart dropped a subpoena off this morning. I told him that you were out of state, but he said that they really needed you."

Suzi heard Carroll groan over the phone. He had planned to spend a few more days working on the case with Ben while doing some sightseeing on the side, but the subpoena changed things. If it had been issued for the defense he would have told Suzi to explain that he was out of state and had not been served in person. He was not about to voluntarily return to testify for a criminal. But the subpoena was for the state, for Jay, a colleague as well as a friend. Carroll knew that his testimony would help to ensure a conviction. He decided to fly back immediately. He was also curious to see what additional information the McDowells could provide.

Suzi gave him a moment before she made a suggestion:

"I could see if he might be able to talk to the judge to get a continuance?"

"No, don't worry about it. It's not a problem. I'll come back. It'll give me a chance to meet with the McDowells again. Get me a flight and see if you can get them to come in tomorrow, say around two?"

"Well, alrighty then. Give me a few and I'll get back to you."

That Carroll was not more upset about having to turn around and fly back to Indianapolis was proof that the Georgia trip was just what he had needed. Suzi's message about the McDowells having new information intrigued him, but he knew better than to speculate. Whatever it was, he would know the answer by tomorrow afternoon. What he was concerned about was that they were obviously going to expect a report about his trip. While he wanted to provide them with as much information as possible, he had to be sensitive. They were still suffering enough. The last thing he wanted to do was to add to it. They had not seen the gruesome crime scene photos. The truth was that he had two persons of interest, Billy Bob McCoy and Lenny Sauls.

It was only mid morning, but he wanted to update Walden on his separate meetings with Billy Bob and Lenny. He also needed to tell him about the subpoena. Ben was planning to have a cookout at his place to introduce Carroll to some people from the community. A stranger would stand out in a small town like Fitzgerald, and Walden's cookout would explain his presence. If he were going to be roaming around town asking questions, they needed a cover story. Their plan was just to stick with their original one, that he was in the publishing business and the two of them were working together. The subpoena meant that the cookout would have to wait until the next trip.

He began a text conversation with Walden;

How's it going? Will you have time for lunch? Carroll texted.

Sure Sportsman About 12:15? came Ben's response.

Do U EVER eat anywhere else? asked Carroll.

LOL Not during the day. Good food & close 2 work.

OK Sportsman CU there Carroll told him.

During their lunch the day before, Carroll had told Walden that he wanted to meet with Ruth Jackson, one of the people questioned during the initial investigation of Thomas McDowell. Although several people said that they had seen him around various locations, Jackson was one of the very few people in town who had actually spoken to the victim at length.

If Carroll was correct, she was also probably one of the last people to speak with him. He had wanted to set up the meeting for the following afternoon, which would have been today, this afternoon, but Walden had told him he needed to wait. Ben had been about to explain why when their conversation was interrupted. They turned to other topics and forgot about the one concerning Jackson. He now needed to clear that up.

He also needed to return Ben's case file. He was lucky that Walden had been able to obtain it, although he still did not know how he had gotten it. Carroll had read and reread the file until he could probably recite it word for word. He had also managed to scan the crime scene photos after befriending the night clerk at the hotel. She had thought he was scanning publishing documents. Unfortunately, even when he combined what he had learned from the case file and the information provided by McDowell's grandparents, he still had more questions than answers.

Carroll had some time before meeting Walden for lunch, so he rode by the locations around town where McDowell had last been seen. He would have to return later, after Ben's cookout, after they established his back-story, to actually talk to people at those places. He arrived at The Sportsman before Walden so he went ahead and took a seat at their booth. He was looking around for Betty when another waitress approached the table.

"Wait'n on Ben?" she asked, acknowledging him either as a friend of Walden's or, if he was not, hinting that Carroll was in a quasi-reserved booth.

"Yep, he should here in a minute," he replied.

"So, you must be Bob," she said, as she plopped down a menu.

"Yep, that's me," he responded, somewhat surprised.

"Well, Betty's off today. So y'all are stuck with me. I'm Pearl."

"Hi, Pearl."

"You wanna go ahead and order?"

"Thanks, but I'll wait on Ben."

"Suit yourself," she said. "I'll check back with you in a bit."

"Thanks, Pearl."

He decided to check in with Suzi while he waited. He pressed the corresponding speed-dial number on his phone.

"Good morning, Carroll Investigative Services," she answered.

"My! Aren't we professional this morning?" he said.

"Bite me. I didn't look at the caller ID," she popped back. "And by the way – not sure what you meant about we. I'm always professional."

"Yeah, maybe with customers, but not with me."

"Well, that's who pays my salary isn't it? – the customers?"

"Fair enough. I'm waiting on Ben and I thought I'd check in."

They started with the McDowell case, going over everything to be sure that both were on the same page, Suzi then updated him on the court status of Linder and some older cases. She also informed her boss of another possible client. They were just wrapping up when he saw Walden's jeep pulling up outside.

"Anything else? Ben's pulling in now."

"Nope, that's it. Go join your Bubba-buddy."

"Actually, he's joining me. I'm already at our booth."

"Our booth?" she chuckled.

"Yes, I've successfully infiltrated their base – disguised as a restaurant, code named, The Sportsman. I've got my own booth."

"I am so proud of you," she quipped.

"Actually, it's not really my booth, " he confessed. "I'm just a co-owner, and being a newcomer, the junior-partner with less stock, but it's a start. It's something I can build on."

Suzi was still snickering when they ended the call.

Walden was momentarily detained in a chat with two locals on the sidewalk. Carroll focused his attention on Pearl as she took the orders from a family at a nearby table. He thought she looked more like a waitress than Betty, although he couldn't have explained exactly why he thought that. Maybe it was because she reminded him of an older version of Flo, from that old TV comedy series, Alice. Betty also looked like a waitress, so much so, that if Carroll would have seen her on the street he would have thought, I'll bet she's a waitress, so it said a lot that, at least in Carroll's eyes, Pearl was even more waitressy.

"Hey, Pearl!" Walden chirped as he entered the restaurant.

"Morn'n Ben, I done told Bob, ya'll are stuck with me today."

"Good! It's about time I had a decent waitress."

"Well, I reckon I oughtta be, after 50 years," she said, walking back toward the kitchen.

"Fifty years? Is she serious?" Carroll asked.

"As a heart attack – and all of them were right here."

"She's worked here for 50 years? This place has been here that long?"

"Add another two decades before she started if you're talking about the restaurant," said Walden.

"That would make her...?" Carroll was doing the math.

"Old!" Ben finished for him.

"How old?"

"Not sure, but ask her to tell you about the time the fish delivery was late."

"I'm not falling for that!"

"Okay, then don't," Ben responded.

Knowing their time was limited, Carroll wanted to get right to business. He handed Walden the case file.

"That was a huge help, Ben. Thanks for trusting me with it."

"Like I said, whatever I can do to help. Any thoughts?"

"Yeah. Like I said before, that's the problem. Too many."

"Now you know how I feel. I stay up at night thinking about it. I keep thinking that there's gotta be something I'm missing."

"Well, I don't know if it'll make you feel better or worse that I couldn't find anything either," Carroll admitted.

"To be honest, both. While I hoped you would be able to find something I missed, I didn't want you to do it too quickly. That would've made me feel pretty stupid."

"One of the most frustrating things is that you can't rule any one part out because it fits somewhere else."

"What do you mean?" Ben asked.

"Okay, why was Thomas McDowell in Georgia in the first place? There are at least four different explanations."

Walden nodded, "He told some people that he was helping a friend with research on their family genealogy, but no one could provide the name of the friend or the family that he was researching."

"Right," Carroll agreed. "Two people said that he told them that he was working a project that documented the history of voting rights for African Americans. He told them that he had been working in the southeastern states for over a year, when in fact, he had been in Georgia less than two weeks and, as far as the investigators could tell, hadn't been to any of the other southeastern states."

They stopped talking as Pearl came back to take their orders, but Ben jumped in before Carroll started with his order.

"Hey, Pearl, Bob wants to hear about the time that the fish delivery was late, but he's afraid to ask."

Carroll could have choked Walden, but he needn't have worried. Pearl's grin indicated that she understood Ben's tactics.

"Well, since Bob wants to know," she said, looking straight at Ben. "It was on a Friday and the fish guy was already three hours late," she began her tale.

"Fresh fish is the special on Friday," Ben explained.

"So here we are," Pearl continued. "The place is packed and everybody's want'n fish. The cook opened the freezer and there were only two catfish in there."

"And the fish delivery guy still hadn't showed up," Ben added, in his unofficial capacity as assistant storyteller.

"There were three of us wait'n tables and we couldn't figure out who placed the fish orders first. Since it wouldn't be fair to just randomly pick two, we decided to give the catfish to the bearded homeless guy that had showed up out back. I told him what was going on and gave him the two fish. A few minutes later he knocked on the back door and said, 'Your fish delivery came.'

"I looked out and saw the crates of fish stacked by the wall, but I knew it wasn't from the regular fish delivery, 'cause I didn't sign no ticket for it. Then I turned around and – POOF! – the homeless guy was gone! That's how long I've been here Bob, since Jesus walked the earth!"

They all had a good laugh. Then Pearl took their orders and started back toward the kitchen.

"I always regretted it," she said shaking her head as she walked away.

"Regretted what?" Carroll asked.

"That I didn't give him some wine too," she said, as Walden howled and slapped the bench.

Carroll knew that he had been set up. He suspected Pearl and Ben had pulled that one before. He would retell Pearl's Jesus Story for Suzi and others when he returned to Indianapolis, but he and Walden needed to get back to business right now.

He reminded Ben where they had left off;

"So, McDowell told some people that he was doing research on genealogy while he told others he was researching voter rights."

"Don't forget the realtor, Josh Stone," Walden reminded him. "McDowell told him that he was looking for a place where his grandparents could retire. He even looked at several homes and also at some undeveloped property as if they were even considering building."

"But his grandparents never mentioned it to me. I'm thinking that it was just part of a cover story he made up after he got down here."

"And the last excuse was that he claimed to be a pharmaceutical rep," Ben noted. "But he never went to any doctors' offices or drug stores so we know that's bullshit too."

"So, we've got four scenarios," Carroll acknowledged. "We'll go ahead and toss out the pharmaceutical rep because that's obviously bogus. I also agree with you on doubting the whole realtor thing, but we can wait on that until you talk with his grandparents."

Carroll continued, "So here's what I'm talking about when I say you can't rule one thing out because it fits somewhere else: McDowell was seen at the local library on multiple occasions. Right? Yet, he never checked out any books and none of the employees or volunteers at the library remembered speaking with him or could even say what he might have been looking at. Being at the library fits both researching genealogy and the voter thing."

"But, why is so important that we have to figure out one or the other?" Walden asked.

"Because if the motive wasn't robbery then what was it? That means that whatever he was doing could have somehow resulted in his death, so we need to find out exactly why he was really here and what he was doing."

Ben nodded, "Several people also reported seeing him walking around town with a pad or small book. What could that be about?"

"Yeah, I looked at those locations. They're all historical places, noted in the Architectural Treasures Tour guide which, more than likely, was what people had seen him holding."

Walden nodded again, "That makes sense."

He was starting to understand and appreciate Carroll's thought process. They talked about the people who had been questioned and discussed each person's statement. They also went over the responding officers' statements.

Carroll pulled out the city map that Ben had included in his tour package. They used a pen to note every place that McDowell had been seen. Then he told Ben about Lenny's disturbing revelation of the beating that he and James had witnessed.

"Do you have any idea of who James might be?" he asked.

Ben shook his head, "Not at all. Guys from out of town stop by Billy Bob's garage a lot. I figured they were mostly people he met on his bike trips."

"How often does he take these bike trips?"

"All the damn time. That's why his business isn't that great. He's damn good mechanic and he's fair about the price, but you never know if he's going to be there when you need him to work on your damn vehicle."

"What about this other black male that Billy Bob beat up?"

"Nope. Not a clue. Are you sure that it wasn't Thomas McDowell?"

"It couldn't have been. Lenny said it happened right after McCoy moved to Fitzgerald. That was at least two months before McDowell got killed."

"Pretty twisted that they videoed the damn beating," Ben said. "Man, if you could just find that video!"

Carroll told Ben about the subpoena. Walden was not just understanding about it; he was impressed that his new friend was voluntarily going back to testify without having been served. He knew most folks avoided court like the plague. Carroll said he would try to return in a couple of weeks. They chatted a few more minutes before stacking their dishes and leaving a more than generous tip on table for Pearl. They stood up and Walden started toward the door, but Carroll grabbed his shoulder.

"Hold on! What about Ruth Jackson?"

Walden palmed his own forehead, "That's right! I didn't get to tell you about her."

They sat down again on the booth seats.

"Okay, there are two main things to remember when you go to see her. One, whatever you do, do not mention my name."

Carroll laughed. "You're kidding, right?"

"Hell, no! I ain't kidding! That woman hates me."

"What did you do to her?"

"Honest to God, Bob, I wish I knew the answer," he replied, shaking his head.

"And the second thing?"

Ben leaned forward, "Just as important as the first."

"Okay? And that is?"

"You need to find a really good bottle of bourbon whiskey."

"Come on, Ben!" Carroll laughed, rising from the booth.

"I'm not kidding! Do you want to get on her good side?"

"Well, yeah. Of course I do."

"Then do what I'm telling you!"

"Did you take her a bottle?"

"Yeah, I did, but not the *right* bottle apparently," he said regretfully. "Make sure it's really good bourbon!"

"Anything else about her I should know?" Carroll asked him.

"Well, yeah, with you being into history and all, if you two hit it off, you might get her to talk about the town after you finish on McDowell."

"Is she a historian or something?"

"Kind of," Ben chuckled. "But, she's mostly just old."

"No wonder she hates you, with a comment like that."

"Okay, let me put it this way: She knew Philander Fitzgerald."

"Uh huh, like Pearl knew Jesus," Carroll laughed.

"You gotta admit that Pearl's Jesus Story was funny as hell, but I'm serious on this one, Bob."

"You're talking about the guy that the town was named after. Right?" he asked warily.

"The very same dude!" Ben said, now completely serious.

Carroll was trying to see where the joke was coming from, but he was also doing the math in his head.

"Listen, Bob. Ruth Jackson's father worked for Philander Fitzgerald," Ben was holding his right hand up as if swearing an oath.

Carroll was stunned, "Holy..."

"Shit," Walden finished for him. "She's like 140 or something."

"Well, thanks a lot for your advice. Although, considering how she feels about you, I'm not sure if I should follow it."

"Trust me," Walden said, as they walked out of the restaurant.

They shook hands on the sidewalk and Carroll promised that he would give Ben an update as soon as he talked to the McDowells about the house-hunting scenario.

Suzi called just as he was climbing into the Escape. She could get him on a flight out of Atlanta at his favorite time, between 5 and 5:30 a.m. but it would have to be business class and she needed to know immediately.

"Grab it," he told her.

"And the McDowells can be here at 3 p.m., but are you sure that you'll be up for that? That's going to be a helluva day for you."

"Thanks. I'll be fine," he assured her before hanging up.

He was disappointed. It was only 1:20, and he had the whole afternoon to do some sightseeing, but he knew if he was going to catch that flight he had get some rest so he could leave for Hartsfield by midnight or one o'clock at the latest. The other option was to pack right now, drive to Atlanta and grab a room there for a few hours. It took him only a few minutes to decide. He would stay in Fitzgerald and try to leave by 12:30 a.m.. It would also give him time to do some research on choosing a bottle of bourbon for Mrs. Jackson. Carroll drank occasionally, but he certainly was not a connoisseur. This meant that he would have to find someone who was. Other than making the suggestion, Ben had offered no specific recommendation, so either he also lacked the experience, or he was testing his new friend. Walden's comment implied that a trip to the local liquor store probably would not be a good idea. He might find something around Atlanta, but then he realized he did not really even know what he was looking for.

Carroll thought of a couple of people that he could ask when he got back home, but then he remembered Bite and Booze. It was a blog by a guy named Jay Ducote that he had found by happenstance while doing research. He had accidentally clicked on a link, causing it to pop up on the screen interrupting his work. He had been about to delete it, when he saw a photo and recipe for *Grilled Jumbo Louisiana Shrimp with Tomatoes*. Carroll read it and was impressed enough that he ended up spending the next forty-five minutes scrolling through Ducote's blogs which covered everything from appetizers and sandwiches, to main courses and desserts, and from beer to fine wine. Carroll had followed Ducote's blogs ever since and had even had some moderate success with cooking, not his usual forte. As soon as he got back to the hotel room, he sat down at the small workstation and pulled up the Bite and Booze blog on his laptop and began searching. He was surprised to find multiple entries on bourbon. Carroll was not sure if he should just choose the highest rating and then try to locate it or if he should pick another, but then he came upon *Jefferson's Presidential Select 21 Year Bourbon*. It was an omen. A bourbon named in honor of one of the Founding Fathers, the author of the Declaration of Independence and our third President. Having already pretty much made his decision, he read Ducote's review:

A different bourbon all together, this whiskey is a blend of 21 and 22 year old barrels that create a smooth and intoxicatingly good product. The scent made my nose hairs perk up with aromas of vanilla and caramel. The taste is like an infused butter with syrup and hint of cayenne for a kick. It is sweet butter upfront with a kick on the back end that is aggressive though pleasant. Smooth, then Kapow and Bam like out of a Batman cartoon. It has cinnamon, spice, and everything nice.

He phoned Suzi.

"You need to find some bourbon," he said when she answered.

"Hold on," she replied.

He could hear the sounds of a drawer opening and then liquid pouring. Suzi came back on the line;

"Okay, so who or what are we toasting?"

"We're not," he laughed. "This is for the case."

"Oh, yeah, it's for 'the case.' Nudge nudge, wink wink. Say no more," she said.

The old Monty Python joke was one of her favorites. He imagined that she was probably jabbing her elbow with the nudge nudge and was winking to the wink winks.

"Any preference?" she asked.

As a matter of fact, yes. Jefferson's Presidential Select 21 Year Bourbon."

"Ooooh! Fancy Shmancy!" Suzi exclaimed. "I suppose I'll have to hold my pinky out when I drink it?"

"No, you won't. I'm giving it away."

"You're kidding. Right?"

"Nope, dead serious."

"Listen Boss Man, this ain't Boone's Farm or Mad Dog 20/20. Hell, this ain't even Wild Turkey. This is fancy and it's probably going to set you back some serious change!"

"It's a serious case," he responded.

"Okay. I guess you've picked this particular one for a reason."

"I have. It's got to be Kentucky bourbon and it's got to be something that she wouldn't normally get in Fitzgerald."

"Well, alrighty then," Suzi replied.

He spent the better part of an hour with her on the phone. It was all business. There were discussions about the current case as well as updates on Linder and some other older ones. Suzi said that she was still waiting to hear from the background and criminal history checks. Carroll told her briefly about Billy Bob's remarks and his violent side and described Lenny's obvious developmental problem and his story about the beating. She agreed with Carroll, that it sounded like Billy Bob was their main suspect and that Sauls was hopefully not involved, but if he was that he was being manipulated by McCoy. He decided he would wait to tell her about the chickens later, partly because he wanted to keep the discussion about the case, but mostly because he wanted to tell those stories in person when he could enjoy her reaction. Suzi being Suzi, she had taken it on her own to do some research on the Indianapolis-Fitzgerald connection and had already compiled some notes for her boss. She told him that she was able to find out quite a bit about Philander Fitzgerald.

"The bourbon's for a friend of his," Carroll informed her.

"Dead people don't drink, boss man. And please tell me this isn't one of those things like people do at Jim Morrison's grave where they just pour it out on the tombstone and waste it."

"No, it's —"

"Because if that's what you're gonna do then they'll never know the difference between Boone's Farm and whatever the hell you told me to write down earlier."

"Trust me," he said, using Ben's line.

Her laughter was not very reassuring.

"I'm gonna get in some beauty sleep while I can," he said.

"That would take a helluva lot of sleep. You don't have that much time!" she warned him.

"Why do I put up with your insolence?"

"Because I'm the best damn office manager you'll ever find," she popped back, "And nobody else would put up with your bullshit."

"Can't argue with either part of that," he agreed.

"See ya when I see ya," she responded.

Carroll had to try to get at least a little rest if he was going to make the midnight drive from Fitzgerald to Atlanta, but he found it almost impossible to sleep during the day. Even when he was a young uniform cop working the graveyard shift, he would get off at seven in the morning and be unable to sleep. This would usually continue for a day or two until he was so exhausted that he could finally sleep, but then he would go for another two or three days. It was an endless cycle.

He pulled out the packet Ben had given him. It contained the map and several brochures with historical information about Fitzgerald and Ben Hill County. He read everything. He could not find anything that connected to the McDowell case, but the information made him want to hurry with his trip so that he could get back and start exploring.

Carroll walked over to the window and pulled the heavy double shades which made the room surprisingly dark. He then did something he rarely did; just to be safe he set the alarm on his phone. He plopped onto the bed, first reading, then watching some TV. He was asleep in less time than he thought it would take, but he still awoke before 10.

Carroll had not really unpacked so he double-checked the room three times before grabbing his luggage. He left the Ridgeway at 11 p. m., an hour a half earlier than planned. He headed north on U.S. Highway 129 and was less than two miles out of the city limits when a massive deer bolted right in front of the SUV. He thought he would hit him for sure, but somehow the collision was avoided. Carroll's radar was up as he cautiously continued north on Georgia's rural highways.

He felt relieved when he finally hit the six-lanes of Interstate 75. Carroll had checked his fuel before leaving to be sure that he had enough to reach the same truck stop he had stopped at on the way down. He pulled in 32 minutes after midnight. After fueling up, he was about to go in to take a restroom break and get coffee when he noticed a Waffle House next door.

He was less than an hour and a half from Atlanta at that point and steak, eggs and a last taste of grits was too much too resist.

Because there was no driveway connecting the Waffle House to the truck stop, Carroll decided to avoid driving back out to the divided street to make a trip to the restaurant's parking area, by pulling the Escape to a spot between the truck stop and the restaurant. He grabbed his cell and keys and headed across the parking lot. The smell of the food from the Waffle House encouraged him to walk faster. He could taste it already. He looked up as he stepped over the curb and his appetite instantly vanished.

A man was walking out of the Waffle House restroom toward the booths. It was Billy Bob McCoy. Billy Bob glanced in his direction. Carroll's instincts kicked in automatically. He brought his cell phone up to his ear, tilted his head down away from the light and turned his body slightly. Luckily, McCoy did not seem to recognize him as he walked to a booth where he joined three other men. The only seat available for him was facing away from Carroll, who then was able to look at the men carefully. Was one of these guys James from Lenny's story, Carroll wondered.

Everything was in Carroll's favor. There was only one street light in the area where he was standing, and it was either blown or had been shot out. He knew that the low light outside and the bright lights of the restaurant's interior made it more difficult for McCoy and his companions to see outside, especially into the shadowy area where he was standing. Two other men, probably truck drivers, were also walking around nearby while chatting on their phones, so Carroll appeared to be just another truck driver.

Then Carroll had another stroke of luck. As he was walking around the side of the building he saw Billy Bob's blue Chevy pickup. He had been unable to get the tag at the garage because he would have been seen, but not this time. From where the men were sitting, their view was completely blocked. What's more, there were two other trucks parked by McCoy's, one on either side. The only other vehicles at the restaurant were parked in the main lot which meant that the two parked by McCoy's truck were likely those of his companions.

Carroll casually walked toward the vehicles as he selected Text on his phone. He touched *Suzi* and then quickly typed in all three tag numbers, double-checking them before walking away. As a precaution, he nonchalantly walked over near the other cars and got those numbers too, just in case he was wrong. Then he pressed *Send*. He walked back around the building, positioning himself as close as he could possibly get to the window without attracting attention.

He carefully studied the men, making mental notes of their physical descriptions and regretting now that he had decided against bringing his telephoto camera on the trip.

"I won't need it," he had told Suzi after she suggested it.

If he had listened to her he could have been sitting comfortably, and more discreetly, in the Escape while taking photos and even video. His cell phone hummed in his hand.

It was a text from Suzi;

WTH? R U still in Fitz?!?

She apparently assumed that he had changed his mind and was still in Fitzgerald or had overslept and was going to miss his flight.

"Almost to ATL," he texted back.

"???? Why RU texting & driving? Random car tags? Just to wake me up?"

It actually was not all that unusual for Carroll to text Suzi after hours, even after midnight. Just as in this situation, it was often the quickest way to preserve evidence or send her notes on something that needed to be addressed at the start of the next business day, but she knew his schedule down to the minute. He had to explain.

"I'm not. Bumped into McCoy et al @ Waffle House"

"Seriously? OMG! Their tag #s? Fantastic!!!"

Carroll continued to watch the men, adding to his mental notebook, as he texted with Suzi. Even though he could not hear their conversation, he could see them clearly. Mannerisms were important, he had learned. They can tell you things if you know what to look for. For instance, that was not the Billy Bob McCoy that Carroll had come to know sitting at that table. Billy Bob was always grinning, even when he was choking his best friend and even when he was violently shaking Carroll or hitting him in the back of the head.

There was something else. Billy Bob might be a good mechanic, but he was no rocket scientist. Carroll could not imagine him in a serious conversation about anything, yet the McCoy he was watching now was composed and serious. He was leaning forward, elbows on the table, talking as if he were an executive at a business meeting. One of the men was jotting down notes as Billy Bob spoke.

As much as he hated it, Carroll knew he would have to confess to Suzi about ignoring her suggestion to take the camera. It would have been a huge asset right now, he thought. He glanced around the parking lot. The same two men were still walking around talking on their cell phones. He also noticed another person, a woman, had apparently pulled off of the interstate and was sleeping in her car. She was more or less sitting upright, leaning over with her head on a big pillow. She probably didn't want to risk sleeping in a rest area and thought the lighted parking lot of the Waffle House safer.

Carroll then did something that had become routine for him over the last couple of days; he did something stupid. I'm a complete idiot, he thought, as he raised his cell phone, pointed it toward the men in the booth and pressed the icon to record a video. He was trying to hold the camera where the light wouldn't reflect on his face as he zoomed in.

He had recorded only about a minute of video when he heard the sound of footsteps. One of the truck drivers was walking toward the restaurant entrance. A car door slammed at the same time and Carroll turned to see the woman who had been asleep in the car also walking toward the Waffle House. He put the phone up to his ear without pressing Stop and began talking to the nonexistent person on the other end of his line.

When he looked back into the restaurant he saw that Billy Bob was on his cell phone, too. Was he making or receiving a call, Carroll wondered, and whom would he be talking to at this time of night?

"Yeah, I'll be there in about an hour," Carroll said to no one as the truck driver walked by.

The driver nodded a greeting as he passed and then held the door for the woman from the car who was behind him. Carroll looked back to see Billy Bob and the three men walking toward the exit. His heart stopped. He had to move quickly before they walked right by him.

It was pure coincidence that he had happened upon McCoy, but he knew Billy Bob would automatically assume that he was following him. Carroll walked away, still holding the phone to his ear and talking to the ghost on his phone. He heard the door open behind him as the men exited. They gave names with their goodbyes, but with his back turned, Carroll could not put the names with the faces he had seen at the table.

"Take care, Kenny. See ya, Zack," said one.

"Let me know, Nate," said another.

Carroll did clearly recognize one voice, McCoy's, as he called out, "I'll call you later today, Jim."

"Okay, dude," Jim responded, although Carroll still could not see which one Jim was.

Carroll turned around when he was a safe distance away and found that he had been correct. He had assumed that one of the men was driving one of the other trucks and that two were likely riding together. That was indeed the case. The three trucks left the parking lot, turning in different directions. Billy Bob turned south on I-75, presumably headed back to Fitzgerald, the truck with the two occupants took a right, heading northbound on the interstate; and, the remaining pickup continued west across the interstate on a county road.

As much as he would have liked to have seen more, it actually worked out well for Carroll. He checked his watch. He needed to get on the road to make it to Hartsfield in Atlanta– and back to Indianapolis.

6

Robert Francis Carroll

It was shortly after 2 p.m. when Carroll whipped his Rover into the alley, slid into his parking spot and boldly exited the vehicle. Despite the fact that it was mid-afternoon with the sun shining brightly in a cloudless sky, it was actually much colder at that moment than it was on the morning that he had left for his trip to Georgia. His old nemesis waited until he was exposed and then charged forward, tossing cups, discarded papers and leaves ahead of the gust in an effort to intimidate him. The cups made a cloppitty sound like horses hooves on the pavement.

He had plenty of time to make it to the back door, but he waited. He did not turn sideways. He did not duck his head. He did not lean forward to brace himself.

The trip to Georgia, although brief, had energized Carroll. Determined, he turned toward the wind, ready to face the full onslaught head-on. He stood firm, welcoming it. He was no longer afraid. He was no longer Robert Carroll. He was Lieutenant John J. Dunbar, in front of the Rebel firing line, holding his arms wide, out to his side, with his head tilted back, completely exposed to the enemy. He expected to look up and see his friend, Ben Walden, Wind Blows His Cap Off, shouting down into the alley from one of bordering rooftops;

"Shu Mani Tutanka O Wachiiiiiii! I am Wind Blows His Cap Off. Do you see that I am your friend? Can you see that you will always be my friend?"

Carroll chuckled at his own joke as he used the key to open the back door to his office.

"Why do you have that dumbass look on your face?" Suzi asked, when he walked into the office.

"Because I am no longer afraid of the alley," he declared.

"Well, aren't you a big boy!" exclaimed Suzi, using a voice like she was speaking to a toddler that had just used the potty for the first time.

"What did Georgia do to you?" she asked as she handed him his coffee cup.

"I'll tell you after this," he said, taking a big gulp.

"After the night you had I don't know if that will be enough. Why don't I hook up an IV and run it straight into your blood stream?"

"Sure, go ahead," he said, extending his arms. "Have you heard from the McDowells yet?"

"Not today, but they'll be here. I didn't ask what they found, but it seemed important. I was just about to run those tag numbers. I've already put other files in your office."

"Thanks, Suzi," as he headed down the hall.

Carroll seldom saw clients in his office. That is what the conference room was for. This was his space. He thought back to his first days as a detective at the Indianapolis Police Department. As a freshman investigator, he had been crammed into a room with two other detectives and two desks. The higher-ups apparently figured having two desks in an office for three detectives would not be a problem. They had even tried to say it would be an incentive to ensure that one of them was out doing field work while the other two were doing paperwork.

It took two promotions before Carroll finally got his own desk and another, to captain, before he ranked high enough to get his own office. His dream back then was to open a professional and successful PI business after retiring from the police department. He even had a name for it, Carroll Investigative Services, or CIS.

Early on he had specific ideas about how his personal office would look. Of course, choosing the right the desk was the most important aspect. When he had finally chosen the office space for his business, the next step was choosing his desk. He had dragged Suzi all over Indianapolis in his quest for the perfect desk. Suzi did not understand his obsession. Ironically, Suzi always had her own desk and office, even when she was doing the secretarial work for two detectives, so it was no surprise to Carroll. How could she ever know how important this was to him, to finally be getting your very own desk?

"This is as important to me as shopping for shoes is to you," he had explained in terms that she would understand.

"Oh, my God!" she exclaimed. "Then we must leave no stone unturned!"

They had searched high and low, store after store for more than a week, but he couldn't find the right one. Then, one day, Carroll finally saw it – his dream desk. It was the Pergola Grand Style Home Office Desk.

"That's it!" he shouted, as she tried to calm him down.

"But it's a home office desk," she pointed out.

"I don't care. I want it," he pouted.

One look at his face was sufficient. Suzi could tell he was adamant. She knew if she didn't give in he would become the equivalent of a screaming two-year-old throwing a tantrum in the checkout line at the grocery store.

"Fine," she consented, but she was serious when she asked, "Can I just steal my old desk from the city?"

"No," he answered firmly, "This is our new office, a fresh start. Everything's going to be new."

He sounded serious at the time, but Carroll later surprised Suzi by arranging for her old desk at the police department to be declared surplus. He then purchased it for her as a retirement present. She was thrilled. He probably wouldn't have had a bigger reaction if he had bought her a new car. Except for its new location, Suzi's desk was arranged exactly as it had been for the last twenty plus years. Every photo and memento was in the place as it had been when the desk sat at their old office just a few blocks away. She was completely content.

Carroll, however, was not. Starting from scratch with the new desk as the centerpiece, he had added a workstation with two computers on one side of the office and a long matching table, especially for spreading out the contents of case files, on the other side. It was on this table that Suzi had placed the case-related material that she had researched for him.

There were four separate files labeled, *Philander H. Fitzgerald, Billy Bob McCoy. Fitzgerald (Town)* and *Lenny Sauls.*

Carroll was anxious to get into the files, but he decided to wait until after the meeting with the McDowells. He did not want to be interrupted once he got started. He did his own research on the computer while he waited. It was not long before Suzi notified him that the McDowells had arrived and she was taking them into the conference room.

Carroll emerged from his office to the sound of laughter coming down the hallway. Unnoticed by the McDowells as he entered the conference room behind them, he had a moment to observe them. If he had not known them before, he would have thought that he was looking at two different people. Their demeanor had completely changed. They were smiling and animated as they talked with Suzi.

It was apparent that, like him and Suzi, the McDowells loved the old TV variety shows. Suzi was concluding yet another Lilly Tomlin character impression, her *Edith Ann,* as she rocked back and forth on her chair, talking in a little girl's voice, "And that's the twuth!" she affirmed, blowing raspberries.

Carroll was shocked as Mary McDowell rose from her chair and struck a modeling pose, hand on hip, as she went into a very good impression of Flip Wilson's *Geraldine.*

"The devil made me buy this dress!" she said in a high-pitched voice.

"Well, maybe you should listen to him more often then," said Carroll.

His unexpected presence and comment caused Geraldine to instantly vanish. Mrs. McDowell dropped into the nearest chair.

Realizing that he had surprised and embarrassed her, he added, "Because that's a great dress."

Carroll was in a good mood too. The trip to Georgia had been just the break he needed and seeing the McDowells feeling better lifted his own spirits. Of course, there was no denying why they were meeting, but he was not in much of a hurry to change the light mood by bringing up the main subject, their murdered grandson. The four of them spent thirty minutes discussing the old TV shows and watching Suzi do more of her impressions before he eased into the discussion.

He explained that robbery was still a possibility and reasoned if that were the case, the offender was likely a transient. Then he told them about another possibility, one that might involve a local person. He did not go into great detail and he did not mention Billy Bob McCoy or Lenny Sauls by name, but he did tell the McDowells that he had two persons of interest. He made sure they understood that a person of interest was not the same as a suspect and that it was his own opinion. He also explained that as far as he knew, the investigating law enforcement agencies had no official suspects or persons of interest. The McDowells were satisfied, even pleased, with his explanation.

Carroll certainly did not describe the crime scene in great detail, but he did tell them about various locations where their grandson had been seen around town. He asked them to think about the locations where Thomas had been seen and to suggest any ideas on why he was there.

"Does that ring any bells? Are there any reasons that you can think of for Tommy to be there?"

The McDowells both shook their heads. It was a complete mystery. They could provide no new ideas or insight. Carroll also asked them if their grandson had ever discussed their retiring somewhere down south.

"No, we never even talked about anything like that," Thomas Sr. answered.

"We've been having more health problems in the winter," his wife said, "but he knew we didn't have that kind of money."

He asked them a few more questions. Then, partly in an effort to bring the topic back to a lighter note and also hoping that it might remind them of something Tommy had said, Carroll told them about the history of the town. He even included a short version of the Chicken Story; however, he did not mention the incident with the hens by the dumpster. That would have entailed giving them more details about their grandson's death than he wanted to reveal at the moment. He just talked about seeing them on his first walk with Ben, how chickens could be seen throughout the town and about hearing the rooster crow from his hotel room on that first morning. He recalled the hen crossing the road with the babies and how people stopped for them.

"Biddies," Mrs. McDowell corrected him.

"I'm sorry?"

"They call baby chickens biddies."

"How'd you know that? You been in the city all your life." her husband asked.

"Tommy said something about them, but Grandpa Joe used to have chickens and he called them biddies, too. Remember?"

Carroll's instincts were kicking in again.

"Tommy said something about them?" he asked. "Was this during that telephone call you mentioned last time?"

"That's right. If he wasn't in town he would always call, two or three times a week."

"When was that call, Mrs. McDowell?"

"It was the last one I got from him. I asked him when he was coming to see me. He said as soon as he got back. Back from where? I asked him. 'From Georgia,' he said. Then he said something about chickens being everywhere," she smiled, but a single tear escaped from her eye.

"And you didn't hear anything else from him?" Carroll asked them both.

They shook their heads.

"Not until we got the call from the police department," Mary McDowell said.

"Do you think that your Grandpa Joe might know something?" Carroll inquired.

"Oh, he died more than twenty years ago," Mrs. McDowell replied. "Thomas was still just a little boy then."

Thomas McDowell chuckled, "I'll bet that's where he got it, too, about biddies. From Grandpa Joe."

"He probably remembered it from his Grandpa's stories when he was little," she agreed.

"Did Grandpa Joe ever live in Georgia?" Carroll asked.

"Not as far as I know."

"Honey, give Mr. Carroll the letter," Thomas Sr. suggested.

Mrs. McDowell reached into her purse and pulled out a plain envelope, which she held on the very tip of the corner as she offered it to Carroll.

"Can you just put that on the table, with the address facing up?" he requested.

She did as he requested. Carroll leaned forward to inspect the letter. It was unopened and addressed to Albert McDowell. Without being asked, Suzi quickly left the room and returned momentarily with a pair of surgical gloves, some tweezers and a clear bag.

"Is Albert McDowell also Grandpa Joe?" Carroll asked.

Mrs. McDowell looked at him sideways, "Of course not. Why would Tommy send something to a man that's been dead since he was six years old?"

Carroll looked up to see Suzi smiling, her eyes watering as she tried to keep from laughing.

"Albert's my oldest brother," Thomas Sr. said. "He's still alive."

"I'm glad that he didn't, but why didn't your brother open the letter?" Carroll asked.

"Albert's in a retirement home, but he still has the house at our family place. I go over there and pick up the mail twice a month."

Mrs. McDowell added, "Except he skipped the first pick up in January because of what happened, and I guess the post office must have lost it because it wasn't in the mail at the end of January either."

Carroll donned the gloves and, holding the envelope by the edges, inspected both sides. Besides the destination address, there was no additional information, not even a return address.

Carroll inspected the postmark.

"When did you get this, Mr. McDowell?"

"Well, let's scc," he pondered. "It was in the batch I picked up this week, but it could've been there for days or even weeks. Like she said, we figured the post office sent it wrong or something."

"What's the date on the postmark?" Carroll asked him.

Thomas Sr. put on his glasses and leaned forward to inspect it.

"January 23rd," he read aloud.

Mrs. McDowell's smile vanished as she suddenly stood up exclaiming, "Oh, my Lord!"

Her husband was confused. He looked at her then back at Robert Carroll.

"Mr. McDowell, the postmark is not the date it came in," Carroll explained, "That's the date that it was mailed *out*."

The elder Thomas nodded at the first part of Carroll's statement, but he looked up at Carroll.

"But – that was after Thomas died," he said, scratching his head. "Who mailed it then?"

"There are only two possibilities," Carroll answered. "Someone who might be trying to help or –"

"The person who killed our grandson," Mrs. McDowell concluded.

"That's right," he confirmed. "You understand that with an open murder investigation, I've got to turn this over to the law enforcement authorities. Right?"

"So, you'll take it to Georgia?" asked Mrs. McDowell.

"I'm sure that it will end up there, especially if there's an arrest and trial, but for the time being I'm going to contact a detective friend at my old office at the Indy PD."

Carroll had immediately decided on his course of action upon first seeing the letter. As a hired private investigator who had stumbled upon evidence in an active homicide investigation, he would follow established protocol and turn the letter over to Jay Stewart at Indianapolis PD.

Receiving the letter this way, from the McDowells, here in Indianapolis, actually worked out perfectly for Carroll in several ways. First, by having it enter the case in Indianapolis, it would allow him to remain semi-anonymous in Fitzgerald, at least for a little while. The longer he could look around without being linked to the investigation the better it would be. As much as he disliked Billy Bob McCoy, Carroll knew he needed more time with him if he wanted to learn more, and he certainly could not do that if he was identified as an investigator.

Another important factor about the letter coming to him here at his office was that he was now part of the chain of custody for this particular piece of evidence and, at least in that respect, he was now officially involved in the case. Also, he had returned specifically to help with Jay's unrelated case, something that his friend would not forget. With this new development, Jay would be named as the case officer for Indianapolis PD's side of the McDowell investigation. A multi-state homicide investigation in his personnel file would look good when it came to job performance evaluations for pay raises or promotions. That is, if they successfully solved it.

The McDowells were afraid the new evidence would not be taken seriously, but Carroll reassured them, saying, "Don't worry. This is important and it'll be treated seriously. Have you told anyone else about this?"

They shook their heads.

"No, no one," said Mrs. McDowell.

"I've got to say that you handled this very well," Carroll told her. "Most people would have just opened it without thinking."

He was not just trying to make them feel better. He was serious. Potentially, this could end up being a key piece of evidence, something that could turn the entire case around.

Carroll was also beginning to wonder if there was some sort of connection to the past, either to someone in the McDowell family or something the young McDowell had accidentally stumbled upon. The question was, what would have caused someone to take his life?

The historical information Suzi had gathered and the little tourist packet that Walden had given him now took on added significance. It was no longer just about Carroll's personal hobby of delving into American history. It was now a matter of finding how the pieces of this puzzle fit together. Carroll walked the McDowells to the door and promised to update them on anything relevant.

He knew Suzi was waiting for them to leave. As soon as the door closed, she blurted out, "Is Albert McDowell Grandpa Joe?" she asked, using the voice of Disney's *Goofy* for more effect.

She looked at Carroll sideways just as Mrs. McDowell had done and, using an elderly voice, she answered, "Of course not. Why would Tommy send something to a man that's been dead since he was six years old? Are you an idiot?"

"You made that last part up," Carroll popped back. "She never said, 'Are you an idiot?'"

"Maybe she didn't *say* it —" said Suzi, her voice trailing off.

Carroll had no defense. He knew Suzi was correct. Mrs. McDowell had probably wondered if they had hired an idiot, he thought.

"I'm going to take this to Jay," he said, holding up the letter in a protected bag.

"Sneak up behind him and flick his right ear lobe," she said. "Tell him it's from me. He always says that he hated that, but I know that he misses me."

"Why don't I just slap him for you?"

"Sure, that'll work. Anything I should do on this end?"

"Keep digging. Find anything and everything you can about Fitzgerald, both the man and the town, and add it to those files. There's got to be some kind of connection."

Suzi nodded, "You know, if that Jackson lady is really old enough to have known Philander Fitzgerald, then you really should talk to her soon."

"That's my number one priority when I get back down there."

"If she doesn't have a heart attack or a stroke first," Suzi replied.

"You know, that's what I love about you. You're so compassionate," he retorted.

"Oh, grow up!" she shot back. "I mean, she knew a frig'n Civil War drummer boy, for Pete's sake! She's older than dirt."

Carroll laughed. Suzi had a point.

"Ben said that she was 140, but he may have stretched it a bit. I'll find out when I talk to her."

"If she doesn't have a heart attack or a stroke first," she repeated.

"If she doesn't have a heart attack or a stroke first," Carroll agreed, now secretly becoming concerned that Suzi might have jinxed him.

The drive to Carroll's old office at the police department took only a few minutes. He felt strange as he made his way down the hall to Jay Stewart's office, his old office. He felt like he was returning to work from lunch, even though he had been retired for years now. Several people greeted him, some with handshakes and some with pats on his shoulder. It feels good, he thought, to still be treated as a coworker by the guys and gals, rather than like one of those PI's.

Jay's door was open, but Carroll gave it a double knock anyway, out of courtesy. Stewart was on the phone, but motioned for him to come in and, pointing to the chairs in front of the desk, invited him to sit. Carroll responded by pointing toward the break room, indicating he would grab a cup of coffee while Jay was on the phone.

He had not had any real sleep to speak of since the night before last and he knew that it was bound to catch up to him at some point during the day. He had started toward the break room, when Jay snapped his fingers to get his attention. He turned around as Jay lifted his coffee cup and tilted it, showing it was nearly empty. Then he held up two fingers and curled his finger around to his thumb, indicating a circle.

Carroll acknowledged Jay's request with a nod. He took Stewart's mug and headed down the hall to the break room.

"Uncle Bob! How ya doing?" shouted a young female voice.

"Hey, Val. I'm good. More importantly, how are you?"

"No worse for the wear," she replied. "I could have used a cop, but where the hell are they when you really need one, huh?"

"Tell me about it! You know, you've really gotta stop doing stuff like that. You're no spring chicken anymore. What are you now, 30?" he said with a wink.

"Quit busting my balls!" Val quipped.

She waited until he put the two mugs down before giving him a hug. Valerie Chow was not actually Carroll's niece. She was the daughter of one of his oldest and closest friends. He had not only gone through the academy with her dad, Carroll was also at the hospital for her birth. She had called him Uncle Bob since she learned to talk. As far as Val was concerned he was just as much of an uncle to her as her mother's two brothers were. Carroll had proudly watched his niece throughout her life. Following in her father's footsteps, she had joined the department at 21 and had gone from patrolman to detective faster than any other officer in the department's history, all on her own merits, without a single bit of help from her dad, Carroll or anyone else. And she was only 29. The remark about being 30 was just a playful jab. He knew she had been dreading it.

"I'll catch up with you before I leave," he assured her, as she headed back to her office.

Val's office was Carroll's old office, too, the one that housed three detectives and two desks, the one he had worked in for nearly fifteen years before being promoted first to lieutenant, then to captain, the supervisory position now held by Jay Stewart.

Carroll opened the double doors of the cabinet above and to the right of the Bunn coffee maker, identical to the one back in his own kitchen. He could not help but smile as he looked up at the cups and mugs on the second shelf. None of them matched. A few were even chipped. There were various styles and sizes, some plain and unadorned, but most had some type of slogan, phrase or logo on them. Those with logos were typical for cops. There was an oversized MADD (*Mothers Against Drunk Driving*) mug, which belonged to Alan Smith, one of the newer guys.

There were two cups sporting different versions of the logo of FOP, the *Fraternal Order of Police*. The dark blue one was Jay's old cup that he kept as a spare, and the lighter blue one belonged to Reggie Stacks, the newest detective. With several of the officers being veterans, there was an assortment that featured the military logos of every branch: US Army, Navy, Air Force, Coast Guard and Marines, some with phrases like, *Be All You Can Be, Semper fi* and *Aim High… Fly, Fight, Win.*

Normally, everyone could tell who was currently working, who was off and who was on vacation just by observing where a cup was positioned on the shelf. As shifts rotated and changed, so did the cups and mugs. If there was a cup that belonged to someone from another shift out front with a different shift then it was likely that the person was here working overtime.

It had been more than three weeks since Carroll had been by, so he had to search for his mug. His large white mug with the U.S. Coast Guard emblem on one side and the phrase, *Always Ready*, on the other had naturally rotated to the back in the left rear corner. It was not intentional on their part. It was just part of the everyday process of the office.

"Nobody puts baby in a corner," Carroll said, retrieving his cup with a grin. He lost the smile as he glanced at the cup to the right of his. It had one simple, but powerful, four-word phrase on it, *My life for freedom*." That had been Ray Wilder's cup. The slogan was prophetic. Ray was an ex Navy Seal who had been shot and killed during Carroll's last year with the department. Ray had walked into a convenience store right into the middle of a robbery. There were three gang members, all armed with handguns. Even though he wore plainclothes, he was recognized as a police officer by one of the robbers, someone Wilder had arrested before.

"He's a cop!" the guy shouted, and before Ray even knew what was going on, he had been shot by all three.

It took them the rest of the year, Carroll's last, to identify the suspects and solve the case. They had arrested two of the men on the night they identified them ; however, the third escaped and fled the state. He was finally tracked down and arrested in Atlanta two years later. Carroll had retired by then, but Jay had invited his predecessor to accompany him to pick up and transport the prisoner back to Indianapolis for the trial. The way Jay explained it, the crime had happened on Carroll's watch and because he had been instrumental in solving it, he deserved the chance to see it through. That was one of the trips that he had thought about on his way down to Georgia just a few days before.

Carroll closed the cabinet and turned to walk away, but he stopped, turned around and reopened the cabinet. He reached into the back, pulled Ray Wilder's cup out and put it on the front row.

"Miss you, buddy," he said, as he closed the cabinet.

He opened the Dunkin' Donuts box on the table and picked out three, one for himself and two for Jay. Val's unmistakable laugh floated down the hall. It was good to hear, but he could not help but think about Ray Wilder's mug in the cabinet. They came very close to losing Val just a couple of months ago when the same thing had happened to her.

She had walked into a package store and realized immediately that, just like Ray, she had walked into an armed robbery; however, her situation was different for a couple of reasons. For one thing, the bad guys did realize she was a cop, probably because she did not fit their stereotypical image. Val is Chinese, a female and very pretty.

The other thing that worked in her favor was that she played to another stereotype which they expected, the female victim. Val screamed and pretended to faint. The bad guys laughed at her as they beat the cashier and another male customer, joking that they had "something different" planned for her. They never got the chance.

Val's fainting ruse allowed her to retrieve her weapon from her concealed holster. She rose to a kneeling position, raising her .40 caliber Glock, as two of the three robbers turned toward her. She and one of the robbers fired simultaneously. Val was hit in the left shoulder. Her shooter took it in the chest. The second suspect also fired at her within a fraction of a second of the first shooter, but the impact of the first shot that hit Val had knocked her backwards, causing the second robber's shot to graze her other shoulder. They both fired again. She took the second hit in her right thigh, but Val's shot struck him in the neck.

The third suspect had jumped behind the counter and was preparing to fire at the now incapacitated Val, when he was overpowered by the cashier and the customer who the robbers were previously beating on. The suspect who was shot in the throat died at the scene. The other shooter died two days later and the third suspect, the one that the cashier and the customer overpowered, will go to trial in a few months.

Val had just returned to work earlier this week. Carroll had been invited to her Welcome Back party, but he was already in Georgia. It did not matter. She knew her Uncle Bob had sat at the hospital with her family for three days straight when she was in critical condition. The bullet in her thigh went straight through, but the one in her shoulder had traveled into her torso causing massive internal bleeding. It wasn't until the third day that she was removed from the critical care unit.

Her Uncle Bob had continued to stop by every day, sometimes several times a day as she improved. Suzi, who felt the same way about Valerie, represented them at her Welcome Back party. She also delivered a gift from Carroll, an oversized pink coffee mug with a flower on it, the one that Val was holding right now. It originally came with the phrase, "I'm made of sugar, spice and everything nice!" on one side, but Carroll had found someone to hand paint another ingredient, matching the existing font, on the opposite side of the mug, adding, "…with equal parts, KICK ASS!"

Jay was still on the phone when Carroll returned. He placed the coffee and doughnuts on his desk.

"Hey, buddy, let me get back to you. I've gotta deal with a jackass that just walked into my office," Stewart informed his caller.

The person on the phone said something back to Jay.

"Yeah, as a matter of fact, it *is* Bob Carroll," he said.

"Terry Bennett said, hello," Jay said, waving at Carroll.

Carroll lifted his middle finger.

"Bob said to tell you, hello, too. Yeah, talk to you later. Bye."

Jay stood up and shook Carroll's hand.

"This means a lot, Bob; you coming back for this. I really do appreciate it," he said sincerely.

Carroll responded sarcastically, "No problem. I couldn't wait to get back to the subzero weather from short sleeves."

"I'll bet!"

"Can we set up a meeting to review your testimony–" Jay checked his calendar, "say, on Monday?"

"Yeah, no problem. I'll just go ahead and block out the whole day so schedule for whatever time is most convenient for you and just let Suzi know."

"Sounds good. Hey, Val's back. Did you see her?"

"Yeah, she was in the break room. She told me to stop breaking her balls," Carroll chuckled.

"She's getting back to her normal self," Jay laughed. "She'll be on desk duty for a few months."

"Do you think she's ready? Even for desk duty?"

"I tried to get her to take more time, but she insisted. So, I figured I'd make sure that she's not on the street for awhile."

"Good," Carroll agreed. "Val's tough. I think she'll be fine, but if I can make a suggestion?" he paused, waiting on Jay's response.

"Of course, Bob. I'd appreciate your input," Stewart responded.

"Even though she's on desk duty, I would get her back on the firing range as soon as possible," Carroll recommended.

"Yeah, that's what the psychologist said, too. As a matter of fact, I was going to ask you to help ease her back into it."

"Great. I'll talk to her before I leave."

"So, what the hell are you doing in *Georgia*?" Jay chuckled.

"If I had to respond in Facebook vernacular, I would just say, 'It's complicated.' It started out as a missing person case, but then turned into an unsolved homicide investigation that, as of about an hour ago, now involves Indy PD."

Carroll pulled the envelope from his folder and placed it on Jay's desk. Stewart sipped his coffee and munched on doughnuts as Carroll brought him up to speed on everything that had happened since he first met the elder McDowells.

"That's where I'm at now," he said.

Jay shook his head, "Man, you happening upon that meeting at the Waffle House – that's crazy! That was a stroke of good luck! Do you have any idea who the others are or what they were talking about?"

"Nope, not a clue. Although, I'm hoping that one might be James from that beating incident. All I can say is that they were having a very serious discussion."

Jay held up the evidence bag containing the envelope.

"Okay, I'll get this to the lab. I've got a connection there that may be able to expedite it. I'll let you know."

"Thanks, buddy. I'll let you get back to it."

"Yeah, I really need to get to work," Jay said, as they shook hands. He took a parting shot at Carroll as he walked out, "–especially now that you've added to my caseload."

Carroll walked back down the hall and into the detective's office. Nothing had changed. Nothing. There were the same desks, same chairs, same phones, same staplers, same clear paper clip holder, ad infinitum. He thought of Yogi Berra's old line, "It's déjà vu all over again."

Alan Smith's desk faced the door so he saw Carroll first.

"Hey, gang, it's Uncle B!" he informed the others.

Most of the younger detectives had also started calling him Uncle Bob or Uncle B. It was not meant to poke fun or in a disrespectful manner. On the contrary, they were motivated by affection and respect.

"What's up, Uncle Bob!" said Reggie, now holding his blue FOP mug. He had obviously been to the break room since Carroll left.

"Hey, boys and girls," replied Carroll.

"Jesus, you're still here?" Val scowled.

"I thought we got rid of you!" she added, but got up to give him another hug.

"So what's up?" Carroll asked.

"Same shit, different day," said Reggie, pointing to the folder on his desk.

Carroll looked down and read the name on the folder.

"Jeez, Flintstone? Again?"

The young detectives cracked up.

"Yep," Reggie chuckled. "This time it was a GameTime store. Damn thing had more alarms than a bank."

"He was wearing a cool outfit though!" Val giggled. "He was dressed like a ninja, all in black – with this thing," she motioned with her hands, "wrapped around his head with just his eyes showing."

Alan shook his head, "Flintstone's got to be the stupidest, noisiest ninja on earth!"

"Poor Freddie," agreed Reggie, "To make matters worse, there were three patrol cars at the coffee shop on the corner."

His comment sent all four of them into more laughter. They spent the next half hour each telling a Freddie Story. It was sort of a tradition. Every cop, uniformed or plain-clothes, who had been there for any length of time had a Freddie Story.

His name was actually Fred Flint. One might think that the addition of stone to his last name would have started in grammar school, but it was not until he was nearly 20 that he acquired the nickname. Freddie, as his friends and family called him, was a notoriously unsuccessful burglar, not a robber. There is a big difference. Freddie broke into closed businesses at night, but he would never do anything violent where someone might get hurt.

Freddie had two problems. To say that he was not very bright would have been a massive understatement. Freddie's second problem was that he was the most unlucky person that anyone could ever meet, this latest incident representing both points.

Reggie's favorite Freddie Story was about the time he broke into a local business office. Freddie had waited until a couple of hours after dark, then picked the lock on the back door and made his way down the hall to a large office area. When he walked in, about 40 people jumped up and yelled, "Surprise!" He had picked the one night that they were having a retirement party for an employee. There was some debate later about who had been scared the most by the confrontation, the office workers or Freddie. Although one lady had fainted, the general consensus was that it was Freddie who was frightened the most. Witnesses reported that when the crowd shouted, "Surprise!" he turned and ran – straight into the wall. He was out cold when the responding cops arrived.

Val's Freddie Story was simple. He had gained entry to a department store through an air duct and had actually gotten away with some high ticket items – cameras, Xboxes, video games. Freddie had finally managed to pull it off, it appeared, at least briefly. However, responding officers found that he had apparently snagged his pants on the way out – tearing his back pocket, which unbeknownst to Freddie, left his wallet, complete with two forms of ID, laying on the ground. Cops were waiting at his house when he came in with the loot.

It was Carroll who informed them of how Freddie's last name was extended. He retold the story frequently for new cops and detectives. Freddie was walking down the sidewalk when he saw an iPod display through a store window.

"It was the first year they were released and iPods were a big deal," Carroll explained.

He reached down, acting out his story. "So, he picked up the most convenient thing he could find to smash the window, a large rock. He tossed it through, snatched two boxes of iPods and got away!"

As with Val's earlier story, Freddie seemed to have finally gotten lucky. Amazingly, the store's video surveillance system had broken the day before. Unfortunately, the rock that Freddie used was a big piece of broken flint, with a shiny smooth surface that was perfect for fingerprints. Had he picked up the rock to the right or the left, both rough and unbroken, he would have finally had a successful burglary."

Some of them had more than one Freddie Story and even though they had heard them all before, they retold them again, getting more and more hysterical as they talked.

Believe it or not, there are a lot Freddies out there. They are job security, Carroll often told new recruits.

Carroll always enjoyed hanging with the young detectives, but he did not want to keep them from their work so he said goodbye and asked Val to walk him out.

"So how are you really feeling?" he inquired, as soon as they were outside.

"I'm good," she assured him.

"You know I've been there, where you are now, so let me know if you have any problems. Okay?"

She nodded, "The only thing that I'm nervous about is firearms requalification next month. I'm afraid that I may freeze or, even worse, faint like a girl when I hear a gunshot."

Carroll smiled at her faint-like-a-girl comment.

"I'll tell you what; why don't you and I hit the range one day next week, just the two of us?"

"Perfect!" she said, giving him his third hug of the afternoon.

"Now, get your ass back to work!" he scolded.

"I already warned you once, old man! Quit breaking my balls!" she snapped as she walked away.

Because he had not gone in to work until after lunch, Carroll had lost track of time. He started to head back to the office but realized it was already after 5. He checked in with Suzi and told her he would see her tomorrow.

He was still sipping on his first cup of coffee as he sat behind his Pergola Grand the following morning when Suzi informed him that he had a call from Jay. He expected it was probably about the upcoming court case, the one for which he had been subpoenaed.

Carroll touched the speaker button, "Morn'n, Jay."

"Hey, Bob. Can you meet me at the lab?"

"Sure, what's up?"

"Well, I thought you'd want to be there when they opened the letter."

"Are you serious?"

Carroll knew that homicides get top priority, but he was still impressed with the turnaround time.

"What time are we talking about?"

"As soon as you can get there," Stewart replied.

Carroll grabbed keys and phone and stepped into Suzi's office to tell her, putting on his coat as he walked in.

Seeing that he was leaving, she quipped, "Headed home? These 20-minute workdays are brutal, aren't they?"

"Very funny! I'm going to meet Jay at the lab to open the envelope."

"Wow! Who lit a fire under their ass?"

"I have no idea. I'm just thankful that it happened so quickly."

Jay was waiting for him in the parking lot at the lab. They entered the foyer and Carroll waited as Stewart walked over to the wall and pressed a button on a keypad. He took a couple of steps backwards to ensure that he was in full view of the wall-mounted camera, then looked up and waved. There was a buzz, followed by a click as the heavy door popped opened. They proceeded through and down a hallway, then into the first room on the left. It resembled an emergency room at a hospital. A person wearing a white ultra-light, one-piece protective bodysuit stood at the counter on the far wall, writing on a form. In addition to the body suit, he wore a hood, made of the same material, which completely covered everything but the eyes.

"I didn't know ninja's wore white," Jay joked as they walked in.

There was a giggle as the person turned around. Even without hearing the voice, Carroll would have known it was a female by the appearance of the eyes.

Jay motioned toward him, saying, "This is Robert Carroll, the pain in the ass that wanted me to push this."

He added, "This is Dr. Patrick," introducing her to Carroll.

Her eyes were still smiling, "Drop the title. It's just, Cora."

"I'll drop Dr. Patrick if you'll drop the *pain-in-the-ass* part and Robert. It's just Bob."

"Okay, it's a deal, Just Bob," she quipped.

There was no attempt to shake hands as one would normally do when meeting someone new. Carroll was well familiar with lab protocol. They would not risk contaminating evidence with a handshake. That could wait until later.

"And by the way," Carroll added, "I only asked him to try and expedite it."

"No worries," Cora replied. "Believe me; I take whatever Jay says with a grain of salt."

"Well, I really do appreciate it."

"Oh, he's paying for it," Cora assured him.

He shot Jay an inquisitive look.

"I'm pretty sure that she's breaking the law," Stewart replied. "I don't think a government employee is supposed to blackmail a detective. I'm taking her to St. Elmo in return for bumping you to the top."

"Mama Carolla's!" she corrected him. "We always go to Saint Elmo."

Carroll realized the two of them were obviously dating.

"I wouldn't have told him earlier," she said, looking at Carroll, "but we're not that far behind, and with it being an open homicide, I just followed normal protocol."

Jay shook his head, "Damn! She played me liked a violin, Bob."

"I did no such thing! You came in and told me that if I could jump on this tonight or tomorrow you would take me to eat at the place of my choice. Am I not correct?"

"Yes," he admitted, "but you didn't tell me that you were caught up."

"And you didn't ask either."

Carroll was enjoying the back and forth between Cora and his longtime friend. He was also thinking that Jay might have finally met his match, in more ways than one. He wondered why he had not known about their relationship. It was not against any regulations. They were both single. He was surprised that he had not seen them together at St. Elmo. It was also one of his favorite places.

St. Elmo is an upscale restaurant located on Illinois Street in downtown Indianapolis. They specialize in steaks, but they do equally amazing things with seafood, chicken and chops. A guy named Joe Stahr opened the restaurant in 1902. He named it after the patron saint of sailors. And by the way, it's St. Elmo, not St. Elmo's, with an apostrophe like in the 1985 movie or the weather phenomenon.

Besides being one of the oldest restaurants in America and having great food, the place is also known for its wine cellar. They supposedly have over 20,000 bottles.

Carroll liked the lounge on the second floor. There was something about the exposed brick walls of the old building that transported him back to the early 1930s after prohibition was repealed. In fact, there are photos of the time on the walls there. The Travel Channel did a feature on St. Elmo, and in 2012, the James Beard Foundation recognized it as one of America's Classics. Forbes magazine even called it one of the world's "10 Great Classic Restaurants Well Worth Visiting."

The place that Cora wanted to go to, Mama Carolla's, was an Italian restaurant located on East 54th street on the north side of Indianapolis. It was also a very popular place. The restaurant is in a 1920s stucco-style home, but everyone likes to sit on the outdoor terrace if the weather is nice. Mama Carolla's is renowned for its homemade meatballs and steamed mussels.

"Are you going stand around bragging about how you connived me out of a meal, or are you going to get to work?" Jay asked.

"I'm going to stand around bragging," Cora popped back, but she was already busily making preparations to open the letter. She had worked the exterior of the envelope earlier in the morning, checking it for prints and DNA samples. That was why she was wearing the protective gear, not to keep something from getting onto her, rather to keep her DNA from contaminating the letter. Going to that much trouble for a small envelope might appear silly to someone unfamiliar with the process, but the exterior of the envelope could potentially have as much evidentiary value as the contents. Entire cases have been proven by fingerprints and DNA obtained from letters and envelopes.

The exterior work having been completed, Cora had called Jay to let him know she was preparing to open it and he, in turn had notified Carroll. Dr. Patrick entered another room and returned with two large packages.

"Suit up, boys. Gloves first," she commanded, handing a package to each of them.

Each was identical to what Cora was wearing, ultra-light one-piece disposable coverall, kind of like onesie for grownups, except the zipper was on the front, which allowed one to dress without requiring the assistance of another. After donning their gloves, onesies and headgear, they joined Cora at the table.

"Ready?" she asked.

Carroll simply nodded.

Holding the letter with a pair of oversized tweezers, she carefully lifted it up to a light mounted on a swivel. She checked the silhouette to ensure the contents inside would not be affected by the cutting of the exterior envelope. Then, using a scalpel, she cut a slit, not on the top or the side where one would normally open it, but lengthwise along the bottom edge of the envelope. She allowed the contents to fall onto the sterile covering on the table. A small piece of paper fluttered to the table. It looked like it had been torn from a pad or notebook.

"That's it?" Jay asked, his disappointment evident.

Carroll was also taken aback. He had hoped for something more. Just what, he did not know, but more than he was seeing here, more than a torn piece of paper. There was writing on it, just one very short line, written with a regular pen. Still using the tweezers, Cora positioned it under the light so they could view it better.

Jay read it out loud, JEP = John Ephraim Paschal?

"Does that name ring a bell?" he asked Carroll.

"No, I've never heard it before, and it's not in the case file either. Suzi and I will get on it after lunch."

"I wonder why it's written that way, with a question mark at the end?" Cora wondered.

"It looks like whoever wrote it might have had the initials, J.E.P., from somewhere and then they located a name that might be a match," Carroll suggested.

Cora and Jay agreed. It seemed the only logical choice.

"I'll check it for prints and DNA, but don't get your hopes up," Dr. Patrick warned.

Carroll's cell phone rang. Seeing it was Suzi, he excused himself and stepped out to take the call.

"What's up?"

"Is Jay with you?" she asked.

"Yeah. Well, actually he's still in the lab."

She paused and then asked, "So, he hasn't gotten a phone call yet?"

"Why do I have a bad feeling about this call?" Carroll asked Suzi.

"Because you already know that it's bad news."

Carroll lowered his head. He knew it. Suzi's remark about Mrs. Jackson's age had jinxed them, he thought. It was not that he was a superstitious person, but he knew that you do not make jokes about old people dying.

"I know," he said. "She's dead."

"Who's dead?"

"Mrs. Jackson."

"She is?" Suzi exclaimed.

"Are you telling me or asking me?" he responded.

"What?"

"That Mrs. Jackson is dead?"

"Oh, my God!" Suzi sniffled, "I am *so* sorry! I didn't know."

"Wait – what?" he asked, even more confused.

"I didn't know that Mrs. Jackson had passed away," Suzi cried.

Carroll suddenly realized that he had created the whole confusing situation himself.

"Okay, wait! Stop! Let's calm down."

He took a deep breath and asked, "What did you call to tell me?

"That the attorney for the defendant in Jay's case, the one you're subpoenaed for, has filed several motions, including one for change of venue. It's probably going to delay the trial. You won't be able to go back to Georgia next week as planned."

"And that's what you called to tell me?" Carroll asked, putting his palm on his forehead.

"Yes," she said, still sniffling.

"There was nothing else?"

There was a loud honk as Suzi blew her nose, "No, I just knew you wanted to get back down there."

"Okay, thanks. I'll be back of office shortly," he said.

"Wait! What about Mrs. Jackson? What happened?"

"Nothing. Mrs. Jackson is fine. That is, unless you have newer information than I do."

There was an uncomfortably long silence over the line. Carroll knew he had made a huge mistake and he braced for what he knew was coming.

"What – in – the – hell – are you talking about?" Suzi asked, her voice getting increasingly louder with each word as she realized her boss had overreacted.

"So, you're saying that she's alive?"

"Yes" he said, embarrassed.

"*Robert – Francis – Carroll*"

He was in big trouble. She had used his full name, something that was reserved for the most serious offenses, something that Suzi and his mother had in common.

"I'm sorry," he said. "I didn't think–"

"And people actually pay you to do just that," she interrupted, "to think! Unbelievable!"

He knew she was shaking her head as she said it. He had no defense.

"I know," he whimpered.

"You need to hurry and get back to the office so I can slap you for making me feel bad!"

"Should I stop and choose a switch on the way back to the office?"

"Don't even try to joke your way out of this one!" Suzi warned him. She was serious.

He decided he would give her time to cool down before returning to the office. He would take care of a few errands and go back sometime around June.

7

Where's Lenny?

Robert Carroll knew there was only a limited number of legitimate reasons to keep him from returning to his office. Once he had used all of the legitimate ones, reasons became excuses and, just as it was when he was in trouble as a child, delaying his punishment would only make it worse. He finally got up enough courage and sulked into Suzi's office mid afternoon.

"Which cheek?" he joked, turning his head back and forth.

"I'll wait until you're not expecting it," she replied without a smile. "It'll be more effective that way."

"Can I go to work now?"

"Sure. Go ahead," she said motioning toward his office, without looking up. "You could've been working for the last four hours if you would have taken it like a man."

He started to speak but checked himself. He knew he would have to hold his smart comebacks for the remainder of the day and possibly even for tomorrow as well. He simply nodded and walked into the break room to get his coffee. The fact that he was standing there preparing it himself was a good indicator of just how upset Suzi was. Her job description certainly didn't include anything about having to prepare his coffee. She had never done it for him or anyone else when they were still at Indianapolis PD. It had begun spontaneously on the morning when they first opened the office.

Carroll had been sitting at his new desk with a big goofy grin on his face when she had walked in and unceremoniously placed his mug on his desk.

"Thanks," he said.

"Don't get too used to it!" she cautioned him, but from that day forward she continued to prepare a cup for him whenever he came back into the office, whether it was the first thing in the morning or from a fresh pot in the afternoon. That is, until today.

Carroll entered his office and walked over to the case file table. He looked at the folders labeled, Philander H. Fitzgerald, Fitzgerald (Town), Billy Bob McCoy and Lenny Dewayne Sauls. He picked up the folders for McCoy and Sauls and sat down at his desk.

He started with Billy Bob's file. The first piece of information was simply a photocopy of his driver's license. Unless Carroll found something in his driver's history to indicate otherwise, his license was current and unencumbered with any restrictions. Ben Walden had already informed him that McCoy had a motorcycle – a Harley, no less, so Carroll was not surprised to see the class M designation for motorcycle. He was surprised, however, to find that McCoy had a CDL, a commercial driver's license, with sub classifications which allowed him to drive almost anything one might see on the roadway, including buses and commercial tractor-trailers.

The next section in the file was McCoy's driver's history. Not surprisingly, it showed two previous convictions for DUI and numerous traffic violations covering at least six states. There were numerous charges of speeding, running stop signs, Too Fast for Conditions, several Failure to Yields and a Failure to Maintain Lane. There were also some serious traffic offenses such as, Leaving the Scene of an Accident Without Reporting, Reckless Driving and not one, but two convictions for Attempting to Elude Law Enforcement. Carroll grinned. It seemed that Billy Bob loved to run from the Po-Po. It was unbelievable that McCoy's license wasn't suspended. Carroll assumed that he had jumped through all the hoops, the probationary licenses and attending the special classes required to get them back. The traffic stuff was just the salad.

The real meat and potatoes of the file was Billy Bob's criminal history. Carroll knew McCoy was from Texas, but Billy Bob had evaded answering his question about anything more specific. He did not know which town or county he was from.

Carroll chuckled to find that Billy Bob was from Happy, Texas. The only Happy, Texas he knew of was from a movie of the same title. He had always assumed it was a fictional place until now, so this was the first time he realized the town actually existed. The movie was a comedy that he and Suzi both liked. Knowing that she would also get a kick out of it, he was about to reach over to hit the intercom button to call her into his office when he realized that it probably was not a good idea. Better let things simmer down some more, he thought.

Carroll scooted from his desk over to the workstation where two identical computers sat side by side. The double computer thing was also something he had planned for his new office from the start. One computer was designated just for research, emails and video communication, all of which obviously required internet access, so it had a high-speed DSL connection. He and Suzi called it the RC for research computer.

The other computer, dubbed the EC, the evidence computer, was strictly for storing and viewing documents, including photos and video. It did not have internet access. Some of his cases, especially those involving big corporate clients like Linder Technologies, involved dealing with patents and other sensitive material. Big companies were not above hacking their rivals to get a jump on the competition. Carroll was so paranoid about internet espionage that he even disliked the idea of having it connected to the electric outlet. He had searched for an alternate power source, even considering a mini solar panel just for the computer.

He adjusted his chair in front of the RC and googled Happy, Texas. Carroll wanted to get an idea of what Billy Bob's hometown was like. The more that he could find out about McCoy the better. He discovered that Happy is located in the Texas panhandle, pretty much where the handle meets the pan. With part of the town being in Randall County and part in Swisher, one might get the idea that Happy is a sizable community. It is not. With a population of less than 800 people, Happy, Texas is the proverbial stop-in-the-road.

Next came the little tidbits of information that Carroll always enjoyed discovering, like how he found out about Little Miss Sunbeam. He learned that dry-throated cowboys originally named the place sometime in the 1800s after they were "happy" to find a plentiful stream both for themselves and for their cattle.

Besides the movie, there are basically only two other reasons why one might possibly have heard of Happy, Texas. It is where Buddy Knox, the famous Rockabilly musician, was born. It's also where George Avila was born — or, rather, where he would have been born if he were real. Avila is the fictional Federal Air Marshal stationed aboard Flight 520 on the TV series, 24.

After reading a little more about Billy Bob's hometown, school, and the general Texas panhandle area, Carroll left "The Town Without a Frown" and returned to his desk and McCoy's file.

From what he had seen in his personal observation of McCoy's aggressive physical behavior, Carroll expected to see some charges on his record that reflected the same. There were plenty. The first started the day after his 18th birthday. For Carroll this was a strong indicator that Billy Bob likely had a long juvenile record, but those records are typically not included in case files.

There was quite enough without them. Like his driver's history record, McCoy's criminal history reflected his travels from Texas throughout the southeastern states. It seemed that not only had Billy Bob been almost everywhere, but that he took at least one companion with him, Trouble. From reviewing his criminal history one would assume that Billy Bob left Texas with one purpose in mind, to get arrested in as many places as he could.

"If that was his goal then he was pretty damn successful," Carroll muttered to himself.

Billy Bob McCoy had been convicted of almost every crime involving the use of force. The terminology varied from state to state, but there were lots of assault-related charges; affray, disorderly conduct, simple assault, aggravated assault, simple battery, inciting violence and so on. The only violent crimes that McCoy had not been convicted of were those relating to sexual violence, such as rape, and the ultimate crime of homicide. But, there's a first time for everything, Carroll thought.

He opened the file on Lenny Dewayne Sauls. There was a copy of a birth certificate and a Georgia Voters ID card, the one that he had seen personally the day he had taken him to breakfast. That was it. There was nothing else. Lenny Sauls' record was, well, Lenny had no record. He was absolutely clean, spotless.

The intercom beeped.

"Ben Walden's calling. In or out?" Suzi asked.

"I've got it. Thanks."

With Suzi still angry at him, it would be good to hear a friendly voice.

He pressed the button to receive the call.

"Hey, Ben! I was actually going to give you a call in a few minutes."

"Should I hang up and let you call me back then?" Ben asked. It sounded more like something Suzi would say and Carroll found himself feeling more guilty for the situation he had created be between them.

Ben continued, "I could act surprised: Hey Bob! Thanks for taking time out of your busy schedule as a master dick to talk to a peon like me!"

Carroll noted the overemphasizing of the slang word for detective.

"Yeah, go ahead," Carroll told him. "Hang up and wait at your desk. I'll call you back when I can work you in."

He heard Walden cackling on the line, sounding like one of Fitzgerald's chickens. Ben stopped laughing, his tone became serious as he continued,

"Listen, Bob. Did you go back by McCoy's before you left town? After you took Lenny to McDonald's?"

"No, I dropped him off downtown. Why?"

"It's probably nothing. I'm just a little worried," Ben responded. "Billy Bob's acting kind of weird and I haven't seen Lenny at all."

Walden's news was disturbing. It had been midmorning when Carroll dropped Lenny off downtown after his McDonald's breakfast, so there was no doubt that Sauls ended up at Billy Bob's garage sometime later that day. Given Lenny's childlike nature, he had probably told everyone he came in contact with about his ride in the "airplane car" and ordering breakfast at the drive through.

Carroll imagined Billy Bob prodding the naïve giant for more information. If McCoy was the murderer and thought that Lenny had talked…

Carroll rubbed his forehead, trying to stop his brain from flashing various scenarios of Billy Bob disposing of the one person who could testify against him.

"Check around as much as you can without alerting Billy Bob. He's paranoid enough to do anything at this point," he told Ben.

"I will, but it may be too late."

"What do you mean?"

"Well, I wasn't going to bother you with it, but someone slashed all of the tires on my truck last night."

"Jeez, Ben! Where did this happen?"

"At my house. It had to be sometime between 11:30 last night, when I parked it and 6:00 this morning."

"Do you think that it could have been McCoy?"

"I've got to be honest. It's the first thing that popped into my head."

"I'm going to check on something, Ben. I'll get back to you in a bit. Okay?"

"Sure thing. I'll keep looking."

Carroll had not yet told Walden about seeing McCoy and the other men at the Waffle House and, until this moment, he had completely forgotten about the few seconds of video on his phone. He had never even looked at it.

He picked up his cell phone and walked back over to the workstation, this time to the evidence computer. He opened the bottom right drawer and pulled out the cord that allowed his phone to interface with the computer. After downloading the video he pressed, Play, and brought it to full screen.

Carroll was surprised. The quality of the video was actually much better than he had expected, even after he zoomed in. There was obviously no sound, but he could see the men clearly. There was a lot of body language going on at that table. And there was also something else.

He pressed the button for Suzi on the intercom;

"Can you ask Frank to come over?"

"Sure, give me a minute."

Carroll replayed the video again, pausing and backing it up. He repeated the entire process several more times, watching it from the start, pausing, going back, pausing and replaying again. He paused again and looked at the frozen image of Billy Bob McCoy. He touched his index fingers against the screen, one on each side of Billy Bob's face, and moved them in opposite directions, enlarging the photo. Carroll frowned. Once again, he flashed back to Suzi's suggestion that he should take his camera and his response, I won't need it. If he had followed her advice then he would be looking at a higher quality photos and better video. Instead he was looking at an enlargement that grew grainy because of the pixel quality.

He stood and leaned in toward the screen. There was something about McCoy's eyes. He had his head down as if he were looking at something on the table while he was talking on his cell phone, but his eyes were directed toward the window. Carroll's knees buckled and he sat back down on the chair. If Lenny had gone to the garage and talked to Billy Bob that afternoon, then McCoy might have arranged the meeting specifically to address the issue of what to do about Lenny. And if Billy Bob had spotted Carroll outside of the Waffle House window as it now appeared, he would have automatically assumed that he had been following him. That scenario actually made more sense than the reality, which was that Carroll had just happened to stop for gas at that particular truck stop.

Where the hell was Lenny Sauls? Carroll wondered. Could he have gotten him killed? He suddenly felt nauseous and the room began to spin. With the exception of going to court or for important meetings with clients, Carroll seldom wore a tie; however, old instincts kicked in and he reached up to loosen the nonexistent tie that was constricting his throat.

Suzi walked in to report on her call to Frank.

"What's wrong?" she yelled, running over to where he floundered at the workstation.

"I think I got Lenny killed!" he said, half gasping. He was still trying to loosen his collar.

"What are you talking about?"

"I think —" he sputtered, reaching again for his tie.

"Wait! Stop!" Suzi commanded, pushing his hands down.

She loosened his collar for him, left the room, and quickly returned with a glass of water and a damp cloth.

"Here," she said, handing him both.

Carroll took a big gulp of water, then wiped his face and forehead with the cloth.

Not wanting another Who's on first? mix-up like the one they had had about Mrs. Jackson's premature death, Suzi asked, "Have they found Lenny's body?"

Carroll was attempting to stand up so he could walk to his desk, but the word body made him nauseous again. The thought of Lenny lying dead somewhere was too much to bear. He took another big gulp of water.

"No, but Ben has been hunting him all day and then there's this," he said, pointing to the computer screen.

He stood and directed her into the seat. Carroll pressed, Play. He let the video play completely through and then replayed it again, pausing it at the point where McCoy was on the phone. As before, he took his fingers and enlarged the image again and pointed at Billy Bob's eyes.

"He saw me."

"Maybe he did and maybe he didn't," replied Suzi, trying unsuccessfully to reassure him.

Carroll shook his head.

"I'm certain of it now. He saw me."

"Okay, so let's say that he did see you. Even if he did, that doesn't mean that he acted on it."

There was a buzzing sound, indicating someone was at the back door. Carroll pressed a computer key and Billy Bob's enlarged frozen face was replaced by a split screen from four live video cameras. Starting from the top left screen and going clockwise, there were views of outside the main front door, the lobby, the conference room and the one on the lower left, which showed a woman looking up at the camera in the alley. Carroll leaned forward and pressed a button on the wall. There was a metallic click, releasing the lock on the rear door.

"Hey, don't shoot! It's me," came a voice from down the hall.

"We're in here," Suzi called out.

"Hey, guys," she said as she entered.

"Hey, Frank," Carroll replied, "Thanks for coming so quickly."

Frank was Frances Sloan. She worked for a nonprofit that assists people with disabilities. They help them with a variety of issues, from medical problems to legal work, even shopping. Sloan worked extensively with deaf mutes so she was fluent in sign language.

Carroll had first met her twenty years before when she responded to the police department to help him interview the victim of a brutal robbery who could not speak or hear. They had worked together numerous times since and had become good friends.

It was Frank who had recommended the office space that he now occupied. Her building was located next door, and she had given him a heads-up on the prime location even before the old occupant had moved out. Carroll had sealed the deal before it ever went on the market.

"So, whatcha got?" she asked.

"Here, take a seat," he said.

Frances replaced Suzi in the chair and waited as he started the video again. She knew what Carroll was expecting from her.

"Who's your main guy?" she asked him, as the video cued.

"The guy right there," he replied, pointing to McCoy, "but I'm interested in all of them."

Carroll let the video play through.

"Again, please," Frank requested.

He played it again. She repeated her request, re-watching the entire video six times.

"What do you think?" he asked.

"Well, I don't know who your source for this video was, but I hope that you didn't pay them money for it," she told him.

It was more than Suzi could stand. Even while he had been texting her from outside of the Waffle House that night she had thought "If only you had listened to me."

"Told ya," she reminded him.

"Oops!" said Frank, realizing that Carroll had taken the video.

"Sorry," she added, giving an apologetic smile.

Carroll brushed it aside. He explained how he had happened upon the meeting and why he had taken such low-quality video.

Frank nodded, "So, what you're telling me is that you didn't listen to Suzi, right?"

"Right," he finally admitted. There was no more denying it.

"Yes!" Suzi yelled, as if her team had just scored a touchdown.

It was just what Carroll needed at the moment. It let him know that she was no longer irritated with him but, more importantly, the levity relieved some of the stress he had been experiencing since first watching the video.

"Okay, you've had your moment," he told her. "Now, can we please get back to work?"

Suzi grinned, "Yes, but I'll be throwing this in your face for years," She warned him.

"Walk me through it, Frank," he requested, as he started the video playback again.

"Most of it is too hard to say for sure, but—" she pointed to the man seated directly across the table from McCoy, "the first thing that I can make out is coming up right here—"

Carroll and Suzi watched in fascination as they always did when Frank was lip-reading. They had worked with her enough to know she would point out only words she was absolutely certain of. If there was any doubt she would not express her opinion.

"This guy right here appears to use the word *suspect*." Unfortunately, we don't know what context it was used in because the next few minutes aren't clear."

Carroll's stomach churned. He knew exactly what she meant by context. Frank knew the man said the word, suspect, but not how it was used. Was suspect a noun as in, Do you think that you or Lenny may be a suspect? Or, was it used as a transitive verb, as in, Do you suspect that Lenny is cooperating with the cops? It did not really matter at this point because Carroll knew both ways spelled serious trouble.

Carroll nodded, "Okay, go ahead."

"The next thing that I'm pretty sure of is that your guy," she pointed to McCoy, "addresses the guy across the table and uses the word "permission." Again, I'm not clear on the context, whether he was asking for, or giving, permission for something. Does that fit anything?"

Carroll didn't want to upset Frank with his dark thoughts, but it did fit. And what it fit was the scenario that Sauls had gone by the garage that day and told Billy Bob enough for him to figure out that Carroll was not who he claimed to be. For all he knew, McCoy probably assumed he was a cop investigating the murder, and the Waffle House meeting was arranged so Billy Bob could get permission to do what needed to be done to get rid of Lenny Sauls. The other problem was, if his scenario was correct, he still did not know who Billy Bob was getting permission from, but Carroll did not really care at this point. All that mattered right now was locating Lenny Sauls.

There were still a few seconds of video left and Frank had two more places about which she felt confident. She pointed to the same guy she had talked about earlier, the one sitting straight across from McCoy, and said, "Right here. I'm pretty sure he either said, either Larry or Lonnie."

Carroll's heart sank. He already knew the answer to his next question, but he had to ask it, "Could it have been Lenny?"

She replayed those few seconds of video.

"Wow! That's it!" she exclaimed. "You're getting pretty good at this Bob. Keep it up and you won't even need me anymore!"

He looked at Suzi, but she shook her head. Like Carroll, she did not want to upset Frank with the fact that they might be discussing a murder which had either already taken place or was about to occur.

"You said one more?" Carroll asked Frank.

"Yep, this one is from your guy again," she said, touching the screen to continue the video.

"It's right here at the end when he's talking to someone on his cell phone. He very clearly uses the word, outside.

"Shit!" Carroll yelled, sledge-hammering the table with his fist, causing both Frank and Suzi to jump. It was amazing how the four words, suspect, permission, Lenny and outside, could create such apprehension.

Carroll now realized that he had been careless. One of the two men that had been walking around outside that night was probably a lookout, just pretending to be on the phone until he saw Carroll taking the video. It was at that point when he probably made a real call to McCoy, telling him that he was being watched. Once again, Carroll replayed the events of that night in his head. Remembering Billy Bob's racist remarks, he ruled out the black truck driver as the lookout. That meant it was either the woman in the car, who was only pretending to be asleep, or it was the white guy on the phone, whom Carroll had assumed to be a truck driver.

"I'm so sorry, Bob," Frank said, realizing she had inadvertently given him bad news.

"No," he told her, holding up his hand. "It's not your fault. I needed to know this. I really appreciate your help."

"Okay. I might be able to pull something else out of it if I can use my own equipment," she said.

"Absolutely, whatever you need. This is important. I'll put it on a disk for you."

"Come on; I'll buy you a cup of coffee," Suzi said, and they headed toward the break room.

Carroll opened the right-hand drawer of the workstation, retrieved a blank DVD and inserted it into the computer to make a copy for Frank. He tried to call Walden but didn't get an answer, so he left a voicemail and then sent the same thing as a text message:

Ben, Call me! Urgent!

He walked to the break room and thanked Frances again just as his cell phone began vibrating in his hand. He answered quickly.

"Hey, Ben," he said. "Any news?"

"No, I was actually hoping that you had some when you left me that message."

"Yeah, I've got some, but it's not good."

He had not had a chance to cover the new details with Walden since he had left, so the first thing he did was to explain about happening upon the meeting at Waffle House. It helped that Ben was familiar with the area. He knew exactly where Carroll was talking about, so he was able to follow his play by play description of what had happened.

Carroll proceeded slowly, explaining each detail. Then he gave Walden some background on Frances, telling him exactly what she did in her job and describing her abilities. He gave Ben the bad news about what Frank had revealed. He waited for Walden's response and was beginning to think that he had lost the connection.

"Ben? You still there?"

"Yeah, yeah," Walden answered, "I'm here. It's just that—" his voice trailed off.

For the first time Carroll suspected his new friend might be in way over his head. He had forgotten that Walden was not a cop or fellow detective. He was a newspaper reporter, a person that usually reported on crimes after they happened, not while they were occurring. And he certainly was not used to being part of a case where his own life could be put in danger.

"So what do we do now?" Ben asked.

"My main concern right now is for Lenny's safety," said Carroll.

"Absolutely," Walden agreed.

"I think you need to notify the police department and sheriff's department. Tell them everything. Tell about me, about what happened at Billy Bob's garage and why we're concerned. I may get myself in some hot water over this, but I'll deal with that later. We need their help to find Lenny."

"Okay, let me take care of a couple of things here at the office and I'll go over there. I don't want to do it over the phone. The sheriff's department and police department are in the same building so I can explain it to them in person. They know me."

"Good idea. If you need to call me while you're there to put me on a speakerphone or something, then just go ahead and do whatever you need to do."

"All right. I'll call you in a few minutes."

Carroll was sitting at his desk with his head in his hands when Suzi walked back in.

"He's probably fine," she said.

He lifted his head but did not respond.

"Have you eaten anything?" she asked.

He had to think about it. His head was splitting.

"No."

Suzi turned around and left the room. He could hear her on the phone a few minutes later placing an order. Then she returned to his office.

"Who?"

"China King," she answered.

"I'm not sure if I'm up for Chinese."

"You'll eat it or I'll force-feed you," she threatened.

"Fine, whatever."

China King was actually one of Carroll's favorite places for lunch. It was just around the corner on North Delaware Street and when they were not in a rush they would often walk there just to get out of the office.

Carroll pulled Billy Bob's file back out to go through it again, partly in an effort to stay occupied, but also hoping that he might find something useful. He was on the third page when his cell phone rang. It was Ben.

Knowing that he might be on a speaker phone audible to a roomful of detectives, Carroll cleared his throat and prepared himself before answering professionally, "Robert Carroll."

"HEY, MR. CARROLL!" screamed Lenny in his technology-challenged voice, "WE'RE GOING TO MCDONALD'S"

"Hey, Lenny," Carroll replied, dropping his head onto his desk with a loud thud.

Suzi, hearing Carroll's, "Hey Lenny," came running down the hall, entering his office so fast that she skidded sideways, hitting her hip on the workstation. He pressed speaker so she could hear Lenny, too.

"So you're going to McDonald's, huh?"

"YEP! WE'RE GOING TO MCDONALD'S!" Lenny screamed. "ME AND MR. BEN IS!"

Suzi couldn't believe how loud he was.

"Oh – my – God!" she mouthed, as she massaged her hip.

It was late afternoon so Carroll couldn't resist asking the next question. He had to know.

"What are you going to order?"

"THREE, TEN, FIFTEEN AND TWO!" Sauls hollered back.

Carroll knew the two probably referred to two Cokes.

He could only assume that the other numbers were meal numbers and not for individual burgers or sandwiches, although it was not inconceivable that Lenny could eat 28 of whatever items he ordered.

"That's sounds great, Lenny! Hey, could I talk with Mr. Ben?" he asked.

"OKAY! HERE HE IS!"

"Hey, Bo–" Walden began, but Lenny snatched the phone back from him.

"BYE, MR. CARROLL!" he screamed, "I'LL TALK TO YOU LATER!"

"Bless his heart," said Suzi.

Ben was back on the line laughing.

"Guess who I've got?"

"What the hell Ben?"

"I was literally on my way to the Law Enforcement Center when I just saw him walking on the sidewalk."

Carroll shook his head, "Unbelievable!!"

"Needless to say, I didn't talk to anyone else yet. Should I follow through?"

"What has he told you?"

"Nothing yet. I knew that you were probably going nuts, so as soon as he got in the truck I dialed your number and just told him to say hello."

"Okay, listen. Do you have some free time to spend with him?"

"Sure. The paper's out, so I'm good."

"Then buy him whatever the hell he wants. Just get him talking and find out everything you can."

"Okay, Bob. I'll call you back after I've talked to him."

"And Ben," Carroll added, "Don't let him out of your sight until we know that he's safe."

"Don't worry. He's not going anywhere. Not until I talk to you."

Nearly two hours lapsed before Ben called back. He explained that they had gone to McDonald's and then, to encourage Lenny to become more talkative, he took him out to the airport to watch skydiving.

"Skydiving?"

"Yeah, they do classes there. It's tandem jumps, but you can go on to becoming a skydiver yourself. Most people just do the tandem thing to be able to experience it."

"No, thank you."

"What a wuss!" Ben taunted. "I did it a couple of times for a news story. It's fun!"

"Uh huh, yeah, right."

"Lenny wants to do it," Walden laughed.

"Don't even think about it!" Carroll warned him.

He didn't see how a parachute could support Lenny alone, much less with a tandem instructor hooked up to him.

Walden summed up their conversation: Lenny told Ben that he had been out of town at a family reunion. He said Sauls spent the majority of their conversation talking about the food at the reunion – who brought what, who "cooked good" and who "weren't a good cook at all, but we ate some anyway so's not to hurt her feel'ns" and of course, what his favorite dishes were and how much he ate.

Carroll asked the question that had been plaguing him since the initial call two hours before, "So what was the three, ten, fifteen and two at McDonald's?"

Ben chuckled.

"If I remember correctly, the three was a double quarter-pounder, ten was ten chicken nuggets, and I think the fifteen was probably barbecue and bacon. At least that's what it smelled like. I didn't get a chance to see much before it went down."

They had a laugh, comparing their experiences with Lenny.

"Listen, Bob. I think maybe we've caught a break," said Walden, steering them back on course. "Lenny told me that Billy Bob was leaving to go on a motorcycle trip."

"When?"

"Later today or tomorrow."

"And where's he going?"

"All I could get from Lenny was Washington. When I asked Lenny which one, he just said, 'You know, the place.' I don't think he even knows about the state."

"So, he could be going to DC, which would take a few days if you throw in some sightseeing. Or, he could be going to Washington state, which means a week and half at the least, if he turned around to come right back, or several weeks if he took his time."

"Right," Walden agreed. "On my way in this morning I noticed that Billy Bob had put a note on his shop window. I'm headed over there right now to read it, so maybe we'll know in a couple of minutes."

"There's a third possibility," Carroll volunteered. "If he's guilty and he thinks he's been named as a suspect, then he could be running."

"It's possible, but I believe it's a legit trip. He takes several every year."

"Well, if that's really the case, then it's good news, because it looks like I'm stuck here for at least two more weeks."

"Hold on," Walden interrupted. "I'm pulling in now."

Carroll could hear the sound of Walden putting the truck into park, opening his door, passing traffic and his reentering the truck

"Was there a note like you thought?" Carroll asked.

"Yeah, I wish I had something better to tell you. It's no help. It basically says he's on a road trip."

"It doesn't give a date for him to reopen?"

Walden laughed, "Nope, but that's S.O.P for Billy Bob. He pretty much works when he feels like it."

"Unbelievable! So what do his customers do if they have a problem?"

"In that case, change S.O.P to S.O.L!"

Carroll chuckled, but he was still worried.

"So, do you still feel like he's really just on a road trip? You don't think he's running?"

"I guess I could be wrong," Walden admitted, "But, I'm telling you, Bob, this is typical Billy Bob McCoy! I mean, seriously! Who else writes stuff like, 'Hit'n the road for another day cuz it's better to burn out than to fade away!'"

"Wait," Carroll stopped him. "What did you say?"

"About what?"

"That line you just said. Was it on Billy Bob's note?"

"Yeah," Walden laughed. "Can you believe it? That's all it said. He just wrote, CLOSED, with a marker, and under it he wrote: Hit'n the road for another day cuz it's better to burn out than to fade away!"

It was Carroll's turn to laugh.

"Billy Bob's gone to Washington state," he informed Ben. "Specifically, to Seattle!"

"And how the hell do you know that?"

"Because I'm a big shot PI! You said so yourself. Remember?"

"I believe I actually called you a dick." Ben reminded him.

"He was quoting Kurt Cobain," Carroll explained.

"Kurt Cobain?"

"Yeah, Ben. You do know there was this band called Nirvana. Kurt Cobain was their lead singer and–"

"Jesus, Bob! I know who Kurt Cobain is! I just didn't know those lyrics were in any of his songs."

"They weren't," said Carroll.

"You know, if you were standing here right now, I would probably slap the shit out of you!"

"Right now I probably wouldn't care!" Carroll chuckled.

He felt a huge weight lift from his shoulders. If Billy Bob was riding his Harley from Georgia to Seattle and back, then they had two or three weeks before his return, maybe even longer.

"Okay, Bob. You got me. Please explain what in hell you're talking about."

"The first part, Hit'n the road for another day, is just McCoy's. The second part, it's better to burn out than to fade away, is actually from Kurt Cobain's suicide note."

"You're blowing my mind here."

"But if you want to get technical, it's actually Billy Bob quoting Cobain quoting Neil Young."

"Okay, now you're just showing off," said Walden.

"The original line came from Neil Young's song Hey Hey, My My — Into the Black, but Cobain quoted it in his suicide note."

"Well I'll be damned! Get out your crayon box and color me impressed Bob! I'm not kidding!"

"I figured you might like to learn some PI stuff in case you ever want to change careers," Carroll suggested.

"Who woulda thunk it? Billy Bob may actually still have a smidgen of a soul."

"At least we know the son of a bitch can rhyme," Carroll joked.

"It's weird. I thought I heard that line before, but I sure as hell didn't know that about Kurt and I can't remember the Neil Young song. Can you sing a few bars of it for me?"

"I would have to go to a few bars before I could sing a few bars," Carroll quipped.

"You're thinking of Highlander," he added.

"That's it!" Ben exclaimed, snapping his finger. "The big scary dude, Kurgan, when he was leaving the church!"

It was yet another connection, a "bro moment" for the two friends. Carroll felt relieved as they wandered from their main subject, McCoy, to discuss Highlander's swordplay, Ramirez, the character played by Sean Connery, the increasing patheticness of each sequel, and of course, the fantastic soundtrack by Queen.

It was Ben who finally got them back on track.

"So you think he's going out there to write poetry on Kurt Cobain's headstone?" he asked.

"He can't. There's not one. Cobain was cremated," said Carroll throwing another tidbit in to impress Walden.

"Come to think of it, Billy Bob went out to LA about this same time last year. That was a month-long trip by the time he got back."

"I hope this one takes as long or longer," Carroll responded.

They wrapped up their conversation, but Walden called back within the hour. He told Carroll that he had bumped into someone who was able to confirm Seattle as McCoy's destination. A friend of Ben's said Billy Bob had called him to say that he had finished repairing his car and was leaving town. He had waited on the guy to pick it up before he left.

"It doesn't make it true just because he told a couple of folks and left a note," Carroll cautioned

He was still worried that McCoy might have fled.

"Well, there's nothing we can do but wait," Ben noted, "And we don't have to worry about Lenny, so there's that."

"You're right. I'm almost done up here, so I'll be headed back down soon. I'll give you a heads-up."

"Yeah, I've been thinking about that," Walden replied. "Why don't you fly into Albany this time and I'll pick you up?"

"I appreciate that Ben, but that's what, an hour from you? And I would need to pick up a rental anyway."

"You didn't let me finish," Walden explained. "I was thinking I could pick you up and you could use my truck while you're here."

"And you'll walk?"

"No, I'll drive my Jeep. I switch back and forth during the week.

Carroll was appreciative, but hesitant about taking advantage of such an offer, but Ben insisted, so he finally relented.

8

Isabella Ruth Jackson

With no need to schedule his trip around Atlanta's rush hour traffic and, more importantly, considering Ben would be meeting him in Albany, Carroll asked Suzi to book him on a flight that would arrive an hour or two later than his normal sunrise time at Hartsfield. ExpressJet, Delta's smaller regional carrier, has three regularly scheduled flights to Albany every day. The flights arrive at Southwest Georgia Regional Airport roughly at noon, 5:00 and 9:30 Carroll's flight, the only one before lunch, was scheduled to depart from Atlanta at 10:50 and arrive in Albany forty-five minutes later.

Scheduling it this way worked out great. It would allow Walden to leave Fitzgerald at a more reasonable hour and it would give them at least two hours to catch up and talk about the case, assuming they would grab lunch in Albany and talk on the ride back to Ben Hill County.

Carroll later decided to stick to his normal schedule for the Indianapolis-Atlanta flight after Suzi informed him there would be a difference of only an hour or so. With ExpressJet's set schedule, Ben's time remained the same, but Carroll would have some brief downtime at Hartsfield.

Downtime – it was a word that would have driven Carroll nuts just a few weeks ago, but it did not bother him at all today. He was surprised at how much he was looking forward to getting back to the little town in South Georgia.

He was especially anxious to meet Ruth Jackson. In addition to discussing the case, Carroll hoped to get the centenarian's perspective on local and national history. He was also anticipating the opportunity to do more sightseeing and explore Fitzgerald's history on this trip. The two top items on his list were visits to The Blue & Gray Museum and Evergreen Cemetery.

Carroll thought he had lucked out with weather. A storm was quickly approaching when they took off from Indianapolis, but because the weather system was moving eastward and they were flying almost due south, they were out of it quickly. By the time he arrived at Hartsfield it was perfect for flying, nearly cloudless. To his delight, Carroll got his most memorable view of Atlanta as they circled to land. The sun hit the gold dome of the capitol and brilliantly reflected back just as they were about to cross over

Interstates 75 and 85.

It was a short distance over to the ExpressJet terminal and the wait to board was not long. The weather continued to cooperate as they left Atlanta for Albany, flying at a cruising and altitude that allowed him to view and appreciate Georgia's landscape below. It seemed as if they had barely left Atlanta when they were told to prepare to land in Albany.

Walden was awaiting Carroll as he walked into the terminal. They proceeded to the baggage claim area where Ben grabbed the two smaller bags, and Carroll pulled the other along behind him.

"Do feel like driving?" Ben asked as they walked to his Jeep, "Or, do you want me to?"

"I would like to, if you don't mind. I don't get to drive in the country much."

"I can't imagine ever living in a big city again," said Walden.

"I don't actually live in Indianapolis. My place is up in Noblesville."

"What's that? Like a suburb? You mean you're on the north side of the city, right?"

"No, I mean north of Indy. Noblesville is a small community. Downtown is not a whole lot bigger than Fitzgerald and it's got a lot of history behind it, too. You would like it."

"So what do you feel like for lunch?" Ben asked.

"Something with grits. I haven't had grits since I left."

"Okay, Pearly's it is then. Take a left out of the parking lot."

Carroll turned left onto Newton road as instructed. He had gone less than two miles when Walden told him to take another left onto Slappey Boulevard. Slappey was apparently one of Albany's major streets. They were soon passing lots of restaurants and other businesses.

"It's just ahead on the right there," Ben said.

Carroll saw a green sign with Pearly's in big white letters across the top and Famous Country Cooking underneath. The best part was still farther down on the sign, Breakfast Any Time.

Carroll perked up, "Now we're talk'n!"

"You wanted grits, right?"

It was not even noon yet, but the parking lot was already full. A line was starting to form at the door and employees were walking to take orders from cars that were lined up for the drive through window. Carroll knew his friend had chosen well.

"Welcome back to South Georgia, buddy," said Ben, seeing the big grin on his face.

"You go grab a table and I'll order," Walden instructed as soon as they got inside the restaurant.

'But you don't know what I want!"

"Trust me," Ben responded.

There were only three tables available. Carroll got the one closest to the window. Walden joined him shortly.

"They'll bring it out to us."

"So, tell me about your truck." Carroll said.

"There's not much to tell. I didn't hear a thing. I just got up the next morning and – BAM! Four flat tires!"

"You still believe that it was Billy Bob?"

"That's what I'm thinking, but I'll never prove it."

"I probably already know the answer to this, but what's your plan for today?" he asked Carroll.

"Ruth Jackson is at the top of my list. And if there's enough time I would also love to find Lenny today and see if he can tell me anything else about Billy Bob."

"You can go see Mrs. Jackson as soon as we get into town, and while you're talking to her I'll try to track down Lenny."

They had been sitting for only a few minutes when a waitress, a girl in her mid to late twenties, brought a loaded tray out to the table.

"Hey, ya'll, I'm Donna. Looks like you both got the same thing?" she asked, double-checking the order.

"Yep," Ben answered. Then pointing at Carroll, "Him first, though. He hasn't had grits in weeks."

"Oh no! Poor baby!" she sighed, looking at Carroll like he was a malnourished stray dog at the back door.

"Okay, that's a Breakfast in a Cup with bacon, eggs and cheese-grits and three buttermilk pancakes with sausage," she said, placing the order in front of Carroll. She repeated the process with Ben.

She gave each a cup of coffee and asked, "Anything else?"

"Yeah, Donna. Could I get a glass of OJ and a glass of milk please?" Carroll asked.

"Sure thing," she said, before trotting off.

They started on their lunch and Carroll gave Walden a rundown on McCoy's criminal and driver's history. He also informed him about Lenny's record, or lack thereof. Ben's reaction was the same as Carroll's had been when he first saw the reports. He was not surprised at either result.

Donna returned with glasses of orange juice and milk as well as another bowl of cheese-grits.

"It's on the house, for what you missed," she said, placing the bowl in front of Carroll.

"Wow! Thanks a lot!"

"No problem," she said as she walked away.

"I sure do like Southern hospitality," he told Walden.

They discussed the case while finishing their meal, then returned to the Jeep for the trip to Fitzgerald. Carroll still wanted to drive, so Ben functioned as navigator.

"Four lanes or two?" Ben asked him.

"Two! Definitely two."

Carroll got enough of four, six and ten lanes every day. He was not about to miss an opportunity to drive through the country if he could help it. Walden guided him toward Fitzgerald taking rural Georgia highways 91, then 32 and finally 107. They were soon passing fields with cows or horses and others with tractors plowing, as farmers prepared for spring planting.

Carroll took the opportunity to give Ben a little historical background about Noblesville. Walden took it all in, asking lots of questions, just as Carroll had when Ben had told him about the founding of Fitzgerald.

Walden was surprised to hear that the notorious John Dillinger and a young car-stealing Charles Manson both spent time behind the bars of the Old Hamilton County Sheriff's Residence and Jail.

"Does the name D.C. Stephenson ring a bell?" Carroll asked.

"Are you kidding? Davis Curtis Stephenson? The politician of the 1920s who was also the Grand Dragon of the Ku Klux Klan? That Stephenson?"

Ben had unknowingly just impressed his Robert Carroll. While Stephenson's exploits were legendary in Indiana, Carroll had not expected someone from rural south Georgia to know the name, let alone details about the man.

"He was a psycho who kidnapped and abused women. He was convicted of rape, kidnapping, conspiracy and second-degree murder," Walden added, as if Carroll did not know anything about him.

Ben had made previous arrangements to have his truck at his office so he told Carroll to drop him there.

"By the way," he said, "I've got that package you sent last week in the truck. Why didn't you just bring it on the flight yourself? You could've saved some money."

"TSA rules, I couldn't bring it on the plane."

"Jesus, Bob!" Walden exclaimed. "What the hell did you send me? Am I gonna get thrown in jail?"

"No. Not unless they've brought back Prohibition," Carroll chuckled. "I followed your advice. It's the bourbon for Ruth Jackson."

"Well, all right then!" said Ben, giving Carroll a pat on the back.

They arrived at Walden's truck. He jumped out and retrieved the boxed bourbon and handed it to Carroll. He was relieved that Ben had not asked him for more details about the bourbon. He was not sure what Ben had had in mind, but Carroll was self-conscious about the amount he had paid for it.

He thanked Walden again for the use of his Jeep.

"Call me the second that you're done!" Ben instructed him.

"I will. Thanks a lot for this, Ben."

"Don't thank me yet," he warned. "I charge twice what the rental companies do."

Ruth Jackson's home was located on Lincoln Avenue on the west side of town. Carroll had rode by during his first trip when he was getting to know his way around town. He had also done some research on the home.

Ironically, Lincoln Avenue is on the side of town where all of the streets are named after Southern generals and it is outside of the original downtown square that Philander Fitzgerald and the city founders created, but the street is not new. In fact, two of Fitzgerald's oldest homes, the Jackson House and the Hageman House, were both constructed in 1896 during the first year of the town's existence.

Carroll suspected that the original owners purposely chose the then-rural location, preferring their privacy. The rest of the older homes are all located in one of the original four wards, within two or three blocks from downtown. The wards were subdivided into four blocks, each containing 16 squares that created 256 identical land lots. This obviously included those on Lee Street, South Main and West Central.

The Jackson and Hageman homes were built at the same time in 1896. Both were constructed from felled longleaf pine trees taken from their respective properties. It would be difficult to appreciate the effort it took to build these homes without knowing something about the trees that were used to produce the lumber.

The longleaf pine once dominated the entire southeastern United States, as much as 24 million acres by some accounts. While the few remaining longleafs of today are still impressive, growing as high as 115 feet with 28 inch diameters, they do not compare with their 19th century ancestors.

The longleaf pines of the 1800s were monstrous. Some reached heights of 150 feet and had diameters of nearly 50 inches. The trees were prized for the amount of usable wood they produced. Longleaf lumber was very versatile, used in everything from the construction of homes and businesses to ship building.

Now, imagine cutting trees of that size – with hand tools, no less, and then hauling them by wagon nearly 30 miles to the sawmill in Tifton. The new lumber was then returned to the same property where it was cut to build the houses.

Carroll was thinking about all of this as he turned into the driveway at the Jackson House. The two-story Queen Anne-styled home was beautiful. It boasted a tower and turrets, and a huge wraparound porch.

The home sat on a forty-acre lot. It was completely surrounded by well-kept gardens with lots of rosebushes, camellias and azaleas. The east side of the property was bordered by a large pond, and the west side and rear were covered by rows of pecan trees.

Carroll climbed the six steps to the porch. The front door was located directly in the center. There were eight large rocking chairs on the porch, four on each side of the front door. None of the chairs matched another. They were all unique, each one a work of art.

He shook his head and smiled.

"Jesus. I'm standing in a postcard. I should be sipping on a mint julep," he said aloud.

Still grinning, he raised his hand as he turned toward the door to give it a knock. It was only then that he realized that the main interior door was standing wide open and only the screen door was closed. Not only that, but standing there in the doorway, behind the screen door was a woman. She was African-American, very petite, probably in her late thirties.

"Hello," he stammered. "I'm Robert Carroll. I'm here to see Mrs. Jackson."

"Good afternoon, Mr. Carroll. We were expecting you," she said pleasantly. She unlatched the old-fashioned hook that held the screen door closed and pushed it toward Carroll.

"I'm Betty," she said, as he stepped inside.

"Hi, Betty. Nice to meet you."

She ushered him through the first door on the left into a very large parlor

"Have a seat and make yourself comfortable, Mr. Carroll. Can I get you something to drink? Some lemonade or sweet tea? Or perhaps you would prefer a mint julep?" she said with a broad smile.

"Thanks. Lemonade sounds great," he said, embarrassed that she had overheard his remark.

He was about to sit when he noticed the photographs hanging on the walls. None of the photos was recent. Some were obviously as old as the town itself. Even with his limited knowledge of the community, Carroll recognized some of the buildings and homes in the photos. He walked around the room looking at each photograph, paying attention to every tiny detail. Betty returned holding a glass of lemonade.

"These are absolutely amazing," he said. "And to think that all of these people are now dead and gone."

"Not all of 'em," came a voice from behind him.

He turned around to see a tiny, frail, elderly black woman sitting in a wheelchair. He immediately noticed a strong resemblance between Betty and the old woman who sat there staring at him. Although the two ladies could not tell it, Carroll was angry and embarrassed – at himself.

Even though he had not verbally expressed the thought as he had done with his careless mint julep comment, he realized he had had preconceived notions about the owners of the home. From what Ben had told him about the history of the town and from his own research, he had just automatically assumed that the owners were white.

"Mr. Carroll, this is my grandmother, Isabelle Ruth Jackson. Granny, this is Mr. Carroll."

"Good morning, Mrs. Jackson. How are you?" he half-bowed.

"You look'n at it," she said, leaving it for him to decide.

"Well, if you feel as good as you look, then you're doing well indeed," he complimented.

She pointed a long boney finger at him;

"You can save your flirt'n for somebody else," she warned. "I'm a widow three times over and I *ain't* look'n for number four!"

"Not flirt'n, ma'am, just being truthful," he replied nervously.

Betty chuckled and left the room.

"You've got a beautiful home. And I love the old photos."

"Betty keeps the house up and most of them pictures is 'bout as old as I am."

As curious as Carroll was about her age, he wasn't about to take the bait. Betty returned with a large glass pitcher of lemonade, bits of real lemons floating on the surface, and refilled his class without asking.

"Betty tells me that you're looking into the death of that boy that got killed."

"Yes ma'am, that's correct, although I'm not a policeman or anything. I'm doing this at the request of his grandparents."

"And how much are you scalp'n 'em for?"

"You'll have to get used to Granny. She tends to say what's on her mind," Betty explained.

"Don't go 'pologiz'n for me!" she popped back. "He knows what I'm talking about."

"That's all right," he told Betty.

Then, looking at Mrs. Jackson he added, "I appreciate direct talk."

"You might as well 'preciate it, cause that's what you gonna get from me whether you like it or not."

"I haven't charged them anything," he said, looking directly at her. "I was going to do it and just let them cover the expenses, but I've decided that I'm not even going to ask for that."

"And why is that?" she asked dryly.

"For two reasons," he answered, still looking her directly in the eye. "First, they're friends with somebody who I used to work with, a policeman, whom I respect and who's done a lot for me."

"And the other reason?" she asked, returning the same eye contact.

"It's the right thing to do and I'm in the position where I can do that right now."

"Oh! So you *rich* then!" she said sarcastically.

"No ma'am. Not by a long shot, but I can afford to do this one thing right now."

Ruth Jackson leaned back in the wheelchair and looked him up and down. She was sizing him up. It took only a few seconds before she nodded her head.

"All right then, you seem like you try'n to do what's right and since you waited for Days of Our Lives to get over before you come by, you can go on ahead and ax me whatever you came to."

"Where would you like to sit, Granny?" Betty asked her.

"One place 'bout as good as another. My ass'll be hurt'n in a few minutes no matter where I'm sit'n."

Betty chuckled and shook her head as she helped her grandmother into a more comfortable padded chair.

"Last time I sat here was when that radio man interviewed me for Story Code," she remembered. "My ass hurt for three days after that."

"That was called Story Corps, Granny," Betty reminded her.

"Didn't make no difference what it was called to my ass none."

Carroll was impressed, "They interviewed you for *Story Corps*? Will it be played on NPR?"

"Naw, probably not," she said. "It'll just be on the radio."

"That's what NPR is, Granny," Betty giggled. "It stands for National Public Radio."

"Well why didn't he just say the radio then?" she snapped, "'stead of try'n to sound *'fisticated* using 'nitials."

"Anyway, it's good that they talked to you and got it on the record," Carroll said.

He winced, immediately realizing that his comment was insensitive.

"Yeah, good thing they got it. 'Cause I could fall over dead any time. Better hurry up and ax your questions, too!"

"I just meant that you've seen some amazing and wonderful things in your life and it's good to know that people will get to hear it from you. In fact, I'm going to be sure to look that up myself."

"I'm sit'n right here in front of you and you wanna hear a recording of me talking. That don't make no damn sense!"

"I would much rather talk to you," he said, now taking the opening that she had given him, "In fact, that reminds me, I brought something, but I left it in the jeep."

Carroll stood up and patted his pockets feeling for the bulge of the key and then he ran his hand into both front pockets.

"I can't seem to find the key," he apologized.

"Well, go on and ax me some questions then," Mrs. Jackson said impatiently.

"All right then. The young man, Thomas McDowell, that came to see you–"

"Yes, nice look'n young man," she interrupted him, "Good manners. It's a shame what happened to that boy," she said, her voice trailing off as she shook her head.

"Do you remember how long that was before he died?"

"Betty might know, but I don't remember."

"This is very important, Mrs. Jackson. I know that it's been a long time, but please try to remember."

"*Please try to remember?*" she repeated in an agitated voice.

"Funny how folks like you always com'n round here 'spect'n me to remember shit from three months to 90 years ago when you can't even remember where you put your own damn car keys that you just took out your pocket five minutes ago!"

"Granny!" exclaimed Betty as she reentered the room, "Mr. Carroll is our guest!"

"I'm sorry, honey, but I'm get'n old and my patience ain't what it used be."

Betty tried to explain to her grandmother, "Yes ma'am, I know that, but you have to contro–"

"–'specially when dumbasses like this sumbitch here keep on axing the same stupid shit over and over!" she interjected.

Ruth Jackson was obviously not in the mood to be lectured to, by her granddaughter or anyone else. Carroll waited for the storm to blow over.

"How 'bout this?" Mrs. Jackson suggested, "Why don't you go hunt for your damn keys while I sit here on my sore ass and try to remember, and we'll see which one of us gets lucky first?"

"I'm sorry, Mr. Carroll," Betty said, obviously embarrassed. "Maybe you could check to see if you left the keys outside while we talk?"

He stood up and although he felt like fleeing in terror, he forced himself to walk calmly out of the house. He wondered how this treatment compared to what Ben Walden had received from her. Carroll stepped onto the porch and saw the Jeep keys lying on the porch. He must have dropped them as he was preparing to knock on the door.

He retrieved the bottle of Jefferson's from the vehicle, fighting the impulse to down half the bottle right there in the driveway, and hesitantly reclimbed the steps and approached the door again. Carroll could hear a muffled conversation, but he could not make out words.

Betty seemed to be explaining that her grandmother needed to help if she could. He heard her walking toward the front door so he stepped back, pretending to be just arriving. Betty put him in a different chair this time, slightly closer to Mrs. Jackson, something that made him extremely nervous.

"Now why don't we start over?" Betty suggested as if she were negotiating a treaty between two warring countries.

"All right then," replied her grandmother.

"Thank you Betty. I apologize if I was out of line Mrs. Jackson," Carroll said as he placed the box on the table.

Ruth Jackson's eyes were focused on the box.

"What's that you got there?" she asked.

"Oh, it's just something that I brought. It's a gift."

"A gift?" she said, raising her eyebrows above her glasses. "Well, lemme see it then."

She reached out with both arms and Carroll handed her the bottle, keeping his hand underneath until he was sure that she was ready for its full weight. She took it and adjusted her glasses.

"Well, what we got here?"

Holding the bottle, she tilted it slightly so the light from the table lamp illuminated the label. She read the label:

"Jefferson's Presidential Select, 18 Year-Old Straight Bourbon Whiskey."

She turned toward Carroll with a look of astonishment before continuing to read the description:

"A limited offering, the Presidential Select is a premium blend that has been aged for 18 years. The Presidential Select is the premier bourbon in the Jefferson's line. The richly textured bourbon boasts a robust nose and taste balanced with the trademarked Jefferson's smooth finish."

She turned and looked at him again. Mrs. Jackson seemed to be at a complete loss for words. He hoped that was a good thing. She noticed a smaller label on the side with handwriting on it.

"Batch No. 13 Bottle No. 0964. Distilled from wheat in the fall of 1991," she read aloud, unconsciously smacking her lips.

Turning suddenly, she shouted down the hall.

"Betty! Go get me two of them good crystal glasses out tha china cabinet. We ain't gonna be drinking this here in no Solo cup. Uh-uh! No, sir!" she shook her head, "Toby Keith can kiss my ass!"

Carroll smiled. Ben would later tell him that he had "done good." He was really starting to like Mrs. Jackson's directness and her sense of humor cracked him up. He expected he had be humming Red Solo Cup for the next week. As they waited for Betty to return with the glasses, Mrs. Jackson nodded toward another chair even closer to her.

"Why don't you scoot to this chair where I can talk to you better?" She posed it as a question, but Carroll knew better. It was an order. He quickly switched seats.

Still inspecting the bottle and box it came in, Mrs. Jackson discovered additional information.

"Jefferson's Bourbon is a collection of ridiculously small batch straight whiskeys produced by skillfully marrying a selection of barrels of various ages."

She cackled, repeating the word, ridiculously, before continuing, "Jefferson's Bourbon pays homage to one of the country's most complex founding fathers, Thomas Jefferson."

She turned and looked behind her to be sure that Betty had not returned, then leaned closer to Carroll, cupped her hand over her mouth and whispered, "Uh-huh, he was a Found'n Father all right! Fathered six young'uns with that Sally Hemings!"

Carroll wasn't sure if he were allowed to laugh or not. The rumor of Thomas Jefferson's affair with his slave, Sally Hemings, was well-known. It had begun even before Jefferson was elected president and continued throughout his life and even after his death. Jefferson had always denied it; however, DNA tests in the 1990s concluded it was probably true.

"The worst part is that she was his wife's half-sister!" Mrs. Jackson said disgustedly.

"Are you sure that's true?" he asked her, treading on thin ice.

"Did it come out my mouth?"

"Yes, ma'am. It did."

"Well, all right then," she said matter-of-factly, as if whatever issued from her mouth was the Gospel.

This was something that Carroll had never heard, but he was not about to dispute her. He made a mental note to do some research on the Sally Hemings-Martha Jefferson family connection.

Mrs. Jackson abruptly sat up as Betty returned, bearing a silver tray with two beautiful crystal glasses and a corkscrew.

"What are you two talking about now?" she asked suspiciously, seeing that her Granny was obviously up to something.

"President Thomas Jefferson, who this bourbon is named after," she said innocently.

"Thomas Jefferson. Oh Lord! I can only imagine," Betty said with a smile.

She had heard her grandmother's remarks about Jefferson's goings-on before. Betty placed the tray on a small serving table, then lifted both table and tray, placing it in front of Carroll. She took two coasters from the tray and put them on the lamp table between Carroll and Mrs. Jackson.

"Mr. Carroll, would you like to do the honors?" Betty asked.

"Thank you, Betty."

Carroll broke the seal and used the corkscrew to remove the cork from the bottle. He did not have to be a connoisseur to realize that the aroma emitting from the bottle indicated it was something very special indeed. On impulse, he leaned over and held the bottle closer to Mrs. Jackson, allowing her to get a whiff. Mrs. Jackson closed her eyes as she inhaled. When she opened them again, they appeared to be wider and more alert.

"Pour it!" she commanded with a broad grin.

He poured both glasses, leaving his on the tray as he handed the other to Mrs. Jackson. He then picked up his glass and extended it toward her.

"To your health, Mrs. Jackson," he toasted.

She touched her glass to his, producing a clink.

"My health is fix'n ta get a whole lot better." she assured him.

They simultaneously raised their glasses and took a small sip. It was just as good as Jay Ducote had described it.

Carroll was speechless. Ruth Jackson was not.

"*Sweet Lord Jesus in Heaven above!*" she exclaimed.

He felt like shouting the same thing, but for a different reason. It was obvious that he had crossed an important threshold.

"It is good; isn't it Mrs. Jackson?"

"Good?" she said, "I'm get'n ready to be 111 and I ain't never tasted noth'n like this in my whole life!"

She took another big sip before adding, "And you can call me, Aunt Ruth."

Carroll caught his reflection in a picture on the wall. He was grinning like he was in a toothpaste commercial. He had done it. He had gone from being that obnoxious whatever she thought he was to her adoptive nephew. And it was not just that. He had wondered about her age from the moment they had met and now, hearing that she was nearly 111, he was trying to do the math in his head.

It was astounding. The woman seated next to him was born just 40 years after the Civil War ended, and she was just ten years younger than the city of Fitzgerald.

"Pour me another one, Bobby," she told him.

"Yes ma'am," he replied with a smile. Now he was Bobby!

He picked up the bottle and tipped it toward the glass. The label caught his eye, Jefferson's Presidential Select. Once again, he began calculating in his head. Thomas Jefferson, the principal author of the Declaration of Independence, the third president of the United States of America, whose name adorned that bottle of fine bourbon, died in 1826. Ruth Jackson had personally known people who gave an account of hearing news of his death.

Betty returned to check on them.

"Well, it seems that you two are getting along fine," she noted.

"And why wouldn't we be?" her grandmother asked. "Bobby is a fine boy."

"So it's *Bobby* now is it?" she said, acknowledging his new promotion with a nod and a big smile.

"Umm huh, he's my lost white nephew," Aunt Ruth giggled as she took another sip.

"How many of those have you had?" Betty asked.

"Just one," she answered. "But I'm fix'n to have another."

"I hope that you're just talking about the one in your hand," replied Betty as she left the room.

Carroll certainly did not want to get on Betty's bad side, but he also did not want to waste a great opportunity. He decided not to start with the murder. Mrs. Jackson gave him another opening.

Reaching back over, she lifted the bottle as if the contents had given her super strength.

"So where did you get this?" she asked.

"To be quite honest, my secretary found it online."

She looked at him as if he were speaking a foreign language.

"You know, on the computer," Carroll explained.

"This?" she asked, lifting the heavy bottle even higher. "You ordered this using a computer?"

"I was told that you were a lady who demanded the best, so I went in search of it."

"Well, you damn sure found it!" she congratulated him.

Ruth Jackson realized that she was going to have to reassess her opinion on computers. It seemed they were more beneficial than she had previously thought. After taking yet another, even bigger, gulp of Jefferson's, she hit Carroll with a question that he was not sure how to answer.

She leaned in, just as she had done when delivering the remark about Jefferson and Sally Hemings, and – in the same secretive whisper – she asked, "How much was it?"

Carroll knew that he had a few nanoseconds to decide how to reply, but he was not sure if he should tell the truth this time. The Jefferson's that he had asked Suzi to find was the 21-year-old vintage. The whole back and forth thing they did about getting Boone's Farm or Mad Dog 20/20 instead was after Suzi found out that the Jefferson's Select 21 was $140 per bottle.

After he had explained how important Mrs. Jackson was to the case, Suzi being Suzi, did her own research and found that the Jefferson's Select 18 was actually better– way better. The 21-year-old was rated at 82.75 and the 18 year old was rated 91.25. Suzi finished her research and walked into his office with the results. Carroll had been impressed and told her to go ahead and order the 18 year old instead.

"Are you sure?" she asked. "It's more expensive."

"It would be, since it's a better product. I mean, how much more could it be?"

"Are you sitting down?" she asked, even though she was standing there looking at him seated behind his desk.

She placed a print out on his desk. He read the line at the top, Price History for NV Jefferson's Presidential Select 18 Year Old Kentucky Straight Bourbon Whiskey, Kentucky, USA. It showed a line on a graph that resembled a heart beat on an EKG chart. Carroll did not know it, but the value varied. It was the old supply and demand trick.

The problem here was that the demand was a lot more than the supply. The graph showed that the price averaged $849 per bottle over a year and for several months rose to an astounding $1648 per bottle. However, Suzi being Suzi, she had found a bottle at $649.

"So?" she asked again.

"Order it," he told her, amazed that the words came out of his own mouth.

He now had a dilemma. He had already told Mrs. Jackson that he was not rich. So, how could he justify spending that kind of money on a bottle of bourbon? She was already impressed with the taste, and he suspected that the price of the 21 year-old bottle at one hundred, forty dollars was more than she would ever pay herself. He made his decision. He would go with one hundred and forty. Then he looked over at her sitting there with a huge grin on her face. She wanted the price to reflect the taste.

"Six hundred and forty-nine dollars," he blurted out.

"*Oh, my God!*" she yelled, putting the bottle down so quickly that she practically dropped it and almost broke both the table and the bottle.

Carroll heard the sound of running coming from two different parts of the house. Betty came in from the main hallway, and a younger man ran in from a door on the opposite end of the room.

"What happened?" Betty asked, visibly upset.

"Do you know how much this bottle cost?" Aunt Ruth asked her granddaughter.

"*Granny*! You 'bout scared me to death!" said Betty.

"Guess!" her grandmother demanded.

"I have no idea. My head don't work so well when I'm having a heart attack!"

"Aw, now you just being mella-dramatic. How about you Henry?" she asked, addressing the young man.

She turned to Carroll and pointed back toward the young man.

"This is my grandson, Henry."

He stood up to shake Henry's hand.

"Bobby bought this on the line!" she explained to them.

Henry laughed, "I think you mean online, Granny, not on the line."

"That's what I said!" she scolded, shaking her long wrinkled finger at him.

"How much?" she asked.

"Eight-five dollars," replied Henry.

"Uh uh," she laughed, shaking her head.

She looked at Betty again, "Come on; how much?"

Betty gave up. "One hundred dollars," she guessed.

"Guess again!" demanded Aunt Ruth. She was enjoying herself. She was the star of The Ruth Jackson Show.

"Just tell me, Granny!" Betty pleaded, "I've got work to do."

"*Six hundred and forty-nine dollars!*" Aunt Ruth said proudly.

The younger Jacksons looked over at Carroll for confirmation. He simply nodded.

Having just met another member of Ruth Jackson's family, Carroll seized upon the opportunity to start moving their conversation toward his investigation.

"So, tell me about your family," he asked Aunt Ruth. "I've only met two so far."

"Well, Betty is my great granddaughter and Henry is my great great grandson. I got six greats, eleven great-greats and four great-great-greats."

"What about your ancestors? How did they end up here in Fitzgerald?"

"Because of my daddy. Mr. Fitzgerald brought him down here after they picked out a spot."

"You're talking about Philander Fitzgerald? The founder of the town?"

"Uh huh, my daddy worked for Mr. Fitzgerald in Indianapolis. He asked him to come down here and help with the construction."

Carroll was speechless; however, it actually made complete sense after he thought about it. Fitzgerald would have chosen men that he knew and trusted in the most important project of his life. And if Aunt Ruth's father had established himself as an honest and dependable man then he would have been perfect for the job.

Mrs. Jackson took a sip from her second glass of Jefferson's Select. What had been more of an interview, turned into a story-telling as she began to talk. She became a river and the words flowed freely downstream. She told Carroll about her family history and recounted stories, some that she had seen firsthand, and others that were told to her by her father and other relatives or friends.

One such story was about something that came to be called the Parade of Unity. To celebrate their amazingly successful first year, the town had constructed a truly impressive building, naming it the Corn and Cotton Palace. It was essentially a venue for big events, a showplace, matching anything in Atlanta, Milledgeville or anywhere else in the state at the time.

The first major event was to be an exposition showcasing the progress that had been made since the colony was established. This included a parade of veterans of both armies. The Confederate veterans were scheduled to march first and the Union veterans would march afterward. People were seriously concerned about the potential for violence because there were still some folks who held deep resentment.

Aunt Ruth pointed to a photo on the wall.

"That's it," she said.

He stood up and walked over to look at a picture of the Corn and Cotton Palace on the wall as she retold the eyewitness account that she had heard from her father;

"My daddy told me that when they opened up them big ole doors on the Corn and Cotton Palace, veterans from both sides marched out together, 'stead of separate, and both bands, the Blue and the Gray, were playing the National Anthem, together."

Carroll got a chill at hearing Aunt Ruth's story. He would later be able to verify it as authentic in several historical records. The soldiers that marched that day renamed their combined unit Battalion One of the Blue and Gray and the parade became known as the Parade of Unity.

"It's really a shame the Corn and Cotton Palace wasn't preserved isn't it, Mrs. Jackson?" he asked.

"Aunt Ruth!" she corrected him.

She started to respond to his comment, but broke into laughter. She held her almost empty glass up, indicating a need for a refill. Carroll turned to pick up the bottle and saw Betty glaring at him with her arms crossed and foot tapping. He stopped and gave her an inquisitive look, asking for permission nonverbally. Betty held up her index finger. One more, that was it. He nodded and poured his Aunt Ruth another glass. Seeing that Betty had turned away, he topped it off after she took another sip.

"The Corn and Cotton was lost before I was born," Aunt Ruth continued, "Like most towns back then, the fire department was mostly just men who learnt how to do it."

She took a deep breath before continuing;

"Now our fire department knew they was the best and they wanted to prove it. So they decided to have demonstration. They set the Corn and Cotton Palace on fire to show folks how good they was at working together at put'n out fires. They let the fire get go'n real good so's it would look better when they put it out, but it got out of hand and it burned down to the ground in minutes."

She finished her story and sat there with a tear in her eye. Carroll did not know what to say. He had apparently asked a question that made her upset. He was about to stand and call Betty when Aunt Ruth suddenly busted out laughing. It was only then that he realized the tears were because she was trying to hold back her laughter to gage his reaction.

"Ain't that the stupidest thing you ever heard?" she bellowed.

Lowered her voice to imitate a man, she said, "Hey, I got an idea. Let's set the biggest building in town on fire to show how good we are. Uh oh! I think we done messed up, boys!"

Carroll couldn't help himself. Her laughter was contagious. Betty returned once again to check on the commotion, shooting him a look as she entered the room. He immediately threw up his hands in a gesture of surrender. He wouldn't give her granny any more alcohol. Betty nodded, wheeled around and left again.

He didn't want to overdo his first visit, especially since it was going so well, but Carroll had to at least ask about the most important topic.

"Aunt Ruth, earlier you said, Folks like you always com'n round here spect'n me to remember. Has anyone else been around asking you to remember anything?"

"Now, that was before I made you my nephew," she said, addressing the Folks like you part.

Responding to his question, she resumed, "Ain't nobody been by in awhile. The last person that came 'round was a young lady, but that was a week or two after that McDowell boy visited."

Carroll literally did a double take.

"I'm sorry; what did you say?"

"'bout the young lady, or the boy?" said Aunt Ruth.

"Both."

"I just told you. The last person that came around here asking about the town was a young lady."

"Was she connected with Thomas McDowell?"

"I didn't think so since it was a couple of weeks later. Folks is always com'n by asking me 'bout the town's history so I didn't pay it no mind. I reckon she could have been."

Carroll could not believe it.

"What was her name Aunt Ruth?"

"Lisa?" she responded, but it was more of a guess.

"Aw, hell. I don't remember," she finally confessed before calling for her granddaughter

"Yes, ma'am?" Betty asked upon entering the room.

"What was that girl's name that came after that McDowell boy?"

Betty thought for a moment. "Laura," she replied.

"What about her last name?" Carroll asked.

"She might have mentioned it, but I don't recall what it was."

He talked with them both for a few more minutes and made some notes. Then he stood up to leave.

"You were very helpful Aunt Ruth! And I loved your stories!"

"Well, then you gonna have to come back, cause I got lots!"

"You can bet on it," he assured her.

"Thank you, Betty," he said, meaning both for her hospitality and her help with Aunt Ruth.

"You're welcome."

"Ain't you gonna take your bottle?" Aunt Ruth asked.

"Ain't mine to take," he answered as he thanked them both again and took his leave.

Carroll called Ben as he was backing out of the driveway.

"He shoots, he scores!!" he shouted like a basketball sportscaster when Walden answered.

"Well, all right, buddy!"

"How about supper?"

"Sure, wherever," Ben replied.

It was after work so Walden was willing to venture further away from downtown. They settled on Mexican, which was about halfway for both.

Ben was already waiting in the parking lot when he arrived.

Walden pulled out a coin, "Flip you for supper," he said as Carroll walked up.

He gave it a good high flick and the coin spun end over end.

"Heads," called Carroll.

Walden caught the coin in his left hand, immediately slapping his right hand over it as it landed.

"Why does everyone always call heads?" he asked Carroll without revealing the coin.

"It has something to do with the weight affecting the way that it spins. The odds are supposedly more in your favor."

"You think so?" he grinned. "Well, let's find out."

Ben removed his hand, revealing a bald eagle, wings outstretched and holding arrows and an olive branch in its talons.

"Sorry, buddy, but you're buying supper" he said with a grin.

"Fine."

"Flip coins a lot?" Ben asked as they walked toward the door. He was openly taunting his friend now.

Carroll responded by holding up his middle finger.

"Awe, don't feel bad, buddy," Walden consoled him. "What's that saying? You can't win'em any? No, that's not it. Well— maybe for you it is," he joked.

Carroll just smiled and let Ben relish his victory, for what would amount to about twelve dollars. He was actually getting a kick out of how much Walden was enjoying himself.

Ben snapped his fingers.

"You can't win them all! That's how it goes."

"You know, you act like a ten year-old sometimes," Carroll said.

"I'm sorry, Bob. Here you go—" he said, tossing the coin to his friend. "Put it toward my supper."

Carroll barely had time to react as the coin twirled toward him. He threw out his right hand to catch it, but ended up knocking it straight up into the air over his head. He tried to grab it with his left hand and missed, which allowed the coin to fall back and hit him square on top of his head before it fell onto the sidewalk. Ben launched into a pretty good imitation of Howard Cosell giving a play-by-play;

"Bob Carroll did his very best, but it just wasn't good enough. Perhaps the aging receiver is past his prime. It's a sad sight—to – see!"

"Very funny," Carroll chuckled, then looking at the coin, he added, "Oh, great! Now it lands heads-up!"

He was still laughing as he bent down to pick up the coin, but he realized that the head looked odd. He picked it up and inspected it. Turning it over, he looked at the date, "1897," he read aloud. Carroll stood there staring at it for a moment. The coin that he was holding was 118 years old.

"That's really amazing Ben," he said, extending his arm to return the coin to its owner.

"I told you, it yours," Ben said. "Put it toward supper."

"Are you nuts? I can't accept this! And it sure as hell shouldn't be spent for supper!"

Ben refused to take it back.

"Seriously, it's yours. Think of it as a welcome back present."

Walden watched and smiled as his friend just stood there, holding it, looking at it and trying to decide what to do.

"Look, I've got several. That shitty thing is the worst one that I have."

"Well then, since you put it that way. Thanks!" he said, still looking down at the coin.

"This thing is only two years older than the town," Carroll said in disbelief. "What a day I've had!"

"Well, technically it's actually one year older than the town," Ben corrected him. "They got here and started working on it in 1895, but didn't incorporate it until 1896."

Carroll didn't answer. He was still staring at the coin, running his fingers over it and thinking about its history. Men who actually fought in the Civil War held this very same coin, he thought.

"So, are we going to eat or what?" Ben yelled, bringing him back to reality.

Carroll recounted every detail of the visit with Aunt Ruth over the course of their meal, being sure to remind Ben of the difference in their receptions.

"I get it!" Ben said. "She hates me."

He confirmed Ruth Jackson's stories about the destruction of the Corn and Cotton Palace and the Parade of Unity.

"You really need to visit The Blue and The Gray Museum," Walden suggested, "Besides all the historical artifacts, there's a great video called Marching As One, narrated by Beth Davis, the museum's founder. It covers all of that stuff and more."

"Could I meet Mrs. Davis too?" Carroll asked.

"Unfortunately, she died in 2002. I knew her pretty well. She was an amazing lady."

At Ben's insistence, Carroll recounted his entire visit at the Jacksons. He started with getting busted by Betty at the front door and included how he went from being treated like a used vacuum cleaner salesman to an adopted nephew, all mostly because of an expensive bottle of bourbon.

"Listen, I wouldn't have succeeded with Ruth Jackson without your help. I really mean it," he told Walden.

"I told you at our first meeting, whatever I can do to help."

"And thanks to you," Carroll added, "I've got a new lead. Now, we've got to—"

"Find out who Laura is," Ben concluded.

Carroll nodded, "We've got to find Laura."

9

Family Reunion

Robert Carroll was trying to figure out how to resolve his biggest problem with the McDowell case as he drove north on Grant Street. Finding out more about Billy Bob had been the main priority when Lenny was missing, but now that they had determined that he was on a road trip and Sauls was safe, he had dropped down a notch to second place.

Identifying Laura, the young lady who visited Ruth Jackson after McDowell's death, was the top priority now. Unfortunately, he was beginning to think it would ever happen. The problem was that the only thing they had to go on was the vague description that Carroll had managed to get from the Jacksons – a very pretty girl in her mid-twenties, of average size and height with black hair. That was it. That was all that he had. With only a first name, and a common one at that, and a very general description, they would never find her. It was an impossible task. Carroll knew that he had to come up with a better solution. But what could it be?

One idea had occurred to him even as he was still sitting there with Aunt Ruth. He could bring in a professional sketch artist to do a facial composite based on information from Betty and Aunt Ruth. He hesitated for two reasons. First, it had now been more than three months since they had seen Laura. While facial composites are a useful tool to identify suspects or witnesses in investigations, their effectiveness averages less than 50 percent if the description is obtained immediately or by the third day. The success rate decreases as the amount of time from the event, actually seeing the person, increases. So, given that more than three months had passed, he was, realistically, looking at a less than a 10 percent chance of getting something that would be useful.

Who was he fooling? His main witness was 111 years old, for God's sake. Factor that into the equation along with the three months of elapsed time, and the probability dropped into negative digits. So, that was his first problem.

The second one was that he was reluctant to bring anyone else into the investigation because it would draw attention. Up until this point he had managed to keep his identity and real reason for being in Fitzgerald concealed, but that was bound to change. The more people that were poking around the more likely the local law enforcement was going to realize what he was up to and he was not sure how they would react.

Carroll was on his way to Billy Bob McCoy's garage. He wanted to see if there was any sign that McCoy had returned. He made a slight detour to stop at a Dollar General store to purchase a roll of Scotch tape before continuing north on Sherman Street. The traffic light at West Central changed from yellow to red. He stopped and pondered his predicament as he waited for the green light. A young lady walking down the sidewalk hurried through the crosswalk just as the light was changing. He waited, giving her the right-of-way. He smiled because she reminded him of Val.

"Val!" he said, popping the steering wheel.

"What an idiot!" he said, looking at himself in the mirror.

He touched his cell phone and said, "Call Val."

"Did you say Call Al?" a female voice asked.

"No."

"Say a command," she said.

He repeated it again, "Call Val."

"Did you say Call Al?"

"No!" he yelled.

"Say a command."

He repeated it more slowly and clearly this time, "Call – Val."

"Calling Ralph Wilson," she said.

"Shit!" he shouted.

How the hell did she get Ralph Wilson from Val, he wondered? He hurriedly canceled the call knowing if Ralph answered he would be on the phone for the next hour or two. He decided to give up on modern technology for the moment. He pulled over and manually selected Val from his list of contacts and pressed Call.

One ringy dingy, he thought of Suzi as he listened to Val's phone ring on the other end. She picked up on the second ring.

"Hey, Uncle Bob!" she answered cheerfully. "What's up?"

"How would you like to take a working vacation?"

"Oh, I know!" she exclaimed. "Can we go on a Caribbean cruise?"

He instantly knew that Suzi had told Val about her deception as a fake temp.

"Very funny," he said.

"Come on Uncle Bob! I know someone who just got back from one and she said that it was awesome!"

She was playing, trying to get him to "fess up" as she called it, but he was not going to fall for it.

"I can't. I don't have any Bermuda shorts or knee socks," he explained.

"I'll buy you some! You can tell Deborah, your new receptionist, to book it for you," she laughed.

"You're really having fun with this, aren't you?"

"Lots!" she giggled.

"How about Fitzgerald instead?"

"As in the writer? He's buried in Rockville, Maryland, isn't he? No reflection on the fine people of Rockville, but visiting a dead guy isn't really my idea of a vacation, Uncle Bob."

"No, not a dead writer. It's a town, Fitzgerald, Georgia."

"Georgia! What the hell are you doing in Georgia?"

"Chasing bad guys."

"Really? Is it a fugitive case?" she asked, suddenly interested.

"No, it's actually an unsolved homicide case that occurred down here, but it has ties to Indianapolis."

"Oh hells to the yeahs!" Val shouted. "How many uncles take their nieces on a murder investigation vacation?"

"Yeah, I know. It's the typical, old murder investigation vacation thing, and I should probably try to come up with something more original."

Val laughed. "Does talking like this make us weird?"

"Probably."

"So, you're for real?" she asked for confirmation. "You want me to come down there for an I.D., huh?"

"That's the general idea."

"Witness or suspect?"

"My gut feeling is that she's just a witness, but I can't completely rule her out as a suspect until we find her and talk to her."

"What kind of 'scrip are you starting with?" she asked, reverting into police slang for description.

"White female, mid to late twenties and average on everything else."

"Yikes!" Valerie exclaimed. "So that narrows it down to a few hundred million people. Who's my witness?"

"You've got two. One is a female in her thirties and–" he hesitated.

"And, the other one?"

"Another female, but older."

Val laughed, "Jeez! It's like pulling teeth getting info from you today. Is she young, middle-aged or elderly?"

"Elderly, definitely elderly."

"Now you're just being evasive. She is alive right?"

"Crap!" he thought. "First, Suzi jinxed me with a quip about Mrs. Jackson dying before I got back to Fitzgerald and now Val is risking another one."

"She's 111 okay?" he confessed.

"Holy shit!" Val yelled. "What if she dies while I'm interviewing her?"

"Quit saying stuff about her dying!" he cautioned her.

"Oh, here we go. You and your whole paranoid jinx thing again."

"I am *not* superstitious," he said, getting overly defensive, "You just shouldn't joke about old people dying."

"Okay, whatever!" she laughed. "What about trauma?"

"None at all. The girl that we're looking for was just a visitor in the home of the two ladies who you'll be interviewing."

Val was good. She was asking all the right questions, the last being extremely important. If a witness has undergone some type of severe trauma such as a physical assault or rape, then it is obviously more difficult for them to talk to anyone about details, especially a complete stranger.

The body's natural defense mechanisms kick in and suppress any memories that could potentially cause severe stress. It is often on a subconscious level and the person might not even realize their memory is being affected.

"No trauma. Well, that's good news at least. So, what you're saying is that I've got to interview a witness that is old enough to have survived the Hindenburg crash, about a person that she saw more than three months ago?"

"Well, actually, at her age she probably could've been on the Titanic, too, but yes, that's correct."

"Sounds fun! Count me in!"

Carroll gave Valerie a brief rundown on the entire case and she agreed to come down immediately.

"What's the soonest that you could leave?" he asked.

"Well, since this is a mobile phone," she stressed the word mobile, "I can actually start walking toward my car right now. I'll go home and grab a bag and hit the road."

"Don't be silly," he interrupted her. "I'm flying you down. I'll have Suzi book you a reservation."

"Cool! This is going to be fun, huh?"

"You do realize how twisted that sounds, right?"

"Well what do you expect? Look who I'm related to!"

"Don't forget your kit," he reminded her before hanging up.

Still sitting on the side of the road, he pressed the button to end the call and then, one, to speed-dial Suzi.

"A gracious good morning," Ernestine answered.

"It's actually afternoon," he said, correcting her.

There was a loud snort, followed by "Picky, picky, picky!" as Suzi's Ernestine morphed into a monotone Pat Paulsen.

"I need you to book a flight."

"What happened?" Suzi asked, dropping the imitation and becoming concerned.

"You're coming back already?"

"No, it's not for me. Everything's fine," he reassured her.

"I'm bringing Val down here."

"Good!" she said approvingly. "You're killing two birds with one stone, huh?"

Besides being an A-1 office manager, Suzi was highly intelligent. She knew that he was bringing Val down to help with the case, but that it would also be helping her as well by getting her out of Indianapolis.

"For when?" Suzi inquired.

"The sooner the better," he answered. "And make it first or business class to Atlanta and then put her on ExpressJet from to Albany."

"Not a problem. Give me an hour," Suzi told him.

He went by Billy Bob's garage and, seeing no sign of him or anyone else, pulled in to have a look around. The note was still taped on the front door: *Hit'n the road for another day cuz it's better to burn out than to fade away!*

He walked around the building looking for signs that McCoy might have returned. Finding none, he reached into his pocket and pulled out the Scotch tape he had purchased. Carroll glanced around to be sure no one was watching before he tore off a piece of tape and carefully placed it across the top corner of the door. He would check it later to see if the door had been opened.

Suzi called him back in less than 30 minutes.

"I've got her booked for in the morning. The same flight time that you like."

While the early morning flight was normal for him, Carroll knew that it was awfully early for Val. She would have to be at Indianapolis International by 4 a.m..

"You might better check with her on that first."

"Did you just have a stroke?" Suzi asked him. "Do you realize who you're talking to?"

"Sorry," he said.

Of course he realized, Suzi being Suzi, she had obviously coordinated with Val on the ticket.

"What's her arrival time in Albany?"

"The same as yours was, about 11:45," she replied.

"That's great, Suzi. Thanks."

After talking to Suzi, Carroll made a beeline to the Barrett-Parrish House, the Bed and Breakfast that Ben had arranged for him to stay in on his second trip. He had initially told Walden that he would be fine staying at the Ridgeway again, but luckily for him, Ben had insisted. It was like going from a life raft to the Queen Elizabeth.

The Barrett-Parrish House was built by J.H. Barrett, known during his day as Captain Jack. Carroll had found quite a bit of information about him during his research on the town itself. Most historical documents referred to Captain Jack as a business man. That was a massive understatement that did not do justice to the genius of the man who one historical author called "a legend in his own time."

Unlike most of the families who flocked to the Colony City from Indiana and other northern states, the Barrett's were a prominent local family. J.H. Barrett was described during his own time as "a Southern gentleman who represents the Southern or "Rebel" faction of this experimental Yank-Reb city."

He owed much of his success to cotton. Besides owning several farms where he grew cotton as well as other crops, Barrett also owned a cotton gin, a cotton warehouse, a cotton oil mill, a fertilizer business, and sawmills in the towns of Broxton and Waycross.

Promotional material for the Barrett-Parrish House Bed and Breakfast invite you to "treat yourself as you enjoy the elegance and warmth of Southern Hospitality at its finest!" Carroll found that the statement should be taken literally because you are actual guests in their home. J.H. Barrett's great great grandson's family lives on the first floor while the seven rooms upstairs are for guests.

Carroll had already decided if he couldn't arrange a room for Val he would vacate his for her and rough it at the Ridgeway. Inquiring at the Barrett-Parrish about a room for Val, he was informed that there was a room that had been reserved but the people were already overdue. While he hoped that the reservation-holders hadn't experienced any serious calamity, he did secretly wish that a minor one, such as a last-minute change in business plans, would make the room available.

Mr. J.H. Barrett himself must have personally intervened from on high because Carroll was later informed that he could have the room for Val. He decided to spend the remainder of the afternoon in his own room where he did some additional research on the case as well as the town. He later went downstairs where he enjoyed reading on the front porch until sunset and concluded his day in the parlor.

He was up early, eagerly anticipating Val's arrival. He met Ben for breakfast, filling him in on the plan to track down Laura. Then he headed out toward Albany.

Carroll watched as the ExpressJet came coasting down the runway. It quickly taxied up to the terminal and passengers began disembarking within minutes. His smiled when he saw Val emerge from the cabin and his smile broadened as she escorted an elderly gentleman from the plane into the terminal. The man thanked her and tried to pay her for her help. Of course,

Val refused the money, saying that a hug would be worth a lot more.

After Carroll received his own hug from Val, they walked over to claim her baggage. She gave him an indication of what was expected from him during her trip. Snapping her fingers, she barked, "You there, boy! Retrieve my luggage!"

He laughed, but he was apprehensive as they waited for her luggage to appear. The worst thing that could happen right now would be for the bag containing her laptop and sketch equipment to go missing. His fears proved unfounded as her pink Hello Kitty suitcase rotated in on the belt.

"How about this weather!" Val said, as she twirled around in the parking lot.

"Nice, huh?" he said.

"Oh, it's better than nice!"

Her eyes widened when she saw Ben's Jeep.

"So what's with the ride?"

"Beats the hell out of a rental doesn't it? It belongs to a friend."

"Hell yeah!" replied Val, circling the vehicle. "Can I drive it?"

"I'd better ask Ben first. It's his Jeep, but he's a pretty laid back guy, so I'm sure he won't mind."

He knew the answer but he asked anyway, "Did you eat any breakfast?"

"Are you mental?" she responded.

"You're lucky I was able to get up and make it to the airport at such an ungodly hour!"

"Silly me," he replied.

"I had some crappy snacks on the plane, but that's all."

"Well, I'm taking you to Pearly's then."

"Sounds southern," she said, trying to speak with a drawl.

"Taste southern too," he said. "But we better hurry because it gets crowded."

He whipped down Newton and Slappey like he was a local native. The parking lot was crowded as they pulled in to Pearly's. Carroll gave Val a twenty.

"I'll grab a table. You go order."

Val reached for her purse.

"What are you doing?" Carroll asked.

"Duh! I'm getting my money."

"For what?"

"Well, I want to eat too!" she said.

"I gave you a twenty already. That should cover it."

"For both of us? No way!" she exclaimed as if he had just told her that elephants roost in trees.

"Way!" he said, trying unsuccessfully to be cool.

"Please don't talk like that in public," she warned him.

"Be sure to get me grits. And you have to try them too." he instructed, as she headed toward the counter.

Val joined him at the table a few minutes later. He asked her about the two flights. As he expected, she had slept the entire time until the flight attendant woke her when the Buckle Your Seatbelt indicator came on as they approached Hartsfield. Carroll was pleased to hear that she did at least catch the view of the Atlanta skyline.

As he watched Val inhaling her breakfast, Carroll couldn't help but think that she might be able to beat Lenny Sauls in some sort of eating contest at a county fair.

"So what the hell are grits anyway?" she asked as she started on her second helping.

Carroll wasn't about to let the opportunity slide by.

"They're grown down here on local farms.

"You are such a liar sometimes!" she said sarcastically.

"Seriously, they come from small trees that are about the same size as peach trees."

She should have gone with her first reaction. He could tell that she was wavering on the whole grits tree thing.

"I'm not kidding," he insisted. "I just finished reading a book last night called, Don't Sit Under the Grits Tree with Anyone Else But Me.

"Uh-huh. Yeah, right."

"Okay, smart ass, google it on your phone right now!"

He knew he had already won when she reached for her phone. She typed in the title of the book and touched the search button.

"Well I'll be," she said, nodding her head. "There it is. Lewis Grizzard," she said, wrongly pronouncing the author's name as rhyming with lizard or gizzard, something that gave Carroll more ammunition to use against her later.

Valerie suddenly burst into laughter.

"Oh my God! Look at the titles of these books! I love it!"

She ticked off the names to Carroll as if he had never heard of any of the books that actually sat on his bookshelf back in his home in Noblesville; Elvis is Dead (and I Don't Feel so Good Myself), Shoot Low Boys (They're Riding Shetland Ponies), My Daddy Was a Pistol (And I'm a Son of a Gun).

The other titles should have been a clue, but Val missed it. Carroll started to tell her the truth about grits, but he decided to bask in his victory a bit longer.

"Do you feel like working this afternoon?" he asked. "Or, do you want to get a fresh start tomorrow?"

"I'm ready," she assured him. "We young people don't need as much rest as you old folks do."

"And who's turning 30 soon?" he reminded her.

"That was really uncalled for!" she pouted.

Carroll called the Jackson residence to see if it would be okay to come by. He heard Betty tell her Granny it was Bobby on the telephone and that he wanted to come by to see her.

"That's Bobby?" Aunt Ruth yelled. "Tell him to come on!"

"Did you hear that? Betty asked.

"I did," he laughed. "We'll see you in about an hour."

He took the same two-lane route to Fitzgerald that he had driven with Ben: Highways 91, 32 and 107, giving Val an opportunity to appreciate the scenery. He used the time to tell her more about the case, Ruth Jackson and her family, and the town. Because doing a forensics sketch can sometimes take as long as four hours, they decided to hold off on the actual sketch part today and use the visit for introductory purposes.

Carroll saw that Aunt Ruth was waiting for them in her favorite chair on the front porch as they pulled into the driveway of the Jackson House. Betty emerged as they were climbing the steps. As he hadn't prepared them in advance, Carroll introduced Val and explained what they hoped to accomplish.

"You're a policewoman?" Aunt Ruth asked.

"I was. Well, I still am," she said, correcting herself, "but I don't wear a uniform any more. I'm a detective now."

"A *detective!*" Aunt Ruth exclaimed in disbelief. "But you just a little thing!"

"Don't let her size fool you, Aunt Ruth," Carroll said. "Dynamite comes in small packages."

He decided not to go into details of Val's shooting back in December. Better to save that for another day.

"So you're Bobby's niece?" Mrs. Jackson asked.

"We couldn't be any closer even if we were blood related," she responded.

Carroll smiled proudly. He felt the same way.

"It's like me and you, Aunt Ruth," he explained.

"Well, then. Since I'm his Aunt Ruth I 'spect you best call me, Granny," she declared.

"Oh wow!" Val exclaimed, looking genuinely happy. "I've got a new granny!"

"Well, I sure ain't new," Aunt Ruth chuckled, "and I wouldn't want to make your real grannies mad or hurt their feelings."

"I don't have one anymore," Val replied, explaining that her only living grandparent was her mother's father. She promptly walked over and gave her new grandmother a hug.

They sat in the same parlor as when Carroll had first visited. They were there only for a few minutes when Mrs. Jackson decided it was time to pop the cork.

"Betty?"

"Yes, ma'am?"

"Will you bring me two–" She stopped, looked at Val, and asked, "Are you twenty-one?"

"She's fix'n to be 30, Aunt Ruth" Carroll answered, as Val shot him a dirty look.

"Make that three crystal classes," said Aunt Ruth, amending her original request.

"I'm not much of a drinker, Granny" Val admitted

"Well, you need to try this at least one time."

As before, Betty brought the classes out on a tray and placed it in front of Carroll. He noticed that since his first visit the Jefferson Select had been properly decantered in an elegant vessel befitting its precious contents. He poured the glasses, serving first, Aunt Ruth, and then Val.

"Health, wealth and happiness," he toasted them.

"Well, at least I got two out of three," quipped Aunt Ruth, adding, "less'n I win the lottery."

Both Carroll and Aunt Ruth watched as Val took a tiny sip.

"Wow!" she said, fanning her face with her hand.

"That'll put hair on your chest won't it?" asked Aunt Ruth.

Val hooked her finger in the collar of her shirt and looked down at her chest.

"Damned if it didn't!" she exclaimed.

Aunt Ruth let out another one of her howls.

"I like this girl!" she declared. "She's got spunk!"

"You have no idea, Aunt Ruth," Carroll warned her.

As planned, they kept the conversation light. Val walked around the room looking at the photos and the antique furniture. When she got to the photo of the Corn and Cotton Palace Carroll retold the story that he had heard from Aunt Ruth.

"You told that good – as if you lived here all your life," she said proudly.

"Well, I had a pretty good teacher, didn't I?"

"I reckon you did!" she said, tooting her own horn.

They spent nearly two hours with her and made arrangements to be back at ten the next morning. Val went over and hugged Mrs. Jackson.

"Bye, Granny. See you tomorrow," she said, giving the appearance that she had been doing it for her whole life.

Carroll drove back into town on Lincoln Avenue, turned left onto Merrimac drive, then right onto West Central and turned into the driveway of the Barrett-Parrish House.

"Nice! Who lives here?" she asked, anticipating another visit.

"We do," Carroll answered. "You've had a pretty long day, so we'll just relax for the rest."

"We're staying here?"

"Yeah. It's a bed and breakfast called the Barrett-Parrish House. It was built in 1912. Sorry, but it's the best I could do on short notice," he apologized.

There were six rooms for guests, all with their own name and theme. Carroll was already in the Lincoln room and Val was given the Cherokee Rose room. After helping her get situated, Carroll began talking about the case until he realized that Val was not holding up her end of the conversation. He looked over to see her eyes half closed and her head bobbing like a toddler past her naptime as she tried to hold it up.

"Why don't you rest a bit and then we'll get a bite to eat later if you want to?"

"Yeah, I think I'll take a little nap," she mumbled.

Val's' nap lasted the rest of the night.

They were up bright and early the following morning. They went downstairs to get coffee. Seeing the fresh pastries, breads and fruit, Val reached for a plate.

"Hold on," said Carroll, "We're meeting Ben Walden at The Sportsman for breakfast."

"I'm just going to get a taste," she explained. "Someone went to a lot of trouble to prepare this. It would be rude to not even try it."

"Well we wouldn't want to be rude would we?" Carroll echoed as Val loaded her plate. Her mouth was already full so she could only shake her head.

He sipped his coffee as she tasted everything on her plate until there was nothing left.

"You ready?"

"Yep," she answered, licking her fingers.

They walked outside and Valerie headed toward the Jeep.

"Where are you going?" he asked her.

"I thought we were going to The Sportsman to meet this Ben guy?"

"We are, but we're going to walk."

"Walk? How far is it?"

"It's just right down the street," he told her. "But if you can't hang with me then I'll drive you."

"Pfffff!" she mocked him. "Hang with you? Not a problem!"

"Uh huh," Carroll laughed. "I seem to remember someone saying, we young people don't need as much rest as you old people do, not long before she fell asleep yesterday."

"Okay, so I was just a little tired," she admitted.

"A little?" he prodded, "You were sitting there with your head bouncing up and down like a little bobblehead in a car window."

"Whatever! Lead the way, old man."

They had walked less than fifty feet when a chicken popped out from between two houses. Carroll had been anticipating this moment since Val arrived. He waited for her reaction, but she was looking the other way and the chicken slipped back into the shrubbery without her noticing it.

They had completed three of the five-block walk when she acknowledged what he liked about the town, "This is pretty nice huh? It's really quiet and pretty."

"Yeah, it is. The Sportsman is right over–"

There was an explosion of sound as two roosters rolled out from between some azaleas in the midst of a mighty brawl, fighting either over territory or some attractive hen.

"What the hell?!" Val yelled as she jumped back, but Carroll also noticed that she placed herself between him and the melee.

"Welcome to Fitzgerald," he said.

"You've got to be kidding me!" Val exclaimed, as she regained her composure.

"Thanks for protecting me," he said. "Those chickens can be pretty tough customers!"

"I reacted to the sound," she explained. "I didn't know they were chickens!"

"Don't be so defensive. That was a very brave thing that you did there, protecting me from the chickens."

He was about to give her a rundown on the chickens when a hen walked out ahead of them.

"Oh, I get it," she said, "It's called The Sportsman. So you have to kill, pluck and clean your own chicken and they'll cook it fresh for you!"

"You're exactly right," he laughed.

Ben was obviously running a few minutes behind, so Carroll proceeded to lead Val toward his booth.

"Morn'n Bob, your booth's ready," Pearl welcomed. "Just you and the lady, or will Ben be joining you, too?"

"Thanks, Pearl. He'll be here in a few minutes," he replied.

They took a seat at the booth. Val sat there staring at him with a massive grin on her face.

"What?" he asked.

"You really like this! You're turning into a regular local yokel, with your own booth and the whole Cheers, *where everybody knows your name thing*!"

"Okay, first, Cheers was a bar." he reminded her. "This," he said, motioning around, "is a restaurant. And second, yeah, I do like it."

Walden entered and joined them. Carroll introduced Ben and Val. He had previously told each one about the other so they both knew what was expected from them. Carroll told Ben about the rooster fight and because he didn't get to explain it earlier, he asked Walden to give Val a condensed version of the Chicken Talk. Then they got down to the serious business of the case.

It was agreed that identifying Laura was their main objective at the moment; however, both Walden and Carroll were becoming increasingly concerned about the whereabouts of Billy Bob McCoy. They were at first relieved when they had found out about his trip as Lenny's safety had been their main focus at the time, but now they were beginning to wonder if Carroll's theory – that McCoy had fled because he was guilty, was indeed, correct.

Carroll informed Ben that he and Val would be spending most of the day with the Jacksons doing the sketches. Like most people, Walden was surprised to learn that doing a properly detailed forensic sketch can take hours.

Val would be interviewing Mrs. Jackson and Betty separately to ensure that neither's sketch would be influenced by the other. The whole process could take half the day or possibly even the entire day. They wanted to get it right so they were not concerned with the amount of time to be spent.

The three made plans to meet again for supper. To Val's delight, Ben gave her permission to drive the Jeep. They chatted for a few more minutes then she and Carroll returned to the Barrett-Parrish House where they loaded her equipment and then proceeded to Aunt Ruth's, with Val driving.

Their visit the day before had paid off even better than they had hoped. Knowing that she would be working with her new granddaughter instead of some stranger, Aunt Ruth was no longer nervous about the process. In fact, she was actually looking forward to it. To make her even more comfortable they decided to do her interview in her day room where her favorite chair was located. This was the room where she read books and watched her favorite programs on television.

To save time, both Betty and Aunt Ruth were present as Val explained that she was going to do a hand sketch, which is what most people think of when they hear the term, forensics sketch artist, while Carroll was going to use her computer program to create a composite sketch.

"A computer can do that?" Aunt Ruth asked.

Val told her that most of the renderings that are shown on TV news are from composites, which are done utilizing a computer program.

"You don't really have to be talented to run the computer program. Even an idiot could do it," she assured them.

Carroll suddenly realized that they were all looking at him and grinning. He didn't mind being the brunt of Val's joke. She was telling the truth. In fact, she was being modest. He had to brag on his niece.

"Believe it or not, you wouldn't know it by looking at her, but Val is old-school when it comes to forensic sketches. She represents a dying breed. There are only a few artists left that do it the old-fashioned way, by hand, using their own natural talent."

While Val was always ready with a quick retort about most anything, any praise in front of people other than her work colleagues usually resulted in her clamming up.

She smiled modestly before she humbly continued;

"The most famous sketch artist in the U.S. is a woman named Lois Gibson," she told them, "She holds the record for the number of successful police artists' sketches at nearly 1,500. She's in the Guinness Book of World Records. I got to meet and work with her at a training conference."

Val gave Aunt Ruth and Betty a brief history of the process as she opened her kit and began pulling out the components;

"Back when Uncle Bob was still a young policeman," she emphasized, "there were no computer programs. So they had to have talented artists that could listen to a description and then draw the person's face."

She explained that around the 1970's, it started to become harder to find artists, especially in smaller communities, so some companies came up with kits that had interchangeable templates that you manually placed on top of another.

"There was one called Photofit that was big in Europe. Smith & Wesson's Identi-Kit was used by most law enforcement agencies in the US. And then, as computers got to be the thing, starting in the mid 90s you had companies popping out programs left and right, like, SketchCop, FACETTE, Identi-Kit 2000, FACES, E-FIT and PortraitPad."

Valerie concluded setting up her equipment and her impromptu lesson simultaneously as she said, "The newest thing out now is a computer program that uses a holistic approach where it attempts to create a likeness to groups of complete faces instead of just focusing on features. I did a lot of research and decided to go with EvoFIT, so that's what Uncle Bob will be using."

Both ladies were impressed with Val's knowledge as well as her ability to relate it. Aunt Ruth wanted to go first, so they took a short break and then Aunt Ruth, Val and Carroll returned to her day room.

It had already been decided that because this was Val's field, she would ask all of the questions and Carroll would simply use Aunt Ruth's responses to Val to do his computer composite.

She began by getting the most basic information about the person she was drawing: Caucasian female, probably in her mid to late twenties, pretty and tanned, of average height and weight with black hair. Then she started to probe for the details that would make this average person unique enough to identify.

"Close your eyes, Granny," Val said. "Think about the shape of her face. How would you describe it in one or two words, like long or..."

"It was lots like your face," Aunt Ruth responded automatically.

"Good. My face is best-described as round."

"Now, what is the thing that you remember the most about her face? What stands out?"

"Her eyes," Mrs. Jackson said. "She had real pretty eyes!"

"What color?"

"They was dark, so I'm guess'n brown."

The process continued with Val asking questions and Ruth Jackson answering them. Val would sketch on a pad and then show it to Aunt Ruth. She would either say something like, "Yes, that looks like it" or "No, the nose was smaller" or "The lips were thinner."

Except for the clicking on the laptop, Carroll remained silent. The only exception was after Aunt Ruth looked at Val's sketch offering adjustments or her approval, Carroll would do the same, showing the computer-generated image to Aunt Ruth and then adjust the image as she directed. This continued for quite a while until Val showed Mrs. Jackson a drawing that she had adjusted to Aunt Ruth's last instruction.

"Okay, Granny, I changed the bridge of the nose and made it narrower like you said," she explained, showing it to her.

"Oh, my Lord!" exclaimed Aunt Ruth. "That's her! I wouldn't have thought it possible!"

Carroll also showed the computer composite. It was almost identical to Val's sketch.

"You sure are talented, child!" Aunt Ruth complimented her.

"What about me Aunt Ruth?" Carroll enquired.

"What did you say about the computer?" she asked Val.

"You don't have to be talented to run the program. Even an idiot could do it," Val replied, which quickly had the three of them laughing.

Checking the time, they discovered that Aunt Ruth's session had only taken about an hour and fifteen minutes, a fraction of what they had anticipated.

Betty was eager to see the sketch, but Val was afraid it might influence Betty's description so they decided to wait until after her interview was over before showing it to her.

They decided to do Betty's interview in the front parlor. It was where she liked to read so it was a setting where she felt relaxed. The move also allowed Aunt Ruth the use of her day room to watch TV. Carroll and Val relocated the equipment, then took a short break before continuing.

The process was identical to Aunt Ruth's. The main questions were exactly the same, word for word. The only difference was obviously when they made the little corrections after showing her Val's drawing or Carroll's computer composite.

Betty's interview lasted an hour and a half, just fifteen minutes longer than Aunt Ruth's, but still far under the projected three to four hour norm. Betty's reaction to the finished product was similar to her grandmother's.

Carroll asked Aunt Ruth and Betty to sit side by side at the table. He wanted to show them that their individual sessions had produced virtually identical sketches. They placed the end products in front of them. Both women were astounded and Carroll and Val were thrilled with the results. The drawings and computer composites from both sessions were virtually indistinguishable.

"How did you find out her last name?" Mrs. Jackson asked.

"Her last name?" repeated Carroll, confused.

"It says right there on the top of all four sketches, Laura Lenu," she said, pronouncing the last name *Lenu* unconsciously adding an *E* where there wasn't one.

Valerie covered her mouth with her hand to keep from giggling.

"That's not her last name," Carroll corrected. "We still don't know what her last name is. That's an acronym. L-N-U stands for Last Name Unknown.

Any other person might have been embarrassed by such a mistake, but not Aunt Ruth. She didn't hold back.

"Why you gotta go using 'nitials 'stead of just write'n the words?"

"That's just what they do Aunt Ruth," he answered. "But, thanks to you ladies, I don't think we'll have to use it for much longer before we'll know her last name. I really believe that we're going to find her now."

10

Looking for Laura Lenu

Now that they had a likeness and the first name of a person that possibly had key information concerning the death of Thomas McDowell, the question became, what to do with it? Unless the investigating law enforcement authorities had recently come up with the same information, it was doubtful that they knew about Laura at all.

This was the main topic that Carroll, Chow and Walden discussed over supper. Ben's opinion was that they should hold on to the information for the time being and investigate it themselves. Val was leaning toward his point of view. Coming from a large metropolitan police department, she had doubts about the ability of the yokels, as she called them, to complete the investigation after three months.

Carroll reminded them of his objective.

"I'm here for his grandparents. I promised them that I would do everything that I could to find out what happened to Thomas McDowell and bring his killer to justice.

"And that's what we'll do Bob," Walden countered, "The police had the same opportunity that you did. They just didn't take advantage of it."

Carroll disagreed. "It was just pure luck that I stumbled on it, Ben. It happens all the time. Sometimes it's in your favor and sometimes it's not."

He wasn't being modest. Investigators, whether they're private or police, like for everyone to believe they're like the super sleuths on TV crime dramas, but the truth is that luck, be it bad or good, is often the determining factor in the outcome of a case.

Carroll stood by his initial assessment. From what he had seen in the report the local and state law enforcement investigators had done everything that should have been done up to this point.

"There are also both legal and ethical ramifications," he said.

"Val, do you believe that Laura, whoever she is, has pertinent information relative to this case?"

"Absolutely, without a doubt," she replied.

"Then put the shoe on the other foot. If this had happened in Indy and you were the lead investigator and you found out that an unlicensed private investigator and an off-duty cop from another state were not only nosing around your open murder investigation, but had pertinent information that they concealed, what would you do?"

"Charge them with obstruction and throw their asses in jail," she replied without hesitation. Carroll had made his point as far as she was concerned. Walden was still resisting.

"But then we're done, we're no longer part of it," he interjected.

"Not if we play it right. Nothing has changed. Val and I are still under the radar right now. Everyone knows that you're still looking into this as a reporter so you can pass this along to the law enforcement investigators and we can continue with our own investigation."

In the end it was agreed that Walden would inform local investigators that they should check into locating Laura. The question now became, how should they proceed with the search for Laura?

"Well what about me?" Val chimed in. "She's supposedly around my age anyway, so why can't I go around looking for my friend from college?

Ben sat up straight and raised his eyebrows. It was the best idea he had heard so far. Carroll ran over the possible implications in his head. He had planned to let Val return to Indianapolis as soon as possible since she had accomplished the task that he brought her down for.

"It's your idea, so you're obviously up for it," he said to Val, "but what about work? Do you have leave or vacation time and are you sure that you're willing to lose it over something that might not be productive?"

"Are you kidding, Uncle Bob? Captain Jay practically barricaded the door to try and keep me from coming back so soon. He had already arranged extended leave time for me, but I insisted on coming back, so I'm sure he'll let me use it."

"Okay, then give him a call and run it by him. He's already familiar with the case."

"So this is what you were working on when you came by our office the last time, huh?"

"Keep it up and you'll make detective yet," said Carroll.

"I thought you already were a detective?" said a confused Ben.

"I am. And a damn good one, too! He's just a grumpy old man trying to be funny."

Carroll already knew that Jay would allow Val to extend her leave time. Although they had not addressed this specific issue when he was in Stewart's office, obviously because the idea about bringing her down to Georgia had not even occurred to him at that time, Jay had told Carroll that he thought she should take more time off. Granted, this probably wasn't exactly what Stewart had in mind, but at least it was giving her time away from the Indianapolis Police Department.

Having decided their course on the search for Laura, the discussion now returned to Billy Bob McCoy. Given McCoy mentioning Washington to

Lenny and the clue in his rhyme, Carroll was fairly confident Billy Bob was referring to the state of Washington when he mentioned his bike trip. That is, of course, if he had truly taken a road trip. There was still the distinct possibility that he was already on the run. This was the kind of thing that kept Carroll up at night. He was both dreading McCoy's return and anxious for it at the same time. Dreading it, because of his concern for Lenny's safety and anticipating it because it would prove that he was not a fugitive – at least not yet.

"What about social media? Facebook, Twitter or Snapchat?" Val asked. "Does he have an account and, if so, has anyone checked to see if he's posted status updates?"

Val and Carroll both looked at Walden.

"No, he doesn't have one," Ben informed them. "Billy Bob says any man that does social media is gay."

"Umm, don't you have a Facebook account, Uncle Bob?" she asked.

"Yes, I do and actually, that's the real reason I brought you down here. Ben and I have something to share with you." he said, reaching over and clasping Ben's hand.

"Very funny, but it's obvious you aren't gay. I mean, look at the way you're dressed for one thing. You have no fashion sense at all."

Carroll's cell phone rang.

"Well speak of the devil," he said, looking at Val.

"It's Captain Jay?"

He nodded as he answered, "Hey, Jay"

"Hey, Bob, Are you by yourself?"

"No, but I don't have you on speaker so feel free to talk about Val. She can't hear you."

Val held up her fists in a threatening manner and then slowly extended her middle finger like it was a hatching bird.

"Sounds like you're having more fun than you should be."

"Tell me about it. I've felt guilty about enjoying it the whole time I've been down here."

"By the way, Val's holding up her middle finger. I'm not sure if that's for me or you. Hold on I'll ask her. Jay wants to know if that's for him or me?"

"It's for both of you if you're going to gang up on me!"

"She said it's for you."

"Yeah, I heard what she said. You can really be a troublemaker sometimes."

"So, what's up?"

"Cora's been updating me on that note, the one with John Ephraim Paschal on it."

"Hold on, Jay. I'm putting you on speaker," Carroll informed him. "By the way," he added, as he touched the screen, "Ben Walden is also here. I've told you about Ben."

"Hi, Ben. Hey, Val," said Jay.

"Hey, Captain Jay!" Val sang out.

Walden was more formal, "Hi, Captain Stewart. You've got two good people here."

"Don't get ideas about keeping them," Stewart warned.

"So, what did Dr. Patrick say about the note?" Carroll asked.

"There are a couple of smudges on it, but no useful prints. There does appear to be DNA evidence, but of course, that will take longer to get back. The problem is that if the person isn't already in the database then it still won't do us much good – that is, unless someone can identify a suspect to test it against."

"I expected that about prints, but the DNA is a surprise. Thanks a lot for getting it expedited," said Carroll. "And be sure to thank Cora too. I know she's probably a lot busier than she said."

"Believe me, she's getting more out of this than she's putting into it."

"Sounds like you've already been to Mama Carolla's? More than once?"

"Let me put it this way, I could probably get a job there moonlighting as a waiter. I know the damn menu well enough. What about the name or initials, anything on that?"

"Suzi's been working on it, but nothing so far. Look Jay, since we're already on the phone, Val's been really helpful down here. Any chance that I could hold on to her for a week or so?"

"Giving her the time off is no problem at all. Is this something that you've already discussed with her that she's willing to do? Val, Is your Uncle Bob holding you hostage down there? Are you under any type of duress?"

"Yes!" she answered. "I'm having to deal with inferior beings. Other than that, I'm fine Captain Jay. I'd like to stay and help if I can."

"All right then, we'll take it a week at the time and see how it goes. How's that sound?"

"That sounds great! Thanks, Captain Jay!"

"Thanks, Captain Jay!" Carroll echoed.

"Don't be a smartass! Anything else?"

"There are chickens everywhere!" Val shouted.

"Of course there are," said Jay, "You're in Georgia."

"No, you don't understand about the chickens," Carroll told him, "but I'll explain later. Thanks a lot Jay."

"I'll look forward to hearing about it," he laughed. "Take care of my detective."

"You know I will," Carroll assured him. "Talk to you later."

"Well, that really worked out well," he said after disconnecting.

Although they did not yet have an official suspect, the news about the DNA was a huge plus if they did ID someone later.

"You've mentioned Jay, but who is Cora?" Ben asked.

"Cora Patrick. Actually it's Doctor Cora Patrick. She's with the Crime Lab. She's been analyzing a torn piece of notebook paper that was mailed to the McDowells. I thought I told you about it?"

"No, but it's good news. Why would someone mail it to them though?"

"That's a mystery. It could be someone with information who's just trying to help," Carroll suggested.

"But, why mail it then?"

"They might be afraid of being implicated as a suspect themselves or, what if they were threatened, too?"

Val raised her hand like she was a student in a class, "Question."

Carroll responded in kind, "Yes, little Valerie Chow?"

"You mentioned Captain Jay and Dr. Patrick and you said something about Mama Carolla's right?"

"Right."

"So, are they dating?"

"Well, that's not any of our business, is it?" Carroll smirked.

"Oh, my God! They totally are!"

"You should go to work for Entertainment Tonight or E," he recommended. "You would be really good on the gossip segment"

"*Segment?* There is no *segment*. The whole show is gossip."

"Does the name, John Ephraim Paschal, ring any bells, Ben?"

"Not right off, but I can sure check on it. Why?"

"That's what was written on the note, John Ephraim Paschal."

"That was it?" he asked. "Just a name?"

"You're right. It's just three words, but if someone is going to give me three words in a homicide investigation I'd prefer a name."

"Fair enough," Walden agreed. "Well, boys and girls, I've got to get back to the office," he said, rising from his seat. "I'll check into this John Ephraim Paschal character."

"Good. Call me if you find anything," Carroll replied.

"We're going to go back to the Barrett-Parrish House to plan our strategy for the rest of the day."

Carroll and Val started their walk back to the Barrett-Parrish. She informed him that she was going to start keeping a tally on chicken sightings.

"And what would the purpose be?"

"Well, duh! Obviously to count the frig'n chickens!"

"Do you really think you can count all the chickens in town? That's impossible," he said.

"Well, I know that it won't be an exact number, but I could get an idea."

"And how do you know that you're not counting some of them twice or even ten times?"

"I don't for sure, but I'm sure that they have characteristics where I could recognize them."

"Such as?" he prodded.

"Colors and patterns being the most obvious!"

"What about voice recognition?"

"I'm not going to even acknowledge such a stupid statement with a reply."

"Said the person who's planning to count chickens."

"You just don't want me to have fun!" she replied, with her lip poking out.

"You do realize that you just used the words counting chickens and fun in the same sentence, right?"

She flipped him off.

"It's an absurd idea, but go ahead and knock yourself out."

"One," she said, as a hen crossed ahead of them.

Carroll awoke at 5 a.m. as usual. Being aware that he was a guest in someone's home rather than the occupant of a cubicle in a hotel, he made a special effort to make as little noise as possible as he went through the steps of his morning routine and then went over the case.

When he did a emerge from his room at 6:00 he was surprised to find that Val was already up and downstairs. In an effort to get started early they decided to grab the continental breakfast. Their plan for the day was for Val to go ahead and start asking around about Laura, while Carroll would start to do some research; however, it was still too early. Most businesses and public offices would not be open for another hour or two.

He decided to give Val a tour of the town during the interim. Even with GPS, she needed to know her way around. He acted as navigator as she happily drove the Jeep. He pointed out locations relevant to the case, including the Ridgeway, where Thomas McDowell had stayed, the crime scene behind it where his body was found and other places where he was seen. Carroll also pointed out some of the community's historical aspects, buildings and the names of streets.

She had added more than a dozen chickens to her total by the time they returned to the Barrett-Parrish House. Carroll planned to start at the Fitzgerald - Ben Hill County Library while Val did her thing. She offered to drop him off, but he said he would walk since the library was nearby.

"Please be careful," he reminded her.

"Yes, I know! It's not a rental. It's Ben's Jeep!" she said, rolling her eyes. "Well, yes, you're right about the Jeep, but that's not what I meant." She smiled and drove off.

Carroll was beginning to feel that he might have caught a break for a change, maybe even several, as he started down the sidewalk. He was thinking his first instinct, about contacting Ben Walden, had paid off. Ben had not only been helpful with the case, he had become a good friend — something that Carroll realized he did not have many of outside of his law enforcement circles.

Another break was that they did not have to worry about Billy Bob McCoy, at least for the moment. It would have been hard for Carroll to focus on anything if he had thought Lenny Sauls was still in danger. The fact that they still did not know McCoy's exact whereabouts was still a cause of concern. Carroll still worried that McCoy might have fled even though Ben kept insisting that Billy Bob would return at some point, but Carroll was not so sure.

And then there was Val. By following the same instinct that compelled him to reach out to Ben, he had brought Val down and, as a result, had obtained a workable image for the search for Laura LNU within less than a day. With Val looking for Laura and Ben working on John Ephraim Paschal, Carroll could focus on other things.

Thomas McDowell had been seen at the library on at least four occasions, more there than any other place in town. He might have even been there even more than that and had just gone unnoticed.

Unlike most people who picked at least one to believe, Carroll's instincts also told him that all of the various stories about McDowell's reason for being in town were fabrications. He was convinced that there was some sort of connection, be it recent or historical, between Indianapolis and Fitzgerald that had led to his death. They just had to find out what it was.

The library was located at 123 North Main Street, five blocks from the Barrett-Parrish House and one block north of West Central. Carroll normally used the sidewalk on the south side of Central for his walks to The Sportsman, but the library was on the opposite side so he went ahead and crossed over before heading into town.

His walk took him by several historical homes, but as he got closer to town he passed newer buildings intermingled with the older ones, including a Wells Fargo Bank on the left, a Harvey's Supermarket, part of a local regional chain of grocery stores, across the street from it, and the Central United Methodist Church.

He crossed Lee Street, the same street where he had sat in the truck receiving his history lesson from Ben, then proceeded east to Main, where he turned north and walked half a block to the library. He was not there to ask questions or draw attention so he tried to remain as inconspicuous as possible.

An elderly lady simply acknowledged him as he entered.

"Good morning. Let us know if we can help you with anything."

"Thank you," he replied.

The obvious assumption about McDowell being at the library was that he was probably also doing research, but there was another possibility. What if there something about the library itself that McDowell was interested in? That is where Carroll started.

He learned that the building currently housing the library was the town's second location. The first had been built three blocks away at 116 South Lee Street, on land that was donated in 1915 after the Woman's Club of Fitzgerald obtained a Carnegie grant to cover the construction cost.

The library had opened on March 1, 1915. Carroll thought it extraordinary that during the first 60 years of its existence, only two women had held the post of librarian. The first, Louise Smith, was there from day one until 1958 and her successor, Pauline Ennis, served from 1958 to 1974.

The library was moved to its current location in 1983. The move from the old location to the new gave the modern community an opportunity to show that the people of Fitzgerald still maintained their spirit of unity. In an amazing display of civic mindedness, people from throughout the county came downtown and, based on the old idea of a fire brigade, where people passed buckets of water to one another, they formed a human book brigade. Instead of buckets of water, they passed books, tens of thousands of them, along a line of people that stretched nearly four blocks, from the old address on Lee Street to the new one on Main. As a lover of books and one who considered libraries at or near the level of a church, Carroll thought that story was an amazing statement of the community's commitment to a public library that would afford equal access to everyone.

His cell phone vibrated in his pocket. He fished it out and checked the display. It was Betty calling. He first thought was that something had happened to Aunt Ruth. Why else would Betty be calling? He placed his finger on the green icon and slid it to the right allowing him to answer the call.

"Hold on Betty," he whispered, as he walked toward the door.

"Sorry, I was in the library," he explained as soon as was outside. " What's up?" he asked, dreading the answer.

"Granny and I just thought that you and Valerie might like a real home cooked meal for a change?"

He exhaled without even realizing that he had been holding his breath.

"Wow! That would be great."

"Do you already have plans for supper?"

"No, I don't, but Val and I are working on separate things today so I need to check with her."

"Why don't you give her a call and just let me know. We can do it another time if you're busy."

"Okay, let me give Val a call and I'll get right back to you."

Carroll touched 4 to speed dial Val.

She answered that phone with, "Jeez – I'm fine!"

"Well that's good to know, but we're invited to supper with the Jacksons. How about it?"

"Well, that depends on where we're going," she answered.

"I just told you – to the Jacksons"

"Oh, I thought you meant like a restaurant. What are they cooking?"

"I don't know. You don't ask that when you're being invited to someone's house!"

"But, what if it's one of those scary southern things?" she asked seriously.

"Scary Southern things? Like what?"

"Well, chitterlings for one! Do you know what those are made from? Pig guts!" she gagged, answering her own question.

"First, they pronounce it *chitlins*," he corrected her.

"– or pig's feet, or their ears, or turkey necks, or–" she continued, still making gagging noises.

"Secondly," he tried to butt in, "I doubt very seriously that they'll try to feed us chitlins."

Val was still gagging and naming items, some of which Carroll was sure that she'd made up on the spur of the moment when he successfully interrupted her;

"Fine, I won't accept it then," he said.

"No, we should go, but ask if I can come to help with the cooking. That way if it's something gross we can have a backup plan to get us the hell out of there."

"Okay," Carroll chuckled, "I'll accept their gracious invitation and then you and I can plot an escape beforehand."

"That'll work!" she said happily. "By the way, how many do you have so far?"

"How many what?"

"Chickens! I'm up to 46! Can you believe it?"

"I'm really starting to worry about you," he said as he ended the call.

The afternoon went much faster than Carroll thought it would. He spent most of it at the library, but he also walked to some of the other locations where Thomas McDowell had been seen around town. He and Val kept in touch over the phone. Neither of them had made any real progress to speak of.

When he had called Betty back to accept the invitation, he did as Val requested, asking if she could assist with preparing the meal; however, he neglected to mention that her idea of cooking was popping a Bertolli's Chicken Portabella Ravioli into the microwave. Betty loved the idea and said they should arrive between 4:30 or 5.

Carroll knew that Val had acted on impulse and had not considered that she would be placing herself in a world totally alien to her, a kitchen. The thought of it amused him.

He texted Val to meet him back at the Barrett-Parrish to freshen up. He was just arriving as she turned into the driveway. She leapt from the jeep and ran to meet him.

"Guess!" she shouted.

"Oh, I have no idea."

"*Guess!*" she commanded.

"Okay, fifty-two."

"What the hell are you talking about?"

"Fifty-two. You saw fifty-two chickens."

"No!"

"Well then, how many?"

"Not chickens. Guess her last name!"

"Who's?" he asked, but then his eyes narrowed.

"Not funny!" said Carroll.

"Okay, fine. If you don't wanna know."

"Are you serious?"

Val lifted her right hand as if she were swearing in court.

"You actually have a possible last name?"

"No," she said, shaking her head.

"Do you or do you not have a last name?"

"Yes," she nodded her head.

"You're really pushing it," he warned her.

"You asked if I have a possible last name. I don't."

"I assume from your cocky attitude that you think you have her real name — *for sure?*"

"We were so close all along and we never even knew it!" she exclaimed.

"What do you mean, close? We didn't have anything!"

"Yes we did!" she insisted. "We only lacked one letter. Come on! Guess!"

"Just tell me."

"Nope, Granny almost had it right!"

"What are you talking about? Aunt Ruth?" he asked as she followed him into his room.

"Fine, if you won't guess, then I'm just going to get ready for supper," she said with a Southern drawl.

"I will strangle you right here and no one will ever find your body!"

"Fine, if you won't guess then I'll just tell you, but it's not as fun."

He took a step toward her. She squealed and jumped over the bed.

"Okay! I'll give you a hint. Think of the name that we've been using and add an A. It's a jumble!"

Val knew that she had made a major accomplishment and she was beyond control at this point. He had no choice but to comply.

"Fine," he sat on the bed.

"We've been using the standard acronym for last name unknown, LNU. So, if I add an A and change the order it becomes–" he suddenly looked up at Val, "Luna?"

"Ding! Ding! Ding! Looks like we've got a winner!" she yelled.

"You've got to be kidding me!" said Carroll.

"Nope! Her name is Laura *Luna*!"

Val was like a windup toy that was wound too tight. She was all over the place, bouncing around the room. He moved from the bed over to a chair to allow her to expend the bottled up energy. It took a few seconds until she fell, face-forward onto the bed.

"Have you got it out of your system now?"

"I think so," she gasped, as if she'd just run a marathon.

"So, tell me!"

"It was my last stop, the Ridgeway Hotel, where McDowell was staying and where he was killed. Of course, I acted like I didn't know anything about that part."

"I told them that a friend from college had moved to town about three months ago, and I came down to surprise her but forgot that I bought a new cell phone last month and didn't have her number stored anymore."

"And they actually believed the crappy story?" he asked her.

"Do you want me to tell it or not?"

She knew that she had the power right now. He nodded.

"So, first I had to listen to the geek behind the counter explain how to swap the numbers on phones so this doesn't happen again, but finally I was able to show them the sketch."

"Oh great," Carroll said sarcastically, "A police sketch. I'm sure they were not suspicious at all."

Val stopped talking and stood, glaring at him.

"Sorry, it won't happen again," he apologized, holding his hands up.

"I've told them that I was a student at SCAD and that I had done a sketch that I was going to surprise her with."

"What's scad?"

"SCAD is the Savannah College of Art and Design," she explained before continuing;

"So, I showed them the sketch and none of them knew her."

"How the hell did you know about SCAD?" he asked.

"Oh! My! God! Can I please just finish? I already knew about SCAD. It's well-known in art circles and since Savannah's not that far away I figured it would play into my story. They also have a campus in Atlanta. So, do you have another question?"

Carroll shook his head. Satisfied that she was now a control, she continued again;

"So, I was on my way out the door when they stopped me and said that I should wait, because Sheila, the girl who covers night shift, was coming in the back door. So, I waited on her and then showed her the sketch and Sheila said, 'Wow! That's really fantastic! It looks just like her!' And I go, 'You know Laura?'"

"And she goes, 'Yeah, we talked a several times.'"

"If you're making all of this up—" Carroll threatened her.

"I swear!" she laughed, raising her right hand again.

Carroll smiled as Val continued, her words coming increasingly faster as she got nearer to the climax of the story. It was something that she had done since she was little girl, talk so fast when she was excited that her words eventually outran her breath. Right on cue, Val stopped talking and took a deep breath like she had just surfaced from a dive below the water.

"And here's the best part," she said, preparing him, "Sheila goes, 'so why do you have her last name jumbled around like that?'"

"Oh, come on!" exclaimed Carroll, stopping her. "If this is some joke that you and Suzi came up with—"

"I promise, Uncle Bob! I'm not kidding! Sheila saw Laura LNU at the top when she asked about last name jumbled around, so I told her that I was probably just typing too fast and I asked her if she had a pen or something."

Carroll was continually shaking his head in disbelief as she continued;

"Sheila grabs a pen and starts to hand it to me, but I know that if she does that then I'm screwed because I still have no idea what to write. I've been standing there the whole time trying to turn LNU into a frig'n name and—"

"So how did you handle it?" Carroll asked, not able to contain himself any longer.

"I said, you found the mistake, so you get to fix it and it'll be a way for me to remember you, like it was a girl thing. I handed her the pen and she crossed out LNU and wrote Luna. I almost shit a brick!"

Carroll checked the door to be sure that it was closed. While residents of the Ridgeway might be familiar with Val's last phrase, he doubted if the guests at their current venue used the phrase very often.

He congratulated Val for her quick thinking in letting Sheila write the last name herself. He told her to phone Suzi to give her the name so she could start a search and then listened as Val went through the same fast-talking, breath-stealing explanation to Suzi over the phone.

They freshened up for supper and headed to the Jacksons', arriving promptly at 4:30. He let Val inform them about finding Laura's last name. Val didn't go into the details that Carroll and Suzi heard. Instead, she just said she was able to get it by showing the sketches to a hotel employee.

The ladies ordered Carroll out of the kitchen, telling him to feel free to explore the house and the garden while they prepared supper. Betty usually did most of the cooking, however today was a special day. As far as they were concerned, they were passing on a recipe to another family member, Valerie. It was a long tradition in the Jackson household. Val was now in the equivalent of Kitchen Boot Camp and Granny was the sergeant-major. She rolled her wheelchair up to the table and opened an old, well-used recipe book.

"Me and Betty could fix this blindfolded. The best way to learn somethin' is by doing it, so you gonna to do this yourself."

Granny was throwing Val into the deep end.

Val read the heading, "Chicken and dumplings."

"I don't think I'm ready for this," she stammered.

"Yes, you are," she insisted. "The first thing we gonna do is make our own seasoning."

"Seriously?" Val asked. "You don't just use McCormick's or something?"

Betty chuckled as she placed a large pot on the stove. From this point on Val followed the recipe, performing each task as Betty and Granny encouraged her accomplishments with "Good job!, Well done!" or, "That's perfect!"

Val's mistakes, which were fewer than expected, were corrected with finesse, "That's good, but you missed one item" or, "Reread that again. I think you missed something."

Boot camp was tough. As soon as she completed one task, they would push her to the next one.

"It's all about being fresh," Betty explained. "If you're spending too much time on one thing, then something else is getting cold."

Granny gave an analogy; "It's kinda like them plate-spinners on The Ed Sullivan Show. You gotta run around give'n all them plates a spin or they'll fall off the stick."

Val nodded politely, but she had no idea what Granny was talking about. She had heard of Ed Sullivan, but thought he had something to do with The Beatles. She could not even try to imagine what plate-spinners were.

Betty retrieved an over-sized measuring cup from the cabinet and handed it to Val.

"Put four quarts of water in that pot." said Betty.

"Add a cup of salt, a quarter cup of black pepper and a quarter cup garlic powder," instructed Granny.

Val was a good soldier. The instructions from the decorated veterans continued, coming faster as she progressed, but she kept the pace, gaining confidence as she improved. She added chopped celery, chopped onions, two chicken bouillon cubes and bay leaves into the pot. After making sure it was all properly mixed, she added the chicken.

"Very good!" complimented Betty. "Now we're going to let that simmer for about forty minutes."

"Now you gonna fix the dumplings," said Granny. "This is the most important part."

Betty placed a large mixing bowl on the table. Val was getting cocky now. Checking the recipe instructions, she put two cups of all-purpose flour and a teaspoon of salt into the bowl, glanced at the book and then picked up one of the measuring cups and headed toward the sink.

"Hold on," said Granny. "I know it just says a cup of water, but it has to be ice water."

"Really? Ice water? Why ice water?"

"It makes it stick better," Betty explained, as she retrieved the water from the refrigerator. "You'll see."

Val mixed the flour and salt into a mound in the mixing bowl. Then, as Betty dripped ice water over the center of the mound, Val used her fingers to knead the dough moving from the center toward the rim. Betty continued to gradually add the ice water as Val eventually formed the dough into a ball.

A massive, thick wooden table, probably as old as the home itself, sat against the right wall of the kitchen. The surface of the table was covered with countless knife marks from decades of use. Betty dusted a sizable amount of flour onto surface of the table. She told Val to place the dough ball onto the center of the table and then handed her a heavy wooden roller.

Granny had wheeled her chair closer so that she could supervise their work. She nodded approvingly.

"Now, you gonna need to roll that dough out until it's about a quarter of an inch thick," she commanded.

Betty took over as Val complied, instructing her to let the dough sit a few minutes.

"Pour that can of condensed cream of celery into the chicken pot and use the ladle to mix it around and pour some over the chicken," Betty told her.

That task completed, Val returned to the dough, cutting it into one inch pieces. She checked the cookbook again.

"Okay, I'm confused," she admitted. "I just cut the dough into one inch pieces, but now I'm supposed to cut those pieces in half?"

Betty, knowing what was coming, was grinning from ear to ear. She had had the same question when she had first cooked chicken and dumplings under the supervision of her grandmother and her mama decades before.

"What's the 'structions say?" Mrs. Jackson asked.

Val read aloud, "Using your hands, pull the pieces in half."

"Well?"

"I just cut them into one inch pieces," Val reminded her. "So, now it's saying cut those pieces in half?"

"Read it again," Granny instructed. "It don't say noth'n 'bout using no knife."

Betty could not help but giggle.

"I asked the exact same thing the first time I cooked dumplings," she informed Val. "They say there's something special about using your hands for certain things when you're cooking."

"It makes a difference," Mrs. Jackson assured them. Go ahead and pull them in half and start dropping them around the pot. Be sure to spread them all around."

She could not see into the pot from her wheelchair.

"How's it look, Betty?" she asked.

"Good. Very good," she answered, "Except, you got some sticking out here."

Betty handed Val two pot holders, saying;

"We don't stir it anymore now, but you've got to make sure that everything is covered so lift the pot just a bit and very gently swirl it around until all the dumplings are covered."

"Now what?" asked Val, awaiting the next instruction.

"Now we wait 'bout 10 minutes and it's done!" replied Granny.

"Holy shit!" Val exclaimed. "I cooked chicken and dumplings!"

She immediately covered her mouth when she realized what she said. "I am so sorry!" she apologized.

"Don't worry about it," replied a grinning Betty.

Aunt Ruth was even more forgiving. "Shit is a good word to use sometimes," she assured her.

Having been banished from the kitchen, Carroll was still roaming around outside. He walked to the back yard and saw remnants of old brick foundations were still visible in two locations. In another section a brick chimney still stood tall, even though there was no building for it to warm. Carroll realized that there had probably been at least two or three barns and some other structures there in the past. An old well, heavily boarded to keep children and animals from falling in it, sat between the chimney and the Jackson House.

Carroll moseyed around for a few minutes and then returned to the front porch just as Henry was arriving for supper. It was the first time Carroll had seen him since his initial visit to the Jackson House.

"Hey, Henry, how've you been?"

"I'm good Bobby, and yourself?"

"I can't complain."

"Sure you can!" Henry grinned. "That's what most people do ain't it?"

"Would it do any good?"

"Probably not," Henry admitted.

"Hey, have you got those sketches with you? Granny and Betty were telling me how ya'll did that. I'd like to see if it looks as much like her as Betty and Granny say."

"Yeah, hold on and I'll go—"

Carroll was halfway down the steps before it registered. He turned back to Henry.

"Wait a second. You actually saw her when she was here?"

"Yeah, but she was on her way out."

"Did you talk to her?"

"Not really. Like I said, I walked up pretty much as she was leaving. She was talking to Granny and I didn't want to interrupt them."

"Did Laura say anything to you?"

"Just nice to meet you when Granny introduced us was all."

"Did she say anything else?"

"No, not to me. She just told Granny to call her if she thought of anything else."

Robert Carroll's heart skipped a beat.

"Call her?"

"Yeah," he nodded, "if she thought of anything else."

"Did you see her hand your Granny a business card?"

"No. She said that she didn't have a card."

Carroll's hopes faded.

"She just used the notepad," Henry added.

Carroll spun around so fast that it made Michael Jackson look like an amateur.

"What notepad, Henry?"

"The one that we keep on the table by the telephone," he replied, pointing into the house.

"Show me!" Carroll said, clearing half the steps in one jump.

Henry led him back into the house and into the same parlor where he had sat for hours during his two previous visits.

"There it is," he said, pointed to the notepad.

Carroll picked it up. "Are you sure that it's the same pad?"

"I speck so. We don't use it like we used to. Me and Betty mostly use our cell phones."

Carroll wondered how far back he would have to look to find a note from three months ago as he opened the little notebook. Henry was right. They did not use the pad much. There on the very first open page was the name, Laura Luna, and underneath, her telephone number.

Carroll now had confirmation that the name Val obtained was correct and, more importantly, he also had a phone number. He thought back to his first visit and remembered that he accidentally knocked the notepad off of the table, picked it up and put it back. That was over a month ago. Too bad that the pad had not landed with that page open that day.

"Supper's ready!" Betty announced.

"Can I take this Henry?"

"Sure. Just pull that page out."

He followed Henry down the hall to the bathroom where he waited as Henry washed his hands and then did the same. He glanced into the kitchen and saw Val standing there with a big grin as the women congratulated her. She still had her apron on. He wondered how she had managed to cook enough dumplings when she appeared to be wearing most of flour.

"Hold on! I've got to get a picture of this," he said, "Suzi and the guys are never going to believe it."

Aunt Ruth, Betty and Val scrunched close and Carroll took a couple of photos. Then Betty and Val both decided that they wanted photos too so he used their phones and took more. It was a big moment for Val and he let her enjoy it. He would wait until after supper to tell her about the notepad.

Aunt Ruth was proud too. She had instructed dozens of family members, her daughters, nieces, daughters-in-law, granddaughters and lots of great-grands, in this very kitchen, and — as far as she was concerned, she had just added another one.

She clapped her hands to get everyone's attention.

"Now, let's have some of Valerie's chicken and dumplings!"

11

The Death of John Tucker

Carroll could hear the voices of Aunt Ruth, Betty and Val talking and laughing intermingled with the sound of dishes and glasses clinking and pots and pans clanking as Val and Betty washed the dishes and tidied up the kitchen. There was something very pleasant about hearing it all together like that. He was smiling. He seemed to be doing a lot of that lately – smiling.

He was not in the kitchen with them. He was across the hall, sitting in Aunt Ruth's Day Room looking at old photo albums that Betty had pulled out to keep him occupied. They had sat at the dining room table talking for awhile after supper was concluded. They probably would have been there longer, but Henry excused himself to go work. Henry was an X-ray technician at Tift Regional Hospital and was currently working on the night shift. He had about a 25 minute drive to get there. He had thanked Val for supper, something that she was still beaming about, and set out for Tifton.

That was Betty's cue;

"Them dishes ain't gonna clean themselves!" she said, as she headed toward the kitchen.

"I'll help," Val volunteered as she wheeled Aunt Ruth into the kitchen to supervise.

Carroll followed along.

"What do you think you're doing?" asked Aunt Ruth, as he walked into the kitchen.

"I thought I would help. What can I do?"

"You can get the hell out of our way," she commanded. "Ain't no man got business in my kitchen, even a nephew."

"Yeah, beat it old man! Get the hell out of our way!" Val echoed, causing Betty to squeal with laughter.

"Betty, since he likes pictures so much, why don't you get some of them family albums to keep him out of our way," Aunt Ruth suggested.

"Yes ma'am," Betty replied, still giggling.

He followed Betty across the hall into Aunt Ruth's favorite room where they had sat the day before. She opened a closet door and slid out three big Rubber Maid storage containers. They were full of neatly stacked photo albums.

"I think she wants Val to herself," said Betty. "Call me if you need anything.

Now, as he sat there hearing the sounds, he came to appreciate that it was part of a ritual that was reserved exclusively for the women of the house. It was tradition.

Carroll returned his attention to the photo albums. Most of the photos had notes about them, identifying the people were in a particular photo and telling where it was taken. He was glad he knew his way around town now. He knew where most of the locations were.

There were a number of photos taken of the Corn and Cotton Palace from different angles, some featuring people and others showing produce or the decorations of the many celebrations held there. What a shame, he thought, that it was gone – due to pure stupidity and arrogance.

The photographs of the building that impressed him the most were those featuring the Lee-Grant Hotel. It was a huge, four-story hotel that actually had held the record as the largest wooden building in the state of Georgia for several years following its construction.

The hotel's construction itself made history. America was still feeling the effects of a depression that was occurring at the time. A decision had been made to make the construction of the massive hotel a public works project. Some historians say that it was the first public's works project in the United States, predating President Franklin Roosevelt's Civilian Conservation Corps and other groups by thirty-seven years.

The Lee-Grant took two years from the start of construction to completion, likely keeping many of the worker's families from falling into poverty. Carroll came upon several photographs that at first puzzled him. They appeared to be aerial photographs of the town. Closer inspection revealed that they were taken from the Lee-Grant's cupola, showing just how high the building really had been. There were photos depicting views from all points of the compass. Carroll was even able to identify a number of buildings that were still standing now.

He decided that he was going to have to pay Aunt Ruth a visit when she could spend some time with him to go over these old albums. Seeing them was one thing, but what could be better than having your own personal historian to narrate?

Carroll was so wrapped up in the photo albums that he did not hear the ladies leaving the kitchen. It took him a while to realize that it was suddenly very quiet in his part of the house. He walked across the hall and poked his head into the kitchen, ready to duck quickly if Aunt Ruth took a swing at him with a broom or something worse.

Finding no one there he made his way down the hall to the front pallor. There was no one there either. He was beginning to think that maybe she was showing them around upstairs when he heard laughter from the front porch.

He walked out to find all three ladies in three of the four large rocking chairs on the right side if you were exiting the house. Betty had obviously brought the little serving table out with them. It sat between Val and Aunt Ruth, where it performed its sacred duty, holding the precious bottle of Jefferson's Presidential Select.

Aunt Ruth and Val were already well into their first glass, but Betty was drinking lemonade.

"Is this still Ladies Only?" he asked,

"I told you we were going outside," Val said, "but you were in La La Land with those old photos."

"Come on and join us," Aunt Ruth said, "Betty brought you a glass, too."

Val was in the rocking chair nearest the front door, followed by Aunt Ruth, then Betty with the vacant chair on the end. He started toward the end, but Betty got up to move.

"Stay where you are, Betty. I'll sit on the end," he told her.

"Me and Granny get to see each other every day. Y'all don't," she said. Completing her move to the chair on the end, she added, "And besides that, that smoke is starting to bother me."

Carroll had not noticed in the dark, but he now saw an orange glow coming from Aunt Ruth's rocker.

"A cigar?" he asked.

"You want one? she offered.

"No, thank you. I don't smoke."

"Aw, come on! Lighten up," Val told him, blowing a puff of smoke and his direction.

"You too? But you don't smoke either."

"And she better not start neither!" warned Aunt Ruth. "A lady ain't got no business smoking cigarettes, chew'n tobacco or dip'n snuff!"

"But, as Granny said, 'Ain't noth'n wrong with a proper *see-gar* on special occasions,'" Val drawled in her over-the-top Southern accent.

Her performance caused a spontaneous eruption of laughter. Carroll stepped toward the serving table and reached for his glass.

"Go on and sit down," Val told him. "I'm always happy to serve my elders."

He eased into the rocking chair and was surprised at how comfortable it was. He had admired the rocking chairs on his previous visits, but he considered them as decorations, works of art, and not functional for sitting, let alone rocking.

Val promptly delivered his glass of Jefferson's. Aunt Ruth opened a wooden box on the same table where the bottle sat, removed a cigar and handed it to him.

"I 'spect I'm probably gonna have to cut that for you too, ain't I?" she said.

"Cut it?"

Once again, all three women erupted in laughter at his expense.

"I already told them that you wouldn't know that!" Val said, "Jeez, Uncle Bob, Even I knew that you have to cut a cigar!"

"'Specially a fine cigar," Aunt Ruth clarified.

"And this one is?" he asked, inspecting the biggest cigar that he had ever seen.

"Presentación Bolivar Coronas Gigantes!" said Aunt Ruth speaking like a native Cuban.

"You speak Spanish?" Carroll asked her.

"Sí, señor. Hago hablar Español!" she replied.

"She lived in Cuba!" Val exclaimed. "How cool is that?"

"*Cuba*? When was this Aunt Ruth?" he asked.

"I first went down there with some friends in '51. Went back the next year and, except for occasional trips home, stayed there until 1959 – well, a few hours into 1959 anyway."

"Wait a minute," said Carroll. "You were there on New Year's Day 1959? When Batista fled and Castro took over?"

"Like I said, only for about three hours. I wasn't able to get on a plane, but some of the bigwigs had boats docked at private homes that wasn't being watched."

He started to ask more questions, but Val interrupted;

"You know you're going to at least need a whole day to cover all your questions, so save it for another time, old man."

He knew she was right. He had already thought of a dozen questions in his head. He wondered if she had ever seen or met Fidel Castro. He held up the cigar, remembering that he still did not know how to cut it.

"Can I cut it, Granny?" Val asked.

"Go on ahead then. Just remember what I showed you."

"Bring it here, Uncle Bob. You need to see this anyway," Val motioned to the serving table.

He went over and squatted down between Aunt Ruth and Val facing the table. The decanter sat on his right; the wooden cigar box was on the left and in between was a small square cast iron object.

"Check it out Uncle Bob!" said Val, holding her cell phone up to illuminate it.

It was obviously very old. It also appeared to be from a store. He read the raised words: *We sell Smokettes 5¢ Cigars*

"You know where that came from?" Aunt Ruth asked him.

"No, ma'am."

"That was from the store in the hotel lobby."

"Which hotel?"

"The bestest and biggest hotel we ever had here," she replied, leaving it up to him to decide.

"This came from the Lee-Grant Hotel?"

"Uh-huh. Got other stuff too, but we ain't gonna worry 'bout that tonight. That'll be for another day."

Val took his cigar and performed the action, instructing him just as Aunt Ruth had done for her earlier;

"You've got to cut it clean and level or," Val lapsed into Yokelese again, "You'll mess up the draw or the wrapper. Okay? Now I'm going to cut the cigar so that an eighth of an inch of the cap is left around the cigar wrapper."

She pulled the lever and presented him with the cigar, sticking it right into his mouth, saying, "Voila!"

Val then reached behind the cigar box and picked up a brass cylinder about the size of a shotgun shell.

"If you're going to be drinking fine Kentucky Bourbon in real crystal glasses and smoking fine Cuban cigars cut with an antique then you have to use an antique lighter to light'em!"

He held the cigar in his teeth as Val pulled her thumb backwards on the notched wheel, igniting a flame.

"Take short puffs to light it up," Val ordered. "Pretend you're a little train. Say, I think I can. I think I can. I think I can!"

"It's hard to do that when you're laughing" he said, as he began to cough and gag.

He had to take a larger than normal sip of Jefferson's to recuperate. He returned to his rocking chair and found that he became accustomed to the cigar much faster than he expected to.

"The house faces north," he noted. "Was that intentional, Aunt Ruth?"

"It sure was. Daddy wanted it to face north. Lots of Yankees built that way, facing north, but there's a lot facing east too, so they can see the sunrise."

"You don't wish you could see the sunrise?"

"My bedroom's on the east side of the house and my bed faces that way. And if'n I wanna watch it here on the porch all I gotta to do is to scoot my chair thataway," she said, pointing at an angle.

"And why out here on Lincoln Avenue?"

"Cause Mama and Daddy didn't like living in town."

Carroll nodded. His assumption about the Jacksons, and probably the Hageman House, wanting their privacy, was correct. It was getting pretty dark. He looked around realized that the streetlights on both sides of the house were out.

"Have you called anybody about these street lights, Aunt Ruth?"

"Which ones?"

"The ones on both sides of the house that are out."

"They out 'cause I want 'em out. I called the power company and told them to come turn 'em off a few years back and they never did so I shot 'em out. They replaced a few times, but I kept shoot'n 'em out so they finally gave up."

"Don't mess with my Granny!" Val yelled at the power company and anybody else who was out there in the dark.

They sat there for quite awhile. He or Val would ask Aunt Ruth a question and sometimes she would ask them questions about their work or Indianapolis, but there were also long periods when no one talked and they just enjoyed the creaking sounds of the rocking chairs, the chirps of crickets and frogs, and every now and then, even the occasional mooing of a cow from somewhere farther down the road.

They were sitting there like that, just enjoying each other's quiet company, when Aunt Ruth suddenly asked,

"Do y'all think you ever gonna find out who killed that boy?"

Carroll was surprised at the question. He had not planned on bringing up the subject tonight. Both he and Val had decided to stay away from the subject for the evening, but Thomas McDowell was always on his mind.

"I hope so, Aunt Ruth. I surely do."

Because she had brought it up, he decided she must want to talk about it so Carroll followed up with a question of his own, a big one.

"Aunt Ruth, I'm not sure how to bring something like this up, but do you think he could've been killed because of his race?"

"I 'spect anything's possible," she said, looking up at the sky, "but people ain't really like that round here. We really never had problems that other places did." She was quiet for a minute and then added; "'cept for that one time with that Tucker man."

"Who was that?" Val asked.

"He was a man that was lynched."

Betty, Carroll and Val's chairs abruptly stopped rocking. Betty's mouth was wide open in surprise, Val looked stunned, but Carroll's face showed no surprise. Given her age, he had expected Ruth Jackson had likely heard or seen something like that in her life.

"When was that, Aunt Ruth? Can you remember?" he asked.

"January 31, 1930."

"You remember the exact date?" said Val.

"It was my mama's fifty-fifth birthday and she nearly died on account of what happened."

"Granny, why haven't you ever told any of us about this before?" asked Betty, amazed that she was learning of this for the first time.

"Cause I reckon I thought it was too bad for y'all to hear."

"Well, you've got to tell me now." Betty insisted.

"You said his name was Tucker?" asked Carroll.

She nodded, "His name was John Tucker, and he lived down in Irwin County."

Betty leaned forward, "What happened, Granny?"

"It was on a Friday, January 31, 1930. I was 26 years old. Daddy had arranged for me to come home from Atlanta for the week to surprise Mama for her birthday. I came in on the train and got to Fitzgerald in the afternoon."

Betty got up from her rocker on the end and moved closer. Val relinquished her seat to Betty and plopped down on the porch, leaning against the front rail facing her new Granny.

"Daddy and Joseph, my younger brother, was there wait'n on me at the depot. We was all hug'n and talk'n 'bout how surprised Mama was gonna be when we heard a commotion and people holler'n. Daddy said that something was wrong. He told Joseph to go on and take me to the house."

Carroll saw Val discreetly typing on her phone. She googled *John Tucker Lynching*, then leaned over, showing him numerous sources verifying Aunt Ruth's account of the incident and Tucker's name as well as the date of January 31, 1930.

Mrs. Jackson said her father went downtown to find out what happened.

"Daddy come home about thirty minutes after we got there and said that a 14 year old girl was murdered down on the Irwin-Coffee County line near Lax. He said people down there were chasing a black man in the woods and they was asking for all of the help they could get. Mama didn't want him to go. She was cry'n. Then I started cry'n too, so he said he wouldn't go. But, later on, word came that the chase was coming northwest toward Ocilla and Fitzgerald, so he said he was taking Joseph and they was going to help."

Carroll had been listening quietly up until this point, but he had to be sure about what she had just said.

"Aunt Ruth, You're saying that your father actually went down there— to help them?"

"And Joseph, too," she reminded him. "Oh, believe me, Mama didn't want neither one of 'em to go. It was cold by then and it was get'n late. She even tried to block the door, but Daddy pushed her out the way, say'n,

'What if that was one of our girls?' He said, 'I gotta go!'"

Robert Carroll turned to his left and looked back at the front door. Having just seen photographs of Ruth Jackson's mother and father, it was not hard for him to visualize the struggle that had taken place just a few feet away from where he was now sitting, even though it had occurred 85 years earlier.

When she started telling the story, Mrs. Jackson had sat completely still in her rocking chair, but she eventually began to rock back and forth slowly. Now her rhythm increased, keeping pace with her story.

"Daddy and Joseph put on their boots and heavy coats, and then they got their shotguns and headed out. They was gone all night. Mama was a mess, say'n things like, 'What if they get mistaken for that other man in the dark?' At one point, she got so upset that she fell out. I thought she'd had a heart attack, but she come back 'round."

Betty appeared to be almost in shock. After all, it concerned her own family. Other than a pause now and then, or a quiver in her voice, Ruth Jackson seemed composed, almost detached from the story. Carroll was thinking she might not ever have told it to anyone, but she had obviously relived it thousands of times over the eighty-five years since it happened.

"Daddy and Joseph finally come through the door about 11:30 in the morning," she continued. "Mama was so relieved that she wasn't even mad no more. They didn't say much about it right then. Him and Joseph was dirty and dog-tired. All daddy said was, 'They killed him,' before him and Joseph washed up and went to bed."

She said her father and brother slept until late afternoon. In the meantime, she and her mother went to town where they learned that the burned and mutilated body of John Tucker was still hanging from the tree at the location where the girl's body was found.

"Folks begin to load up in vehicles to ride out there – some because they didn't believe the story, and others because they wanted to be sure that he was dead," she told them.

More details surrounding the events began to emerge as people who rode out to the site began to return, reporting back to families and friends. It had started with a misdelivered letter. A 14 year old girl named Mary Beth Wilcox had walked down the road to a neighbor's farm to deliver a letter which had gone to her house by mistake. She had been on her way home when John Tucker passed her with a load of corn on his mule-driven wagon. The sheriff suspected Tucker had stopped ahead of her, possibly pretending to be working on harnesses, and grabbed her as she walked by him. She tried to escape and a violent struggle ensued.

"Some folks said John Tucker raped her and then stabbed her," Mrs. Jackson remembered. "Some said he killed her first and raped her dead body. Then he threw her in a mud puddle and took off."

According to Ruth Jackson's telling, word had spread quickly when the girl was found minutes later and people from the community arrived in the area. Tucker was spotted on the road. Still on his wagon, they easily chased him down in a car. He jumped off and ran into the woods along a stream. The Irwin County sheriff, W.C. Tyler, was notified. He gathered his deputies and called for help from the other surrounding law enforcement agencies.

It was around this time when a young Ruth Jackson was being met by her father and brother at the train. More people had begun to arrive from the surrounding areas and it was not long before there were several hundred. At least half a dozen bloodhounds were brought in from various agencies, and they quickly began tracking Tucker through the woods.

The dogs lost the scent only a few times before finding it again. Tucker was running in a northwesterly direction toward Ocilla. It was at that point when Mrs. Jackson's brother and father joined the search. The posse would track Tucker until dawn.

"It was about three o'clock in the morning when they came up on a cabin," Aunt Ruth resumed. "They was try'n to surround it when John Tucker ran out the back and headed toward the woods. Several men shot at him but they all missed."

"Joseph told me that not long after Tucker ran outta that cabin, some more men arrived to join the group. One of 'em looked at him and my daddy and yelled, 'What's them niggers do'in here with guns?' They aimed their shotguns and rifles at daddy and Joseph, but some other men jumped in between 'em and said, 'They do'n the same damn thing here that you are, try'n to catch a murderer!' After that, daddy and Joseph were told to stay close to the sheriff and the men who helped 'em."

It wasn't hard for Carroll to imagine what the two Jackson men faced that night. Mob mentality is a scary thing even today, but it was far worse for a black man in the South in 1930, especially after the rape and murder of a teen-aged girl. The fears of Ruth Jackson's mother were well founded and, had those white men not intervened, Ruth would probably have lost both her brother and father that night.

"They chased that man nearly twenty miles— all on foot," said Ruth Jackson said, shaking her head in disbelief. "Until finally, the track led'em to a farm house in Mystic."

"They was quicker this time," she reported. "They surrounded the house, but the man who lived there told 'em there wasn't nobody else inside. Sheriff Tyler and his deputies decided to search the house anyway.

They found John Tucker hiding in the kitchen. Joseph told me that that mob near 'bout went crazy when they found out that the man who lived there was try'n to hide Tucker. They wanted to lynch 'em both right there, but Sheriff Tyler talked 'em out of it."

The sheriff had intended to transport Tucker to the county jail, but the mob wanted to take him back to where he had killed the Wilcox girl. Sheriff Tyler knew what would happen if they did. He tried unsuccessfully to reason with the mob. He was told that he could keep Tucker in his custody as long as he followed their instructions.

"The sheriff put John Tucker in a car with him and two of his deputies," said Aunt Ruth, "He was ordered to follow a farm truck with about a dozen men ride'n in the back of it and Joseph said there must've been close to a hundred cars and trucks follow'n along behind 'em."

Ruth Jackson had become increasingly more animated as she told her story, raising and lowering her voice at times and aiming an imaginary rifle in her frail hands as she gave the account of the men confronting her brother and father. She paused, taking a sip of Jefferson's and a couple of puffs off her Bolivar before continuing;

"When they were come'n in to Ocilla, the farm truck with all the men in the back turned right on the road toward Lax, but the sheriff tried to pull a fast one. Sheriff Tyler floored it!' Ruth Jackson shouted as she stomped on the rocking chair's gas pedal for emphasis.

"He went straight ahead try'n to get to the jail! The men in the back of the truck and some in cars following the sheriff started shoot'n at his car! You know how on TV they always show a car explod'n when the gas tank gets hit?" she asked. "Luckily for the sheriff and deputies that ain't always the case. Several bullets hit the car. A shotgun blast hit the gas tank. It didn't blow up, but the gas drained out the tank. A bullet went through the radiator, too."

Perhaps as part of some pitiful attempt to appear to remain legitimate, the mob still allowed the sheriff to maintain custody of the prisoner; however, there was no longer any doubt about their final destination. The caravan proceeded through town, passing right by the Irwin County jail. More vehicles pulled in behind them, and they paraded to the place where the girl's body had been found the previous afternoon.

"Onliest thing daddy said about it was that the crowd pulled John Tucker out the car and stretched him up to a tree, piled sticks and limbs and stuff up underneath him, poured gas on it and set on fire. Several folks shot him, too."

Mrs. Jackson had stopped rocking. Everyone had. Betty and Val were wiping tears. It seemed that the crickets and frogs had even stopped singing.

"That's all my daddy ever told us about it," she said, "but later on I was able to get Joseph to tell me more. He said they put John Tucker up against the trunk of that tree and wrapped chains around him, but they didn't set him on fire right then. The men first cut off his fingers and toes, one joint at a time. A couple of 'em even wrapped the pieces in handkerchiefs and stuck 'em in their pockets to keep as souvenirs. Then they pulled out his teeth with pliers and he was stabbed with a pole. Joseph said there was at least a thousand people there by then, all screaming and go'n crazier each time they did somethin' else to him."

She looked over at Betty and Val. "They did worser stuff than that to him before they put him up to a tree limb and finished him off," she said, leaving it up to them to decipher what was worse than she had already described, what she could not bring herself to say now. Finally, after they done all that, they burned him."

Tucker's body stayed there all day. Thousands more came out from surrounding towns and counties to see it. Some brought their entire family. It was not until sunset that the sheriff and his deputies took him down and buried him.

Carroll had developed a new theory as he listened to Ruth Jackson's account of the lynching of John Tucker. What if Thomas McDowell had been investigating it? Is it possible that his digging around about a lynching that occurred 85 years ago could have led to his own death? Most of the offenders were probably long dead, but it was certainly possible that some were still alive. After all, Ruth Jackson was here. He was sure that relatives of the Wilcox girl still lived in the area.

If the Tucker lynching was connected to the McDowell murder then what about Billy Bob McCoy? How did he fit in – if he fit in at all? McCoy was not even from Georgia, much less the local area. Then Carroll remembered the men at the meeting in the Waffle House. Was it possible that they were somehow connected to the event and had involved Billy Bob, knowing of his racist views?

"Aunt Ruth, did Thomas McDowell ask you about any of this, or did you tell him this story?" he asked.

"No, I ain't never talked about this to nobody 'cept my brother, Joseph. And he's been gone for nearly 65 years."

Carroll did the math. Joseph was her younger brother and that seemed an awfully premature death.

"What happened to your brother, Joseph, Aunt Ruth?"

"He got killed in a car wreck in 1950."

She shook her head, saying, "That sure sounds like a long time ago when you say it like that, but it don't seem like it to me."

Carroll had questions about the accident that claimed her brother's life. He was now wondering if the accident had not been one at all, but now was not the time to ask. Aunt Ruth looked emotionally and physically drained. He gently steered the conversation back to more pleasant topics, asking her questions about her mother and father and her grandparents.

It wasn't long before they were all laughing again, the Jefferson's Presidential Select no doubt contributing to their speedy recovery. In fact, Aunt Ruth was on another roll, ranting about President Herbert Hoover, something that Val thought was both hilarious and fascinating. Carroll thought that they should end the evening on a good note.

"Well, I'm just going to have to admit it," he said, with a yawn. "I can't keep up with you young folks!"

"Ha! I knew it!" Val exclaimed. "Can't hang like you used to. Huh, old man?"

"Why don't y'all finish your drinks and I'll straighten up," said Betty, rising from her chair.

"I'll help!" volunteered Val, as she jumped up, too.

"You all right, Aunt Ruth?" Carroll asked as soon as the women were inside.

"Um huh," she answered, taking another sip. "I've been want'n to tell Betty 'bout that for a long time. Just didn't know how to do it."

"I feel like I've intruded on your personal life" Carroll confessed. "Making you talk about things you'd rather have kept private."

"Oh, don't you worry none about that. This was a good thing. And if you worried about Betty, she's tougher than I am. I shoulda told her as soon as she was old enough."

Sensing that her adoptive nephew was still apprehensive, she added, "If you got more questions about it then go ahead and ask 'em if you want to."

"I might have some later, but I'm about ready for bed. Gotta get my beauty sleep, you know."

"Yeah, you could sure use some," she said grinning as she looked him up and down. "You 'bout a pitiful sight!"

He chuckled as he gave her a hug and helped her into her wheelchair.

"Of course, I don't need none myself," she added.

"What's that, Aunt Ruth?"

"Beauty sleep."

"No, you can't improve on a rose," he replied, using a line that had gotten him rebuked, but was now accepted as sincere.

They all said goodnight, hugs were exchanged and for the first time, Betty gave one to Robert Carroll.

"Thank you, Bobby," she whispered.

Val was on her iPad the minute that they got into the Jeep, pulling the information about John Tucker up before he was out of the driveway.

"So, do you think there could be some kind of connection, between McDowell and Tucker? " Val wondered.

"I don't know. It seems like McDowell would have brought it up if there was, but maybe he was planning to do it in a later conversation?"

"Listen to this," she said, looking at her computer screen. "Up until John Tucker, there hadn't been any documented lynchings in Georgia since the mid-1920s, but after Tucker, there were five more that same year and four of those were less than 70 miles from here."

"There was the one in Ocilla, one in Montgomery County, one in Darien, which is in McIntosh County, and two separate lynchings in Thomasville.

"Where was the sixth one?"

"Someplace called Cartersville, in Bartow County."

"That's north of Atlanta," he said. "Let's look into the others. There could be connections between them, but I doubt it. Sadly, that was something that happened during that period."

"It's just unreal, you know?" Val said. "It's one thing to read about this stuff, but to sit and listen to somebody talk about it that was actually connected?"

Carroll had to agree. Aunt Ruth's revelation had been a real shocker, even to him.

"Well, something else happened tonight that you need to know about," he said.

"Is that your way of telling me that I missed something important?"

"No. Don't get so defensive. You were busy cooking your famous chicken and dumplings."

"I am a pretty damn good cook, ain't I!"

It was a statement of fact, not a question, but he acknowledged it, saying, "I'll admit you are, but while you were cooking I was able to verify Laura's last name."

"Seriously? How?"

Carroll handed her the piece of the notepad that Henry had given him.

"Holy shit! You verified the name and got a phone number, too? And you waited all night to tell me?"

She balled her fist and hit him hard on his right shoulder.

"Ow!" he yelled. "This is elder abuse!" he warned her.

"Just be glad that you're driving."

Val looked at the telephone number.

"The area code is 3-1-0," she noted.

"That's Southern California, the L.A.-Santa Monica area."

"Well, that's not good news then is it?" she asked.

"Maybe, maybe not. Lots of people have distant area codes for their cell phones nowadays. Look at it this way— it's a new lead. Why don't you text the name and number to Suzi and Jay so they can start checking on it first thing in the morning?"

She was already on it.

"This could be a real break huh?" she said excitedly.

"Yeah. You did some really good work getting that name."

"Well, you did too. I guess that you're at least still half a detective even if you're old!"

"Thanks a lot. I appreciate those kind words."

"You're welcome!" she replied cheerfully, as she continued to scan the results from her Google search.

The following morning brought renewed energy to the investigation. Val pulled out several sheets of printed material. She had obviously stayed up quite late reading up on the John Tucker lynching.

"I found out more about Tucker's past," she said as she unfolded a Georgia travel map on the table. "I don't know if he was born there, but Tucker spent most of his life around Hawkinsville in Pulaski County. It's about three counties north of Irwin County."

Val said there were also more detailed accounts of what happened before the mob got control. She reported that Tucker supposedly confessed to Sheriff Tyler and his deputies giving details that matched what they had found at the scene. For two years prior to the murder, Tucker had lived at the home of M.J. Williams near Mystic where he had performed various chores around the farm and residence. He was married and had a child.

"Get this," she said, preparing him. "John Tucker had a previous rape conviction and he was an escaped convict who had been serving a ten year term in Pulaski County."

Val discovered that Tucker had been caught prowling around a house in Ocilla the year before. He had been locked up briefly, but was released when charges were not pressed against him.

"So, any thoughts?" Carroll asked her.

"Are you kidding? I'm surprised that my brain hasn't exploded! Tucker was probably guilty of murdering the girl, but it would've been better to have a confession and a trial. I know lynchings happened, but hearing a living person describe all that medieval torture stuff was unreal. It's not like he was going to get away. I just don't understand how something like that can happen."

"I was up late last night too," he told her. "Look this up, The Tragedy of Lynching by Arthur F. Raper. It's an analysis of more than 20 lynchings that occurred during that same year, 1930. It was done by a commission of Southern scholars and investigators in 1932."

"So, if it covers 1930, then John Tucker should be in there right?"

"He is. Read that book and you'll understand how it happened. Each lynching is examined in great detail, including the formation of the mob, behavior of the police, and the economic background of the area where the crime occurred."

Val was already clicking away on her keypad.

"I'll tell you what," she said, "why don't you trot down and fetch my breakfast and I'll get to work?"

"Do you require that immediately Madame? Or may I first take a brief walk for some morning air?"

"Make it very brief!" she commanded. "And remember, I like the ones with blueberries."

"I'm going to call Suzi, too," Carroll informed her, "and make sure she got the text from last night."

"Good. Go now– and don't forget to count chickens," she reminded him.

"Wow! Isn't this a surprise," Suzi answered.

"What do you mean? I told you I'd call today."

"Yeah, but from Val's last text last night, I didn't think either of you would be up this early."

"What did she say?"

"Let's see; I think it was something like, 'We're drinking bourbon and smoking cigars!' What the hell are you teaching her?"

"The fine art of being a detective. Believe it or not; yesterday was amazingly productive."

"Yeah, I actually agree with you. I've already started checking on Laura Luna. The problem is there's a buttload of them."

"That figures. What about John Tucker?"

"No more than the accounts of the lynching that you already sent me, at least so far. I've got a call in to the McDowells to see if they might be related or at least know the name, but they haven't called back yet."

"And last, but not least, anything on John Ephraim Paschal?"

"Zilch! And believe me, I've checked everywhere," she told him. "But, don't worry. I'm still on it."

"One last thing; exactly how much is a buttload?"

"Google it," Suzi responded.

"Give me a call if anything pops up at all okay?"

"You've got it. Hug Val for me."

Upon returning to the Barrett-Parrish House, he found Val already downstairs getting her own breakfast.

"Was I gone that long?" he asked.

"No, I could smell it coming from downstairs and I finally just couldn't take it anymore."

"We're running a little late this morning," he noted as he picked up a plate. "Anything good left?"

"Well let's just see," she said, looking around as she grabbed several choice pastries. "No, it doesn't look like it. Not much left, sorry."

"You have no shame."

"Not when it comes to these I don't. Oh, guess what? I found that book by Arthur Raper and downloaded it as an EBook," she added.

"You're kidding! Wasn't it published in '33?"

"Yeah, you were right, but it was republished in 2003, and more recently, it was added as an EBook. Lucky for us, huh?"

Even though it was convenient for their research, Carroll could not get used to the whole EBook phenomenon. He was old school. He preferred real books, hardbacks. One of the most important factors in designing his house had been planning the room that was specifically made to be his library. He already had seven book cases in it and was about to add an eighth.

"So what's the plan this morning?" Val asked.

"Well, I would like to update Ben and see if he's found out anything, especially about Billy Bob or John Ephraim Paschal. Do you feel like walking down to The Sportsman?"

"Are you mental? Do you see my plate?"

"Fine," he said. "I'll go meet Ben and then I'll go to the library and see if I can find anything on John Tucker. Do you need anything else?"

"Yeah, I think I still have room for grits," she decided.

12

Evergreen Cemetery

The week had started out very well for Robert Carroll. Bringing Val down had instantly paid off, producing, first, the sketches of Laura and, then, a possible last name, Luna. It was as if someone had lit two candles in the darkness.

Then he had had the good fortune to bump into Henry and find the notepad which not only verified that Luna was indeed Laura's correct name, but it also gave them something they never even dreamed of, finding a phone number. That was two more candles.

Aunt Ruth's story about John Tucker had become yet another possible lead. They just needed to find that one connection. He thought perhaps this was where John Ephraim Paschal fit in. That name had to be significant for someone to mail it to Albert McDowell. It was a fifth candle.

But, then, they ran out of new candles. Even worse, those that were burning started fading one by one. They were now flickering and the slightest breeze would snuff them out.

Suzi had found dozens of Laura Lunas but not the one for whom they were searching for. Carroll gave the phone number to Jay. As Indianapolis PD was now part of an open homicide investigation, he had been able to obtain a subpoena for the phone records, but they were still awaiting the results.

Despite doing an amazing amount of research they had thus far failed to come up with anything to connect Thomas McDowell to any of the leads. Suzi had heard from the McDowells. They were not related to John Tucker, nor had they ever heard of him. There was absolutely nothing on John Ephraim Paschal. It was like he had never even existed. And there was another thing that kept gnawing at Robert Carroll; he still did not know where Billy Bob McCoy was.

He was feeling disappointed as he made the drive from Southwest Georgia Regional Airport in Albany back to Fitzgerald. Carroll was putting the blame where it was most deserved, on himself. He knew better than to get too optimistic about a case, but Val's youthful enthusiasm was contagious; and, he had let it get the better of him.

He tried to remember back to when he was a young detective and expected to break every case within hours, or days at the most. His supervisor, Lieutenant Paul Rabon, had warned him against that type of thinking.

"Don't let it get you too cocky," Lieutenant Rabon had cautioned him. "You'll start missing the little things, the details that will solve your case. You guys are like a bunch of unbridled colts," he would say while adjusting his pipe. "It's my job to rein you in."

Carroll had forgotten to pull the reins. Not Val's, he thought. Being overly optimistic was natural in a young detective. He forgot to pull his own reins.

Knowing the four month anniversary of McDowell's murder was in just a few days was also a painful reminder for Carroll. The farther they got from that date, the less of a chance they had of solving the crime. It's a well-known fact; the first 48 hours of a homicide investigation are the most critical. After that, hours become days, days become weeks, weeks become months, and– Carroll did not even want to think about years or decades.

He often joked about his old nemesis, the Cold Wind, hiding in the alley back in Indianapolis, but Robert Carroll knew there was something far worse than the cold wind – a cold *case*. He thought about the contrast of the way that the week began and ended.

The only real productive events of the later part of the week were two more nights of home cooked meals at the Jackson home. Val discovered that she had a new passion, cooking. As much as she enjoyed cooking the chicken and dumplings, it was not until Ruth Jackson planned an even bigger supper, inviting other relatives over, that Val felt as if she had really accomplished something in the kitchen.

"Just wait until you taste this girl's cooking!" the Jackson matriarch had told them.

That gathering had also given Carroll the opportunity to meet and learn more about the extended family, in particular and the history of the town in general. As much as Val was enjoying herself, she was also now fully vested in the McDowell case. She found that she was as frustrated as he was. They discussed the situation and came to a conclusion. Jay Stewart was working on the case in Indianapolis, but they knew, as captain, he had other responsibilities that demanded his time and attention. Carroll and Val agreed that one of them needed to return to Indianapolis, at least for a week or two.

She had made the choice that she should be the one to return, saying, "You're more effective down here. With Suzi in the office, you can just make a phone call and get almost the same result as you would if you were in Indy. I've run out of options here, but I can go home and work these new leads through Indy PD."

She was right, of course. He would likely be doing the same kind of research at his office that he was doing in Fitzgerald. One of the remaining flickering candles was the subpoena for the phone records. He was expecting the results from the subpoena for the phone records any day now. With his luck, he worried that he might get off of the plane in Indianapolis to find they had located an address right here in Ben Hill County or somewhere in Georgia.

Valerie also wanted to meet the McDowells and she hoped to do it at their home instead of the police department or at Carroll's office. He liked the idea, especially if she met them at their home. Val had a natural ability to instantly connect with people and the more the elder McDowells talked with her the more likely they might remember something important.

Carroll also felt that it would give them some encouragement to know that in addition to him and the Georgia authorities, a detective from the Indianapolis Police Department was now also working on the case full time.

They called Suzi to inform her of their decision. All of the morning flights were full so he asked Suzi to book her on whatever was available. That turned out to be a flight leaving Atlanta at 10:30 p.m. that very night. ExpressJet's latest flight from Albany to Hartsfield departed at 5:30 p.m. and arrived in Atlanta less than an hour later. That's a layover of four hours, so he offered to drive Val to Atlanta instead.

"Well that's just stupid," she told him. "You're going to drive a seven hour roundtrip so I don't have to sit and read or work on my laptop or watch TV for three or four hours?"

She was right again, of course. She reminded him of it twice on their way to Albany. Besides disappointment about the lack of progress with the case, he was experiencing another negative force, guilt. Carroll felt guilty about Lenny Sauls.

He had told Lenny that he would see him as soon as he got back. It was not a lie. He had planned to, but bringing Val down had changed that plan too. As much as he wanted her to met Sauls he could not risk it. He could just hear Lenny telling Billy Bob about Uncle Bob's pretty Chinese niece that was here visiting.

McCoy was already suspicious enough without throwing yet another stranger into the mix. Carroll had told Val all about Lenny and she wanted to meet him, but she also understood that it could endanger the case and more importantly, Lenny, in the long run. So, for the entire week Carroll had been using alternate routes, avoiding the streets Lenny usually walked on so they wouldn't accidentally bump into one another. Then it happened. As they were coming through town on Thursday, Val pointed down the street to the giant in the middle of the crosswalk.

"That's *got* to be Lenny, right?" she asked.

It was Lenny. He spotted the Jeep at about the same time that Carroll made an abrupt turn through a parking lot to avoid him. Lenny was still more than a block away, but he started jumping up and down and waving like a castaway on a desert island who was trying desperately to signal a passing ship or plane.

"HEY, MR. CARROLL! HEY, MR. CARROLL!" he screamed in his drive-thru voice.

Luckily, Carroll was quickly able to make the turn and Lenny was too far away to see that he had a passenger. He felt terrible enough about it, but Val threw fuel on the fire.

"Damn, Uncle Bob. That was cold! Look at him!" she said with her lip poking out.

Now Val was gone, too.

He checked the time. Her ExpressJet flight should be touching down at Hartsfield right about now. He decided that he would just grab something at a fast-food place and spend the rest of the day going back over the case to see if he could find anything he might have overlooked. He had already decided on what his main priority was for tomorrow. He would find Lenny. Carroll needed to get Karma back on his side.

His cell phone rang.

"Hey Suzi," he answered.

"Okay, before you freak out, I'll just tell you that it's mixed news," she prepared him.

"The phone records came in," he guessed.

"Yes, and like I said, it's good news, bad news. The good news is that you're right, even with the Southern Cal area code, she was in Georgia. The last activity was around Atlanta."

"I don't like the *was* and *last activity* part."

"Yeah, I didn't think you would."

"When?" he asked.

"The last call in or out was on the day that Thomas McDowell was killed."

"Shit!" he yelled. Then he hit the dash and yelled some more. Suzi had anticipated this reaction. She had made sure that he was not on speaker just in case someone walked in. And she also held the receiver away from her ear to protect her own hearing.

She gave him a moment to vent and get it all out.

"You okay?"

"Yeah, sorry about that. I know you and Jay are just going with what you have."

"Remember what you told me when I screwed up? Don't worry about it," she reassured him.

"It's just that– three, no, four months have passed now! I mean, I didn't think she would be GPSing herself for us, but, Jesus! If she hasn't used it in four months then she could be anywhere!"

"Look," said Suzi in an effort to ease his mind. "We literally just got this within the hour so give us some time to work it and save your freak-out mode for later. Deal?"

"Deal," he agreed. "Val's in Atlanta right now. Should we hold her there overnight just in case?" he asked.

"It's up to you and Val, but what if nothing pops up?"

"Why not let her come on home as planned?" Suzi reasoned, "You're less than three hours away from Atlanta and I could always put her on a plane to meet you there if needed."

"You're right."

"As usual," she pointed out. "I'll call you if there are any changes."

"Thanks, and thank Jay, too."

He focused his attention on Laura Luna. Both Aunt Ruth and Betty had commented about how Val resembled her in certain ways. They specifically mentioned her physical stature, dark eyes and dark hair. Luna is a common Latin American surname, especially in Argentina and Brazil, a demographic well represented in Southern California.

Of course, he hoped she was still in Georgia, if not in Fitzgerald, possibly in the Atlanta area.

He called Val.

She answered with, "Hey, you miss me that much already?"

"Yes, but I also have some mediocre news," he told her.

"Well, then, I'll probably give you a mediocre response."

"The phone records came in. That's the mediocre news. The bad news is– "

"Wait," she interrupted. "You only said mediocre news. You didn't say anything about bad news."

"I was trying to be tactful. The bad news is that the last activity was on the day that McDowell was killed."

"Shit!" she yelled, giving the same response he had.

Carroll heard her apologizing to the people sitting near her in the terminal.

"I'm so sorry!" she told them. "But my dog died."

"You don't even have a dog," he said in her ear.

"Shut up," she whispered.

He could hear bits of muffled conversation. She had apparently placed her hand over her phone.

He heard Val say, "Thank you very much. He was a good dog."

Carroll was still chuckling when she returned to the call.

"Okay, I'm back. So, should I stay here in Hotlanta tonight?" she asked, using her now-perfected Southern drawl.

"No, you know that if you do that, then of course nothing will happen."

"Well, I'm going to have to start calling you Debbie Downer! Fine, I'll just go back to Indy where at least I know that I'm loved and appreciated."

"Anything else?" he asked her.

"Yeah, about that 3-1-0 area code, Luna is a popular name in South America, especially in Argentina and Brazil."

"You don't say?"

"Yeah, it really is. And LA has a sizeable population of both, so she could be there."

"Good to know," he told her.

"Of course there's another possibility," Val offered.

"Which is?"

"Which is that she's a foreign national and she may have already returned to South America."

"Why do you say things like that?" Carroll exclaimed.

"Um, because we're talking about the case and it's a definite possibility? Oh, wait, I'm sorry." she apologized, "I forgot about your, Don't jinx us, rule."

"I am not superstitious!" he insisted.

"Uh huh, sure you're not," she chuckled.

"Have a good flight and call me tomorrow."

Carroll called Ben and brought him up to speed on the phone records. He also wanted to double check with him on the continued use of his Jeep. He was saving a lot of money by not having to rent a vehicle, but as convenient as it was and as much as he was enjoying it, it was yet another source of guilt for him.

"Look, you bring this up almost every day and it's starting to get on my nerves," Ben told him. "So why don't we do this; let's swap. I'll drive the Jeep and you take my truck?"

"That's even worse! Your truck is what – a year old? At least the Jeep is older."

"Then quit worrying about it. If I was buying your gas too, then I would probably draw the line there, but you even had the oil changed and paid for that. I usually swap back and forth driving them during the week anyway."

"Okay, forget I mentioned it," Carroll told him.

"Look at it this way; you can't really claim to have had the real Southern experience unless you drive a pickup truck."

"Fine, I'll swap for one day." Carroll relented.

"Good! Call me when you get back to town."

As painful as it was for Carroll to get this frustrated about a case, there was a beneficial side effect; it usually caused his brain to kick into overdrive. That is what was happening now. He did feel some relief, knowing that they now had the phone records, which were bound to provide something sooner or later.

He started going back over every aspect of the investigation, trying to figure out where he could have missed something. He had found multiple accounts of the lynching of John Tucker and had read and reread them all. Val had downloaded the eBook of Arthur F. Raper's The Tragedy of Lynching on his laptop. Even though he had recommended it to her, it had probably been 20 years since he read it, so he read it again.

Raper's book provided the most detailed account of the incident and went into just as much detail about the aftermath. It contained editorials and letters to the editors from newspapers throughout Georgia and all over the country. The book also included eyewitness accounts and as well as information about how local religious institutions reacted to the incident, some against, but most indifferent or even supporting it.

It made Carroll recall a quote by the religious philosopher, Blaise Pascal: "Men never do evil so completely and cheerfully as when they do it from religious conviction."

An electric shock suddenly shot through his head.

"Jesus!" he yelled, as he slid the Jeep to the shoulder of the roadway. He suddenly felt as if he had been slapped like that old Skin Bracer commercial again. He grabbed his phone and called Suzi.

"How did you run the check on John Ephraim Paschal?" he blurted out, as soon as he heard her pick up.

"Well, hello to you, too!" she popped back. "What do you mean, how did I run it? Like I always do, through–"

"No, I'm talking not about the networks" he interrupted her, "I meant, how did you spell it?"

"I can read and write. I spelled it just like it was in the letter."

"Run it again, but drop the H in the last name, then call me back."

"Will do."

He started to pull back onto the roadway, but he decided to wait. He knew Suzi was running it right now and it would be no more than five or six minutes before she called him back.

His cell phone rang in less than two. Carroll slid the icon to answer it, but did not say anything.

"So, do you want your cookie now, or later?" Suzi asked him.

"Yes!" he yelled. "I knew it!"

"What made you think of that?" she wondered. "One stupid letter made the difference!"

"It was completely by accident," he admitted, "I was thinking of a quote by Blaise Pascal and I realized the spelling was different."

"Oh silly me! I quoted him three or four times today already, but I missed it."

"Who *are* you?" she asked. "Who the hell is Blouse Pascal?"

"Not Blouse, it's Blaise," he corrected her. "You make him sound like a shirt."

"Whatever. So who is this Blouse dude anyway?" she asked, intentionally pronouncing it incorrectly just to irritate him.

"Not is, *was.*" Carroll explained, "You know how Mozart was writing symphonies and operas when he was just a child? Well, that's the way Blaise Pascal was with mathematics, physics, writing, religious philosophy and even making new inventions."

"And I thought the bumper sticker, My child is an honor student at Dipshit Elementary School was obnoxious," Suzi joked.

She added, "Try, My child is a child prodigy in mathematics, physics, writing, religious philosophy and inventing stuff. I hope his papa drove a big carriage, because he sure needed one big ass buggy bumper for that sticker!"

"Will you just please tell me what you found?" he pleaded.

"Well, don't yell again, but you're not going to be talking to him."

"Okay, so he's obviously dead."

"Either that or he's gonna be in Guinness because he's been holding his breath for 150 years."

"I hope you're enjoying yourself, dragging it out like this," he told her. "You might as well dig another grave, because you're killing me here."

"Fine! He's actually buried there in Georgia at– "

"Evergreen Cemetery," Carroll said, finishing for her.

"Evergreen Cemetery in Fitzgerald, Georgia," she confirmed.

Carroll tried to remember, how many times he had started over to Evergreen Cemetery since he had been in Fitzgerald. At least three or four that he recalled. If only he had made that trip. He would have probably seen the tombstone and it would all have connected.

"The next time that you see me I'm going to bend over and I want you to kick my ass," he told her.

"Hold on," said Suzi. "Let me start the recorder, then I want you to say that again, so when you're wearing your ass for a hat I'll have a defense in court."

He was already chuckling, but Suzi's last comment put him over the edge. Levity was just what he needed at the moment. Carroll was laughing so hard that his eyes were watering. He reached for a napkin on the passenger seat to wipe his eyes and noticed the tourist packet that Walden had given him during his first trip to Fitzgerald.

"Give me a sec, Suzi," he said, as he touched the button to put the phone on speaker-mode.

Still parked on the shoulder of the roadway, he reached over and picked up the packet.

"I've got a couple of brochures about Evergreen Cemetery that Ben Walden gave me," he informed her.

"Only two? You should've asked for more. You can never have too many cemetery brochures," she joked.

"Very funny. The first one's about the historical aspects of the cemetery," he said. "It gives details about some of the people buried there."

Carroll quickly scanned the names. He was both relieved and disappointed to find that John Ephraim Pascal was not listed among them. He knew that Suzi would never let him hear the end of it if he had been walking around with information about Pascal the whole time.

"He's not listed," he told her.

"Too bad," she answered. "Just out of curiosity, what's the second brochure about?"

"New arrivals."

"What?" she chuckled, before going into involuntary snorts.

Carroll knew Suzi would not him let hang up until he explained himself. He opened the second brochure, which contained the basic information on how to obtain a burial plot at Evergreen.

"Okay. Listen to this," he said. "There are two steps to secure a burial plot: Step one is to purchase the site. You can get a plot for $375, but city residents get a discount of $50.

"A discount is always nice," said Suzi.

"Step two is purchasing a burial permit," he informed her. Those are $325. But again, city residents get a discount, although this one is only $25.00."

"Hey, that might not seem like much, but it s still a tank of gas," she noted, quickly adding, "– for whoever you're leaving behind."

"Hey, listen to this," said Carroll. "You can purchase a plot at the funeral home like normal, but if funeral homes freak you out, you can do it at City Hall. That's convenient."

"I'd like to pay my power bill please. Oh, by the way, let me buy a grave while I'm at it," Suzi cackled.

Carroll continued, "And for another $25.00 you can purchase an Improvement Permit; although, the brochure doesn't go into details about what kind of improvements you can make."

Would a swimming pool be considered an improvement?" she asked.

"Probably," he snickered. "Uh-oh. You're not gonna like this," he warned her. "No pets are allowed."

"Well, that does it. I was considering getting planted there, but not if I can't take Lolo," she said, referring to her cocker spaniel.

It was the kind of back and forth they did at the office daily and Carroll had missed it. They joked around a few more minutes. As usual, it was Suzi who got them back on track.

"So, what's next?" she asked.

"Dig everything up on Pascal you can find."

"Okay," she responded, "I'm making a couple of assumptions here. First, when you say dig, you mean that as in research, and not actually digging up a dead man's body. After all, we've been talking about a cemetery for ten minutes. And, two, that you're talking about the dead guy in Georgia, not the bumper-sticker Blouse in France."

"Yes on both," he chuckled.

"And can I do this tomorrow since it's nearly seven o' clock?"

"Oh, crap! I'm sorry! Of course. Thanks, Suzi. Have a good night."

"You, too. Nice job on Pascal," she said. "No kidding."

"Thanks."

Carroll wanted to go straight to the cemetery to search for Pascal's grave, but the brochure clearly stated that the cemetery hours were from 7:00 a.m. until dusk, noting anyone entering the cemetery after hours is subject to misdemeanor arrest. The last thing he needed was for locals to see a stranger with a light in the cemetery. He smiled, imagining calling Suzi to bail him out of jail for that one.

The new information obviously changed Carroll's priorities for the following day. Lenny Sauls would have to take a backseat to John Ephraim Pascal. Carroll returned to his room at the Barrett-Parrish House where he spent the remainder of the evening learning as much as he could about Evergreen Cemetery.

Walden had told him that, in addition to being named after the famous cemetery in Gettysburg, Pennsylvania, the original Fitzgerald settlers had also used other references to its' namesake. For instance, they had named the lanes between graves in Fitzgerald's Evergreen after roads at Gettysburg. It had a Taneytown Road, Cemetery Ridge Road, Emmitsburg Road and Seminary Ridge Road. Carroll studied the maps and layout. Although he would take the brochures with him, he wanted to be as inconspicuous as possible.

Because it was a bit foggy, he forced himself to wait until 7:30 before going to Evergreen the next morning. There were markers located throughout the cemetery with numbers that corresponded to those on his guide, so he was not as self conscious about having it in his hand. He realized that a cemetery such as this probably had frequent visitors from out of town looking for relatives or just people like him, who were interested in the historical aspects of it.

John Ephraim Pascal was not mentioned in the brochure, so that meant that Carroll was going to have search for his burial plot on foot. He decided to start with the numbered guide, one through twenty-six, hoping that he would locate the Pascal gravesite along the way, buried among them – that is, if he were there as Suzi's research had indicated.

The first marker was for Sgt. John C. Buckley, Company G, 4th West Virginia Infantry. The notation stated that Sergeant Buckley was awarded the Congressional Medal of Honor for "gallantry in the charge of the volunteer storming party" on May 22, 1863 in one of the most famous battles of the Civil War, the Battle of Vicksburg.

The second marker was for Capt. David Timothy Cummins. Captain Cummins served in Company H, 64th Ohio Veteran Volunteer Infantry. Carroll presupposed that Veteran Volunteer Infantry meant that Cummins was a veteran of previous wars.

Carroll was impressed with the details mentioned in the brochures. Several went beyond the typical dates of birth and death and their rank. For instance, the brochure noted that Captain Cummins' family left from Minatare, Nebraska and met up with two other families, the Davises and Twisses in Ft. Scott, Kansas on their way to Georgia. They stopped for six weeks in West Plains, Missouri for the birth of a new daughter into the extended Cummins family. There were also details about what they did after they got to the new Colony City.

Jerome Moss, another resident of Evergreen, served in Company K, 16th Wisconsin Infantry in the Union Army. He was a drummer boy under Sherman. The brochure included a quote from Moss: "I lied about my age to get in, but would have lied 1000 times to get out." He later became an optician in Fitzgerald.

The notation by the entry for W.J. Crawford simply states that he "marched up with Robert E. Lee."

It is highly doubtful that Infantryman J.M. Mosher of Company A, 64th Illinois imagined any future at all while he was a prisoner at the infamous Andersonville Prison, especially one that included staying in South Georgia if he ever got out of Andersonville. Mosher not only survived, he was one of the original settlers of the colony where he founded and operated Fitzgerald Artificial Stone Works, the company that manufactured granitoid from which many of Fitzgerald's beautiful, first homes were constructed. Many of those original first homes still stand, as Carroll recently noticed.

Carroll spent a long while standing at number seven, the grave of the Rev. Joseph Wilmer Turner. He died in 1908, but he must have defied death hundreds of times. Reverend Turner was a confederate soldier in the Virginia Artillery, Leake's Battery under Gen. Robert E. Lee. He fought in some of the most vicious battles of the war including Antietam, the Second Battle of Bull Run and Spotsylvania. No wonder he became a preacher, Carroll thought. Reverend Turner was one of the first to arrive in the colony, when it was known as Shacktown. He immediately founded Saint Matthew's Church and remained its vicar until his death. He performed the first wedding and first funeral in the colony. He served on the school board. Reverend Turner was so beloved by the community that when he died, schools and businesses closed for two full days while his body lay in state.

There was no indication whether or not he was a soldier in either army, but Fred Bingham obviously deserved a place of high respect in the community as he was the lead carpenter for the massive Lee-Grant Hotel which was the largest wooden building in the state of Georgia.

Private Lewis Clute of Company H, 1st Wisconsin Calvary, swore an official affidavit shortly before his death, hoping to dispel the rumor that C.S.A. President Jefferson Davis was wearing a dress at the time that he was captured by the Union Army. The affidavit reads:

"Mr. Davis was plainly seen by him and that the statement he was garbed in female attire was entirely false and without foundation whatsoever."

Number nineteen was the Denmark Family plot. They were related to and part of the group that accompanied Captain Cummins on the trip south. Not long after they had departed, a storm had blown in, and young Charlie Davis had been killed by a lightning bolt in Nebraska. He was buried there along the trail. Mrs. Twiss was knocked unconscious, but she survived.

Henry Bruner, Company M, 1st West Virginia Calvary, became the last surviving Union veteran in Fitzgerald. He died at the ripe old age of 98 on October 30, 1940. He was actually born in Germany and had immigrated to America in 1854.

Another grave that Carroll found particularly interesting was that of Gen. William Joshua Bush. Although the word, General, is carved on his tombstone, he achieved that rank in the years following the war through his work with veterans organizations. Bush enlisted as a private with the 14th Georgia Infantry from Wilkinson County, also known as the Ramah Guards. He fought General Sherman's army at Cross Keys, Atlanta, Milledgeville and Duncan's Old Field. He surrendered to the Union Army at Stephen's Station, Georgia at the end of the war. General Bush was actually the last of Georgia's 368,000 Confederate Veterans when he died on November 11, 1952 at the age of 107.

Of course there were many other tombstones, usually adorned only with a name and date of birth and death and the ranking of the grave's occupant. It was among these that Carroll found John Ephraim Pascal at last. It was unfortunate that he was not included among the more notable people in the brochure. That would have provided more information. Besides his name, the only other engraving on the tombstone was the date of his death, September 29, 1895. There was no date of birth.

While he would have loved to have as much detail about Pascal as the brochure offered on some of the other veterans, Carroll was thankful for what he had discovered. And it was an important discovery. Although he did not yet know how it all connected, it was now evident that Thomas McDowell's death was somehow linked to a man named John Ephraim Pascal who, more than likely, fought for either the Confederacy or the Union Army.

13

Planes: Real and Imagined

Funny how time flies when you're enjoying yourself in a graveyard, Robert Carroll thought. He had been in Evergreen Cemetery for nearly an hour when he finally located the grave of John Ephraim Pascal. He probably would have spent even more time there, but he had made an important decision yesterday. He decided he was going to determine what his goals were for each day, and, after setting them, he would immediately move on as he accomplished each task.

Having achieved his first major objective of this new day, it was now time to move on to the second. He was going to spend some time with Lenny Sauls. He called Ben Walden to see where Lenny might be this time of the morning.

"Well, if Billy Bob was back I would say you should check at his garage, but since he's not, Lenny could be just about anywhere."

Walden gave Carroll directions to the Sauls residence a couple of miles north of Fitzgerald. Carroll knew his way around the community enough by now to bypass going through town. He left the cemetery and turned right onto Benjamin H. Hill Drive which, like the county, was named after the famous Georgia politician of the Civil War era.

In researching the local community, Carroll had also learned a lot about Benjamin H. Hill. Like Philander Fitzgerald, Hill was another historical figure of whom Carroll had never even heard. He found that he liked the guy. Ben Hill was not one who had reacted out of heated emotion from the fiery rhetoric of the day.

While other politicians were either inciting or joining the mob, Hill's was a voice of reason. Unlike most of his peers whose kneejerk reactions did more harm than good, Hill truly had been a thinker who encouraged comity and discourse. He cautioned his fellow Southerners against joining the mad rush to secede from the Union, imploring them to give the newly elected president, Lincoln, an opportunity to work with them to resolve their differences without resorting to all-out war.

It was not as if he was totally against the idea of war. In fact, Hill thought that war was imminent; however, he knew that the South was not yet prepared, and he argued that they could use the delay to properly prepare for the war.

Carroll's phone rang as he was approaching East Central Avenue. He checked the display.

"Hey, Val," he answered.

"Hey, Uncle Bob. Are you where you can talk?" she asked.

"Yeah, I'm on my way to pick up Lenny."

"Are you sitting down?"

"Well, I'm driving, so yeah, I'm sitt– "

"You're taking all of the fun out of it!" Val interrupted. "You're supposed to play along."

"I'm sorry," he said, "Let's start over. Hey Val!"

"Hey, Uncle Bob. Are you sitting down?"

"Wait, hold on," he made some noises that could either be associated with the act of sitting or someone having a minor seizure.

"Okay, go ahead," said Carroll.

"What was that noise?"

"You told me to sit down, so I was sitting down."

"But, you're driving! So, why would you–"

"I will get on a plane and fly up there and hurt you."

"You're so gullible." she laughed.

Val would have prolonged it if possible, but she could not contain herself.

"Laura Luna is in Los Angeles!"

"Are you sure?"

"Well, she was as of the day before yesterday. We've got both credit and debit card activity."

"Do you have an address?" he asked.

"Yep, through her credit card statement."

Anticipating his next question, she quickly added, "I've already contacted the Los Angeles County Sheriff's Department and I really lucked up."

Val explained that she had talked to several people at LCSD as she had gone through the normal protocols that involved putting a multi-agency investigation together. She was eventually put through to the homicide unit of their detective bureau where she found Sgt. Judy Johnson.

There had been an immediate connection between the two female detectives. Both had broken gender and racial boundaries in their respective detective bureaus, although Johnson had done so a couple of decades ahead of Val. Through discussion, they realized they had likely even met, if not formally, at least by being in proximity, as they had attend some of the same training conferences over the last two or three years.

Val gave Sergeant Johnson the background on the murder and the information that she had on Laura Luna.

"That was about 15 minutes ago, so I don't expect anything until probably this afternoon," Val told him.

"That's great news! So, are they just going to grab her if they find her?"

"Depends," answered Val. "Judy said that the address is in an area near the school where USC students live, so she's probably a student there. If she thinks nobody's on to her then she might just be doing her regular thing. If that's the case then we'll consider our options, but if we decide that she's a flight risk, then, yeah, they'll go ahead and grab her."

"Nice work," Carroll replied. "I guess that you know that I'll be on pins and needles here, right?"

"No more than I am," she assured him.

She promised to call him the moment she heard from Sergeant Johnson.

Carroll followed Ben's directions, going north on Bowen's Mill Highway, which was also Georgia State Route 129. He was glad he had accepted Walden's offer to continue with their arrangement in lieu of a rental. Carroll had initially told the McDowells that he was waiving his normal fee and would require only reimbursement of his expenses, but Ruth Jackson's question, asked during their very first meeting, had made him change his mind.

It was not her question exactly; it was the way that she phrased it. If she had asked a more general question such as, what is your normal fee, he probably wouldn't have had a second thought about his response. Or, if she had wanted to know about this specific case, she could have had asked, what are you charging them?" He probably would have also answered that one without thinking about it, but that is not what she had said either.

"How much are you scalping them for?" she had asked.

He remembered it had actually stung at the time. He literally had reached up and felt the back of his neck. And it was that one word that did it.

She had used scalping in the modern sense, as if he were reselling tickets to an entertainment event at a preposterously elevated price for the sole purpose of personal gain. Ruth Jackson was a mother, grandmother, a great grandmother— even a great great great grandmother. She could truly empathize with the McDowells and she honestly wanted to know how someone could profit from such a tragedy and actually be comfortable living with it.

Her question forced him to realize that he was dangerously close to crossing over to the other side. He recalled a conversation with an attorney friend about a big trial, where Carroll asked him in the same honest way, "How can you use the term pro bono without any feeling of guilt when you know that you're going to be benefiting from taking the case?"

"What do you mean?" his friend responded.

"Well, pro bono means for the public good, right?"

"Yes, and I'm not charging him anything for it, so what's your point?"

"Well, let's be honest," Carroll replied, "You're not charging him a fee, but win or lose, you'll be getting a lot of free publicity with this case, and if you do pull it off and manage to win then it's even more valuable to you."

His friend gave him a knowing wink, "Exactly!"

Carroll's point had gone completely over his friend's head. He was doing it for the publicity, not for the public good, The concept of doing something because it was the right thing to do, with absolutely no other motivation, was either alien to him from the beginning, or the line had somewhere become so indistinguishable that crossing it no longer bothered him at all. Carroll never wanted to cross that line. That was why he had made the decision that he would not even ask to be reimbursed for expenses on this case; it was the right thing to do.

That meant that Carroll had to be careful with his spending, so Ben's offer had taken on added significance. He would be saving several weeks in rental fees and he was grateful. Walden still insisted on swapping vehicles for a couple of days, so Carroll was now driving his new Ford pickup.

He took a right on Joshlyn Road and began counting the homes on the left. He was looking for the fifth one. Carroll had not yet met any of Lenny's family, and he felt more comfortable knowing that he would be arriving at their home in a vehicle that was familiar to them.

He slowed down after he passed the fourth residence, anticipating the driveway after the curve. Sadly, the home was pretty much what he expected to find. The house was old, but not historic. Besides needing a good scraping and a few coats of paint, it was in terrible disrepair. The yard was covered with debris and there were six vehicles scattered around the property.

Only one of the six looked as if it might start, but upon closer inspection he saw that they had obviously been mowing around it for months. One vehicle had the hood partially open, another had no hood at all; and, two vehicles were up on cinder blocks.

One car, an old, beat-up rusty Pontiac Trans Am, a Bandit wannabe, was parked or more likely, pushed, under a monstrous oak tree. The engine hung, suspended on a chain, from one of the oak's massive branches.

There were also cats, two on the porch and others sleeping on, in and around the vehicles. Carroll tooted the horn, an action which immediately caused two reactions. He was not sure exactly which occurred first, but barking dogs appeared out of nowhere and everywhere. The cats jumped two feet and exchanged places with the canines, instantly disappearing into the nowheres and everywheres.

Lenny emerged from the house.

"Hey, Mr. Ben!" he yelled upon seeing Walden's truck.

Realizing that it was not Ben, he bent down and squinted.

"Hey, Mr. Carroll!" he yelled, after his eyes adjusted to the morning glare. "Why are you in Mr. Ben's truck?"

"He's letting me borrow it." Carroll replied.

"But, where's your airplane car?" he asked, looking terribly disappointed.

Carroll could not help but grin. He remembered giving Lenny the ride to McDonald's during his first trip. Lenny had said the Ford Escape's interior looked like an airplane. He even made airplane sounds with his mouth during that first ride. As far as Sauls was concerned they had almost been riding in an airplane.

"That wasn't my car," Carroll explained. "It was a rental car."

"Well, what kind of car do you have?"

"I actually have a Land Rover."

"Can we go get it?" he asked.

"It's not in Georgia. It's in Indiana."

"Well, we could drive Ben's truck and go get it," he said, as if Carroll didn't understand the whole concept of go get it.

"It's too far away."

"Is it in Atlanta?"

"No, it's further than that. It's in another state. I have to take a plane to get there. That's why I don't have my Rover."

"You rode in a real airplane?" Lenny asked, his eyes widening. "For real?"

"Yeah, I did."

"Was it fun? Or, were you scared?"

"No, I wasn't scared. I like flying."

"I would like to ride an airplane," he said seriously.

"Have you already been to town today?"

"No, not yet."

"Well, have you had breakfast?" Carroll asked.

"Yeah, I ate early this morning. Mama made breakfast before she went to work."

Not wanting to lose the opportunity, Sauls quickly added, "But I ain't had no lunch though."

"Why don't you tell them that we're going to town then?"

"Ain't nobody here 'cept me," he said, as he opened the passenger door and climbed in.

Then Carroll asked a useless question, "So where do you want to go eat?"

"I like McDonald's," Lenny answered as if they had never even discussed food before.

Carroll headed south, driving through town on Grant Street. He was hoping against hope that Lenny had forgotten something they had discussed during his first ride, but Sauls let him know that in addition to being the size of an elephant, he also had the memory of an elephant.

"Remember you told me I could drive when you came back?" he reminded Carroll.

"Well, that was when it was my vehicle," Carroll explained, attempting to weasel out.

"But you said the airplane car wasn't yours. You said you rented it. You have a red rover."

"Yes, the one that I drove here was a rental. But mine is a Land Rover, not a red rover."

"Land Rover," Lenny repeated, nodding his head. "So why don't you just rent an airplane car again?"

"Well, there's not a place here that rents them," Carroll answered, glad to be off the hook.

"But you can buy'em at the Ford Place," Lenny informed his ignorant chauffer.

"I already have a car. I don't need another one."

"But it's in India," Lenny reminded him.

Carroll decided to let the misnamed venue of his Rover go, saying only, "I'm not rich, Lenny. I can't just buy a vehicle everywhere I go."

"But, they don't know that," he reasoned, "You could just pretend and do what they call a test drive."

Carroll smiled. He should have known better than to make such a promise. He thought about trying to explain about insurance and liability, but he started to get a headache.

"Here we are at McDonald's!" he said thankfully, adding, "I've got to go to the bathroom so let's go inside. Okay?"

Lenny was already disappointed about not getting to drive. Now Carroll was taking away the drive-thru. His frown deepened as they walked into the restaurant. Sauls ordered his standard meal for lunch or supper; three, ten, fifteen and two.

Carroll went to the restroom after telling Lenny to get a booth. He returned shortly to find Sauls nowhere in sight. He checked around a side area where more seats were located, but Lenny was not there either. He stepped outside, but did not see Lenny in any direction.

Carroll's heart was beating faster. He flashbacked to the times when his son wandered away; once at the mall when he was three and then a year later, at Disney World. It was the same feeling, except this time he was missing a kid who was six feet, five inches tall, weighed nearly three hundred pounds and was 34 years-old.

Carroll was dialing Ben when he heard voices coming from behind the building;

"Thanks for the help, Lenny!"

"You're welcome," Sauls shouted.

"No, you can't come through this door," someone explained. "You have to go back around to the front."

"Okay, bye Jake!"

Lenny came around the building from the northwest corner of the restaurant.

"Hey, Mr. Carroll, where's our food?" he asked, evidently concerned Carroll might have eaten it all.

"They haven't brought it out yet. Where were you?"

"I was helping Jake take out the trash."

He held the door for Lenny as they went back inside. Their orders were sitting on counter.

"See?" Carroll said, proving that he had not betrayed Lenny.

They proceeded to a booth where Lenny divided his order into groups on his tray and carefully counted to be sure that he had not been shorted.

They chatted over their meal. In reality, Carroll chatted while Lenny did a lot of nodding and occasionally managed to insert a response between gulps. As Carroll expected, he found out that Billy Bob had indeed quizzed Lenny about what they did during their first ride.

When asked about it, Sauls replied, "He mostly wanted to know what you and me talked about."

Besides wanting to know the content of the conversation, Billy Bob had asked Lenny if he knew where Carroll was from and why he was in Fitzgerald. He had even suggested that he needed to be careful around Carroll, telling Lenny, "You don't know noth'n about that man."

They were back in Ben's truck riding and talking when Carroll noticed a green sign with a plane and an arrow on it. He turned in the direction of the arrow. Carroll was pleasantly surprised when he arrived at the local airport. He expected to find not much more than a dirt or asphalt strip and a windsock. True, it was not Hartsfield International or even comparable to Southwest Georgia Regional in Albany, but the runways were bigger than he had thought they would be. They also had a fairly new terminal and, judging by the number of hangers, apparently more pilots around than he would have thought.

Carroll parked where he thought Lenny might be able to see a plane take off or land, turning the truck around so they could sit on the tailgate. Unfortunately, there was not any flying activity at the time. Lenny constantly scanned the sky for any sign of a plane as they talked.

"So have you always lived here, Lenny?"

"No" he shook his head, "I don't live at the airport. I live on Joshlyn Road," he reminded the ignorant Mr. Carroll.

"Not at the airport.   I meant have you always lived here around Fitzgerald?"

"Yes sir, since I was borned."

Carroll asked him about his hobbies. He found out that besides fishing, Lenny did most of the work on the vehicles at the house. His Uncle Richard, his mama's brother, finds and purchases cheap junky vehicles and Sauls repairs them to where they would at least run. Then they sell them. Lenny was apparently better at it than Carroll realized. He said that he could usually fix one every week or two.

"Except for that Oldsmobile," he said. "I can't get the parts for it no more. Mama told Uncle Richard just to get shed of it!"

He asked Lenny if he gets paid for his work.

"I get half of it and Uncle Richard get's half of it. He said that we usually make twice what he pays for 'em, sometimes a lot more. Mama puts my part in my bank."

Carroll hoped that he meant a real bank and not a piggy bank.

A silver SUV turned off of Ward Road into the terminal parking lot, and Lenny immediately began to jump and wave.

"Do you know who that is, Lenny?" Carroll asked.

"No, but maybe he's gonna fly an airplane."

Seeing a frantically waving man in his mid-30s, the driver stopped.

"What's wrong?" he asked.

"Nothing," Carroll assured him. "He just gets excited about planes," he explained, trying to be sensitive to Lenny's presence.

"Bob Carroll," he said, offering his hand toward the window.

"Alan Sangster, Bob," he replied, accepting the handshake.

Lenny ran up and introduced himself.

"You related?" Alan asked.

"No, we're just friends," Carroll responded without elaboration.

"I haven't been up in a couple of weeks, so I'm just taking it for a spin around the block if Lenny wants to watch."

Lenny suddenly appeared to be concerned.

"Ain't cha worried that a truck or a car might hit one of the wings, Mr. Alan?"

Sangster grinned and looked down at the ground.

"He didn't mean he was going to drive it on the road, Lenny," Carroll explained, "A spin around the block is just a figure of speech. He's going to fly it."

Sangster looked at Carroll and nodded, acknowledging that he understood that Lenny was basically a giant kid. They followed him to his hanger. Alan asked them to wait by the bay door as he entered through the back. Carroll and Lenny soon heard the hum of a motor as the big door began rising, eventually revealing a Piper Seneca. The small twin engine six-seater was not brand new, but it was in beautiful condition.

Lenny was more than thrilled. Carroll was beginning to worry that he might be too excited. He tried to calm him down to keep him from hyperventilating, but Sangster was obviously enjoying Lenny's enthusiasm. Alan let him have a look inside and then he said the words, "Do you want to ride?"

The question caught Carroll completely by surprise. He was momentarily at a loss for words. So was Lenny; however, his response left no doubt that he was ready to go.

He yelled and clapped his hands and emitted a high-pitched, dolphin-like sound that he produced when he inhaled. Carroll had heard a mild version of it before, but it did not compare to what he was hearing now.

Carroll was trying to figure out a way to decline Sangster's invitation without appearing ungrateful or making Lenny hate him for causing him to miss such an opportunity. Carroll was not worried about Alan's flying ability or the condition of the aircraft. His concern was about Lenny. After all, Carroll had not even met his family yet. He wondered what kinds of liable actions Lenny's mother might bring against him if her son had a stroke or heart attack as a direct result of the excitement.

"That's really nice of you Alan, but I don't think—" Carroll began.

Alan, misinterpreting his hesitation, interrupted with, "Oh, no problem at all. I was going up anyway. It won't make much difference."

"Okay, let's go!" Lenny shouted as he ran up to the plane.

There was no going back now. Alan took Lenny through the whole process, patiently explaining the entire preflight procedure. They started with an external inspection.

"Where do I sit?" Lenny asked when they were finished.

The only place that could accommodate Lenny's size was the double seat in the back. Carroll acted as copilot. Sangster and Carroll both offered Lenny a barf bag, but he declined, assuring them, "I don't get sick on any of the rides at Wild Adventures."

They were taxiing out to the runway within minutes. After taking off, Alan circled Fitzgerald, giving Lenny an opportunity to get a good look at his favorite places, including Billy Bob's garage, and, of course, McDonald's. He made three passes over Lenny's house, banking low enough for Lenny to see his mother taking groceries out of her car. Mrs. Sauls certainly did not know why a plane was flying over her house or that her son was excitedly waving from inside, but Lenny swore that she waved back.

Sangster had planned only to take a spin around the block, but it turned into an hour-long ride. Of course, Val called back about halfway through it. Carroll started to text her that he would call her in a few minutes, when Alan, seeing that he had a call, reached over and unplugged Carroll's headphone set from the plane's console, showing him that it would fit his phone.

"Hey, Val," Carroll answered, trying not to shout like Lenny at a drive-thru over the drone of the plane.

"Hey, Uncle Bob," she said. There was a short pause before she asked, "What's that noise?"

"Plane engines. I'm on a small twin engine plane with Lenny."

"Yeah, right."

"No, seriously, we were at the airport watching planes and just got lucky. I've taken some photos."

"Uh huh. Anyway, I just wanted to give you an update. Sergeant Johnson verified that Laura Luna is a student at the University of Southern California and she is in class today."

"That's great news!" he said.

"Judy and I have talked about it and we both believe that Laura probably feels safe now, thinking that no one can track her down on the West Coast."

"I agree," he said, feeling relieved.

"Captain Jay helped worked out something with LCSD on surveillance."

"That's some real nice work Val. No joke!"

"Thanks, Uncle Bob!"

"I'll call you back when we land."

"You're not kidding are you? You're really on a plane?"

"Yep. Talk to you in a bit."

Alan banked the plane around to the west causing Lenny to do one of his sonar squeals. Carroll felt like doing one himself, but he did not speak Dolphinese.

His mind was three time zones away. He knew there was a young woman who had answers to many of his questions who was sitting in a classroom in California. He wished that Alan could just keep going and fly the Piper Seneca to Los Angeles.

Carroll spent the reminder of the flight thinking about what could go wrong with the Laura Luna situation, the worst possibility being that if she got any indication they were on to her she would be gone in a heartbeat. He agreed with Val and Sergeant Johnson in thinking that Luna was a witness rather than a suspect. If they considered her a suspect they would obviously apprehend her immediately. They had more options for the latter.

Surveillance was the best one, especially if they were able to get an order for her phones. He knew that he could have pulled it off if he were still on the job, but he had to keep reminding himself that this was an open homicide investigation and his involvement was limited.

Carroll was almost certain it was Laura Luna who had mailed the clue to the McDowells in an effort to help without having to talk to anyone and expose herself personally. Partly in an effort to occupy his mind with something else, he sent photos from their plane ride to Val, including a couple of an excited Lenny peering out of the window and one where he was waving directly at the camera.

They touched down about 35 minutes after Val's call. Alan was going to the terminal after putting up his plane, so Carroll and Lenny thanked him and jumped into Ben's truck. As soon as he sat down in the truck he called Val.

"Did you get the photos?"

"I did! It is so cool that you were able to do that for him," she said. "He's just a big teddy bear!"

"He is that! Anything new?"

"They were going to see a judge for the order when I talked to her earlier. It sounds good. We're waiting on Sergeant Johnson to call back, but it's almost lunchtime out there so it may be a bit later."

Val told him more about her conversation with Sergeant Johnson as they discussed how to proceed.

He made her promise once again to call him as she received information and before hanging up said, "Hold on, I've got someone with me that I want you to meet when you come down here."

Carroll put the phone on speaker.

"Lenny, do you want to say hello to Val?"

"HEY, VAL!" he screamed, not knowing who Val was.

"Hey Lenny! How are you?"

I'M FINE!

"What?"

"I'M DOING FINE!"

"I'm sorry, but I didn't hear you?"

"I – SAID – I'M – DOING – FINE!"

"What?" she repeated.

Carroll took the phone off speaker.

"You know that I'm going to get you back for this right?" he told her.

"What are you talking about? He's so soft-spoken, I could barely hear him."

He handed the phone to Lenny. He and Val talked from the airport all the way to Lenny's house. Val promised she would meet him if she ever came to Fitzgerald. Carroll waited by the truck while Lenny ran inside to get his mother. He was not sure what kind of reception to expect – being a stranger, who had not only driven her son around town, but had taken him on a plane ride as well.

Mrs. Sauls turned out to be very gracious. Lenny had apparently told her everything that he knew about Carroll which was, basically, "he's helping Mr. Ben at the paper." She was even okay with the unauthorized plane ride and played along when Lenny said, "I saw you waving back at me, Momma!"

"I wondered if you could see me," she told him.

Carroll checked in with Val twice more during the afternoon, but nothing had changed. He was back in his room, pulling up his email when she called again, saying, "Hey Uncle Bob, you're on a conference call so try and act professional, okay?"

"I'll do my best," he promised.

"Captain Stewart's with me in our office," she said, "and we've also got Sgt. Judy Johnson of the Los Angeles County Sheriff's Department with a couple of her people."

"Hi, Bob and Jay," Judy said, "I think I'm going to have to kidnap Val and bring her out to L.A."

"Thank you. I've been trying to get rid of her for two years," said Jay.

They made some more chitchat to get acquainted. Then Jay got down to business.

"Bob, I've talked to Sergeant Johnson several times now. I've told her about your experience and explained that the whole reason that we were able to find out about Laura Luna is because of your work. You've really done a great job putting this together and we all want to keep you in the loop."

"Thanks, Jay. I appreciate that. Speaking of loops, have you contacted the Georgia authorities about Luna?"

"I have. I've spoken with the Special Agent in Charge of the GBI office that's handling the investigation and we're coordinating information with them."

Carroll wondered if Jay had mentioned anything to the GBI's S.A.C. about his trips to Georgia as an unlicensed private investigator there, but he did not want to ask during a conference call. He made a mental note to ask him later.

Sergeant Johnson informed them that she had received approval for the wiretaps, a misleading term nowadays because modern technology obviously allows cell phones to be intercepted wherever they are. She explained that the judge had been reluctant to authorize it at all and said he had limited the surveillance to a short term of only forty-eight hours, with the option to extend it if he was shown results that justified it.

"I know that we're the newest agency to get in on this," said Judy, "but from what we're seeing here, I think we're looking at a witness and not a suspect."

She added, "My suggestion is that you go ahead and get someone out here ASAP. Luna's obviously going to have to be interviewed and we've got an extremely limited amount of time here, especially if that forty-eight hours doesn't yield anything new."

"I don't want to speak above my station here," said Carroll, "but I really believe that Val and Sergeant Johnson should be the primary officers to deal with her, at least at the beginning."

Jay agreed, "She's obviously scared to death already. Val and Laura are only two years apart in age so that should help some."

"Can you come out with her, Jay?" Johnson asked.

"I would love to, but it's impossible for both of us to go right now."

The group discussed the options, and it was decided that Val would fly out, and that she and Sergeant Johnson, both in plain clothes, would make the first contact with Laura Luna, with others in the area serving as backup.

"Bob, is there any way that you could go, too?" Jay asked. "You've been on this longer than anyone else and you've had contact with Billy Bob, the closest thing we've got to a suspect."

Jay wanted to be sure that Sergeant Johnson was okay with his proposal. Carroll was technically a civilian.

"Would that be okay with you, Judy? Bob's technically retired, but he's still certified. We still bring him in on cases here in Indy."

"That's fine on our end." she replied.

Carroll felt like doing one of Lenny's dolphin squeals, but he said, "Let me call Suzi and I'll get back to you," trying to sound calm and professional.

He knew that Laura Luna was the best lead they had and now he would finally meet her in person. He also knew he had Jay to thank for it. He had almost asked to go himself, but it had worked out much better coming from the commander of a detective bureau at Indianapolis PD.

Carroll called Suzi and asked her to contact Val and coordinate their flights, arranging for them to arrive in Los Angeles as closely together as possible. Suzi phoned back to inform him the earliest flight that she could arrange for them was a redeye for the following night. Carroll would arrive in L.A. at 3:30 a.m., and Val would get there an hour later. They would then take a cab to a hotel near the airport and rest for three or four hours. Sergeant Johnson would be picking them up personally.

Carroll broke his normal pattern and asked Suzi to splurge for a seat in business class. He knew he would be restless and the extra space would benefit him as well as the unfortunate person who would have been forced to endure his shuffling in coach. He tried to force himself to relax. He put on one of those blindfolds and listened to music. It actually worked – sort of. He did not actually go to sleep, but he did zone out for awhile.

Carroll arrived at LAX and was able to be at Val's gate when she arrived. They were both pretty wound up, but Val had actually managed to get some real sleep during her flight; so, Carroll suggested they go ahead and get breakfast out of the way.

"How about Waffle House?" Val suggested. "You could even snoop around outside first and watch people through the windows."

"Very funny, but they don't have them here."

"Don't have what, windows?"

"Waffle Houses. They don't have them in Southern California."

"Well, we'll stop and let you peep in some random windows then." she volunteered.

Carroll asked the cabbie to take them to a close place for breakfast but quickly changed his mind. Val had never been to L.A., and it did not look as if she was going to have time to be doing much sightseeing on this trip.

"Just go to any fast-food drive-thru," he told the driver.

"Are you mental?" Val asked. "I've flown all night and you're going to make me eat in the room?"

"No," he said.

Carroll looked at the driver's ID on the dash.

"If it's okay with Raphael, we'll eat while he shows us around town and then I'll take care of whatever's on the meter as well," he said, slipping Raphael a fifty dollar bill.

"Welcome to L.A.!" said Raphael.

Raphael took them through L.A. down Sunset Boulevard, Rodeo Drive and Santa Monica Boulevard. They got out and took some photos at Mann's Chinese Theater and a couple of other places. They still had time to kill so Carroll told him continue on to Santa Monica. Val yelled for Raphael to stop when she saw the Santa Monica Pier. She got out of the cab and put on her ball cap. Then she jogged onto the pier in slow motion with her head lowered. When she got to the end she stopped, looked out at the Pacific Ocean, then turned around to look behind her, and ran back off of the pier.

When she was a few feet off of the pier she stopped and looked at Carroll and Raphael, obviously waiting for a comment.

"Well?" she asked.

"Well what?" shrugged Carroll

"Wasn't it cool?"

"I'm sorry, but I guess that I missed something."

She looked at Raphael.

"Very well done!" he congratulated her. "You looked just like him!"

"Thank you," she said, bowing low before returning to the cab.

"What the hell did I miss?" Carroll finally asked.

"Seriously?" she half-yelled. "Forrest Gump! After Jenny left? At the end of his first run when he decided to turn around and run back until he came to another ocean?"

"Sorry," said Carroll, "I should have known. That was really excellent."

Val flipped him off.

Because he had already confirmed the hotel rooms and was going to have to pay for them anyway, they decided to head to the hotel and use the rooms to freshen up.

Val called him about thirty minutes later.

"Judy's downstairs," she informed him.

"I'll meet you at the elevator."

"She's waiting in the lobby," Val told him as they rode down.

Carroll could never explain it, but he knew a cop can spot another cop a mile away. So it was when they got to the lobby. Carroll pegged Judy Johnson as a cop the second he saw her mingling among the two dozen people.

Of course, she did the same. Even though there were four other people on the same elevator and a dozen more exiting two other elevators Johnson waved to Carroll and Val as they stepped out. She and Val hugged as if they were old friends.

"It's so nice to meet you," Judy told her.

"Yeah, same here. This is Uncle Bob."

"Hey, Uncle Bob," she chuckled, relieving him by greeting him with a handshake instead of a hug.

"Hi, Judy, I really appreciate you doing me this courtesy."

"Oh, it's not a problem at all," she replied, "But if you get maimed or killed then you understand that we don't know you and we'll just dump your body in the La Brea."

"Completely understandable," he replied. "We would do the same, but we don't have tar pits. We just use the White River."

Sergeant Johnson drove them to her office and introduced them to the team she had put together for the effort: AJ, Taylor and Margo, were all plain-clothes detectives. Four uniformed officers would be strategically patrolling the perimeter.

"That's ten of us," Johnson noted. "I would rather be safe than sorry."

They had nearly two hours before Laura Luna would finish her last class for the day. She lived in an apartment just a few blocks west of USC and rode her bike to campus, so it was not like they were facing a high-speed chase.

AJ was the youngest detective. He could easily pass for a student. He would be riding a bike following Luna. Margo would be covering the north side and Taylor would have the south. Carroll and Val would be riding with Johnson who would be parked near Laura's apartment.

The plan was to wait until Laura got off of her bike at her apartment and let Val casually approach her and calmly explain the situation. There would be plenty of help if Luna decided to bolt. They chatted and compared stories to kill time. Carroll thought it was not much different than their old office at Indy PD. In fact, it probably was not much different than any law enforcement agency anywhere.

Sergeant Johnson informed them it was time to go. They wanted to be in place an hour early in case Luna left class ahead of schedule. Judy drove, of course. Carroll was riding shotgun and Val sat behind him. Judy pointed out some landmarks here and there as they traveled to the USC campus. They came in on MLK Jr. Boulevard and took a right onto Vermont, passing the Los Angeles Memorial Sports Arena. She turned left onto Exposition Boulevard and, after a few blocks, took a right onto Raymond Avenue and then pulled the Toyota Highlander to the curb.

She radioed to confirm that everyone was in his assigned position. It was just under one hour before Laura Luna emerged from the building as scheduled.

A.J's voice crackled over the radio, "Stand by. Looks like she's getting ready to leave campus."

There were no 10-4's or Rogers. There was no need. Everyone knew what was expected. Other than AJ, who was following Luna, and Sergeant Johnson, who was in command, the others would transmit only if there was a problem, or if they had an urgent question.

AJ radioed again, "Okay, here we go, boys and girls. She's crossing Vermont."

"Let's do this nice and cool, everyone. Just stay back," Johnson reminded them. "We don't want to spook her."

There was no radio chatter. They all waited quietly.

"She's continuing westbound on 37th," radioed AJ.

"Which 37th, AJ?" said Sergeant Johnson.

"There's more than one?" Carroll asked.

"Yeah, there are three," Judy laughed.

Carroll thought he heard her incorrectly.

"Did you say three?" he asked.

"Yeah, I know it's crazy. There's a West 37th Street, a 37th Place and 37th Drive. I could strangle whoever thought that one up."

"You're kidding!" replied Val. "Are they all in the same area?"

"Yep! They're each one block apart."

She pointed to the cross street just ahead of them. "That's West 37th Drive, and continuing straight ahead, you've got 37th Place next and then, 37th Street."

She radioed AJ for clarification again, "Which 37th is it AJ?"

"Sorry, it's Street. West 37th – Street," he clarified.

That was three blocks north of where they were sitting.

"Looks like she's turning–" said AJ, but his transmission was abruptly cut off.

"I didn't get that, AJ. Which way did she turn?" Judy asked.

They heard brief static over the radio followed AJ's voice, "Oh shit!"

The radio keyed again. They could clearly hear the sounds of a scuffle and AJ grunting.

"Margo and Taylor, get up there!" Johnson ordered.

"I'm on it!" replied Margo.

"I'm only half a block away, Sergeant!" Taylor assured her.

Johnson started the Toyota and had shifted into drive as the radio crackled again;

"He's okay," Taylor informed them. "Everybody hold up. Stay in your positions."

"What happened?" Sergeant Johnson asked.

"I'm replacing AJ behind Luna," Margo informed them. "She's still on her bike. I'm following half a block behind her."

"What the hell happened to AJ?" an irritated Sergeant Johnson asked again.

Taylor keyed his radio to answer, but all they heard was laughter. Then he called again, explaining, "I'm sorry, Sergeant. AJ was attacked – by a dog."

"I'm 10-4," AJ radioed. "I'll need a change of clothes though."

Margo interrupted with, "Luna is turning onto her street. You better scoot, Sergeant!"

Sergeant Johnson whipped the Highlander onto the street. She had to hurry, but she could not come flying down the street. That would frighten Laura for sure. They had originally planned to put Val out far enough ahead so she could be walking down the sidewalk like another student. However, Luna was already getting off of her bike at her apartment, so Judy pulled right up to the curb near her. Val jumped out within a few feet of Luna.

"Thanks for the ride, Aunt Judy!" she adlibbed.

Johnson slowly pulled out as if she were leaving.

"Hey, it's Laura right?" Val said as she walked over to Luna.

"Yeah, are you new here?" Laura asked. She was smiling, still unaware of what was happening.

Val offered her hand.

"I'm Val," she said, as Laura took her hand, she added, "Listen, Laura, everything's okay, but I'm a police officer."

Luna did not even look surprised. She just started crying.

"I'm so sorry!" Laura sobbed. "I didn't know what else to do!"

She had not realized that the SUV was still sitting in the street. Judy and Carroll were now standing behind Val. AJ, Margo and Taylor watched from different positions as two marked Los Angeles County Sheriff's Department patrol cars blocked the street on both ends.

"I wanted to say something, but I was so scared!"

"It's okay," Val reassured her.

"I know I shouldn't have left, but I was afraid that he would kill me, too!" she cried.

"Who, Laura?" Val asked.

"I don't know what his last name is. Thomas just called him, Billy Bob."

14

Chasing Jeff

Knowing that Laura Luna was the last person to see Thomas McDowell alive and hearing her say that he was meeting someone named Billy Bob, was enough to officially name him as a suspect. It was a combination of professionalism and shock that kept Robert Carroll from leaping into the air and yelling, I knew it! Val, on the other hand, was a cucumber cool. She simply glanced up at him and nodded as she informed Laura that she needed to go with them to give an official statement.

Luna agreed. After handing her backpack to Sergeant Johnson, Val accompanied Laura inside the apartment to secure her bike. Judy waited until Luna was seated in the back seat of the Highlander with Val before thanking and dismissing the team of officers over the radio. Then they headed to the office.

It had been predecided that Val and Margo would conduct the interview. Adding Margo, another young female officer, as the required second detective on the interview team was a strategic move, an effort to alleviate some of the tremendous pressure that Luna was expected to be feeling.

As he stood in the adjacent room with Sergeant Johnson, watching through a one-way window, Carroll knew she was about to see another area where Val excelled. One of the most difficult things to do when interviewing a witness in a homicide investigation is to keep them calm and willing to talk after advising them of their Miranda rights. It is intimidating enough to be questioned by a cop, but being on the receiving end of you have the right to remain silent takes it to a whole new level.

In addition to informing Luna of her rights, Val would also have to get her to sign the form saying that she understood and voluntarily waived them before any questions could be asked without an attorney present. That is when witnesses usually clam up. Val carefully and patiently explained the entire procedure to Laura, point by point.

When she was sure that Laura was comfortable, Val pressed a button and began speaking;

"This is Detective Valerie Chow of the Indianapolis Police Department.

Also present is detective Margo Vega of the Los Angeles County Sheriff's Department. The date is Thursday, April 23, 2015 and the time is 12:34 p.m., Pacific Time. We are interviewing Laura Luna in reference to an ongoing multi-jurisdictional investigation into the death of Thomas McDowell III on or about December 19, 2014 in Fitzgerald, Ben Hill County, Georgia. This interview is being conducted at the Los Angeles County Sheriff's Department. It is being videotaped and recorded."

Val asked Laura to give her full name, date of birth, Social Security number and current address. She also asked her about her previous education and verified that she was currently a student at the University of Southern California.

She then placed two Miranda forms on the table, putting one in front of Luna for her to follow along as she read the other. Val had Luna initial each line indicating that she both understood her rights and wished to waive them.

Miranda having been read, understood and waived, it was now time to begin the actual interview. Val asked a few more general questions before she got to the main topic.

"How did you become involved with Thomas McDowell? Did you know him previously?"

"No, not at all," Laura answered. "A friend told me about an ad on a message board at school where someone was looking for a research assistant to do short term work."

Luna went on to explain that this was a week or two before the Thanksgiving holidays. It was perfect for her because she would be out of school from then until the second week in January, it would allow her to do some actual historical research in an area which would be beneficial to her education; and, it would obviously provide some financial income.

The first contact Laura had with McDowell was from an email he sent after her initial response. There were several subsequent emails and phone conversations before they came to a mutual agreement. The initial plan did not include a trip to Georgia for Luna. She was to do the research from her home in California and forward the results to McDowell by email.

"What was the nature of the research that you were asked to do?" Val inquired.

"It was historical research, surrounding the creation of the town of Fitzgerald, Georgia. Thomas lived in Indianapolis. He explained how that city and Fitzgerald, Georgia are connected historically. He said that he was working on a project that would be used partly to celebrate Fitzgerald's 125th Anniversary."

"So, you were working on a project that wouldn't come to fruition for five more years?"

Carroll smiled. Val's question was calculated for affect. She wanted Luna to know that the young police detective who was questioning her had done her homework, too.

It worked. Laura had assumed that she would be questioned by the police at some point, but she had expected it to be a man, someone she thought – more like the older guy who had been standing behind Detective Chow at her apartment earlier. Luna would have never made her out to be a cop, much less an Indianapolis detective who knew that the obscure little town of Fitzgerald, Georgia was incorporated in 1896.

"Yes, I guess so, from Thomas's point of view," she agreed, "but my work was to be completed by the end of January."

"Did he explain anything else about it?" Val asked.

"No, but he didn't really need to. It was pretty basic stuff as far as research goes. However, I found it interesting because I had never even heard about Fitzgerald before."

"Why would a person in Indianapolis look for a research assistant at a California university?" Val wondered. "Surely the educational institutions in Indiana and Georgia could've helped with projects that were connected to their own states? Did you ask him about that?"

"No, it didn't even cross my mind. I just assumed that he had done his homework and wanted the best."

Realizing she had probably come off sounding conceited, Luna quickly added, "I'm not speaking of myself personally. USC is known worldwide as a leader in research. That's why I chose to go there. I was just one of several grad students who applied after seeing the ad. I felt pretty good about it and after a few emails and a couple of phone interviews, I got the job. I just lucked out."

Luna's explanation was unnecessary. Even without a search warrant, Sergeant Johnson and Val had been able to find out quite a bit about their young interviewee. Actually, it was Laura's mother who unknowingly provided most of the details – through her Facebook account.

By first going to Laura's Facebook profile they had found a link to her mother's page. There were posts dating back to 2008 when she first established her Facebook account, apparently to chronicle Laura's academic achievements from her high school days to the present. Mrs. Luna was proud of her daughter. And rightly so. Laura continued to maintain a 4.0 GPA despite being involved in a plethora of extracurricular activities. She was the president of the school's award-winning debate team as well as the student council.

Val appreciated Laura's humbleness, but she knew that Luna did not just luck out. Thomas McDowell had chosen his assistant well.

"Is there anything else about the project that was unusual?" Val asked, casting a wide net.

"Not to start with," Laura responded thoughtfully. "I liked Thomas's enthusiasm. He was very passionate about his project. From our earliest conversations he would say things like, 'We have to bring those people back to life. We have to make those of today understand why those of yesterday would climb on horses and wagons to ride hundreds of miles under harsh conditions, only to live for several more months in an equally harsh environment, as they established a colony in former enemy territory.'"

In the beginning, Luna sent her work to Thomas as planned; however, he later asked if she would be willing to travel to Georgia if he covered all of the expenses and threw in a bonus. McDowell explained that he was spending far too much time in the local library when he should be out doing other things. He reasoned that Luna would not only free him up, but it would allow her to access resources there that were not available online.

Laura did not agree right away, mainly because she wanted to check him out first.

"Working online for someone you've never met is one thing; traveling across the country to meet them in person is another entirely," she pointed out.

In the end she had decided to go. She explained that her professor and a few other people knew Thomas personally and they assured her that he was a good guy who was working on a legitimate project.

There were two factors in her decision to go to Georgia. She was keenly interested in seeing the town that she had been researching, and Thomas had tossed out yet another enticement: The city of Fitzgerald operated a museum. It was full of relics, photographs and documents, none of which were available online.

She had flown into Atlanta during the morning of Wednesday, the 17th, and then on to Albany where McDowell had arranged a rental car for her to drive to Fitzgerald.

"And what happened when you got there?" inquired Val.

"I didn't get to Fitzgerald until about seven and I was pretty beat, so we only met for about thirty minutes. Thomas was very nice and professional, but he seemed to be tired, even more so than me – and he also seemed nervous."

"What made you think he was nervous?"

"I don't know – a couple of things. Like, we heard people walking by on the catwalk a few times. He would get up and go over to look through the peephole or from behind the curtain. He also checked the locks on the door twice. I just thought it was odd."

"So, you met for only about thirty minutes that first night. What was that about?"

"We went over my work. I was telling him about some letters and journals I'd read online. That's when he told me that he had also discovered an old journal with the initials J.E.P. on it and later found the name, John Ephraim Paschal. He asked me if that name had popped up and I told him no. He tried to act like it wasn't a big deal, but I could tell that he was disappointed."

"So it was you?" Val asked, without elaborating.

Luna paused, realizing that she had just opened herself up.

"Yes, I mailed it," she admitted as her eyes teared up. "I wanted to help after– but I–" she tried to continue before she broke down and sobbed.

Val interrupted, "The time is 1:19 p.m.. We are suspending the interview to take a break."

"No," Laura objected. "I want to keep going."

Val and Margo allowed the recordings to continue as they asked Luna once again if she needed a break.

"I want to keep going," she repeated. "The sooner we get back to it, the sooner it'll be over."

Val and Margo exchanged looks. Margo nodded.

"Okay, for the record, we'll continue," said Val.

Sergeant Johnson and Carroll stood watching through the one-sided window as Luna wiped her eyes and nose with tissue, and then gulped from a glass of water.

"She's good, Bob," Judy acknowledged. "I know some of that is natural ability, but Val and I have talked pretty often and she gives you a lot of credit, too."

He had been thinking the same thing. Well, not the last part so much. While Judy Johnson's comment was certainly nice to hear, Carroll expected it was more of the former than the latter, but he also knew that he had had a little something to do with it.

"Thanks, I'm really proud of her," he said, but his eyes were focused on Laura Luna, not Val.

Watching them through the window had convinced him that Luna was neither a suspect nor a conspirator in the murder of Thomas McDowell. He had pretty much felt that way from the beginning, but Carroll knew that you never close that door completely until you are absolutely positively sure. It was her reaction to something that Val said before the interview started that sealed it. Val did not even ask a question. She had made a statement trying to calm Luna down to reassure her:

"We haven't named you as a suspect. You're not under arrest."

"A suspect?" Luna had responded in astonishment.

Her reaction was genuine. While she did have a fear of being arrested, Carroll instantly knew that the thought of being considered a suspect had never even crossed Luna's mind. She was more concerned that she could be charged with some form of obstruction for fleeing Georgia and not giving a statement. An obstruction charge was still possible – but now unlikely.

"About that note that you mailed Laura," Val resumed, "was that your handwriting or Thomas's?"

"Mine," she responded. "I was just making notes so I could do research on him later."

"Did Thomas spell the name for you?"

"No, I just wrote it down myself. Why is that important?"

"We just have to know to confirm hand-writing analysis," Val answered.

It was a half-truth. She threw a knowing look toward her unseen Uncle Bob through the window. During Val's visit to Fitzgerald, Carroll had told her about his revelation on the misspelling of John Ephraim Pascal's last name after recalling the quote from Blaise Pascal. Carroll's theory, just having been proven correct by Luna, was that whoever wrote J.E.P. = John Ephraim Paschal was the person who sent the note. He had further hypothesized that it had been a simple error as whoever it was likely just jotted it down as McDowell dictated it. That was indeed the case.

"What else happened during that first meeting?" Val inquired.

"He told about a woman named, Ruth Jackson. He said that he wanted me to talk to her."

"Did he elaborate on why he wanted you to talk to her? And did he give you any specific instructions?"

"It was mainly because of her age. She's 110, so she's seen a lot," Luna explained, not knowing that the young detective she was addressing had not only met with the centenarian, but was now her "adopted" granddaughter.

Laura continued, "That, and the fact that her father actually worked for Philander Fitzgerald, the man the town is named after. Thomas did say that I should just throw that name – John Ephraim Pascal, into the conversation when we were talking about other people to see if she reacted to it."

"And that's all you covered on that first night?"

"Uh huh. I went to see Mrs. Jackson the next day. I brought the name up, but she didn't remember it at all."

"That was on the eighteenth?"

"Yes, that's correct."

"You mentioned someone named, Billy Bob?" Val reminded her.

"Yes," she replied, before blowing her nose again. "That night, we were–"

"I'm sorry, Laura," Val apologized, "When you say, That night, what night are you talking about?"

"Oh, the eighteenth, the same night," Luna clarified. "We were still talking about my visit with Mrs. Jackson when Thomas got a phone call. I couldn't hear the other person's voice, but Thomas called him Billy Bob twice. When he got off the phone he told me that he had to meet someone who might have information on Pascal."

"What time was that?"

"It was probably around nine or nine-thirty."

"Think back, Laura," Val instructed her. "Did Thomas mention your name to Billy Bob or give any indication that there was someone else in the room with him?"

Luna paused, replaying the one-sided phone call in her head.

"No, it was a brief conversation. Thomas ended our meeting as soon as he got off the phone. He told me that he would call me in the morning. But the sirens woke me up first and people at the hotel told me what happened. I just grabbed my stuff and got out of there!"

Laura broke down and started crying again.

"Okay, why don't we take a break?" said Margo as she rose from her seat. It was clearly not a question or a suggestion this time. She escorted Laura down the hall, showing her where the bathroom and break room were located.

Val waited until they were gone before she walked into the adjoining office where Carroll and Sgt. Judy Johnson waited.

"Nice work, Val!" Sgt. Johnson complimented. "Damn, Bob, I'm gonna have to steal this girl for sure!"

"Good job," he agreed, giving Val a hug. "You covered it well."

"Thanks!" she blushed. "I'm glad I made notes. I almost forgot about the spelling, but it made perfect sense. Thomas never realized that Luna spelled the last name wrong."

"I'm going to contact the GBI. I've been talking to John White, the S.A.C. on the case," Judy informed him. "I'm sure that they'll want to start looking for Billy Bob McCoy immediately," she said, as she headed toward her office.

"Margo and I are going to take Laura home. Do you want to ride, Uncle Bob?" Val asked.

"No, thanks. I'm going to call Suzi and then Ben. He needs to watch his back until they find Billy Bob."

"Okay, I'll be back in a few."

"Don't forget to get that computer info while you're there," he reminded her.

Val wheeled around. "Didn't you just watch me in there? Do you actually think I would forget that?"

He grinned, "You did forget, didn't you?"

"Yeah, I did. Thanks!" she said, holding her index finger in front of her lips in a shhh position. "Don't tell Judy."

After thinking about it, Carroll decided that he should call Walden first. McCoy could be anywhere. Better safe than sorry, he thought as he dialed.

"Hey, man, where the hell are you?" Ben asked.

Sorry, I didn't have time to tell you, but I'm in LA."

"L.A.? Did you find Laura Luna?"

"Not only did we find her, but we just had a great interview with her. That's why I called. Is there any sign of Billy Bob yet?"

"No, why?"

"I don't think he's coming back. He's probably on the run. If he really did go to Seattle, then he could have slipped across the border into Canada, but I'm starting to be doubtful about that whole bike trip scenario."

"You don't believe that he went to Washington?"

"Nope, I think it was just a ruse to give him a helluva head start. He could be in Mexico or even some place in South America by now. Billy Bob called Thomas McDowell while Luna was in his hotel room – just before he was killed."

"Holy shit! What about?"

"To arrange a meeting. We don't know if it was a set up to kill him or a real meeting where something got out of hand and escalated to murder. The good thing is that McCoy probably didn't even know McDowell had someone else in the room."

"If that's the case, then you might be right about Canada or Mexico," Walden concluded. "Is that all?"

"No. You need to watch your ass!" Carroll warned.

"Why?"

"Because I could be wrong. He could still show up."

"Well, that's just great to hear."

"Don't worry; we're notifying the GBI right now, and they'll be looking for him."

"That's good to know. He'll stand out like a sore thumb around Ben Hill County. Anything else?"

"Yeah there is. There wasn't anything in the case report about a journal being found, but has anything been said about that?"

"Like McDowell's Day-Timer or something?"

"No, not his," replied Carroll, "Something historical, with the initials JEP on it?"

"I haven't heard anything like that at all," said Ben. "Wait a minute," he added as his brain kicked into gear, "J.E.P. – Could that be John Ephraim Pascal?"

"The very same. Are you trying to take my job as a detective?"

"Well, I am a journalist, you know."

"There are two possibilities with the journal," noted Carroll, "Either the police have it and they are keeping it quiet due to the evidentiary value, or–"

"The killer took it," Walden concluded.

"Watch your ass! I'll come back as quick as I can."

"Okay! You take care, too, Bob."

Carroll immediately dialed Suzi.

"You two really know how to drive somebody crazy!" she answered. "What's going on?"

"We got Luna. Val really did a fantastic job with the interview."

"That doesn't surprise me at all," she said. "I trained you both very well."

"Yes you did," he admitted.

"It looks like Billy Bob McCoy is our guy. Sergeant Johnson has already notified the Georgia Bureau of Investigation."

"Congratulations. Is there anything that I can do on my end?"

"Why don't you contact the McDowells. Tell them that we located Laura Luna and that she is cooperating, which has led us to a suspect, but don't give them his name or any details."

"That's one call that I'll be glad to make, thanks!"

"One last thing," said Carroll. "Call Jay and give him an update. Then ask him if he needs Val back in Indy. If so, then book her a flight home. And if not, get us both on a flight to Atlanta as soon as possible."

"Okay, give me 30 minutes."

"I'm in a generous mood. I'll give you thirty-five."

"Guess which finger I'm holding up?" Suzi asked.

Sergeant Johnson returned and said that the GBI was putting out a BOLO for Billy Bob McCoy. His truck was still at his shop where it had been sitting for weeks, so he was probably still on his Harley. Carroll was still talking to Judy when Val called his cell phone.

"Is everything okay?" he asked.

"Are you sitting down?"

"Don't even start with your sitting down and standing up bullshit," he told her. "Spit it out!"

"Let me put it this way," she said. "I've got you an early Christmas present!"

"What is it?"

"Laura handed me the CD, then she reached into her backpack and pulled out a jumpdrive!"

"So my Christmas present is that I get the information in two formats. Gee, thanks."

"No, your Christmas present is that the jumpdrive belonged to Thomas McDowell!"

"What's on it? How did she get it?"

"To answer your first stupid question, we won't know what's on it until we look at it, will we?"

"Touché," he responded, giving her the point.

"And on your second question, it was a lucky accident, at least for us. She thought she was picking up her jumpdrive off the table as she was leaving his hotel room, but she grabbed the wrong one.

"How long before you're back here?"

"Margo says about 20 minutes."

They actually made it back in fifteen. They crowded behind Sergeant Johnson's desk as she inserted the jumpdrive into her computer. They were surprised at the number of files it contained. Carroll scanned the list of folders. He recognized several historical names from the cemetery. There was also a folder for Ruth Jackson as well as one on Billy Bob. Carroll wondered if McDowell had never known Billy Bob's last name or if he just omitted it for some reason.

"Where do you want to start? Judy asked.

"How about this," Carroll suggested, "Have you got four spare jumpdrives?"

"Sure. Can you grab them, Margo?"

"Got it," she responded, trotting out of the room.

"Let's put the Ruth Jackson file on one jumpdrive," Carroll said, "John Ephraim Pascal on one, the file on Billy Bob on another and Chasing Jeff on the last jumpdrive."

Margo returned and inserted a jumpdrive into the computer. Sergeant Johnson downloaded and Margo replaced it with another as the process continued.

"Okay, now what?" Judy asked as she completed the task.

"Now we each take a jumpdrive and see if anything stands out," Carroll answered.

"What the hell is Chasing Jeff?" Val asked.

"I have no idea," Carroll admitted, "but it's too interesting to pass up."

"I'll take that one if it's okay?" Margo volunteered.

"Why don't you take the Billy Bob file since you know more about him and have actually met him," Johnson suggested to Carroll. "Okay," he agreed, "Val you get John Ephraim Pascal and that leaves Ruth Jackson for Sgt. Johnson."

Judy directed Val and Carroll to a couple of desks where computers were available. Val inserted her jumpdrive and opened the file.

"Holy shit!" she yelled.

"What?" Carroll asked as he jumped up and ran over to her computer. Margo and Judy did the same.

"He's got subfolders labeled Notes of JEP Journal and Photos of JEP Journal!"

Val opened both folders. Sure enough, one contained detailed notes that McDowell had obviously made about the JEP journal. The other folder had numerous photographs of the actual journal, including photos of individual pages. Carroll stood behind Val looking at the computer screen momentarily before issuing an order;

"OK, new rule," he said, "No more yelling out or I'll be jumping up every two seconds and running over to someone's computer. Let's give it thirty minutes and then stop to compare notes."

They all agreed as they hunkered down at their assigned desks and got to work. Carroll's one and only find was a good one. McDowell had a Word document where he basically just typed notes.

One entry stood out:

Rcvd call 12/18/14 9:22 p.m. from "Billy Bob" Sounds 20's or early 30's. Real country bumpkin! Will call back at 2 a. m.

Not only did this fit with the coroner's estimated time of death, it narrowed the timeline down even more. The coroner estimated that the time of death was between midnight and 5 a.m.. It also pointed to one suspect, Billy Bob McCoy. Carroll suspected that McCoy had called Thomas back at 2 a.m. as planned and then had likely ambushed and murdered him in the parking lot.

It was a major find, but Carroll was greedy for more. So he was disappointed to discover that the Billy Bob file did not contain any new information about him. It appeared that McDowell had simply done a Google search and then used two pay sites, Intelius and PeopleFinders, to search for Billy Bob, but McDowell didn't even have a last name, much less a birthday or Social Security number. He had literally entered Billy Bob Fitzgerald Georgia in the search engine and hoped for a miracle. Of course it had not happened. There were no results.

Carroll changed his strategy, focusing not on what little Thomas McDowell had found about McCoy, but when he did the searches. From the date and times on the saved files, he saw that all of the searches on McCoy were done between the time McDowell received the call that Laura Luna mentioned and 2 a.m., when he was killed.

The detectives gathered in the conference room when the thirty minutes were up. Judy had ordered lunch, so their conversation also included some smacking and one amazingly loud burp from Val. Carroll started by revealing the two main points he had discovered: the first being that McCoy was the probable killer as he had suspected and that the time of death was narrowed.

"I also believe the phone call that Luna heard was the first time that Thomas had any contact with Billy Bob," Carroll told them.

"How do you figure that?" Margo inquired.

"There's nothing mentioning McCoy anywhere until that note," Carroll replied, "but after it, Thomas spent the next couple of hours online trying to find out anything he could about Billy Bob."

Judy reported that she had not found any new information in the Ruth Jackson file, so she had started going through McDowell's original jumpdrive.

Val took her turn, saying, "The entries from John Ephraim Pascal's journal that Thomas seemed to be focusing on were all various dates in May of 1865."

Margo perked up, raising her eyebrows. "1865?" she repeated. "Those are all dates that are also in the Chasing Jeff file. Do we know who Jeff is?"

"Not is, was," Carroll informed her. "Jefferson Davis, the president of the Confederate States of America."

"Oh, come on!" Judy laughed. "you're saying that this homicide is somehow connected to the Civil War?"

Carroll shrugged. "What does the evidence say?" he asked, knowing that an experienced detective would arrive at the same conclusion.

"How the hell did you even know that?" asked Margo.

"He's a real big, geeky nerd when it comes to history," Val explained.

The three ladies proceeded to enjoy a big laugh at his expense.

"Jefferson Davis was captured just nine miles from Fitzgerald," he added, proving to be the real big geeky nerd Val said he was. "But that was on May 10th of 1865, before there was a Fitzgerald,"

"What do you mean before?" Sergeant Johnson asked.

Val jumped in, giving them a brief history lesson of both Fitzgerald and the final days of the Confederacy, accidentally showing she had some nerdy qualities of her own. She explained that when Jefferson Davis was captured in the woods near Irwinville in May, 1865, Fitzgerald did not yet exist.

"The settlers didn't start arriving in what would become the town until 30 years later," Carroll concluded.

"Okay, this is just weird," Judy admitted.

Margo nodded in agreement, "I've worked on some strange cases before, but nothing like this."

Carroll was open to ideas, "So what do we have here?"

"That somebody still hasn't surrendered from the Civil War?" Margo suggested.

"Well, we are talking about the South," he jokingly reminded them, "but this town doesn't hold those old grudges."

"What's the oldest motive in the world for murder?" he asked.

"Theft, to take another's money or possessions," said Johnson.

"Hold on a sec," Val yelled as she ran back to her computer. Carroll, Margo and Judy followed. She backed out of the file and returned to the main folder on John Ephraim Pascal, then clicked on it to bring up the list of subfolders and opened another file, Confederate Treasury

"I've got that same subfolder under Chasing Jeff!" said Margo.

Seeing where they were headed, Judy scoffed, "You can't be serious! Confederate money would've been completely and totally worthless after the war."

"Would Confederate money be worth something today?" asked Margo. "I'm not speaking so much in terms of monetary value but more like as something collectible that would be valuable?"

"Maybe, but you guys are missing the point," Carroll told them.

"Which is?" Val prodded him.

"Jefferson Davis fled south after Robert E. Lee surrendered on April 9, 1865," he reminded her and informed Judy and Margo, "The Confederate capital was in Richmond, Virginia, so their treasury had to be moved as the Union soldiers approached and only part of the treasury was Confederate paper money."

Carroll stopped to see if they had figured it out yet. The big geeky nerd was starting to enjoy himself.

"So what was the other part if it wasn't paper money?" Margo asked scratching her head.

"Silver and gold coins, silver and gold bullion and a chest of silver jewelry."

"Oh, come on! Seriously, Bob?" Sergeant Johnson stammered. "You're bullshitting me, right?"

Carroll responded with a smile and continued, "The problem was that they left in such a hurry that it wasn't actually counted, but it was estimated to be about $10 million in today's value."

"Whoa! Whoa! Whoa!" Margo shouted, putting her arms out to keep her balance as if she were about to topple over.

"You're telling us that there's ten million dollars out there somewhere?" Val asked him.

"No, most of it has been accounted for one way or another." he said, still teasing them.

Val ran up and hit him hard on the shoulder, yelling, "Quit doing that! Just tell us! How much is unaccounted for?"

"At least three," replied Carroll, rubbing his shoulder.

"Three what?" Judy asked.

"Million," he responded nonchalantly.

Margo was now standing motionless with her mouth wide open. Judy was grinning but was shaking her head, either because she thought it a joke or because she finally thought it to be possible.

"Actually, it's three and a half million that's still missing if you want to quibble about numbers."

"I think $500,000 would be something to quibble about," laughed Val.

Judy spoke very slowly and clearly as she asked, "You are saying that this has never been recovered?"

"Nope! It's out there somewhere. Besides that, there's also the chest of jewelry that was never recovered."

Margo was still standing in the same position with her mouth open. Judy gave her a gentle pat on the cheek to bring her back.

"We should go to Georgia!" Val yelled, "All of us! We could be like– The Goonies! Uncle Bob could be Sloth!"

Her comment once again sent the ladies on a laughing binge.

"Is she like this all the time, Bob?" Judy asked him.

"Oh, yeah, she's a real riot," he answered, "Maybe I should arrange for her to do her own TV comedy special as her birthday present. It's coming soon. How old will you be, Val?"

Her laughter evaporated and she flipped him off again.

"Somebody's cell phone is vibrating," Margo reported.

They began to search for their phones as the sound of intermittent vibration continued. Carroll patted his empty pockets.

"It's mine," he said, trotting toward the conference room table.

He checked the screen as he grabbed it, "Hey, Ben, What's up?"

"Billy Bob is back." Walden informed him.

"Do they have him in custody?"

"No," he replied. "No one has actually seen him yet, but I went to the garage; and, the tape has been broken on the corner of the door. I looked through the window and some things had been moved around inside."

"Have you reported this yet?"

"Yeah, I just did. This is all starting to make me very damn nervous, Bob. When are you coming back?"

"Soon! Let me check with Suzi. Just be careful and stay around other people until he's caught."

Carroll disconnected with Walden and called his office.

"I was literally reaching for the phone to call you!" Suzi told him. "Weird, huh?"

"Weird seems to be a good word for today," he acknowledged.

"Okay. First, Jay said that you can keep Val – forever," she chuckled. "Now, how fast do you two want to get out of there? Because I can have you both on a plane tonight."

"Make it tonight," he said immediately.

"Alrighty then! Give me a few minutes."

"Thanks, Suzi."

He told the others about Ben's phone call.

"Val and I are flying out of here tonight," he informed them.

"I should probably check with Jay first," said Val as she pulled out her cell phone.

Carroll shot her a look.

She rolled her eyes, "Oh, of course! You've already done that haven't you? You don't even ask me if I want to go! You just drag me all over the country against my will!"

"So, you don't want to go to Fitzgerald and search for a murderer and treasure?" he asked.

"Well, when you put it that way, sure! Let's go!"

Suzi called back a few minutes later with their flight schedule. Carroll asked Sergeant Johnson if she could arrange a ride to a hotel where they could get some rest first. Then he called Walden again to inform him that they would be coming in tonight.

"I've gotta admit that I'll feel a hell of a lot better when I know that you are back," Ben confessed.

"See you in a few hours," said Carroll. "Like I told you earlier, just be careful."

Carroll and Val managed to get hotel rooms near LAX, but they might as well have stayed at Johnson's office. After downloading the four jump drives onto her work computer, Judy had given them to Carroll, so he and Val both ended up downstairs at the workstation for hotel guests, sitting in two terminals.

"We're looking for two things in these files," Carroll said, "tracking the movements of Jefferson Davis himself and the Confederate treasury. Although they were bound for the same destination, they didn't travel together."

"You don't really believe this treasure stuff, do you?"

"No, this myth has grown over the decades," he said, "but, it looks like whoever killed Thomas McDowell believed it. So we follow the clues that he was following, and maybe we'll find our killer."

Val shook her head in disbelief, "It's just so unreal, following the pursuit of the Confederate president to catch a murderer in the 21st century?"

Carroll had to agree. It was bizarre to say the least.

"Both Davis and the treasury started from the same place, Richmond, Virginia, on the same day," he noted, "but they went by different routes for part of the way and only ended up simultaneously at the same locations a few times."

Val inserted a jump drive and opened up the Chasing Jeff file.

"So, according to this, they left Virginia around midnight on—" she checked the date and continued reading, "April 2, 1865. They left from Richmond on the very last train out and arrived in Danville, Virginia around the middle of the afternoon the next day."

"That would've been on April the third," Carroll noted.

Val reached up and lowered imaginary glasses to glare at him; "Yes, you are correct. It was the third of April. The third usually follows the second."

He smiled and took his turn reading:

"The treasury sat in a guarded railroad car in Danville from April 3rd to the 6th. During this time the treasury clerks exchanged the Confederate paper money for silver coin at a rate of seventy dollars to one dollar."

"With an exchange rate like that it would've been a great time for Yankees to go on a vacation in the South, huh?" Val quipped.

Carroll continued, "Around 6 p.m. on April 6th, an order was issued to move the treasury by rail further south to Charlotte, North Carolina."

Val had abandoned her terminal. She now stood behind him, reading over his shoulder.

"But the train stopped in Greensboro where Major General Joseph E. Johnston, CSA, and his soldiers were paid $1.15 each, a total of $39,000. So we can subtract that amount from the total," she said, jotting down the figure.

"Actually, it's going to be somewhere around $74,000" Carroll told her.

"What are you talking about?"

"See right here?" he pointed. "Another $35,000 was removed to go with President Davis and the Cabinet."

"Listen to this," he continued, reading a quote:

"It was at Greensboro that Davis learned the full details of Appomattox, given in a personal letter from Robert E. Lee, the reading of which left Davis weeping."

"You really love this stuff, huh?"

"Yeah, I do," he confessed. "I'm usually just watching this stuff, as you so eloquently put it, on the History Channel or reading about it in books, but now I've met and talked to a woman who actually knew these people!"

Val returned to the other computer. They continued to compare notes as they opened files on the jumpdrives. The train carrying the treasury arrived in Charlotte on April 8, a full week ahead of President Jefferson. It was stored in the former U.S. Mint, but Capt. William Parker, the officer in charge of guarding it, thought Union troops were closer than they actually were, so he made a decision, on his own initiative, to move it farther south. President Davis' wife, Varina, and her children were already in Charlotte and Captain Parker, fearing that they would be captured, convinced her to join his company for protection.

Jefferson Davis received a telegram on April 15, 1865 informing him that President Lincoln had been assassinated. It was devastating news. He feared that it would provoke an even harsher response from the Union Army. He was right. General Lee had already surrendered to Grant, but now efforts were stepped up to end the war and defeat the remaining troops. They were also determined to capture Davis, offering a $100,000 bounty for him. He finally arrived in Charlotte, N.C. on April 19.

Davis stayed there for six days trying to reorganize; however, he received even more bad news, again by telegram; General Joseph E. Johnston had surrendered what was left of the Confederate Army, some 89,270 soldiers, to General William T. Sherman. It was the final blow. Knowing that he had no army left, Davis left Charlotte on April 26.

Because federal troops were on every other side of him, the only possible avenue of escape for the fleeing ex-president was through Florida. He planned to either secure a boat to escape through the Gulf of Mexico, or to skirt westward, along the coast, but Davis also knew that getting through Georgia would not be easy. Some 13,500 Federal cavalrymen were stationed in Macon, a logistically perfect location for patrolling southeast and south-central Georgia.

Carroll had constructed a timeline of the movements of President Davis with his Cabinet and the treasury caravan, which now included Mrs. Davis and their children

"The treasury was usually a week, sometimes two, ahead of President Davis throughout the evacuation," Carroll pointed out.

Val was no longer poking fun at him about being a history nerd by this point. She was as much into the historical aspect of the research as she was for the investigation.

"Listen to this," she said, shaking her head in amazement, "The weight of the treasury was at nearly 10,000 pounds. From April 8 to May 2, the treasury was loaded then unloaded from train cars to wagons, from wagons to train cars, and from wagons to different storage locations at least eleven different times by the men. That's incredible!"

"So you're not bored with this history stuff anymore?" Carroll asked.

"I was never bored with it and I wasn't making fun of you either," she assured him. "I just knew that you were really enjoying this."

She added, "In fact, we wouldn't be this far along if you weren't such a big old, geeky history nerd."

"I think using both geeky and nerd in the same sentence is being redundant."

"So, now you're giving me English lessons as well as history?"

He hated to burst her bubble about finding a lost treasure, but Carroll pointed out several more legitimate deductions from the treasury where soldiers were paid along the way.

"Yeah, you're right," Val laughed. "They paid soldiers all right. They paid Union soldiers!"

"What are you talking about?" he asked.

"A Union cavalryman, First Lieutenant Joseph Yeoman of the 1st Ohio Cavalry, and twenty of his men were disguised as Confederate Calvary. They were bouncing around all over Georgia and South Carolina, intermingling with the Southern troops looking for Jefferson Davis."

This was news to Robert Carroll. He knew more about the Civil War than the average person, but he had somehow missed this.

She continued, "There was another big payout to soldiers totaling $108,322.90 on May 4th. Soldiers received $26 each and that included Lieutenant Yeoman and his men. And here's the kicker, they also got reward money for the capture of President Davis!"

"Well, I never heard that one before," Carroll admitted.

"I'll confess," Val said, "this is all very interesting. It really is, but do you really think it's going to help us catch Billy Bob, if he's the real killer?"

Carroll was glad to hear Val use the word if when referring to Billy Bob as the murderer. All of the evidence was pointing directly at McCoy, but something was still gnawing at him. He could not put his finger on it, but there was something about Billy Bob that was not right from the start.

Returning to the pursuit of Jeff Davis and the Confederate treasury, Val and Carroll filled in their timeline chart with the last few entries. Jefferson Davis arrived in Washington, Georgia, late on the morning of May 3, only to discover that Varina and the children had left just the day before.

Wanting to catch up to his family, Davis quickly held what would be his last cabinet meeting and ordered Major Raphael Moses to carry $40,000 to Augusta for distribution to returning Confederate soldiers. Davis left the following morning, May 4, in an effort to catch up to his family, just as the wagon train carrying the Confederate treasury arrived in town.

According to records, the treasury was down to $144,700 by this time. Capt. Micajah Clark, whom Davis had appointed C.S.A. Treasurer only hours before, dispensed more than $56,000 to various cabinet members and soldiers.

Captain Clark then sent $86,000, in gold and bullion, to Lt. Cmdr. James Semple. He was supposed to deliver it to Charleston or Savannah to be shipped to a foreign bank for deposit on account of the Confederate Government. Instead, Semple, Edward M. Tidball, an employee of Semple's, and William Howell, President Davis' brother-in-law, divided the loot among themselves and kept it.

Having now completed the treasury portion of their timeline, Carroll and Val concluded tracking the last four days of President Davis' freedom. Jefferson Davis had no idea how close Union soldiers were as he was trying to catch up to his family on May 6. Lt. Col. Henry Harnden of the 1st Wisconsin and 150 of his troops were on patrol between the Ocmulgee and Oconee Rivers on the southeast as Lt. Col. Benjamin Pritchard's 4th Michigan Cavalry was patrolling along the west bank of the Ocmulgee with 300 men.

President Davis finally caught up to his family on the morning of the seventh, but rumors of the Union soldiers also caught up to them. Varina begged her husband to abandon the slow moving wagons for horseback.

He finally relented, but a severe storm blew in on May 8. Between the bad weather and their almost walking-dead horses, they made very little progress.

In fact, the wagon train carrying his family caught up with him late that afternoon at the Ocmulgee River ferry near Abbeville, Georgia. They broke camp just north of Irwinville around 5 p.m. on May 9. Union troops discovered their location during the night, and they were quietly surrounded. After a brief firefight in which as many Union soldiers were accidentally killed when they fired on each as were actually killed by the Rebels, Jefferson Davis was captured at daybreak on May 10, 1865.

Carroll put both of his elbows on the hotel desk and rubbed his forehead.

"What the hell are we missing?" he asked.

"Why do you think that we missed something?" said Val.

"Because Thomas McDowell was going by the exact same information and someone killed him over it."

"But how do you know that for sure?" she asked.

"What do you mean?"

"I mean," she hesitated, trying to build up the courage to say it, "What if you're wrong? I just don't see a connection between any of this and his death."

"It's there. We're just missing it. Remember, Laura said that Thomas was nervous?" Carroll reminded her. "McDowell was onto something and it frightened him. Unfortunately, his fears proved to be well-founded."

Carroll and Val were beginning to go over the files again when his phone vibrated and hers beeped.

"Suzi," Val predicted, beating him to it.

There were only two people who would be sending them simultaneous text messages: Suzi and Captain Stewart. If they had received the messages earlier during the day, it could have been a toss-up as to which one sent it but knowing that it was three hours later back in Indy, they figured it wasn't likely to be Jay.

They checked their phones.

"It's Judy!" Val said in a surprised voice.

They pulled up their messages to find the same one from Judy:

Probably a stupid question, but you did run a search for John Ephraim Pascal on Ancestry.com?

Carroll looked at Val. She shook her head.

"I didn't either," he admitted reluctantly.

"Judy must have searched and found something on Ancestry.com and just assumed that we did, also."

Val went to the website and entered John Ephraim Pascal and the birthday and date of death from his tombstone.

Among the results was a notation:

John Ephraim Pascal, Company E, 15th Mississippi. Assigned to guard detail of President Jefferson Davis. Captured on May 10, 1865 at Irwinville, Georgia.

"Holy shit!" Val yelled, "If Pascal was with Davis then he possibly would have had information about the treasury!"

This history stuff was starting to grow on her.

15

The Return of Billy Bob McCoy

Suzi had taken Carroll's get us booked on a flight to Atlanta as soon as possible, as literal as he had meant it. He knew they had a better possibility of getting a quick flight in the middle of the night. Because ExpressJet flew into Southwest Georgia Regional Airport only during the midmorning and afternoon, he also knew that it was going to necessitate either a layover of several hours or renting a vehicle and driving for at least two. Carroll wanted to get to Fitzgerald as soon as possible, so he chose the latter. They could still be there before daylight.

They arrived at Hartsfield-Jackson International just after 2 a.m.. There was at least one upside of arriving in Atlanta and driving a rental down: He had a wider selection from which to choose.

"When you reserve a rental, make sure it's an airplane car," he had instructed Suzi.

"I guess I've been stuck in the office longer than I thought," she responded. "The last time that I looked the cars were still being driven on the ground."

"A Ford Escape. It's for Lenny," Carroll explained.

"Well, since it's for Lenny then," she said.

He and Val lugged their luggage out to the rental area.

"At least it's blue," he said as he unlocked it.

"I like it," Val said, "You don't?"

"Actually, I do. The last one was red – really red. I felt like I was driving a Red Delicious."

Val opened the driver's door and jumped in. "I'll drive."

"Are you sure? You're not tired?"

"Twenty-nine," she said, pointing to herself. Then, pointing at him, she added "Ninety-nine!"

"You're a bit off on the age there."

"Yeah, I know you're really only 89. I was just fooling around."

"No, I meant on your age, not mine," he replied, settling into the passenger seat.

"I'm still twenty-nine!" she insisted.

"But which birthday are you closer to? Your twenty-ninth or thirtieth?"

"You know, there is such a thing as carrying a joke too far," Val warned.

"Who's joking?" he said, throwing her an overly serious look that made her crack up.

"You'll need to take I-285 east to I-75 South and—"

"Who's driving here?" she interrupted.

"Fine, I'm going to sleep."

He intended it as a joke, but he was soon out like a light. He woke up two hours later.

"Where are we?"

"On Highway 107," she answered.

If they were on Georgia 107, they were only about 20 miles from Fitzgerald.

"Wow, I can't believe that I slept that long. You should've woke me up to take a turn."

"I knew that you needed all of the beauty sleep that you could get."

Carroll chuckled, remembering a similar comment from Aunt Ruth.

It was pushing five o'clock in the morning, so they decided to stay up and work until they got tired.

"Let's get breakfast," he suggested.

"Where's the Waffle House?" she asked.

"There's not one in Fitzgerald, but they've got a Huddle House."

"A Huddle House? So, do we have to wear football shit like shoulder pads and a helmet?" she asked.

"It's a regional franchise that competes with Waffle House for customers."

"Right, because everyone wants to serve drunks in the middle of the night right?" she added sarcastically .

"We're not drunk," he reminded her.

"Speak for yourself, old man. I've been drinking since we left Atlanta," she said, pretending to slur.

Val drove into town and turned left onto Grant Street and then left again into the Huddle House parking lot. They were there for over an hour, eating breakfast and discussing the ramifications of discovering that Pascal had accompanied President Davis on his odyssey from Richmond, Virginia to Irwinville, Georgia.

"Wait a minute! Hold on!" Carroll said. "I just remembered something about another person that's buried in Evergreen Cemetery."

He pulled out his notebook and flipped back several pages

"Here he is. He was a Union soldier. Private Lewis Clute, Company H, 1st Wisconsin Cavalry."

Carroll read his notes out loud, "On hand for the capture of Jefferson Davis, May 10, 1865.

"So," said Val, "We've got a Confederate soldier who was guarding President Jefferson, and a Union soldier who was there for the arrest, living together in the same obscure settlement 30 years later? That can't be a coincidence!"

"Let's see what we can find out about Private Lewis Clute," he suggested, but Val was already typing on her iPad.

"Private Lewis Clute," she reported," Born on December 18, 1842 in Livingston County, New York and died on April 12, 1914 in Fitzgerald, Ben Hill County, Georgia.

She scanned the page and added, "There's a discrepancy about his birthday. The 1900 census of Fitzgerald shows he was born in December of 1836, not '42."

"I don't think that's anything too significant," replied Carroll. "I've run across a lot of errors like that from that period.

"What would be significant," Val offered, "would be to find out more about Clute and Pascal. Do you think that they had some sort of connection before the war?"

"Now you're on the right track," Carroll agreed. "They could've even been related. That war split families apart, so it's certainly a logical possibility. Even if they didn't know each other before the war, they met when Davis was captured at Irwinville."

Carroll suddenly felt too strong hands grab his shoulders from behind.

"What the hell are you doing back in Fitzgerald?" a male voice drawled.

Carroll was about to grab the butter knife when Val jumped up. "Hey, Henry!" she said, giving him a hug.

"Sorry, did I scare ya?" Henry asked, seeing that Carroll looked a little pale.

"No, I'm just tired. You're out early though."

"I'm back on days at Tifton Regional. Headed out now."

"How's our Granny?" Val asked him.

"The same. Mean as a damn snake!" he grinned. "She's gonna wanna see y'all."

"I'll give her time to get up and call her in just a little bit," replied Val.

"Good, I'm run'n a little behind so I'll catch y'all later."

"No, I'm just tired," Val mocked in a deep voice as soon as Henry was outside.

"What? I am tired," Carroll said.

"Yeah, right! You thought it was Billy Bob! I thought you were going to have a heart attack!"

"Don't be silly. He wouldn't risk being seen in a public place right now."

"Uh-huh. You should probably go check your shorts." she advised.

Carroll wasn't about to admit it, but McCoy was the first person he had thought of when he felt those hands. He tried to call Ben, but it went straight to his voicemail. He was momentarily concerned until he realized that it was the day that they published the newspaper, Walden's busiest day. He started to leave a message but decided to send him a text instead:

We're back in town. Let me know as soon as you have some free time, he texted.

Val got up to order them both a second helping of grits just as his cell phone vibrated with a return message from Ben.

Not at work. At ER-Dorminy Medical Center.

Carroll knew that Walden's mother had been sick.

Is it your mom? He texted back.

No, she's fine. I'm the patient, Ben replied.

He stopped Val before she ordered.

"Let's go."

"What's wrong?" she asked.

"I'm not sure, but Ben is at the emergency room at the hospital."

Dorminy Medical Center was on Perry House Road which was not far away so they got their quickly.

"Ben Walden?" Carroll asked the lady at the desk.

She got up and walked through a door. A doctor came out in a couple of minutes.

"Good morning," he said. "Are you related to Mr. Walden?"

"No, we're just good friends and we also work together," Carroll explained.

"I'm Doctor Terrell. He's going to be okay. I'll take you back there."

Val waited in the lobby while the doctor escorted Carroll through the big double doors.

"Was he in an accident?" he asked as they walked.

"No. I'll let him give you the details."

He followed the doctor into an examination room where Ben had obviously just finished getting dressed. His head was bandaged as were several places on his arms.

"What the hell, Ben?"

"Do you still think that I'm just being paranoid?" Walden said, grinning painfully.

"For the record, I never thought that you were paranoid," Carroll corrected him. "What's the old saying? You're not paranoid if they're really after you," he joked.

Ben laughed, an action that caused him to wince in pain.

"I kept telling you to be careful didn't I?" Carroll reminded him.

"And I thought I was," replied Ben.

"Was it Billy Bob?"

"I really hate to sound like your typical dumbass witness, but I really can't say for sure. I never even saw his face."

"So what happened?"

"I worked really late last night and I was walking to the truck when I heard a sound behind me. I started to turn around, but he grabbed me from behind before I knew what was going on."

"Jesus!" Carroll exclaimed.

"Yeah," Ben chuckled. "That's exactly who I was calling, but he didn't show up to help. The guy had a knife in his right hand so I grabbed his arm and just fought like hell!"

Walden said the person was apparently hiding behind a dumpster in the alley. The guy banged Ben's head against the dumpster in an attempt to knock him out – or kill him.

The bandages on his arms covered scuff marks and cuts from where they also hit the wall during the struggle.

"It's weird, but you know what I remembered? That day when Billy Bob jumped on Lenny's back. So I started spinning around and got him off the same way. I hit the panic alarm on my truck and ran back toward the back door of my office. I thought he was dead on my ass. When I got to the back door I fumbled with my keys at the lock, expecting him to grab me again, but I guess the alarm scared him off."

"Is there anything that I can do?" Carroll asked.

He felt as if Ben's injury was his fault.

"Yeah, I could use a ride back to the office."

"You're going back to work?"

"Just for little while. I think it will actually help me to stay busy for a few hours."

"You're probably right," Carroll agreed.

"I'll pull the car around," Val volunteered as Carroll helped Ben into a seat in the lobby of the ER.

They took Walden back to his office. There were a couple of patrol cars parked in the back and a detective was taking photos near the dumpster. If he had been working a case in Indianapolis, Carroll would have introduced himself to the detective. But he was not in Indianapolis. He wasn't even in Indiana. He was in Georgia.

They waited to be sure that Ben made it inside. Not because they were worried about him being attacked. The law enforcement presence would prevent that. Carroll and Val were more concerned that Walden's head injury might cause him to stumble, but he insisted on walking in unassisted.

Carroll checked the time. They were already downtown, so he decided that they should get to work immediately.

"Let's go to the library first," he said.

On the way over he told Val that they needed to check local records for anything on John Ephraim Pascal or Lewis Clute. She would go through old newspaper records while he checked other resources.

Carroll was still most interested in finding out more about Pascal. He knew that he died on May 29, 1895, very shortly after arriving in the new colony, but he did not know how Pascal had died. He was only 29 years old, the same age as Val was now, when his life had ended. He suspected that it was most likely due to an accident or possibly even something more sinister.

By contrast, Clute's life and death were well-documented. Depending on which of the two years of birth that one used, he was either 72 or 78 when he passed away. Either was a respectable age in 1914.

Carroll was so focused on reading that he did not see Val come up behind him. She tapped him lightly on the shoulder and whispered into his ear;

"Guess."

"Guess what?" he whispered back.

"Guess what killed John Ephraim Pascal?"

Using his finger, he motioned for her to come closer.

"I don't know what killed Pascal," he whispered back, "but I know what will kill Valerie Chow if she keeps it up."

"Okay, it was either a falling tree, a pile of logs, an ax or a saw."

He reached toward her throat like he intended to strangle her. She grinned and pointed to the table where she had been working. He walked over to the table and found an old news story.

Local man killed in logging accident

One man was killed and another was hurt on Tuesday morning during a logging operation. John E. Pascal died shortly after the accident, which occurred about two miles west on the property of Robert H. Solomon. William Hargrove was also injured in the accident, but he is expected to survive. Mr. Pascal, a Confederate veteran had only recently arrived in the colony; however, he had already established himself as a reputable member of our community.

The article didn't give the specific details of the accident, but Val was right with her choices of guesses. It certainly could have been any of those things. How unfortunate, Carroll thought. The man had survived some of the bloodiest battles of the war only to die in an accident just as his new life was beginning. He was about to return to his own seat when he glanced back at the article.

"What was Ruth Jackson's maiden name?" he asked Val.

"Um, let me think," she squinted. "I know it started with an S It's on the tip of my tongue."

Carroll pointed the article.

"Holy shit!" Val whisper-shouted, causing a couple of people to look their way, before she covered her own mouth with her hand and sat back down, red-faced.

"That's it, Solomon!" she whispered, this time remembering where she was.

The location, about two miles west, certainly fit the property where the Jackson home now sits.

"Let's go see Aunt Ruth," he said.

They replaced the research material, gathered their things and headed toward the door.

"Did you find everything that you were looking for?" asked a sweet-looking elderly lady.

"Yes ma'am, we did," Carroll replied. "Thank you very much."

"Well come back to visit us again," she said with a pleasant smile.

Then, looking at Val, she added, "Just please remember where you are."

"Thank you," Carroll repeated as Val fled from the building.

"Wasn't she really sweet!" he said as soon as they were outside.

"You're going to have to drive," Val informed him. "I'm not feeling tall enough to see over the steering wheel right now."

Ruth Jackson was sitting on the porch when they arrived. Carroll thought that Henry may have called to tell her that they were back in town, but he could tell by her reaction that she did not know who was pulling into her driveway in the blue SUV. The frown on her face flip-flopped when they emerged from the vehicle.

"Well, what a nice surprise!" she squealed. "I didn't know y'all was back!"

"We just got back in this morning," he told her.

"Well, how's the weather up there?" she asked, referring to Indianapolis.

"Val might be able to tell you a little about that because she was up there for a few days," said Carroll, "but we've actually been in Los Angeles."

"In California? Ain't ya'll something! What were ya'll do'n there?"

Val gave Carroll a look to see if she should give any of the details. He gave her a nod. Ruth Jackson was actually doing a favor by asking the question. He was completely wound up with the recent events: contacting Laura, finding the jumpdrive, the assault on Walden and the discovery about Pascal's death.

His first impulse had been to jump out of the rental car and run up to Aunt Ruth firing questions at her as he bounded up the steps, but he was trying to force himself to wait and do the cordial visit thing first. Her question would definitely speed things up.

She was keenly interested in the details of how they located Laura Luna way out in California. Val told her about the stakeout near her apartment, something that thrilled her, and about the interview.

Carroll mouthed the word, library, to Val.

Taking his cue, Val said, "So, we got into town really early this morning and decided to eat breakfast and – Oh! – we saw Henry there! Then we spent most of the morning at the library doing more research."

"As a matter of fact Aunt Ruth, we found a newspaper article about an accident that mentioned a man named Robert H. Solomon."

"My daddy?" she asked, confirming that it was indeed her father's property.

"Yes ma'am, Val continued. "It happened before you were born, but there was an accident here where a man got killed."

"They was two bad accidents here before I was born," she informed them.

"Two?" asked Carroll.

"Uh huh. Mama and daddy told us about 'em. They happened just a few weeks apart," she said.

"The one that we read about was a logging accident," Carroll informed her.

"That was the second accident. It happened a few weeks after the first one," she corrected them.

"The first one was when my oldest brother, Joseph, wasn't noth'n but a tiny little boy his own self. He always said it was the first memory he ever had."

"What happened, Aunt Ruth?" Carroll prodded.

"First thing they done when they started clearing the land for the house was to dig a well. Daddy was gonna let Joseph help draw up the first bucket of water, but there had been a heavy rain that morn'n and it must've made the ground soft."

"Daddy felt the ground giving way under his feet so throwed Joseph to my uncle just as it caved in. Another man fell first and then daddy fell, too. The dirt was up to his stomach, but the other man was covered up all the way to his neck."

"Your father obviously lived because this happened years before you were born," Carroll said, "but what about the other man?"

"They dug him out. He had a broke leg, but he lived through it– until three weeks later."

"Why did he die?" Val asked. "Did he have internal injuries or did the leg get infected?"

"No. Mama always said that's what was so bad about it. He lived through one thing only to get killed by sump'n else," Aunt Ruth said as she shook her head.

Carroll wanted to be sure that he was hearing this correctly. "Aunt Ruth, are you saying that the man that they dug out with the broken leg was the same one that died in the other accident?"

"Uh huh, that's right. Him and two other men was rope'n down the log wagon when the ropes broke and the logs rolled off on top of him. The other two was able to get out the way, but his broke leg slowed him down."

She pointed a long boney finger, saying, "It happened right over yonder where that big ole rock sits."

"So you're saying that John Pascal, the man who got killed by the logs, was the same man that they dug from the well?" Val asked, also wanting confirmation.

"I never knew what his name was, but if it was in whatever you was read'n, then that was his name. Mama said that was such a nice young man. He was always try'n to help around the house."

It was the first time that Carroll realized how hard life must have been then in the new colony. Up until that moment he had envisioned veterans parading through the new streets while festivals took place in the Corn and Cotton Palace and grand balls and gatherings were held at the Lee-Grant Hotel. His romantic notion of a utopian paradise for the people and the community were further dashed by Aunt Ruth's next statement:

"Most everybody in them early days had stories 'bout sump'n bad that happened to their family."

Aunt Ruth got real quiet for a minute and just rocked back and forth. Carroll was concerned that the memories might have been too depressing for her.

"Dang if'n I ain't hungry!" she said suddenly slapping her knee, dispelling his concerns. "Y'all want some lunch? Betty ain't here, but I can fix sump'n."

"Why don't we take you out to lunch instead?" he suggested.

"Depends on where you think'n bout going," she replied bluntly.

"Where would you like to go?" Val asked her.

"Lemme see," she thought, rubbing her chin. "Today is Turkey and Dressing day at The Sportsman."

Carroll nodded, "That'll work. Do you need to change or get anything?"

"What's wrong with what I got on?"

"Not a thing! You can't improve on a rose," he said, hoping that she had not taken his remark badly.

"A rose!" she scoffed. "You done used that line before," she reminded him. "This was a farm, so I know what bullshit is," she added, but she was grinning. "All I need is my shoes, lessen you think they'll let me eat barefooted?"

"I'll get them, Granny," Val volunteered. "Where are they?"

"Right there by my TV chair in my room," she yelled.

Val returned with her shoes, slippers actually, and helped her put them on as Carroll retrieved the wheelchair. He wheeled her out and helped her onto the back seat of the Ford Escape.

Val was attempting to buckle Aunt Ruth in when she decided that she wanted to "scootch over to the middle where I can see better."

"What kind of car is this, Bobby?" she asked, leaning forward to peer between the seats.

"It's a Ford Escape."

"Daddy's first car was a Ford, too — 'cept they called it a Model T. He ordered it in 1909. Mama said they brought it in on the train with two more just like it for other folks. Daddy still had it when I was born."

Carroll shook his head in disbelief. Henry Ford didn't start producing Model T's until October of 1908 so the Solomons' Model T was among the first ever produced.

"Didn't look noth'n like this though," Aunt Ruth confessed as she continued to inspect the interior. "This looks more like an airplane."

Carroll smiled.

As they entered The Sportsman, it became apparent that the people of Fitzgerald obviously felt the same way about Ruth Jackson that Carroll and Val did. Every man stood when she entered and several people greeted her by name.

They were served promptly, but it seemed as if they would never finish their meal. Every person in the restaurant stopped by to speak to her, either on their way in or out.

"You're like a real celebrity, Granny!" Val pointed out.

"It's just cause I'm so damn old," she acknowledged truthfully. "I recall they used to do General Bush the same way before he died," she added.

"Who was he, Granny?"

"He was the very last Confederate veteran," Carroll interjected, proudly sharing his knowledge. "He died in 1952 at the age of 107."

"We'll ain't it nice of you to remind me of how damn old I am after I just said it! Did ya think I forgot?"

Carroll winced. He had goofed again, but Val could not stand it. She sputtered out sweet tea as she began to laugh. Ruth Jackson quickly joined her. It was only then that Carroll realized that she was playing with him. They finally finished their lunch, but Aunt Ruth insisted that they have dessert.

"You ain't never had banana pudd'n like this," she promised, "...'specially from no restaurant!"

She was right. He was not sure where they put it all, but they consumed copious amounts of the southern delicacy. They had to sit for another 30 minutes just to digest enough to move.

"We got time to ride around a bit?" Aunt Ruth asked as they left the restaurant.

"Sure. Whatever you want," he answered.

Carroll could not have imagined a better afternoon. They rode up and down the streets and avenues of Fitzgerald as Ruth Jackson pointed to houses and buildings, recollecting stories, some that she knew from personal experience and others that she had been told by her parents or family members.

She would say something like, "See that building over yonder? That's where *this happened* or *that happened*."

Some stories were absolutely hilarious while others were terribly heartbreaking, confirming what she had said earlier, that most every founding family had at least one sad story, or several, somewhere in their history.

Carroll's cell phone rang. It was Rosie, another of Ruth Jackson's granddaughters. They had met her at the supper when Val cooked for their family during her first trip. He had left a note on the front door, noting the time they'd left and explaining where she was, with his phone number at the bottom.

He pulled into the R&M Grocery parking area on North Sherman and pressed the button to accept the call.

"Hi, Rosie."

"Hey, Bobby. I just wanted to check. Is everything okay? Judging by the time you put on your note, I must've pulled in just after you left and it's—"

He automatically checked his watch and was astonished to find that they'd been gone for nearly four hours.

"Yes, we're on our way back now. She just wanted to ride around town," he said apologetically.

Carroll put the phone on speaker mode to reassure Rosie that they had not kidnapped her grandmother.

"It's Rosie," he informed Aunt Ruth.

"Y'all check'n up on me like I'm a teenager!" she hollered from the backseat.

"Did you get that?" Carroll asked Rosie.

"Yeah, I did," she laughed. "That's fine. Take your time. Betty's not going to be able to come this evening, so one of us will come spend the night with her tonight."

"Can I do it? Can I stay?" Val asked.

"That's okay with me if it's okay with Granny," Rosie said.

"Me and Val will be just fine!" Aunt Ruth declared.

"Well, all right then," Rosie acknowledged, "Y'all just try to be home by midnight. Me or Betty will be over by eight o'clock. Have fun!"

Carroll pulled out of the parking lot into the westbound lane of Sultana Drive and was preparing to turn left onto Grant Street when he heard yelling.

"Mr. Carroll! Mr. Carroll!"

It might actually be midnight before I get her home at this rate, Carroll thought, as he pulled into the vacant gas station on the right. Lenny came running up behind them. He came around to the driver's window and peered inside. Carroll was not sure if Lenny was more excited to see him or the Escape.

"Did you buy it for down here?" Sauls asked excitedly.

"No, but I rented it just so you could ride in it."

"Can I ride now?" he asked opening the rear door. "Hey, Mrs. Jackson," he said, just noticing the other occupants.

"Hey, Lenny," she replied.

He looked at Val and scratched his forehead. Carroll had planned to introduce her to him during this trip, but he wanted to do it later. Lenny's abrupt appearance required an adjustment.

"Lenny, this is Val. Remember?" said Carroll. "You talked to her on the phone when we had the airplane ride?"

Lenny ran back around to the other side, opened the door and gave Val a hug.

"You said that you would come see me when you came here from India!" he remembered.

"And, here I am!" she said ignoring the fact he had changed her state to another country and her nationality from Chinese-American to Indian.

"Is it okay if we take that ride tomorrow, Lenny?" Carroll asked.

"What time?" he inquired as if he had to schedule it.

"Val and I will pick you up at 9 a.m. and we'll take you to the drive-thru at McDonald's. I'll even let her drive and you can sit up front so you can order for her."

"OKAY!" he nodded satisfactorily. "Bye, y'all!" he waved, slamming the door and resuming his stroll.

"He's so sweet! He's just a big Teddy bear!" Val sighed.

"He's a good boy. He's lucky to be alive at all." Aunt Ruth informed them. "He was dead, but they brought him back."

Carroll turned completely around to look at her.

"Lenny?" he asked.

"Uh huh. They was on a trip going someplace when he was about three or four and he fell into a motel swimming pool. He was under water for almost five minutes before somebody saw him. They pulled him out and did that autoficial recitation on him and brought him back to life."

He and Val both smiled at Aunt Ruth's autoficial recitation, but they let it go.

"He was in a coma for five months before he come out of it. He ain't never really growed up in his head like his body did," she explained. "Doctors said that the only thing that saved him was that it happened in January. They said if the water would've been warmer he'd be dead."

Carroll felt a tinge of guilt. He had just assumed that Lenny was born the way he was – not too bright. He glanced at the rearview mirror to see Lenny waving as they pulled away. Carroll already had a soft spot for the big guy, but Aunt Ruth's story had made it bigger.

He took her straight home and, as it was then mid afternoon: Val decided to stay. Aunt Ruth made Carroll promise to return for supper, saying that she was going to teach Val some more about Southern cooking. He agreed and drove over to the old train depot on North Johnston Street that housed the Blue and Gray Museum.

Carroll had been eager to set aside enough time to be able to spend a couple of hours looking through the museum's artifacts. There were numerous pistols, muskets and bayonets in addition to a surprisingly wide variety of swords and daggers, many of which had actually been used on the field. There were also numerous flags, hats and clothing items from both union and confederate veterans.

He remembered visiting the grave of Sgt. John C. Buckley at Evergreen Cemetery and reading about him receiving the Medal of Honor. It is one thing to read about something and another thing entirely to actually see it, he thought, as he stood there looking at Sgt. Buckley's Medal of Honor displayed in the museum.

In addition to the Civil War related artifacts, there were numerous household items from the period; plates, cups, pots and pans, paintings, decorations as well as things used in daily life around Fitzgerald. One of Carroll's favorite items was the massive mantelpiece from the original Lee-Grant Hotel.

As much as he wanted to see the entire museum, Carroll knew he did not have much time before the museum closed, so he focused on looking through the shelves of notebooks that contained old photos. There were also a number of drafts and sketches, some in great detail, showing the locations of existing creeks and ponds as well as proposed avenues, streets and even parks. He tried to photograph them the best that he could with his cell phone.

Carroll was particularly interested in finding any photos of Lewis Clute or John E. Pascal. He had been thumbing through the notebooks and, although he had not yet found any photos of Clute or Pascal, he did find several of the very first workers laying out the streets of the town. He examined them closely, studying the features of the men. Could one of them be Clute or Pascal?

Carroll was frustrated as he picked through the tenth notebook, but then, on the second to the last page, he saw it – the name, Lewis Clute. He quickly took the notebook to a nearby table for better light. Carroll studied every feature of a man who died long ago. Then he noticed something else. Clute was standing in front of a building that looked strangely familiar. It took him a few minutes to realize that it was the Standard Supply Company on East Central, the same building that Ben had pointed out to him during their very first walk.

Carroll made a mental note of where Clute was standing. He felt an urge to go there, to stand on that exact spot, although he had no idea why. He flipped the last page of the notebook over and saw a photograph of Clute and a younger man. The notation read;

Former adversaries, now friends! Lewis Clute and John Pascal.

There they were – together.

He wrote down the number of the notebook before returning it to its proper place on the shelf. He was about to reach for another notebook when he checked the time. He was going to be late for supper if he stayed longer.

Carroll hurried over to the Jackson House to find that his timing was perfect. They had just finished setting the table when he walked in.

"This was all put in the freezer fresh," Ruth Jackson said as she placed the last dish on the center of the table, "but it ain't the same as cook'n it right out the field. Y'all gonna have to come back during the summer when the vegetables are all fresh."

"I don't think it could get much better than this," Carroll declared as he inspected the table.

There were turnip greens, a squash casserole, field peas, green beans, creamed corn, fried green tomatoes and sweet potato soufflé. It would n0t be until weeks later when he was reminiscing about the meal, that he realized that there had not been any meat. Of course, after finishing supper they had to retire to the porch and cap off the evening with some Jefferson's Select and fine Cuban cigars, something to which Carroll found he was getting accustomed.

"Your cell phone's vibrating, Uncle Bob," Val informed him.

"Who'd be bother'n you this time of night?" asked an irritated Aunt Ruth.

Carroll grabbed his phone from the counter and checked the display before answering, "Hey, Ben. You feeling better?"

"Yeah, as a matter of fact, I am, but I just got a weird letter."

"From who?"

"That's the weird part. I don't know. It came in today's mail, but I just opened it."

"What's it say?" Carroll asked, walking away from the others.

"It's really just a note. Hold on; I'll read it to you," Ben replied. "Billy Bob McCoy is back in town. He will be at the Waffle House by the truck stop at exit 142 on I-75 at 1 a.m.."

"Jesus, Ben! It's already 9:45 now!"

"Yeah, I know. I wish I would've seen it earlier."

"The first thing you've got to do is notify the GBI. Hang up and do it right now! And then call me back!"

Carroll was trying to think of an excuse to leave as he walked back toward the front porch. Val, knowing that something was up, tried to help:

"Are you wimping out on me and Granny?"

"Yeah, I'm pretty stuffed with all that great food!"

"Who was that calling you this late?" Aunt Ruth demanded.

He knew better than to lie, "It was Ben Walden, Aunt Ruth. I'm supposed to meet him early tomorrow and he just wanted to confirm it. I'm going to have to get to bed early."

He did not even have to lie. One o'clock in the morning is early.

"Ben Walden," she repeated, trying to place the name. "Is that Velma's boy?"

"I'm not sure who his mother is."

"Does he work at the newspaper?"

"Yes ma'am, he does."

"Uh-huh. I don't much like that boy, but me and his mama are pretty good friends."

"Why don't you like him, Aunt Ruth?" Carroll asked, hoping that he could help Ben solve his question.

"For one thing he always calls me Miss J! Miss," she emphasized, "Like I'm an old maid that ain't never been married. And I don't much like the J part neither. Makes me sound like I oughtta be rap'n on a music video!"

"And," she added, "he wrote a story 'bout me one time and used the word elderly four times!"

"Wow!" Carroll said trying to sound equally insulted, although, he thought elderly was a mild and fair description of her. After all, if she were made of wood he could have used the word antique. He gave her a peck on the cheek and made an excuse for Val to get away from the porch.

"Do you need your phone charger, Val?"

"Yeah, thanks" she said, jumping from the porch to the ground.

"So, what the hell's going on?" she asked when the coast was clear.

"Ben's got a lead on where Billy Bob will be in a few hours."

"Fantastic!" she said, but then realized that she'd painted herself into a corner and could not go with him.

"Shit! Shit! Shit!" she said, muffling her face into her sleeve.

"I'm glad that I didn't tell you in the library," he joked.

"You knew about this in the library?" she whisper-yelled, reaching over and hitting him – hard.

"I wouldn't have volunteered to spend the damn night!"

"Calm down!" he said, holding his hands up in I surrender position. "I just found out when he called. It's not like I'm doing anything. We're giving it to the GBI. I'll just watch from a safe distance."

"But you'll get to see the bastard handcuffed," she said, nailing his arm again.

"Look, if you want, I'll call Rosie and tell her that we have an emerg–"

Val took another swing at him, but he dodged it.

"I'm not backing out at 10 p.m.! Get the hell out of here!" she said, closing his door for him.

He started the vehicle and began to back out. Val ran up and tapped his window to get him to stop. She opened the door and gave him a prolonged hug.

"Be careful!" she ordered.

He called Ben as soon as he was headed east on Lincoln.

"Did you call the GBI?"

"Yeah, they're all over it. There's no way that Billy Bob's leaving there without handcuffs on."

"Do you want me to pick you up at the Barrett-Parrish House?"

"No, It's late and I don't want to disturb the guests. I'll walk down to the corner of Lee and Central."

"11 o'clock?" Ben asked.

"Will that give us enough time to get there and find a place out of the way?"

"Yeah, more than enough. They told me where to park so we can see without being in their way or being spotted by Billy Bob."

"Okay, I'll see you at eleven."

At least I have my camera and video equipment this time, Carroll thought, as he pulled out a padded backpack and checked the contents. He also verified that the batteries were all charged. He tried to kill time going over the case files, but he was too wired up. Finally, just when he thought he could not stand it any longer, he checked his watch and calculated the walk to meet Ben at the intersection. It was time.

He left the Barrett-Parrish House and walked west on Central toward the intersection of Lee Street. He looked to the right as he approached it, imagining the massive Lee-Grant Hotel looming in front of him instead of the Harvey's Supermarket that now occupied the space.

Carroll reacted instinctively when he heard the unmistakable sounds of a vehicle making a high-speed turn coming from behind him; the screeching tires and the whine of an engine whose driver had his foot on the floor. He casually, but quickly, stepped behind some shrubbery as the vehicle came into view.

It was a Ben Hill County Sheriff's patrol car that passed him. The blue lights were on, but the siren was not, that is, until the driver approached the red traffic light at the intersection. The siren erupted into Yelp mode. Another siren, wailed as a second patrol car came from the south side of town. And then another one came – and another.

Carroll remembered that the Law Enforcement Center was on Appomattox Road on the southwest side of town and guessed the parade of patrol cars was coming from there. An ambulance flew by, with brilliant red LED lights flashing on every conceivable surface, like a noisy, lit up Christmas tree.

Carroll's stomach churned as he thought about the attack on Ben in the alley behind his office. He pulled out his phone to call Walden. It rang once, but he disconnected when he saw Ben's Ford pickup approaching from the east on Central.

"What's going on now?" Carroll asked as he quickly jumped in.

"I'm feeling a lot better," Ben replied. "I just hope that they get that son of a bitch tonight."

"No, I meant with all of the sirens?"

"What are you talking about?" Ben asked.

"There were at least three patrol cars from the sheriff's department, two city cops and an ambulance that came through town just before you got here."

"Which way did they go?"

"North on Sherman."

"Well, I came straight in from my place on 319 and didn't see any crossing from that way. Hop in and we'll ride up have a look around."

Carroll buckled up as Ben popped his console, dug underneath papers, assorted condiments, pens, napkins and other items and pulled out a walkie-talkie-sized police scanner. He plugged it in to the accessory power outlet, formerly known as the cigarette lighter, and touched the button to turn it on. They were immediately bombarded by a blast of radio communications from law enforcement, firefighters and emergency personnel.

One of the best things the then-new Department of Homeland Security did after 9/11 was to standardize radio communications for law enforcement and other emergency agencies throughout the country. Most of them used the Ten Code. Almost anybody knows that 10-4 means okay and 10-33 indicates an emergency, but depending on the agency, some of the numbers mean different things. While 10-4, 10-33, and several others remain universal, many departments have adapted their own versions. This often makes it extremely confusing when multiple agencies come together when responding to a big emergency – like what happened on 9/11.

The ten code that is in use by the majority of local, state and federal law enforcement agencies today is an accepted version; however, the National Incident Management System, which falls under FEMA and the Department of Homeland Security, is encouraging departments to abandon the ten code for plain language.

"I keep it off most of the time because it just gets on my nerves," Ben said as he turned up the volume on the scanner.

Typical of most agencies, the communications Carroll heard on the scanner were the responding units using a combination of plain language and the ten codes. The problem is that many departments, especially those in smaller communities, still cling to the traditional ten code. Carroll had carefully studied the local ten code before making his first trip.

"10-57-PI!" someone said, giving the code for a hit and run accident with injuries.

Carroll heard another all too familiar sound as several officers simultaneously keyed their mikes, talking over each other in excitement. When two or more people try to transmit at the same time it produces noise similar to Jedi fighters twirling their lightsabers.

An alert dispatcher took control saying, "All units, 10-3, 10-33 traffic!"

She was essentially telling them to stop talking, unless you have an urgent message.

After order was restored, a calm older male voice came on and said, "I'm 10-8, 10-76 to 10-57," which translated to I'm in my car on the way to the location of the hit and run.

"Do you know who that was?" he asked Ben.

"Yeah, that was the sheriff."

Not good, Carroll thought. A sheriff would not be coming out this time of night unless something major was going on. There was nothing more for nearly a minute, then, "10-79," came an officer's voice over the radio.

It was a call to have the coroner respond the scene. There was a fatality. Carroll started to get a terrible feeling in his gut. He looked over at Walden.

"It's not him. It's probably an accident," Ben said, but it sounded more like he was trying to convince himself.

The blue lights up ahead indicated that there were more patrol cars at the scene than just those that had passed Carroll earlier. Besides the EMS unit, there was a fire truck as well as several private vehicles with red LED lights flashing, probably volunteer firemen or first responders. Ben grabbed his camera and notepad as he opened his door.

"Coming?" he asked.

Carroll shook his head, "I'll just wait here."

Knowing that the sheriff was on the way, Carroll did not want to overstep on his turf or attract attention to himself. A sheriff of a small rural community would quickly spot a stranger, so Carroll hung back and watched. The flashing blue and red LED lights made it difficult to see exactly what was happening in front of the vehicles, but he could still see Walden pretty well.

Ben was almost up to where the officers and rescue personnel were working on a patient when he stopped walking. He stood there, watching for a few seconds, and then he collapsed to his knees, dropping his head to the ground with his arms over his head. The posture reminded Carroll of when he was in grammar school in the early '60s when they would have those stupid nuclear drills after students watched a film featuring Bert the Turtle showing you how to Duck and Cover!

Robert Carroll knew two things as he watched Ben Walden: He knew that it was Lenny Sauls lying up there on the roadway, and he knew that he was dead. Ben remained cowered on the ground in the same position, doubled over with his arms over his head.

Carroll knew that his friend was hoping that it would shield him from the pain, but Carroll also knew it was a futile effort, just as useless as those stupid Bert the Turtle drills would have been against a nuclear bomb. The duck and cover was not going to help you one way or the other. You were either going to live through it or not.

He started to trot up the street toward Ben, but a deputy had also seen Walden collapse, and, he arrived just before Carroll did.

"You okay, Ben?" the deputy asked, putting a hand under his arm for support.

"I'm alright, Tony. Thanks," he said, even as he fell down again.

Ben finally regained enough strength to stand up with the aid of Tony and Carroll. Walden looked at him and tried to say it, but he could not get it out. He did not have to.

"Are you sure?" Carroll asked.

Ben nodded.

"He's gone," he managed.

16

Carroll in Wonderland

Carroll knew that Ben wanted to get far away from there as quickly as possible, but, his friend was in a unique position. Ben was the local journalist, their guy, from their newspaper, whom they all knew, not one of those news people from Albany. He could get information that could possibly help them with the case.

"I really hate to ask you this, Ben, but do you think you could get closer to some of the law enforcement people and see what you can find out?"

Walden appeared shocked that Carroll could be so unemotional about Lenny's death and ask him to do such a thing, but he quickly came to his senses and realized that not only could he help the case, but he had his own job to do, too.

"Yeah, you're right. Wait on me at the truck," he said.

Ben took a few seconds to compose himself before he started back toward his deputy friend.

It wasn't that Carroll was unemotional. A lifetime of training and experience had automatically kicked in, and he compartmentalized what had just occurred. He would deal with the emotional aspects of Lenny's death later. Carroll kept his attention focused on Ben. He could not allow his eyes to drift to the sheet-covered hulk just beyond him.

"Go ahead, Ben," Carroll silently urged him. "Get up there!"

He knew there was a very brief interval when Walden was more likely to get useful information. It is during those few minutes when they are transitioning from a lifesaving response to a crime scene. There was still time. After that they would not get anything until there was an official statement, that is, unless Ben had some damn good LE contacts, Carroll thought.

He watched as Ben worked his way through the maze of law enforcement and medical personnel, moving from person to person. He could see Ben talking with people, but he could not hear anything from such a distance.

Carroll was also observing the group of law enforcement personnel. Who would it be he wondered? Which one would take control? He imagined if Val was on a scene like this back in Indianapolis. He knew she would be having a stroke right now as she watched people traipsing all over an active crime scene. She would have already been issuing orders and having nonessential folks moved out of the area.

As much as Carroll wanted Ben to get information, he also wanted to be sure that Lenny's killer was caught, and the longer people were allowed to contaminate the crime scene, the more likely they were going to lose good evidence.

An unmarked, black Chevy Suburban pulled up, blue lights flashing. An older man got out. He stood by the SUV, quickly surveying the scene before he started toward the mob, shaking his head as he walked. There he was, Carroll thought. He guessed that it was the sheriff or, if not, he was at least a detective or a commander of some higher rank. Carroll could not hear what the man was saying, but he could imagine it. Pointing to the crowd, he issued orders and the deputies began moving people away. Ben came trotting back to the truck shortly afterward.

"Who's that?" Carroll asked, pointing to the older official.

"That's the sheriff."

Carroll nodded. "That's what I figured."

"So what did they say? Did you get anything?"

"Some," Ben said. "A witness heard it first. They ran outside and saw a truck speeding away – Billy Bob's truck! The son of a bitch even threw out a beer bottle!"

"Please tell me they are treating the bottle as evidence!"

"Yeah, I saw one of the deputies mark it with a tag."

"Do you know who the witness is?"

"Well, I didn't want to ask too many questions, so I just walked around and mostly listened."

Walden pointed to a house with knee-high grass in the yard.

"That house is vacant," he said. "So, unless someone like a homeless person was sleeping in it, I doubt that the witness came from there."

"What about this house?" Carroll asked, indicating the home nearest their truck on the west side of the highway.

"Yeah, that belongs to Mrs. Carolyn Parrish. She's standing in that group with some other neighbors from further down the road. That's her there on the right."

"Is this Mrs. Parrish a reliable witness?"

"What do you mean, reliable?"

"Is she competent? Is she elderly? Is her eyesight good? Does she drink? Does she have any kind of problem that might affect her credibility as a witness?"

"Sorry, Bob. I'm still rattled. Yeah, there's no reason to discredit anything that Mrs. P says. She's only in her 60s and her health is fine. She doesn't wear glasses and she's a teetotaler; doesn't drink at all."

"Okay, next question. Does she have any reason at all to lie about Billy Bob?"

"Not that I know of. She probably doesn't like him very much because of his rough reputation, but I've never heard her say that."

Carroll could see that Ben was starting to come back to reality, but he was still pretty shaky.

"I gotta tell you, Bob, I may get kicked out of the He-Man Club for this, but I've got to admit that I'm scared shitless. You may be used to this kind of stuff, but I sure as hell ain't."

"I've seen a lot of bad things, Ben. You don't ever get used to it – not really. You just deal with it the best way you can."

"So, what do we do now?"

Carroll had already been thinking about that while Walden was still at the scene.

"Have you ever seen Lenny out this late at night?" he asked.

"No, never" Ben replied.

"That's what I thought."

"So, what would make him come out at 11 p.m.?"

"Did he have a cell phone?" Carroll asked.

"No."

"I doubt that anyone would have called their house phone. That would have alerted his family and left a traceable number," Carroll theorized. "So it wasn't a phone call that lured him out. That means that someone had to prearrange a meeting with him."

Ben shook his head, saying, "I don't know. It's hard for me to believe Lenny could keep from blurting that out to his family."

Carroll agreed, but he could see it happening. "It depends on what they told him."

"That still doesn't answer my original question; what do we do now?" Walden wondered.

"I don't see this being happenstance at all – that Billy Bob's back and Lenny is killed?"

Ben agreed, "It could be the main reason the meeting was planned, to report that Lenny has been taken care of."

It was a sobering thought, one that had immediately entered Carroll's mind even as he had watched Ben on the ground.

Walden started the truck. They normally would have headed north on that very road to get to I-75, but because it was now blocked after being declared a crime scene, he turned back toward town. He took a right on a county road to get across to Highway 90 and proceeded toward Interstate 75.

Ben called the number he had been given by one of the GBI agents, putting the phone on speaker for Carroll to hear. They learned that the GBI had already been informed of Lenny's death and that McCoy was the main suspect. As a result, they had brought in more agents and upped their surveillance of the meeting area.

The agent in charge explained that this new development obviously complicated matters. Walden and Carroll would have to stay away from the area entirely. Ben was obviously disappointed as he looked over at his passenger, but Carroll nodded. Of course the GBI was right. The two of them being in the immediate area could jeopardize the entire operation, including the safety of the agents. They could not risk the chance that McCoy might spot them or that they might be confused as suspects by the many law enforcement people who were now converging on the truck stop.

Ben suggested getting off of the interstate at the exit before the truck stop, but Carroll did not like the idea. Billy Bob would also be coming from the south as they were. What if he also turned off there for some reason? They could not take a chance of being seen.

"No, let's go on past it to the exit on the north side," he said.

Walden called the number again to inform the GBI of their decision to wait an exit north. Ben was assured that they would contact them as soon as it was over.

That was almost two hours ago.

Ben wanted to leave. He believed the agents had just placated them to keep them out of the way, but Carroll convinced him to wait. He could not even begin to count the stakeouts he had participated in over his long law enforcement career. He explained that, from his personal experience, it was actually unusual for a stakeout to occur on time. The norm was a delay of thirty minutes to an hour or more. He reminded Ben that even though they had been sitting there for two hours, they had arrived early and the one hour mark was just approaching. There was still hope.

That hope ended after another thirty minutes passed when Ben finally received a phone call from the GBI informing him that they were calling it off. He was told to sit tight and an agent would be by to see them momentarily.

A few minutes later a Dodge pickup approached from the east on the county road, not from I-75, and turned into the parking area. It parked behind them. A second truck, this one a Ford, exited from the interstate and pulled in to join them.

They exited their vehicles. Carroll was impressed. It was doubtful that anyone would have made them out to be law enforcement officers. They got the proper introductions out of the way. The driver of the Dodge was Special Agent George Hampton. His "girlfriend" riding shotgun was Agent

Dawn Matthews. The two men in the Ford were Agent Rodney Hall and S.A.C. John White, the special agent in charge of the regional office. There were other agents and law enforcement officers involved in the stakeout, but these were the key players.

Carroll had been dreading his first meeting with the Georgia authorities. He feared they might hold a grudge for him becoming involved – seeing him as a retired; out-of-state busy body, however, it soon became obvious that his LE friends in the Atlanta area and Jerry Hall at the FBI must have paved the way for him.

He had expected either complete rejection or, at best, indifference, the same attitude that a Southerner might give an annoying gnat – a periodic swishing out of the way. On the contrary, they genuinely appeared to appreciate that Carroll had been able to obtain additional information.

Wanting to keep the good vibes flowing, he suggested that Walden should first give them his statement about the letter as he handed it over to the GBI. Upon first learning about the letter from Ben, Carroll had instructed him on how to secure it to maintain its evidentiary integrity. He and the others listened quietly as Agent Hampton took Ben's statement about receiving the letter. He also asked Walden some questions about the assault on Ben in the alley on the previous night. He was clearly embarrassed about the ordeal – not so much that he was assaulted, but more because of his inability to defend himself. He also seemed frustrated that he could not furnish them with more detailed information about his attacker, but that was typical of an assault, especially one occurring at night in a poorly lit area with the assailant attacking from behind the victim.

John White spoke up after Hampton concluded the impromptu interview.

"Most people probably wouldn't have been able to fight him off. Nice job," he said, giving Ben a literal pat on the back.

The others chimed in with their agreement.

"Thanks," Walden replied.

"As far as your job goes," Agent White continued, "It would be better if we could hold off on a news story until we get McCoy in custody. Can you work with us on that?"

"I get the exclusive?" Ben asked. "Not just other papers, but TV media, too?"

"Not a problem," White assured him.

"Agreed," Ben said, as they shook on it.

Feeling much better about his semi-official status in Georgia, Robert Carroll was now able to participate in the conversation at the grownup's table.

"I don't want to overstep here, but Laura Luna, the woman who was working with the victim, told us about an old journal with the initials J.E.P. on the cover. I'm not asking for any details about the contents, but was it recovered?"

"No," replied White, "the first we heard of it was from your partner, Captain Stewart in Indianapolis."

Carroll appreciated that White didn't evade the question. He also liked the your partner remark as it confirmed they considered him an insider, not a gnat.

"That's what I was afraid of," Carroll frowned, "It means the killer probably took it."

The agents agreed with Carroll's assessment about the missing journal. The group ended up sitting on the tailgates of the two trucks, talking for another hour. Carroll got another morale boost when, just before leaving, the agents gave him cell numbers where he could contact them. He gave them his number as well as Valerie Chow's number.

Carroll and Walden purposely took their time returning to Fitzgerald, arriving in town at six in the morning, just as The Sportsman was opening for the day. Carroll was not one who required much sleep on a normal day and the last three had been anything but normal. That old feeling was back, and he was now running on pure adrenaline.

As one might expect, the normal gossip and political discourse that normally dominated daily discussions throughout the restaurant had been discarded. The death of Lenny Sauls was the one and only topic. When it had occurred just a few hours before, people assumed it was a terrible accident, most likely caused by a drunk driver, but word gets out quickly in a small community. By now everyone knew that not only was it no accident, but Billy Bob McCoy was the main suspect.

As difficult as it was for him, Ben still had a job to do – reporting on what had occurred. He could still do a general story without revealing the details of the investigation that he had been privy to. He told Carroll that he thought it would also be a way for him to help memorialize Lenny. Walden took out his notepad and went from table to table asking people the same two questions:

"Did you know Lenny?" And, "what kind of person was he?"

There was not anyone in town who didn't know of Lenny and most of them actually knew Lenny enough to say something about him. Ben eventually returned and took his seat at the booth. He slid the notepad across the table and spun it around so Carroll could scan the comments.

The responses were all very similar. It sounded more like a young child had died. The word sweet was used over and over. Carroll would have given the same type of answers if he were asked the question:

He was just a big kid.

Lenny was a good boy.

He was always smiling.

Lenny was a gentle soul.

He remembered that just from talking to Lenny on the phone and seeing the photo of him in the plane, Val had decided, "He's just a big teddy bear!"

"Oh, shit!" Carroll exclaimed, "Val's expecting me to pick her up. We were supposed to take Lenny for a ride at 9 a.m.!"

He checked his watch. It was twenty-five minutes to eight.

"Can you run me back to my car, Ben? I've got to get over to Aunt Ruth's before someone else tells them."

"Sure," Walden replied, rising from the booth and grabbing his notepad. "I'll get the check. Meet me at the truck."

Carroll was instantly blinded by the morning sun as he exited the front door of The Sportsman. The glare caused him to accidentally bump into a man who was standing at the newspaper box.

"Excuse me," Carroll said, pointing the blame at the sun.

"No problem," said the man. "You wouldn't happen to have four quarters would you?" he asked, holding up a dollar bill.

"Yeah, I think so," replied Carroll, digging into his pocket.

"Sorry, but I only have three," he apologized after counting.

"That's enough for a paper," the man said, handing him the dollar.

Carroll did not feel right shorting the guy a quarter so he just gave him the change. "Don't worry about it," he said, refusing to take the dollar.

A lone cloud drifted between them and the sun, providing some temporary relief. Carroll's eyes adjusted, enabling him to see the man clearly for the first time.

"No, I insist," the man said, forcing the bill into Carroll's hand. "Thanks a lot," he added as he turned toward the newspaper box.

"Sure thing," Carroll called back as he climbed into Ben's truck.

He heard the sounds of the individual coins falling into the box and then the lid slamming closed as the man got his newspaper. Carroll waited until he had closed the truck door before he looked at the note the man had been folded in the dollar bill:

Lamplighter Pub

Tifton

3:00 PM

Ben climbed in and started the truck. Carroll was about to ask him if he wanted to ride to Tifton, but he decided that Walden had enough pressure on him today. He could tell that Ben was still afraid that Billy Bob might assault him out of nowhere – or, even worse, just walk in firing a gun. Carroll would take Val instead.

Walden dropped him off in front of the Barrett-Parrish House. Carroll went in just long enough to change his shirt and have a quick look in the mirror. He would come back and shower and shave before driving to Tifton. He decided that he would take Val with him.

Carroll climbed the steps to the Jackson's porch and saw that the front door was wide open as usual. The ladies were obviously up. He tapped on the screen door.

"Hold on," Val yelled from down the hall.

He could tell by the way she came bouncing down the hall that she had no idea about what had occurred during the night.

"Since I didn't get a text or a phone call last night, I'm assuming that he didn't show," she said as she unlatched the screen door.

"No, he didn't show."

"Wait until you see the shirt that I bought for Granny," she laughed.

"You two went shopping?"

"No, it's just a t-shirt. I saw it online after my first trip so I ordered it and brought it with me."

He was about to tell her what happened when Aunt Ruth wheeled into the room.

"Did you tell him 'bout my shirt?" she asked.

"I just told him I got you one, but I didn't tell him what it said."

"Well let me stretch it so you can read it," Aunt Ruth said, rising to her feet before they could help her.

She turned around to face Carroll, turned like a model and tugged the bottom down so he could read the large words that covered the entire front:

I Love Jesus ... but I Still Cuss A Little.

"Whatcha think?" she asked.

Maybe it was because of how stressed out he was, but Carroll laughed harder than he normally would have.

"I think that Val may have found the most perfect t-shirt in the world for you."

"Me too!" she agreed. "Betty's gonna fall out when she sees it! She's gonna say, 'A little?'"

"What time is it?" Val asked suddenly. "We've gotta get Lenny."

There was no avoiding it, so Carroll decided to go ahead and get it over with quickly. He was actually surprised that they had not already heard about it.

"Hold on. Have a seat," he said to her.

Aunt Ruth had already plopped back into her wheelchair. Val took the seat beside her. She knew him well enough to know that something was wrong. Knowing that Billy Bob was back and that he was probably the person who had slashed Ben's tires and later assaulted him, Val went with her first instinct.

"Is Ben okay?" she asked.

"Ben is fine," he assured her.

Val's next instinct was that something must have happened to someone in the Jackson family. She imagined that Henry had been in an accident on his way to Tifton this morning; however, she was not about to ask that question. Val was about to take Ruth Jackson's hand when she thought Uncle Bob isn't looking at her; he's looking at me. She also saw that it was after 9 AM and they were late.

"Is it Lenny?"

He nodded.

Aunt Ruth leaned forward in her chair. It was a silent request for more information.

"He got hit by a truck last night."

Ruth Jackson put her hands on her knees and shook her head, "Lord have mercy. That poor sweet child."

Val wiped one solitary tear from her left eye.

He would give Val more details later, but that was all they needed to know right now.

"What about the meeting?" Val asked, now talking in code.

"He didn't show up for it." Carroll answered.

"Was this before or after?" she didn't have to say the words, Lenny got killed.

"The meeting happened after, or what would have been the meeting," he corrected himself.

"So you went on to the place anyway. Were the other people there?"

"Yes, I did meet with them for about an hour and a half and it went very well."

"That's good," she said with a smile, but she wiped more tears.

"You and I have another meeting at three this afternoon with some new people," he told her.

"For two people who ain't from 'round here, damn if ya'll ain't the meet'nest people I ever seen in my life," Aunt Ruth declared.

"Might as well be a church committee!" she added as she spun her chair back toward the kitchen. "Let's get some coffee."

Val laughed and Carroll smiled. Ruth Jackson knew exactly what she was doing. He knew that Tifton, the town where Henry worked, was southwest of Fitzgerald, two counties away. The driving time was no more than 40 minutes, so there was no real rush. He and Val ate lunch with Aunt Ruth and also visited briefly with Betty after her arrival.

Once they were on the road, Carroll gave Val all of the details of the previous night, from start to finish. Then he handed her the note that was wrapped up in the dollar bill.

She read it out loud, "Lamplighter Pub, Tifton, 3 p.m."

"Is this from your GBI friends from last night?"

"No, definitely not," he answered.

"Okay, are you expecting any trouble?"

"No, there will not be any trouble. I know that for sure."

"How do you know?"

"Just trust me," he said.

"It's a pub," he added, "So when we get there I want you to stay in the car for a couple of minutes or so, and then go in and walk to the bar and have a seat like you don't know me."

"What do I need to do?"

"Just be observant. The place is right down the street from a college, so there are students in there all the time. You could even carry a book or something to take notes."

Carroll walked through the front door of the Lamplighter Pub precisely at three o'clock. The man who had given him the note at the newspaper box was already there. He was seated in the far left corner, facing the door with his back to the wall. He gave a nod to Carroll as he entered. Other than a man and woman with two kids at a booth near the front, there were no other people in the restaurant. The man stood up and extended his right hand as Carroll approached the table.

Carroll accepted the handshake with enthusiasm.

"Hey, Jerry!"

"Hey, Bob! I heard about your night. How are you holding up?"

"To tell you the truth, I'm kind of running on autopilot right now. Ask me again later."

"Look, I'm really sorry for the melodrama with the note, but we didn't have much of a choice after what happened last night."

"Yeah, I didn't think that you drove all the way from Atlanta to Fitzgerald just to buy a newspaper."

"Well, you sure played it cool outside of the restaurant," Jerry replied, "I know that it hasn't been that long, but for a minute I thought you didn't even recognize me."

He added, "And then I really got worried, thinking that Lenny's death might be messing with your head?"

"No, I'm okay. You've just got to tell me what I've walked into here, Jerry."

"I will, but you know how things work. We've got to jump through some hoops to keep it straight, okay? You need to read this 3-0-2," he said, sliding a folder across the table.

The FB-302 is the standard form used by all FBI agents to summarize interviews and report on cases. The 302 contains details from the notes taken during the interview and any other pertinent information they deem relevant to their investigation.

By showing Carroll the form, Jerry was clearing the way for his involvement in whatever was going on. Carroll saw that some of the notes on the 302 were about him, although whoever initially wrote it did not have much information. They had his first and last name and a detailed physical description.

He thought he had done a pretty good job of staying under the radar, but the agents had gotten the tag number from the rental vehicle that Carroll had used during his first trip to Fitzgerald. That was how Jerry had become involved.

Val walked into the pub, looking like a student with her backpack slung over her shoulder and went straight to the bar. The position worked out great because Jerry could not see her from his seat against the wall, but Carroll could see her clearly. Val began typing on her phone. Carroll's immediately vibrated on the table.

"Sorry, Jerry, but I need to check it," he said, as he picked up the phone and read the text:

3 cars + a motorhome just pulled into parking lot. Not local tags.

Carroll casually placed the phone back on the table, screen facing down, and smiled at Jerry.

"So, I'm here for a reason. What are you up to?" he asked.

"You know that we're here don't you?" Jerry chuckled. "Is she yours?"

"Who?"

"The student who walked in a couple of minutes ago."

"She's not a CIS employee. She's actually a detective from my old office."

"She's down here from Indy PD?"

"Uh huh, that's Valerie Chow," he replied, smiling broadly.

"Seriously? That's Donnie's kid? Jesus! Am I that old?"

"We both are," Carroll chuckled. "She's a helluva detective. She's handling Indy's end of a homicide investigation. She even conducted an interview of one of the main witnesses in L.A."

"Okay," Hall replied. "Bring her over."

It was another good sign. Carroll motioned for Val to join them. She gave him an Are you sure? look and he nodded.

"Val, this is Agent Jerry Hall, FBI," Carroll told her. "He already knows you."

"Well, I can take that two ways," she joked. "Good or bad?"

285

"It's all good. I know your dad," Hall answered. "And I actually even met you once, but I think that you were wearing diapers at the time."

"She still does," Carroll quipped.

"Bite me," she fired back. "So what's going on?" she asked.

"I'm not sure," Carroll admitted. "But, I think we're about to find out. Aren't we, Jerry?"

Hall took a deep breath as if he was preparing to dive underwater.

"Okay, it will be easier if we include some other people in the conversation," he told them. "Come with me."

They left the pub and followed him to the motorhome that Val texted about. It was basically like a moving house and probably cost about as much, thought Carroll. He saw three men seated in the motorhome as they entered. Two were in their late twenties or early thirties. One was black and one was white. The other man, another black male, was probably in his fifties.

"Bob, this is Lou Ramsey," Hall said, introducing him to the older man. "He's the S.A.C. down here."

Carroll shook hands and introduced Val professionally as he always did in LE meetings; "Detective Valerie Chow, Indianapolis PD."

Jerry turned to introduce the younger white male, who stood up, allowing Carroll to get his first good look at him.

"Oh, come on! You've got to be shitting me Jerry!" Carroll exclaimed, palming his own forehead.

"Sorry, buddy," Hall chuckled.

Robert Carroll felt as if he had walked through the looking glass. It would not have surprised him if a giant rabbit had come out of the bathroom and rushed away after checking his watch screaming, I'm late! I'm late!

Carroll began to get that all too familiar, sinking feeling that he had experienced before when a case completely falls apart. He looked pale.

"Bob, meet Special Agent Nathan Pafford." Jerry said.

"Nate, this is my old buddy, Bob Carroll, one of the best detectives you'll ever meet."

"Yeah, I'm sure that you're really impressed with me," Carroll said sarcastically.

"I am. No joke. I was sure that you were on to me," said Pafford.

Val looked completely lost. She knew something was going on, but she had not put the pieces together yet. Carroll did it for her.

"Agent Pafford, this is "Detective Valerie Chow, Indianapolis PD." he said.

Carroll waited until she was shaking Pafford's hand before he dropped the bomb on her; "Val, this is Special Agent Nathan Pafford – also known as Billy Bob McCoy."

Carroll was proud of her. He knew that her little head was about to explode, but she just smiled and nodded.

The last man stood waiting for Hall to introduce him.

"Bob, this is Special Agent William Mitchell."

Carroll laughed again as he shook Mitchell's hand. He was the man that Carroll described as the black truck driver who was talking on his cell phone outside of the Waffle House that night.

Jerry motioned for Carroll and Val to have a seat.

"Get comfortable. This may take awhile," he warned.

Hall explained the situation, which was basically that Carroll and Val had stumbled into a major FBI undercover operation. As a result, they were unknowingly about to expose Pafford, who was working undercover under the name of Billy Bob McCoy. Pafford had successfully infiltrated a radical hate group that included seventeen high profile targets in twelve states.

Hall informed them that the FBI did not have any targets in Ben Hill County or the surrounding area. In fact, most of Pafford's targets were not even in the state of Georgia. The whole point of establishing the nonexistent Billy Bob McCoy as a resident of Fitzgerald, besides playing into the stereotype of the Southern white redneck, was to have him far from the targets of the investigation. That way, it would be difficult for them to track "Billy Bob" down unless he wanted them to. Pafford was only at the garage enough to make his cover appear legitimate. The rest of the time he was on his bike or in the truck working undercover all over the country.

"Nate is really good," Agent Ramsey informed them. "He's into this group further than we've ever been."

Ramsey said that when Carroll showed up at Billy Bob's garage on that first day, Pafford first thought he was connected to the groups that he is investigating. The assumption was that Carroll was there to verify that he was for real. That is where the 302 on Carroll started. They really did not have anything on that first day, but when Carroll brought the rental car in to be checked, Pafford was able to obtain the tag number and VIN.

It was easy from there. A subsequent search revealed that the Escape was rented by Carroll Investigative Services. Pafford got his name and did a background check. When FBI agents saw that Carroll was an ex Indianapolis detective and had worked with Jerry Hall on several cases, including the famed Little Joey Serico case, they contacted Hall to make sure that Carroll would not blow Pafford's cover if he was informed that his private investigation was jeopardizing the federal case – and, quite possibly, endangering Nathan Pafford's life.

When Carroll left Fitzgerald after his last trip the FBI adopted a wait and see status. There would be no need for further action if he had concluded his work in Ben Hill County, but then, he returned again after the California trip. They had intended to contact Carroll's office and set up a meeting within the next few days to work everything out, but the events of last night obviously had made the situation more urgent.

"We sure as hell didn't see anything like this coming," Hall said.

Although the FBI was not officially involved in the investigation of the murder of Thomas McDowell, the case was obviously beginning to interfere with their undercover operation, so they had quietly checked into the McDowell case.

"I did some nosing around after I found out what you were up to," Jerry reported, "and there's nothing that we can find to suggest that McDowell's murder was anything other than a robbery or a fight."

"So I assume that Billy Bob's motorcycle trip was to get him out of town while you tried to figure out what to do?" Carroll asked.

"Well, that, and I was able to do some more work in Texas," Pafford confirmed. "But, then we got concerned about my cover story in Fitzgerald. The closest I came to Seattle was listening to Nirvana. I've mostly been sitting on my ass in the Atlanta Field office."

"We don't know if his cover is blown or not right now," said Hall. "We don't think so, but we obviously have to be sure before he goes back under."

He added, "You've got to understand that this operation is at a crucial point right now. We certainly don't want to hinder a homicide investigation, but if Nate's cover is blown before we finish, then everything that we've done over the last year and a half is for naught."

"In the meantime, we had to get some of his case-related material for the Atlanta office," Ramsey informed them. "So Nate slipped back into town with the intention of grabbing some items and cutting back out again."

Pafford continued, "Some bad guys were expecting me, as Billy Bob, to be driving his truck to a meeting, so I had to come get it. The plan was for me to get the truck and drive it to Rochelle where we had a semi with an enclosed trailer to hide it in, but when I got to the garage the truck was gone!"

"Nate calls me and says, 'Lou! They stole my damn truck!'" Ramsey laughed.

"Hell, we all laughed about it at first because we thought that it had been stolen by a – you know – a regular thief," Jerry added.

"So I'm literally hiding in the damn woods," Nate told them, "waiting on Lou to call me back, when all hell breaks loose with the sirens. I got one of those feelings, you know? Something told me to just – go! I had just gotten out of the building when the local cops swarmed the place!"

Pafford had called Ramsey while he was still hiding in the woods. Ramsey had several concerns. The first was that Pafford was not known to any local or state law enforcement and that someone might overreact before he had a chance to identify himself. It rarely happened, but undercover agents have been accidentally shot by cops in the past.

The other problem was, if Pafford did reveal his real identity to the local cops and deputies, word was bound to get out sooner or later, and the whole community would eventually know. His undercover status would be blown and their case would be over. So, Pafford waited in the woods while Lou Ramsey called their headquarters in Quantico to report that they had an agent who was possibly in danger.

Lou continued, "I checked an aerial photo and told Nate to hike to a big field just out of town near the intersection of 319 and 107. They sent a chopper from Moody Air Force Base outside of Valdosta to pick him up."

"We grabbed the motorhome and met them at Robins Air Force Base in Warner Robbins below Macon and debriefed Nate as we headed down here to meet with you, Bob," Hall concluded.

"That's when I found out what happened to Lenny," Nate said, "when we met at Robins AFB."

Nate was emotional as he added, "I mean, I loved the guy! He was like my giant little brother."

Ramsey asked a blunt question: "Is there any possibility that the truck was stolen and Lenny happened to be out at the wrong time?"

Carroll shook his head, "No, I believe Ben Walden is right. Somebody lured Lenny out last night. It was no accident. Sauls was murdered."

"Speaking of Walden," Jerry said, "I know he's your friend and I think he's actually a good guy, but we can't have anyone else knowing about this right now. You had to know because of the conflicting investigations and Detective Chow is cleared, but that's it."

"No problem," Carroll replied.

He knew they were right.

"Like I said earlier," Jerry continued, "the FBI isn't involved in this homicide investigation but, if we do accidentally happen to run across some information, we will pass it on to you. The sooner your case is solved the sooner Nate can get back to business as usual."

"Obviously, he can't even peep out the window right now," Lou added.

Jerry sat down across from Carroll, "Why don't you update us on your case up to this point so we know what to look out for?"

"Because if we don't know, then how can we accidentally find anything to help you?" added Lou.

It was one of Suzi's, nudge nudge, wink wink, say no more, moments. They were going to help with the homicide investigation, but it would be totally under the table.

"Have you got your backpack, Val?" Carroll asked.

"Yeah, it's in the car." she said.

He looked at Jerry, "Have you got a computer in this dump?"

"It didn't come as standard equipment," replied Hall, "but we might have added one or two."

Val ran to get the case file. Then they settled in and went over the McDowell case again – and again. They had been going at it for over an hour when Jerry decided to order four pizzas from the Lamplighter Pub.

"Please tell me that this motorhome came with beer, too?" Carroll pleaded.

It didn't, but Carroll solved that by doing a beer run to a grocery store a couple of blocks away.

Even though Suzi had never met or even talked to Lenny, Carroll dreaded telling her what had happened. He had told her so much about Sauls that he knew she felt as if she did know him. He also wanted to tell her about the revelation of who Billy Bob McCoy really was. Carroll called her as he drove to the store.

As expected, Suzi was heartbroken about Lenny, but like Carroll, she had been around this type of work a long time. She had seen it all. So, after giving her a moment for some sniffling and nose honking, Carroll told her about Billy Bob.

"Well, knock me over with a feather!" she said.

"Yeah, that's how I felt. Although, it was more of a baseball bat than a feather," he corrected her. "Val handled it good though, at least as far as they knew. I could tell that she was about to have stroke."

"I can't wait to hear her version," Suzi laughed. "She'll probably say that you were about to have a stroke."

"That might not be far off. This thing has sure knocked the wind out of my sails."

"Listen, if you called to whine, then you better make it red and throw in some cheese and crackers, because I don't have time for your bullshit," Suzi admonished him.

"Wow, thanks for the support!"

"And you can knock off the sarcasm too. You already knew on some level that Billy Bob didn't fit. You told me so yourself. You let people's opinions sway you off course."

"You're right," he admitted.

"Okay, so I found three good things about this whole mess," Carroll decided.

"So?"

"You already said one of 'em. Even though I'm an old cop, my instincts are still pretty damn good. I just need to follow them more."

"Excellent! Number two?"

"Well, by accidentally stumbling onto the FBI case, it's brought them on board. Not officially, of course, but they're going to be providing me with some help and even resources, on a limited basis."

"And the last one?" Suzi inquired.

"This can be good for Val. This case will probably open some doors for her. It's her first big multijurisdictional investigation. She could change her career path with this thing if she wants to."

"Bite your tongue! Are you trying to get her to leave Indy PD?"

"No, of course not. But, she should know that she has choices – like the opportunity to go to Los Angeles or to the FBI, if she's interested."

He added, "I know Judy Johnson, at the Los Angeles County Sheriff's Department, wasn't kidding when she said that she would steal her. And a young attractive Chinese agent who has a helluva brain? The FBI would roll out a red carpet for her!"

"You're right." Suzi confessed. "You can mention it to her, but don't do it with too much enthusiasm."

"Okay, how about this? You could go to LA, Val, but you need to know that it's probably going to fall into the Pacific Ocean after an earthquake any day now."

"Very good! I like how you handled that," Suzi complimented.

"Or, what if I said, Val, you can go to the FBI and make damn good money, have an excellent retirement plan and travel all over the country, maybe even the world, but you might get jet lag sometimes."

"You need to work on that last one," said Suzi.

"You think so?"

"Well, I'm proud of you! You went from a whiney little girlie-man to optimism! I'm just going to have to start calling you Optimist Man! I'll get you some bright red leotards and top and sew a big O on the chest and you can wear a blue cape!"

"Guess which finger I'm holding up?" he said, stealing her line.

"Probably your right index finger – because it's on the way to your nose."

"Dammit! Why can't I think of comebacks like that?"

"Call me if I can help from here."

"Thanks."

Carroll made a mental note to bring up the career thing with Val when he had a chance. He then decided to call Ben and make sure that he was okay while he had the opportunity, but he did not mention where he was. They had been chatting for a few minutes when Walden delivered a zinger:

"Lenny's mother called me looking for you."

Carroll got a queasy feeling in his stomach. He was glad he had not eaten any pizza yet. It might have come back up. He suspected Mrs. Sauls blamed him for Lenny's death and he did not know if he was ready to take the abuse that was probably going to be coming his way, even though he understood it.

"Oh man," Carroll sighed. "She probably wants to kill me!"

He winced, immediately regretting using those words.

"No, you don't understand," Ben corrected him. "She wants you to be a pallbearer at his funeral."

Carroll was stunned. He was glad that he was sitting in Ben's jeep. He sat there trying to comprehend what was happening.

"Are you there Bob?"

"Yeah, yeah I'm here. I'm just shocked that she would ask me. When is it?"

"Yeah, I know. She asked me to be one, too. She's going to call me back. I'll get the details and let you know."

"Okay. Thank you, Ben."

"Take care, buddy!"

Carroll returned to the motor home, rejoining what had started as a meeting but had now become a throng. They had gone from formal introductions to working comrades to friends within less than two hours. It was no longer Agent Mitchell, Agent Pafford or Detective Chow. They had quickly moved on to using first names during the first thirty minutes and they progressed from there, going from Valerie, Nathan or William, to Val, Nate and Will.

The younger guys even followed Val's lead when Carroll reentered the motorhome and she asked, "Hey, Uncle Bob, did you get beer?"

"Yeah, Uncle Bob! Where's the beer?" echoed Nathan Billy Bob McCoy Pafford.

"You can't bring it out of the restaurant unless you're going into their courtyard area," he explained.

"What kind of bullshit is that?" Val yelled, instantly sending the guys into roaring laughter.

"We need to get you in the Bureau, working undercover," Nate said. "You're a natural!"

There it is, Carroll thought, the confirmation that she fits right in. Like he had told Suzi, they would roll out a red carpet for Val.

Jerry returned to the motorhome balancing the four pizzas in his arms. The conversation was intermittent for the next few minutes as they sampled each pizza. It was another thirty minutes before they got back into the case.

During that time Carroll had been able to clear up some things and he also impressed the young agents when he answered a question that Val asked Pafford.

She looked at Nate, "Lenny said Billy Bob beat the hell out of a black guy while someone named James videoed it? What the hell was that about?"

Carroll interrupted before Pafford could answer.

"Can I take a shot at that, Nate?" he asked.

"Sure," he answered, eager to know if Carroll had figured it out.

"I'm thinking that James is one of your targets," Carroll began, "but he's just a rung on the ladder. He was there as a witness to watch and record the proof that you're a real badass. The real target at the top of the ladder is whomever James is giving the video to."

Jerry Hall started smiling as Carroll continued; "You were expected to find a suitable, random victim to beat the shit out of, except you didn't just happen upon any random victim."

He turned and looked at Will, "Your random victim was fellow agent, William Mitchell. You guys probably rehearsed that beating like two Hollywood stuntmen."

"We might have rehearsed it, but I had bruises from that damn thing for a month," said Will with a grin, confirming Carroll's hypothesis.

"Nice work, Uncle Bob," Nate conceded.

"I'm also thinking that everyone I saw outside of the Waffle House that night was an agent, right?" Carroll asked.

Nate nodded, "Yep, you already know that Will was on one phone. The others – the woman in the car and the other guy on the phone were agents, too."

"The guy sitting across from me at the booth was an undercover agent with me, but the other dude with James at the booth is a bad guy," Nate informed him.

"I was in the back of the tractor-trailer rig behind you." Lou clarified. "We don't know how the hell you found the meeting, but we almost had a stroke when you showed up."

Carroll confessed that it was totally by accident. They talked a little while longer, but it was almost 6 p.m., so Lou wrapped it up. Before disbanding, everyone exchanged cards and phone numbers. Lou said he would try to arrange another meeting in a few days.

"So?" Carroll asked Val, as they got into the Escape.

"So, other than me having a damn heart attack when you said the name, Billy Bob, and my brain being like scrambled eggs right now, I think it turned out rather well."

He started to bring up the you can change your whole career thing right then, but he decided it was not the right time. Val was still running on adrenaline and that conversation needed to take place in a different atmosphere.

If the revelation that Billy Bob McCoy was really FBI agent Nathan Pafford did not put their investigation back on square one, it sure put them on the second one. Val was in a good mood despite the setback, and Carroll hated to spoil it by bringing up Lenny. However, he realized he needed to find a suit for the funeral, and there was a mall just a few blocks away.

"I'm sorry to bring this up, Val, but I talked to Ben while I was outside, and Lenny's mother wants me to be a pallbearer in his funeral."

"Why would you hate to bring that up? Yeah, it's sad, but it shows that she must believe that you were good for him. You did say, yes, right?"

He nodded, "I just meant that I need to go try and find a suit. There's a mall nearby."

"No problem," she replied. "You can try stuff on and I'll criticize it."

"I think that you meant critique."

"No, I didn't," she grinned.

A phone rang.

"Mine or yours?"

"Mine" she said, digging out her cell phone.

"Hey, Betty," she answered. Val listened and then said, "Hold on a second Betty."

"Aunt Ruth asked if we're coming for supper," she told him.

"Do you want to go?"

Val just looked at him like that was the most idiotic question that he ever could have asked her.

"Yes, thank you," she replied, deciding for them both. "We've got one stop and then we'll be on the way from Tifton."

"How are we going to eat more food after having just eaten pizza?" he asked after she hung up.

"Just? That was almost an hour ago!" she responded, implying that it was his second idiotic question in a row.

Val was right. He expected that he would have to fake eating supper, but he somehow managed up a healthy appetite. The Jackson ladies had another surprise for them.

"How much longer are y'all gonna be here on this trip?" Aunt Ruth asked.

"I'm not sure, Aunt Ruth. We actually had a minor setback today."

"Minor?" Val blurted out. "And the Grand Canyon is a ditch."

Carroll kicked her under the table.

"The reason that she's asking is that we've talked about it, and we would like to invite you to stay here," Betty explained.

"No, we couldn't do that," replied Carroll. "It's a very generous offer, but the Barrett-Parrish House is very nice."

Val returned the under-the-table kick, both as payback and also for his refusal of their offer.

"I'll only charge y'all half of whatever they are," said Aunt Ruth.

"She's just kidding," Betty said.

"The hell I am!" Aunt Ruth shot back, but she was grinning.

"We sometimes have to be in and out pretty late," he explained.

"Well, you know how to turn a damn key don't you?" Aunt Ruth shot back sarcastically.

Betty insisted again, reminding them that she and her grandmother only used the downstairs area. The bedrooms, bathroom and sitting room upstairs were almost never used. It would be very similar to what they were used to at the Barrett-Parrish House.

"We would love to accept your gracious offer," said Val, deciding for them both again.

They were on the porch, enjoying their evening drinks and cigars when Ruth Jackson brought up Lenny.

"Betty, did you find out when that Sauls boy's funeral was gonna be?"

"No ma'am, they haven't announced the details yet."

"Well, be sure to find out. 'Cause I wanna go. I was think'n bout that boy today. We was some of the last people that spoke to him while he was on this earth."

Carroll felt a pang in his heart. He took a sip of whiskey to keep from getting choked up. He knew that someone had talked to Lenny Sauls after they did, and he would give anything to know exactly who did actually talk to Lenny last – because whoever it was is likely to be the one who killed him.

"Uncle Bob will be able to tell you when the funeral is," said Val. "They asked him to be a pallbearer."

Betty looked surprised, "They did?"

Carroll simply nodded.

"Come on over here a minute," Aunt Ruth commanded, motioning for him.

Carroll did as ordered, "Yes ma'am?"

"Lean down here," she said, giving him a peck on the cheek when he was in reach. "I'm proud of you!"

"That's very nice, Bobby," Betty agreed. "Seems like you already meant a lot to that boy."

Carroll had to admit that he was certainly getting attached to both the community and the people in it. Having accepted their invitation to stay there was making them both feel like they were part of her family now for real.

Val and Carroll decided she would start immediately, while he would go back to the Barrett-Parrish for one more night. He would make the transition tomorrow. She said she would go with him to get her bags.

"Stay here and relax," he said. "I'll grab your stuff and bring it back in a few minutes."

Carroll called Ben as he was on his way to the Barrett-Parrish.

"Just checking in," Carroll said when Walden answered.

"Thanks, Bob, but I'm okay. We had a big family supper at my mom's. My brother and his family are here from out of town."

"That sounds nice."

"Yeah, it was. It got my mind off of stuff – at least for a little while. So, I'm letting them stay with my mom tonight and I'm just getting to the hotel now."

"Hotel? What are you talking about Ben?"

"Listen, Bob. It's embarrassing and my family doesn't know it, but I've been staying in town since the thing happened at my office. You've seen where I live, Bob. I don't have a neighbor for a mile on either side!" he said, no longer attempting to hide his fear.

"I'm sorry, Ben," said Carroll, "I had no idea that you were having such a hard time."

Walden chuckled, "I told my mother that I was having headaches, but my head is fine. I'm just scared shitless, if you want to know the truth."

"Have you already got your place for tonight?"

"No, I'm just pulling in now, but I'm sure they've got vacancies."

"Don't do that. Come on over and stay at the Barrett-Parrish."

"Look, I know that we've gotten pretty close in a short time, but I just don't think of you in that way."

"You should know that I don't take rejection well," Carroll pouted.

"All joking aside," he resumed. " Val's staying at the Jacksons', so you can have her room. What do you say?"

"A free room at the Barrett-Parrish? Well, let me think about that for three-tenths of a second," he pondered, "I guess I could, if you insist. Are you on your way there now?"

"Yep, half a block away." said Carroll.

"All right. I'll be there in five minutes."

That was another thing Carroll liked about Fitzgerald. You could answer almost anyone with I'll be there in five minutes and still arrive early.

Carroll met Ben outside. Walden exited his truck with a bag tucked under his arm.

"Let me help you get your stuff," said Carroll.

"You're looking at it," Walden informed him. "I finally told my brother about everything tonight after supper, after he promised not to tell mom."

Ben added, "He's going to ride out to the house with me tomorrow so I can get more."

Carroll realized his friend was even worse off than he thought. He felt a twinge of guilt. He should have picked up on it already, he thought. Walden had been beaten nearly unconscious just a few blocks away, in downtown Fitzgerald, no less. He knew a killer was still out there; so, why would he risk being caught at home, a mile from anyone?

Carroll had planned to spend the evening reviewing his notes and going back over the jumpdrives from Luna, but he decided to focus instead on being a better friend.

"Where can we get a beer?" he asked.

Ben checked the time before he answered, "Not too many places to choose from this late. But there is one place—" he said, turning the pickup around.

Carroll's stomach groaned when Walden turned into the parking lot at Pizza Hut, but he did not say anything. He could not tell Ben that he had already eaten pizza – a lot of it – earlier today. He felt bad enough as it was. Ben was visibly nervous, obviously worried that Billy Bob McCoy was going to walk up behind him and plant a slug in the back of his head. Carroll had to somehow reassure him without revealing that McCoy was really an FBI agent working on a separate undercover investigation.

So, instead of making an excuse, Carroll just played along. He ate pizza as if he had not eaten it in weeks. And, after a few beers, it did not really matter anyway.

Carroll was a little irritated when he awoke the following morning at his usual time of 5 a.m.. He actually hoped the long hours of the last two days, coupled with the emotional and stressful events would've made him sleep later. He lay there in bed for several minutes, hoping he might be able to go back to sleep, but it did not work.

He filled his travel mug and quietly tiptoed down the hall past Ben's room and two other guest rooms. He tried not to step too heavily on the stairs as he descended to the lobby.

Emerging from the house, he was greeted by not one, but two roosters, crowing on either side of him. One would crow and then the other would answer. Or, was it the other way around? It was Dueling Roosters – in stereo no less!

He was not sure why, but Carroll found himself at the Ridgeway Hotel. He started to park by the dumpster as he had done on his first morning in Fitzgerald, but he remembered that the truck could be pulling in to empty it at any moment; so, he pulled into the grocery store instead.

He intended to walk over to the now nonexistent crime scene, hoping yet again that his brain might pick up on something that he had missed before. He was almost to the dumpster when he thought he heard whispering.

Carroll froze. Luckily, he happened to be in the perfect spot. The security lights from the hotel parking lot were blocked by the big magnolia, the home of the ninja chickens, and he was standing in its dark shadow.

Carroll strained to hear, pivoting his head and angling his ears like radar antenna, searching for the sound of extraterrestrials. Although he could not make out the words, there was no mistaking it now. Someone was talking in a very low voice, and it was coming from the backside of the hotel.

He instinctively crouched lower and stealthily eased toward an even darker spot, but then he saw the silhouette of a man walking away. Carroll crept along the edge of the magnolia shadow hoping to get a look at the whisperer, but the man had disappeared. Frustrated, he was about to leave his hiding place to search for the man when he heard a car door close. Then an engine started.

Knowing that he was about to lose his chance, Carroll stepped out from the shadow. He looked toward the area where the sounds had originated. It was a used car lot.

His brain kicked into overdrive. Was someone stealing a car? Could that have been what had happened to Thomas McDowell? Did he accidentally interrupt a car thief who panicked and killed him? Then he saw it. A car was pulling out from behind the lot without its headlights on!

Carroll fumbled for his cell phone and attempted to dial 911, but he dropped it. The phone flopped back into the dark. Fortunately, the screen was glowing from his dialing attempt. Diving, he grabbed it again and held it firmly as he dialed 9-1-1. He waited for the 911 operator to answer as he watched the car approaching a street light. He knew he had to get a good description of the vehicle for the police.

Then Carroll's heart stopped. He quickly pressed the button to end the call before it was answered as he watched the car, a marked patrol car, pull onto the street and turn left. His cell phone rang.

"Crap!" he said as he checked the display, then pressed the button to accept the call. He really didn't have a choice.

"This is Ben Hill County 911," a female voice said. "Do you have an emergency?"

"No, I apologize," he replied. "I meant to dial 411 and I saw that I had called you by mistake. That's why I tried to hang up."

He realized how stupid that sounded. The four and the nine were not even in close proximity on the phone. There was a short pause before she said anything.

"So, everything's okay then?" she asked.

"Yes. Yes, everything's fine," he answered, trying hard to sound normal, even while he was thinking I'm such a dumbass!

"And can I have your name, sir?"

He knew that he had to tell the truth. It was probably already showing up on their Enhanced 911 system.

"My name is Robert Carroll. I'm visiting from Indianapolis and I'm staying at the Barrett-Parrish House, but everything is fine."

"No problem, Mr. Carroll. It's a frequent mistake," she said. "I hope you enjoy your time in Fitzgerald."

"Thanks, I am enjoying it," he answered, as the two ninja chickens clucked from above his head.

17

The Missing Man

He had heard the saying many times before, and he thought he had even been there before; but, Robert Carroll knew there was absolutely no doubt about it this time. He was between the proverbial rock and the hard place.

He was supposed to be meeting Ben for breakfast shortly. They had not had much time to talk since Lenny's death, and he knew Walden was bound to have questions about what he and Val had done the previous day.

Carroll hated knowing that Ben was walking on eggshells, afraid that Billy Bob McCoy was lurking behind every bush, tree and trashcan, but he knew that he could not tell him anything about Agent Nathan Pafford, at least not yet.

Something else was bothering Carroll. He had been able to get a good look at the patrol car when it passed under a street light as he was babbling to the 911 operator. It was not a police car as he had first thought. It was a deputy sheriff's patrol car. Although he could not be certain, the profile looked like Ben Walden's friend, Tony.

He texted Val,

"Are you up yet?"

"Of course! I'm a Southerner now!"

"Meet me outside."

"Only if you don't have more bad news!"

"News, but not bad," he texted.

Val was waiting for him by the street. She hopped into the passenger seat, and he filled her in on what he had seen just a few minutes earlier.

"So, are you actually thinking that this Tony guy may be involved somehow?" Val asked.

"I'm not sure, but I've just got a feeling that something's not right about him."

"Uh huh. Just like you had the feeling there was something wrong about Billy Bob McCoy," she reminded him.

"And I was right. I knew he wasn't who he said he was, but it just didn't end up with him as the suspect," he reasoned.

"Fair enough. I'll give you that one," Val conceded.

"Is Aunt Ruth up yet?"

"No, she wasn't when I came out."

"Then, go and grab your hard copy of the original case file."

Val jumped out, trotted back to the house and quickly returned with the file tucked under her arm.

"What am I looking for?" she asked as she opened it.

"The responding officers," Carroll replied. "Who was the first?"

"Let's see–" said Val as she thumbed through the file and then trailed her finger down a page.

He knew he was onto something when she could not even respond with her usual holy shit! She just turned toward him with her mouth wide open in amazement.

"Well?" he wondered. "Say the name."

"You already know the name – Deputy Tony Webb!"

"I'm betting that it was also him in that car this morning," said Carroll. "And he was also at the scene when Lenny was killed."

"But, what about the witness who saw Billy Bob's – I mean, Nate's undercover truck? Did Tony Webb have time to steal it, hit Lenny with it, dump it and then return to the scene like he was responding to the call?"

"Maybe, maybe not," Carroll answered. "He could've hidden the pickup somewhere nearby, but they still haven't located it. If it turns up close, then the timeframe fits and he could be our guy."

As much as he was dreading it, Carroll went to The Sportsman to meet Ben as planned. They had been talking only a few minutes when Walden got a call from his office informing him that the GBI had concluded the autopsy on Sauls, and they were releasing his body to the family.

Carroll was relieved, both for Lenny's family and also for himself. As he expected, Ben said he would have to cut their breakfast short so he could get back to write a story in time to make the next edition.

"Do you want to go ahead and run out to your place right now?" Carroll asked. "Or, do you want to do it later?"

"I probably better do it before I go to the office," Ben decided. "I doubt that I'll leave once I get started."

They wolfed down the rest of their breakfast and headed toward Walden's truck. Carroll pressed the button on his key to lock the Escape as he walked by.

"I really appreciate this, Bob!" Ben said, as he turned right onto Central and headed toward his house.

Carroll had been there only one time. That was before the tires were slashed on Walden's pickup, before he was assaulted in the alley, and before Lenny was killed. Carroll tried to consider the situation from Ben's perspective. As far as he knew Billy Bob McCoy was now the official suspect.

As they drove up the lane to the house Carroll realized how remote the location was. The lane itself was not much more than a farm path. It extended from the highway past a field and into the woods to the cabin-like structure by a large pond.

The exterior was actually pretty well lit at night. There were a couple of automatic street lights that the power company had installed when Ben first built the place, and there were also motion lights on all four corners of the residence; but, that really would not matter if he were caught out here alone. Ben flipped on the lights and entered the house, trying his best to act normal.

"I've got a case of beer in the fridge. Look in the utility room on your right and get the blue cooler. We'll ice those suckers down when we get back to town."

"Sounds good," Carroll replied.

He retrieved the cooler and carried it to the kitchen. Ben pulled the case of beer from the refrigerator and placed it into the cooler.

"I'll grab my stuff," said Ben.

Carroll picked up the cooler and placed it outside of the front door before returning to the living room. He scanned through Walden's bookshelves.

"Hey, Ben, do you loan your books?" he shouted.

"Not as far as anyone else knows," he yelled back from his room. "I get real nerdy about my books."

"I'm exactly the same way."

"Good, that's what I figured. Go ahead and pick two or three if you want, because I'm not coming back here until that son of a bitch is in jail."

Carroll winced at hearing Ben's response, but he began browsing through the titles on the bookshelves. It was hard to decide from all the choices.

He finally picked three and was just sitting down to flip through one when Walden yelled, "Oh shit!"

Carroll ran to the bedroom, "What's wrong?"

"That!" Ben said, pointing toward a window.

At first, the window appeared fine, but then Carroll saw there was a gap of about half an inch at the bottom. The window was not completely closed.

"That damn window was locked!" Ben assured him. "Believe me. I know it was locked!"

Carroll inspected it closely without touching it. "I believe you," he said.

"How could that be?" Ben wondered. "How the hell can someone get through a locked window without breaking it?"

It was not that difficult. Carroll knew plenty of burglars who could have performed the same trick.

"When were you here last?" he asked, trying to establish when the burglary could have happened.

"I haven't been here in three days, so it could've been any time between then and now," Ben replied.

"Look around and see if anything is disturbed or missing, but try not to touch anything."

Walden closely inspected each room and determined that someone had searched the house. Whoever did it tried to cover their tracks by reclosing doors and drawers, but there were several things that were misplaced.

"I can tell he went through almost every drawer, but I'll be damned if I can find anything missing," he reported.

Carroll knew that Ben's he went through almost every drawer comment referred to Billy Bob, but again, as bad as he felt about it, Carroll knew that he could not say anything. He told Walden that he thought he should notify the sheriff's department. Ben dialed the non-emergency number that he always called as a reporter.

They heard a vehicle coming down the lane about ten minutes later and walked outside. Carroll did his best to appear unfazed when deputy Tony Webb emerged from the patrol car. For his part, Webb gave no indication of anything other than a deputy responding to a call. He covered all the bases, carefully checked the area, asked the right questions and filled out an incident report. However, that is what a smart person would do, Carroll thought.

They determined that Ben's Jeep was undisturbed. The alarm was still on and the doors were locked. More importantly, it was parked under one of those metal sheds on dirt that was undisturbed. If anyone had stepped near it, there would have been tracks. Deputy Webb used his cell phone to call for a detective.

Two sheriff's detectives arrived shortly after. They checked for prints and took a number of photographs before coming to the consensus that Billy Bob was the likely suspect, but was not likely to return. They told Ben that they would place a special patrol on his home anyway as a precaution. This meant that deputies would be dropping by frequently and unexpectedly.

Carroll could not fault the detectives. If Jerry Hall had not contacted him, Carroll would have been saying the same thing. Walden thought about staying home, but he was still uneasy, so he and Carroll went ahead as planned and loaded his stuff and the cooler into the pickup.

"Would you mind driving the Jeep back to town, Bob?"

"No problem. Where to?"

"I would rather park it where there's people, like in a 24 hour shopping center or a grocery store for the night. How long are you going to keep the rental?"

"I can turn it in at any of their locations any time. I actually planned to do it after I gave Lenny his ride," Carroll said as his voice cracked.

"Sorry to bring that up, Bob. I need to get back to the office, so why don't we return the rental tomorrow? You can go back to driving one of mine. I would rather you or Val be using it than have it sitting somewhere."

"Okay, we can do that, but only if you'll keep one of the rooms at the Barrett-Parrish. It's paid-up until the end of the week. After that it's all on you."

"But, today's only Monday," Ben pointed out. "That's too much. I can't accept that."

"Like I couldn't accept driving your jeep and your truck?"

"Fair enough" Walden acknowledged.

"So, Val's going to be staying with the Jacksons, huh? That's nice."

"We both are," Carroll informed him. "I'm moving over there later. That's what I'm talking about with the room."

"I swear! How do you do it? The woman hates me, but you're moving in!" he laughed.

"What can I say? I'm just a lovable guy," Carroll retorted.

Ben dropped him off at the driveway to the Barrett-Parrish House. Carroll was on the phone talking to Jerry Hall by the time he walked to the Ford Escape.

It is one thing to think that a law enforcement officer might be involved in criminal activity, but vocalizing that thought to another officer, especially to an FBI agent, was taking a big step. It was only the fact that he and Jerry were so close that allowed Carroll to freely express himself.

Neither of them would ever accuse a police officer of a crime without absolute proof. However, Carroll was more than 700 miles from home, and he had to consider the possibility that if Tony Webb was dirty and was involved in the murder, he and Val could end up the same way if they weren't careful. He wanted Hall to know what they were working on.

Carroll returned to the Jackson House for lunch, arriving early enough to spend some time with Ruth Jackson. They were rocking on the front porch when Ben called to say that Lenny's funeral would be at 11 a.m. the following day. Rosie and Betty were also there and were supervising Val as she prepared the meal.

After lunch Carroll managed to pull Val aside to inform her about what had transpired up to that point. With this latest revelation about Webb being at so many of the incident locations, especially at McDowell's murder scene before daylight, the FBI was no longer a silent partner. If he was crooked and involved in a murder, then the FBI could legitimately investigate it.

They would have access to Tony Webb's POST file. POST is the Georgia Peace Officer Standards and Training Council, the organization responsible for certifying the state's law enforcement officers. POST's mission statement says that it will "provide the citizens of Georgia with qualified, professionally trained, ethical and competent peace officers and criminal justice professionals."

Carroll would spend the remainder of the day back at The Blue and The Gray Museum while Val would continue her work in her room at the Jackson House. Unfortunately, although both of them found some new and interesting information, there was nothing that moved the case any further along.

A person passing through Ben Hill County on the following morning might have guessed that it was the funeral of some local son or daughter that had been killed overseas while serving as a soldier, or that a prominent politician had died. They would never have expected that it was the funeral of a thirty-something-year-old boy that drew the community together in such a display of emotion.

Black ribbons and wreaths had begun appearing on the doors of businesses and homes on the morning after Lenny died. By the day of his funeral, almost every business in town and many of the homes were displaying them. McDonald's even closed for half a day so all their employees could attend the funeral. The Sportsman did likewise even though they knew that, at least in Lenny's eyes, they played second fiddle to his beloved Macky Dee's.

The church service was very nice, but brief at the request of Lenny's family. Ben had not been able to include all of the comments about Lenny in his article, so he supplied the preacher with them. Many were read during the service, producing lots of smiles and tears as heads bobbed up and down approving the words about their boy.

The longest portion of the funeral was the wait after they arrived at Evergreen Cemetery. The hearse arrived near the front, of course, immediately followed by limos carrying his family and then, the pallbearers. After carrying Lenny's casket from the hearse to the gravesite, Carroll and the other pallbearers lined up shoulder-to-shoulder behind it, facing the family and other mourners.

The long wait was due to the fact that it took nearly twenty minutes for all of the vehicles to arrive, park and for people to gather at the gravesite. Lenny's mother and family sat under the tent. A space was also provided for Ruth Jackson's wheelchair, both out of concern for her health due to her age and also out of respect for her position in the community. Henry stood behind his grandmother with Val on her right and Betty on the left.

Carroll scanned the crowd and was surprised to find that he recognized many of those in attendance, if not by name, at least by their faces and occupations. In addition to familiar faces from McDonald's, The Sportsman and Barrett-Parrish House, he saw a few others, like the sweet elderly lady from the library who had delivered the zinger to Val on her way out. Besides, Lenny's mother, the person who broke Carroll's heart was Sheila, the girl who worked at the drive-thru window at McDonald's. She quietly cried through the entire service.

However, Carroll was a bit disappointed to find that one face was not among the mourners. He did not see Alan Sangster. Carroll thought that Alan had made a special bond with Lenny and he expected to see him there. The news story had dominated local newspapers and TV stations so there was no way that Alan had not heard about it.

In fact, Carroll saw that a reporter from WALB, the local NBC affiliate, was filming from a respectable distance. Carroll smiled, knowing that Lenny would have liked to have been on TV. He decided that Alan was probably out of town. At least, that is what he convinced himself. He hoped that he was not just sitting at home with his feet propped up.

Carroll noticed a man standing alone, apart from the crowd of mourners, but close enough to hear the service. He held a cell phone and appeared to be talking to someone. He knew that it wasn't anyone from the GBI or FBI. They would have been more discreet.

"Do you know who that guy is?" he asked Walden.

"No. He looks vaguely familiar, but I can't quite place him."

"We need to try and get his tag number before he leaves."

Ben nodded.

The preacher finished his graveside remarks, and Carroll was waiting for him to conclude the service when he noticed Val was trying to quietly get his attention. She pointed behind him just as other people in the crowd began pointing in the same direction.

Carroll turned around to see four small private planes approaching, flying low and in a perfect finger-four formation.

"So there you are!" Carroll thought as he spotted Sangster's plane.

He immediately felt guilty for even considering that Alan could have been sitting at home. The flight leader was a single engine Piper Cherokee. The leader's wingman was a Cessna Skylane. Alan was second-element leader in his Piper Seneca, and his wingman flew a Maule.

At first Carroll wondered why Sangster wasn't the leader, but then he swallowed hard, realizing that Alan occupied the most important position, at least for a few more seconds until, right over the cemetery, Sangster banked hard, up and away from the group, which then formed the missing man formation.

The crowd broke normal funeral etiquette when they burst into spontaneous applause and cheers. The whole community knew of Lenny's love of airplanes and many of them had heard about his flight from Sauls himself. He had told everyone who was interested, and some who were not, about his one-hour flight. It was his favorite topic.

Carroll turned back around to see the stranger with the cell phone saluting the planes with a broad grin. It was now obvious that he had been helping to coordinate the flyover.

"Never mind about the guy," he told Ben as he watched the planes flying away.

As he was turning back toward the crowd, Carroll noticed a black SUV with dark tinted windows parked on the opposite side of the cemetery. It had apparently arrived separately and was not part of the funeral procession. Two men, both wearing dark suits, stood by the SUV, with their backs to Carroll as they also watched the planes.

The planes faded into the clouds and the two men turned back toward the SUV and Carroll. He smiled and gave a nod of acknowledgment to Agents Williams and Pafford. The two men returned the gesture. The people never saw him, but Lenny's friend, Billy Bob McCoy, was also paying his respects.

After the funeral, Ben followed Carroll to the rental dealer to return the Escape and then took him back to pick up the Jeep. Neither of them had much to say. There was one person; however, to whom Carroll did want to talk. He waited until he was in the Jeep and called Sangster as he was driving to the Jackson House.

"That was really nice, Alan," he told him.

"How did it look?" Sangster asked anxiously.

"Damn good. Very professional. It was really a nice surprise."

He heard Sangster breathe a sigh of relief. It was the answer he wanted.

"We trained all day yesterday. Everybody was sworn to secrecy, but I was afraid the word had gotten out."

"I can assure you that everyone there was completely surprised and impressed. In fact, I spoke with Lenny's mother after the service, and she asked me to have you call her."

He gave Alan her number. He also told him he would like to fly again pretty soon if possible and he would like to take Val.

"Sure, any time," Alan replied. "Just let me know a day ahead of time if you can."

Carroll was not in the mood to work on the case. He spent the remainder of the day with the Jacksons. They talked for awhile before Mrs. Jackson told Henry to take Carroll outside to, "Keep 'em outta my hair. Go out and put 'em to work" she commanded, saying the women had things to do in the house.

Carroll liked the idea.

"What can I do to help?" he asked Henry.

"I was about to go split some logs for firewood."

He followed Henry to an open shed that covered two large, but neat, stacks of logs which had been cut into lengths of about two feet.

"That's oak and that's pecan," Henry said, pointing to the stacks respectively.

"We just gonna take these logs and stand 'em on end, side by side, and then split'em."

They placed ten logs in a row, standing them on end like a lineup of utility pole rejects.

"You ever used one of these?" Henry asked, as he picked up a big heavy tool that looked like a sledgehammer on one side and wedge-shaped on the other.

"No," Carroll answered. "But I've used an ax plenty of times."

"Ain't much difference – just a little heavier. It's called a straight peen." Henry informed him. "We gonna use the wedged end."

He placed himself squarely in front of the first log and swung the heavy tool back, up, and over his head, bringing it down into the log with Thor-like power – instantly splitting the log into two almost identical pieces.

"You've got to hit'em right dead in the center," he instructed.

Henry then walked down the line, destroying the entire row with amazing rapidity and precision. He turned around and gave Carroll an appraising look – as if he were not sure about his older, adopted Yankee relative.

"You feel up to it?" he asked with a broad grin.

Thinking I'm not about to wimp out, Carroll grabbed the tool and swung it back and around just as he had seen Henry do. He hit it correctly, but it did not split completely. He had to tap it again to finish it off.

"You did it right, but you backed off," Henry observed. "You gotta follow through with it all the way to the dirt."

He took the wedge and demonstrated again, explaining, "When you bring it up and over from behind your back, as soon as you start that downward swing, put the power on it and the weight of the hammer will help do the work for you."

He grunted, completing the process and perfectly splitting another one.

Carroll tried again, this time successfully completing the effort. He found he was not only up to it, but that he actually enjoyed the work. They took turns splitting and stacking, with Henry first humming, then singing, to keep the rhythm. Henry was pleasantly surprised when they finished splitting both stacks before they had to clean up for supper. He had originally hoped to conquer at least one stack.

Val had asked if she could cook chicken and dumplings again, except this time with no one helping her. Carroll made an observation when she finally emerged from the kitchen a little less than an hour later.

"Well, at least you don't look like the Pillsbury Doughgirl this time," he said, referring to the amount of flour she had gotten on her body during her first attempt.

He complimented her more appropriately after their meal. Everyone did. Val was beaming. She just received the Jackson Seal of Approval, which, in her eyes, was more important that Good Housekeeping's any day.

Carroll received a call from Jerry Hall just as they were finishing up with supper.

"I won't keep you," Hall said, "I know it's been a tough day there. Will and Nate said it was a nice service. They especially liked the flyover. That was a nice touch."

"Yeah, I thought so, but I can't take credit for that one. That was a complete surprise to me, too. It was nice of Nate and Will to attend, even if people will never know they were there."

"Nate insisted on going and Will went with him as backup. I was a nervous wreck until they got back. Listen, I put some of our geeks up in Quantico on that name that you were most interested in, John Ephraim Pascal."

"I really appreciate that," said Carroll, knowing that Jerry had other ongoing cases to worry about.

"It's no problem now that I can honestly say that this research is directly related to our case because it affects the safety of our main agent."

"You're absolutely right," Carroll agreed.

"It's certainly not their average area of research, so it kind of broke up the monotony. They're actually getting into the historical aspect of it."

"Have they found anything?"

"I don't know how any of this will help you. These people have been dead for decades, but the two names that popped up several times were Robert H. Solomon and L.B. Creslein. Does either of those ring a bell?"

"The first one does. I'm actually staying with his daughter, but this is the first time that I've heard of Creslein. Do you know what the initials stand for?"

"No, sorry. Like I said, the name popped up several times, but all they have are the initials. They're still working on it though."

"Thanks a lot, Jerry! I'll see what I can do with this."

"Hold on," Hall said before Carroll disconnected. "Did you say you're staying with his daughter? That would make her–" He paused to do the math.

"Old," Carroll helped him. "She's 111."

"Well, knowing how you are about history, I imagine that you're wearing her out with questions. Take care, Bob. I'll call you if anything else comes up."

"Thanks again, Jerry. I'll keep you posted."

After he thought about it, that name, Creslein, did seem vaguely familiar. Carroll was sure he had seen it somewhere, but he did not remember it coming up in McDowell's research. Was it at the library, on some of the material they had discovered online, or among the photos he had seen at the Blue & Gray Museum? He decided that he would go back to the museum first thing in the morning.

Carroll suddenly realized there was another possibility: Evergreen Cemetery. Although Creslein had not appeared in the historical brochure, Carroll thought he might be among those buried in the cemetery. That might have been where he had seen the name. He checked his phone. It was 9:57. Frustrated, he plopped back into a chair. Like the museum, it would also have to wait until tomorrow.

He tried to go through McDowell's files using the laptop, but that lasted less than thirty minutes. It was more than he could stand. The more he thought about the cemetery, the surer he was that he would find somethin there. Aunt Ruth was tired and had already gone to bed. He informed Betty and Val that he was going out to check on something.

"Do you need some help?" Val asked.

"No, not right now, but if I'm right, we'll have a busy day of research tomorrow."

Carroll went to his bag and removed a small LED flashlight that was not much larger than a Sharpie marker. He grabbed his phone and headed to the Jeep. He paused in the front yard and checked the flashlight before leaving. LED technology still amazed Carroll. If he had pointed it skyward, the beam from the light would have looked like the old search lights during the bombing raids of World War II. He pressed a button to change the setting, dimming the light. That was all he would need where he was going. He certainly could not risk attracting attention in the cemetery after hours.

Carroll decided he would give himself ten minutes. If he couldn't find it by then, he would just have to wait until tomorrow. He parked quickly and jumped out, running through the cemetery from grave to grave like a madman.

The light reflected so brightly off of the headstones that he stopped and checked the setting again. It was on the lowest setting, but it still seemed awfully bright. He used his fingers to partially cover the lens as he continued his search. The light began to burn his fingers.

A car approached on the highway. He stopped and killed the light, resuming only after the vehicle's taillights had disappeared around the curve. Another car approached from the other direction a few minutes later, coming so suddenly that Carroll was forced to jump behind a tree to stay out of its headlights.

The vehicle's brake lights illuminated just as it passed him and the car suddenly spun around, bolts of blue lightning suddenly flashing from the roof.

"Oh, shit!" Carroll said aloud.

One of two things was about to happen: If it was just a random cop or deputy then he could be warned or even arrested. That was the best option. If it was Tony Webb and if he was right and Webb was involved in McDowell's murder, then he could be shot.

In an effort to show compliance, Carroll stood up, freely exposing himself. He began trying to think of how he would explain himself to whoever emerged from the patrol car. To his surprise, the car sped away, the driver turning on the siren as he entered the intersection and turned back toward town.

Carroll breathed a sigh of relief. It was a Fitzgerald police officer, and he or she had obviously received a call as they were passing. Carroll decided not to push his luck, so he started toward the Jeep. And then he saw it, the tombstone was right in front of him:

L.B. Creslein.
Born November 12, 1837
Died January 21, 1896

As he looked at the headstone, he suddenly remembered that he had seen that name somewhere else. He reached for his cell to call Val, but it was not there.

"Dammit!" he yelled at the dead soldiers.

Carroll returned to the Jeep and searched the interior for his phone. He tried to recall if he had had it when he left the Jacksons, but he was not sure.

He started the vehicle and headed toward town, steering with his left while fumbling around with his right hand in an attempt to find the phone.

He passed Walmart on the left and the Ford dealership, then Calhoun Road, on the right. The Jeep made a – ba`DUMP! – sound as he crossed the railroad tracks. He read the next street sign; Appomattox Road.

"Almost there!" Carroll thought, just as there was a loud bang!

Robert Carroll did not know what had happened. He was not sure if his eyes were opened or closed. He could not see anything. There was an incredibly loud, high-pitched whine that drowned out all other sound. Then he remembered; he was in the Jeep. He knew that he had been in an accident.

The noise was coming from the motor; the accelerator was stuck. Carroll fumbled for the ignition switch to turn it off, but it was not where it should be. Then he realized that it was he who was not where he should be. The Jeep was upside down. Still not able to see, he reached in the direction he expected to find the ignition, groping until he found the key and turned it off.

He heard the sound of someone running. Then someone was touching his shoulder shouting, "Sir! Sir! Are you okay?"

"It's just one vehicle," another voice said, "–on Benjamin Hill just west of Appomattox."

"Benjamin Hill wasn't at Appomattox!" Carroll yelled, before slipping into unconsciousness.

18

Carroll in Wonderland, Part 2

He woke up, but he was afraid to open his eyes. What if he could not see? He had no idea how long he had been out. Was it hours? Days?

He thought about that movie, The Dead Zone, where the guy was in an accident and awoke in a hospital thinking that it had been only minutes, when five years had passed. He tried to sit up.

"It's okay," a voice reassured him. "Calm down."

He gradually opened his eyes. It was blurry at first, but his vision cleared up quickly.

"What day is it?" he asked.

He almost added what year but thought better of it.

"You've got that backwards," the nurse said. "I'm supposed to ask you those questions."

He looked down to check his limbs. He moved his legs and wiggled his toes.

"You're fine," she reassured him. "You're a very lucky man. Amazingly, nothing's broken. Just some scrapes and bruises"

She helped him to a sitting position.

"Thanks," he said.

"Weren't you a pallbearer at Lenny's funeral this morning?" the nurse asked.

"Yes. Yes, I was," he replied, thankful that her this morning meant that he had not been in a coma for five years.

"Can you tell me your name?"

"Robert Carroll."

She proceeded through the typical questions one would expect after such an accident: "What is your birthday? Do you know what day it is? What year? Who is the president of the United States?"

"We're pretty sure that you're okay," she said. "But, you kept yelling Benjamin Hill wasn't at Appomattox so they wanted to be sure. So, are you some kind of history professor?"

"Not exactly," he replied, looking around. "Did they find my phone?"

"They picked this up, thinking it was your phone, but it's just a radio or something," she said, handing it to him.

Carroll looked at it closely and then tried to put it in his pocket. Realizing he was in a hospital gown, he asked, "Where are my clothes?"

"On the counter behind you, but you're going to be here a while. We've got some more tests to do."

She left the room, saying that she would be right back, but Carroll was up before the door was completely closed. He dressed quickly, then poked his head out to see if the coast was clear. He left the room, walked down the hall, and, went out of the ER through the double-doors.

The hospital was just a few blocks from the Jackson home. Carroll jogged straight up Perry House Road and across a field to Merrimac. Then he cut through Shenandoah Drive to Lincoln Avenue. His cell phone started ringing as he arrived at the Jackson House.

What the hell? Did I have it the whole time? he asked himself.

Then he saw the light from his phone flashing in the grass just in front of him. He must have dropped it before he left.

He picked it up and answered without looking at it, "Ben?"

"Sorry, wrong answer, but you do get points for both names having the same number of letters!"

"Val!" he exclaimed. "Has Ben called?"

"No, where did you go and when will you be back?

"To the cemetery and I am back."

He was walking toward the steps when Val opened the front door, still holding her phone to her ear. It took her eyes a few seconds to adjust and find him in the dark.

"Where's the Jeep? And why do you look like you've been jogging?" she wondered.

"Wrecked and because I have," he answered. "Do you realize that you tend to ask questions in pairs?"

"Holy shit! We've got to get you to the hospital!" she yelled, leaping from the porch.

"Been there; done that. I'm fine," he reassured her. "I'm just winded. We need to talk before we go insi– "

He was interrupted as Henry's truck came flying down Lincoln Avenue. He overshot the driveway and stopped in the street.

"Are you okay?" he yelled, as he jumped from the cab.

Carroll nodded, "How did you know?"

"I stopped by the hospital to check on my schedule and heard about a search for a missing patient who was found in a wrecked Jeep. I knew you were driving Ben's today. "

Henry was able to fill in some blanks. He said that witnesses reported seeing the Jeep traveling down Benjamin Hill Drive when sparks flashed from underneath, and it suddenly flipped for no reason.

"They ran over and found you hanging upside down in your seatbelt. They dragged you out and called 911."

The adrenaline that had propelled Carroll's run to the Jackson home was beginning to wear off and he stumbled forward. Henry and Val helped him into one of the rocking chairs on the porch and then quietly pulled two more chairs close together.

"Listen. What happened to me was no accident," he told them, as he dialed Ben on his cell.

"Bob! Are you okay?" Walden answered. "I'm at the hospital looking for you. Hell, everybody's looking for you!"

"Yeah, I'm sorry about your Jeep, Ben."

"The Jeep? Screw the Jeep! That's what insurance is for! What about you?" Walden asked again.

"I'm fine. What do you mean everybody's looking for me? Am I in some kind of trouble?"

"Trouble? No, you dumbass, they already said that you weren't drunk or anything. The right front tire of the jeep blew out and you flipped at least two or three times. They just want to be sure that you're not lying out there dead somewhere!"

"Did you see the tire yourself? Have you looked at the jeep?"

"Jesus Christ, Bob! Will you forget about the damn Jeep? It's not important right now!" Walden insisted.

"Actually, it's very important," Carroll corrected him. "A witness said they saw sparks from underneath it just before it started flipping. Tell the police to check near the right front tire."

"What are you saying, Bob?"

"That it wasn't an accident."

Carroll could tell that Ben was trying to comprehend it all.

"Someone did this – on purpose?" he asked.

"Yes, that's exactly what I'm saying. Listen, Ben. I need to ask you something. Who was the first officer that found you in the alley when you were attacked behind your office?"

"It was Tony. Tony Webb from the Sheriff's Department. You met him a couple of times. Why do you ask?"

"Because he might be involved in McDowell's death."

"Tony?" Ben exclaimed. "No way! I don't believe it!"

"I don't have the proof yet, but I saw him yesterday morning, before daylight, behind the Ridgeway. He had hidden his patrol car in that used car lot next door."

"But that doesn't mean that he had anything to do with Thomas McDowell getting killed," Ben insisted.

"It's not just that. He was the first to arrive at the murder scene, the first to get to your office in town when you were attacked, even though he's a county deputy. He was the first one there when Lenny was killed. And the first to arrive at your house after you reported the break-in. Also, there's more that I can't tell you right now."

"Have they caught Billy Bob?" Walden asked excitedly.

"No, but I can promise you that you don't have to worry about McCoy. There's one more thing: Have you ever heard of someone named, L.B. Creslein?"

"Jesus Howard Christ! Another damn name? No, I haven't heard of him, but I'll get on it."

Ben did not know it, but his Jesus Howard Christ made Carroll smile despite all of his aches and pains.

"Look, I've got some work to do. You need to be somewhere around people tonight, either at the Barrett-Parrish or your mom's. I'll call you in the morning."

"Bobby, about what you said about Tony Webb," Henry interrupted. "There's something else you should know about him."

Carroll leaned forward on the rocking chair. Henry was the same age as Webb, they had grown up in the small community; so, it was likely that they knew each other. This could tie everything together.

"Tony's been seeing a girl who works at the Ridgeway," Henry informed them.

It wasn't exactly what Carroll was anticipating. He was thinking, trying to work out how this bit of information could tie him into the murder of Thomas McDowell when Val jumped in.

"Is it Sheila?" she asked.

"How the hell did you know that?" Henry asked. "And, how do you know her?" Henry's questions confirmed Val's suspicion.

"I met her briefly when I was looking for Laura Luna. She mentioned that she was separated from her husband and I noticed bruises on her arms. That's typical of spousal abuse. I asked her about it and she said that's why she finally left him."

Carroll felt like a little kid watching the air seep out of his balloon. He quickly formed his own theory about the rest of the story, hoping to prove that he was not totally oblivious to the obvious.

"My turn," he interrupted, "I'm guessing that Tony probably met Sheila after he answered a domestic abuse call at her home, and their relationship began from there."

Henry shook his head, not in disagreement, but acknowledging that both Carroll and Val had impressed him.

"Well, Sheila and Tony knew each other from high school," he said, "But, yeah, that's when they started seeing each other. Actually, it was after Tony and some other deputies had to go out there several times after her husband beat her. I only know about it because my wife is friends with her.

Sheila was worried about people finding out before her divorce was final."

"Do you see any way that either Sheila or Tony could've been involved in Thomas McDowell's death?" Val asked Henry.

"Well, they say anything's possible, but I just can't see it," he responded. "Jimmy, that's her husband, the one who beat her, told her that he was gonna kill her. I really think Tony was just trying to protect her.

It was happening again. Just as it had when Billy Bob McCoy was his main suspect, Carroll saw his theory on his newest suspect falling apart. Tony probably had arrived at the McDowell murder scene so quickly because he was in the area seeing Sheila. He could have even been with her in the hotel when it happened. Just as Carroll had not seen it among the used cars, the killer probably would not have noticed the patrol car if Webb had hidden it in the same place.

Other pieces of the puzzle fell into place, or – to be more precise – fell onto the floor. Besides explaining why a deputy, who should have been out patrolling the county, arrived at the murder scene before officers from Fitzgerald PD, it also explained why he was always close around town. He was protecting Sheila. Carroll sadly watched as his imaginary balloon sputtered away, blowing raspberries at him as it crashed and died a horrible death on the floor.

With his Tony is the bad guy theory being bashed into a million pieces, it was time for Carroll to move on to something new. He reached into his pocket and pulled out the device that the nurse had given him. He placed it on the serving table that usually held the Jefferson's Select.

"What is it?" asked Henry.

Val leaned forward and inspected it closely.

"It's a transmitter," she answered for Carroll. "Where did you get it, Uncle Bob?"

"The nurse gave it to me at the hospital. It was picked up by someone who stopped to help. They thought it was my phone."

"I don't understand," Henry admitted.

"Ben's tires were slashed several weeks ago," said Carroll, "probably as a warning to back off, but he didn't listen. So, he was beaten up in the alley behind his office as a second warning. That still didn't stop him. Then, yesterday, I went with him to his house and we found that someone had broken in and searched it."

Carroll knew that Val was aware of the earlier incidents, but she didn't know about the burglary. Henry was learning about most of this for the first time. Carroll paused to be sure they were both up to speed before he continued.

"What we didn't know yesterday was that someone placed this magnetic tracker on his Jeep. I'm betting that the cops are also going to find some kind of device that was used to blow the tire."

"So, this was probably meant for Ben," said Henry.

Carroll nodded, "Whoever planted it could have put it on at any time since he parked the Jeep three days ago. We brought it to town and parked it, and it sat there until I picked it up this afternoon after the funeral."

He added, "All that they needed to do was to wait for the tracking device to show that it was moving again. Only a few people know about me, so they just assumed Ben was driving."

Looking directly at Val, Carroll added, "But now everyone at the hospital knows that it was me driving, not Ben. I don't think it's a good idea for us to be staying here."

She nodded in agreement, silently acknowledging that they might be endangering the Jackson family.

"And just where do y'all think you going?" Ruth Jackson asked.

They turned around to see her sitting in her wheelchair behind the screen door.

"Granny! What are you doing up?" Henry asked.

"How the hell am I supposed to sleep when Val's run'n in and out the house and you come screech'n up in here in your truck? You done woke me up so you might as well come on in the house," she said, abruptly wheeling her chair around, she snapped, "And don't be think'n y'all are go'in nowhere neither!"

"It really would be safer for everyone if we left, Aunt Ruth," Carroll reasoned.

"Well it ain't gonna happen!" she shot back as she wheeled herself down the hallway, adding, "Now, y'all come on in before you make me mad."

They proceeded into the house as ordered, all suddenly feeling like little children again. Betty was up too. She and her grandmother had heard most of the conversation and had obviously made their own plans.

"Y'all can use the dining room table so you'll have more room," said Betty. "I've already got coffee going."

That was it. There would be no more discussion. It was settled. Val and Henry went upstairs to retrieve everything they needed for the dining room work station – her backpack containing her iPad, Carroll's laptop as well as another small suitcase of notes, books and other printed material. It was just after midnight when they sat down at the dining room table.

"So where do we start?" Val asked.

"With John Ephraim Pascal," Carroll told her. "Now that we know that Pascal worked for Aunt Ruth's father, it can't be a coincidence that McDowell came by to see her and then sent Laura to ask about him again."

"But she didn't remember him," Val reminded him.

"That's not entirely correct. She didn't remember the name, because she never knew it. But she sure remembered the two stories didn't she – even though they occurred years before she was born?"

"Pascal died shortly after arriving in the colony," Carroll said, pointing through the wall of the house toward the yard.

"Just a couple of hundred feet from where we're sitting," he added. "And from the time that he arrived until he died, most of his time was spent right here working for Aunt Ruth's father. Coincidence?"

He gave them more catch-up time before he proceeded. He looked at Val, saying, "The reason why Aunt Ruth knows Pascal's name now is because you found that article. She's always known the story of how he died. She just didn't have a name to go with it."

"I done heard my name at least five times while I was com'n down the hall," Ruth Jackson said as she rolled into the room with a tray of homemade apple turnovers on her lap.

"I reckon y'all ain't got much else to talk about, huh?"

"We were talking about Pascal, the man who died in the accident," he told her. "There's got to be some kind of connection, Aunt Ruth."

"Well I don't know what it could be," she replied.

Betty followed her in with some plates, cups and the coffee pot.

"Let's get a little something on your stomachs and then we'll get out of your way," she said.

Betty was right. The pastries and coffee did the trick. They were now ready to focus on work. The two ladies collected the dishes and started out of the room. Aunt Ruth was halfway out the door when she asked, "What about the cemetery, Bobby?"

Carroll turned toward her, "What?"

"When you first got back and come up on the porch, you said you'd been out to the cemetery. Why in the world would you go out there at night?"

Carroll could not believe it. The wreck must have rattled him more than he had thought. He had completely forgotten about the call from Jerry Hall and his trip to the cemetery until she asked the question.

"L.B. Creslein," he responded.

"Who?" Val asked.

"L.B. Creslein. Jerry Hall called me right after supper. They've been running checks on Pascal. He told me that besides Aunt Ruth's father, who we all knew about; they found another name, L.B. Creslein."

There was a crash as the tray that had been sitting in Ruth Jackson's lap hit the floor. Everyone turned to see her sitting in her wheelchair holding her head.

"Granny!" Betty shouted, as the group simultaneously rushed toward the Mrs. Jackson.

She raised her arms, holding her hands palm outward, as a sign for them to stop, "Just gimme a minute," she said.

She sat back up and turned her wheelchair back around to face the others. It was immediately obvious to Carroll; Aunt Ruth may not have known the name of John Pascal, but there was no doubt that she recognized L.B. Creslein's name.

"L.B. Creslein also died before you were born, but you know that name don't you Aunt Ruth?" he asked.

She hesitated momentarily before she answered him;

"I do. Yes sir. I surely do."

Carroll could almost hear the tape rewinding in her head as she replayed the memory. He forced himself to wait, to give her the same space from his questions that she had demanded physically from them seconds before. It took her only a moment to regain her composure. She sat up and took a deep breath.

Carroll looked over at Betty. Like him, she had forced herself to back off and sit down. He could not begin to imagine how she was feeling. Betty had been hearing some incredible stories about her own family for the first time. It had started with the one about the lynching of John Tucker and now Betty wanted to know about L.B. Creslein.

"Who was he, Granny?" she asked.

"He was the man that your great great Uncle Jebediah killed."

"What?" Betty exclaimed, her mind reeling again, "When was this?"

"It was another one of them things that happened before I come into this world, so I don't rightly know the exact date, but I 'spect Bobby might know it," she said, looking at Carroll.

"January 21, 1896," he reported.

Aunt Ruth nodded her head, "They said it was in the wintertime."

She paused again, taking another deep breath and conserving her strength, as if she were preparing to climb a mountain.

"Ain't nobody ever talked about this since my mama died."

Looking at Henry, she began, "Jebediah would've been your great great great uncle. Most folks called him Jeb. He come down here with Daddy in 1895 on the very first work crew when they was surveying and clearing the land."

Perhaps out of habit, or, possibly to help soothe her own nerves, she began to slowly rock back and forth in her wheelchair just as she had done in the rocking chair on the porch when she told stories.

"Like I done said, Daddy didn't wanna live in town. He said that he had enough of that kinda liv'n in Indiana. He was gonna have him some land down here in the country. So, he come out here and staked this out."

Carroll looked over to see that Betty was discreetly videoing her Granny with her cell phone.

"That Creslein man showed up a few days after the other one got killed by the falling logs. He come by one day and said that he had already claimed this land. My daddy told him that they had checked first and it was free and clear."

Aunt Ruth said Creslein tried to argue about it, but her father had already done everything possible to make absolutely sure that it was legal. The dispute intensified over the next several weeks.

"Mama said Mr. Fitzgerald hisself asked the sheriff, a man by the name of Paulk, to come here and settle it. Sheriff Paulk came and said that, according to the paperwork, this land belonged to Robert H. Solomon, my daddy."

Val was on her computer as soon as Aunt Ruth mentioned the name Sheriff Paulk. She googled Sherriff Ben Hill County 1895. She was hoping to confirm Ruth Jackson's story as quickly as she had done with the others she had previously told, but Val looked at Carroll and shook her head in disappointment. She turned the lap top so he could see the screen. He took his pen and scratched on his notepad, then spun it around in front of Val:

Ben Hill County wasn't formed until 1906.

Change county from Ben Hill to Irwin.

She read his note and wrote him a one-word response: Nerd!

He just smiled and waited as Val changed the county name and clicked enter again. The results showed that a man named Jesse Paulk was the sheriff of Irwin County from 1893 to 1896.

Aunt Ruth had continued telling her story, explaining that L.B. Creslein tried to buy the land, offering her father nearly double what he paid for it. Creslein said the land had sentimental value to his family.

"But daddy found out that he wasn't even from Georgia. He was from Virginia," she explained.

"He was from Virginia?" Carroll asked.

"Uh-huh, 'Least, that's what Mama told me."

"So, what happened with Creslein, Aunt Ruth?" he asked.

"He ended up buy'n the land on the east side of us and behind us. They was a crick that used to come through here, but he dammed it off from his property."

She pointed east, "That's why there's them ponds on that land today. They don't ever dry up. Made my daddy so mad he couldn't hardly stand it!"

The dispute continued between Creslein and the Jackson family, eventually intensifying to a point where he began to threaten them physical harm.

"Mama was out hang'n clothes one morn'n when he come 'cross into the yard," Aunt Ruth said, "He come up behind her and grabbed her. She was able to fight him off the first time 'cause he was so drunk, but he got up and come back at her. He hit her in the head and knocked her out."

She paused yet again, for longer this time, unsure if she should finish what she had started.

Betty walked over and took her hand, pleading, "You've got to tell me, Granny."

She lowered her head, "Uncle Jeb came up just as he was climb'n on top of her. He pretty much went crazy. He grabbed Creslein by the hair from behind, snatched his head back and cut his throat as he dragged him off Mama."

Betty appeared to be in shock as she continued to hold onto her Granny's hand. The elder Jackson said her Uncle Jeb carried her mama back into the little wood shack that served as their temporary home until the current house was finished. Her father arrived home shortly afterward.

"Aunt Sally, Uncle Jeb's wife, took care of Mama, while Daddy and Uncle Jeb got rid of him."

"What do you mean got rid of?" Henry asked warily. He had somehow managed to keep his composure, but the realization that his blood relatives were in fact, bloody relatives, was too much to hear.

It took quite a bit of encouragement from Betty and Henry before their grandmother would say more. She took yet another, even deeper, breath before she concluded, "They waited til dark; then they put'em in the wagon and hauled him up to where the railroad tracks curve away from town. They hid the body in the woods. Daddy come back home, but Uncle Jeb stayed there 'til he heard the train com'n. Then he dragged 'im out and put him on the track. Everybody just thought he got drunk again and passed out on the track."

Ironically, when the sheriff arrived at the accident, he said they had been planning to arrest Creslein on charges related to an assault in Irwinville and for warrants on debts that he owed. The room was silent for several minutes as each one of them processed what they had just heard.

"I spect you gonna have to tell folks about this now?" she asked Carroll.

It was obvious that Ruth Jackson was wondering if she had done the right thing in revealing such sordid details about her own family.

"I'm definitely going to have to check into it more; but either way, it won't have any repercussions on any of your family."

"Least, not the ones that's liv'n," she said, obviously concerned about the reputation of her father's family name.

She suddenly sat up straight as if someone had relieved her of a heavy load that was weighing her down.

"Well, now that I done told it, I want his stuff outta my house."

"What stuff you talk'n about, Granny?" asked Henry.

"That Creslein man's," she said, as she casually added, "Betty, can you get me sump'n to drink?"

Betty stood mouth agape. Carroll and Val both looked at one another.

"Granny, are you saying that something of Creslein's is still in this house?" Betty asked, obviously dreading the answer.

Ruth Jackson pointed her finger at the ceiling, "It's up there in the attic. Daddy and Uncle Jeb hid it. They put it up there as soon as the house was finished. Been there ever since."

"Where's it at, Granny?" Henry asked.

"I done told you!" she yelled impatiently. "Up in the attic!"

Betty knew her grandmother was still upset. She tried to deflect some of the scorn from Henry;

"No, Granny, he means what part of the attic and what should he look for?"

"I'm sorry, baby," Aunt Ruth said, taking Henry's hand. "It's gonna be way back in the northwest corner in a big ole trunk with straps around it."

Henry and Val were hurrying toward the stairs even before she had finished speaking. The access to the attic was on the second floor. Henry led her through the small door by the end of the stairway and up another short stairway. The attic was huge and covered the entire house. The Jackson items were grouped into sections. One contained old pieces of furniture; others had lots of boxes and containers of clothes and papers. The Christmas decorations were all together in another area.

It would have taken forever to search without Ruth Jackson's help. Henry and Val followed her directions, bypassing the bulk of the main items, and proceeded to the northwest corner. They were beginning to think that she had made a mistake. They had searched and found nothing. They turned to leave when Henry spotted it. It sat alone, in the most remote place that it could have been, wedged into a corner and covered in almost 120 years of dust. They had to duck under the beams to drag it out.

Val and Henry hauled the trunk down the stairs into the dining room where Carroll and Betty had spread out some sheets to collect the dust and whatever creepy-crawlies might emerge from it.

"When was this last opened, Aunt Ruth?" Carroll asked.

"I don't rightly know," she responded. "They might've looked in it when it first happened, but I don't know if they did. They never said noth'n else about it. I know it ain't ever been moved since I been here and I ain't never told a soul."

A shiver ran up Carroll's back, and he literally got goosebumps. He had found a lot of interesting clues over his career but nothing compared to this. Aunt Ruth didn't care to be present for the opening of the chest, so Betty took her to her day room.

Carroll asked Henry if he wanted to open it. It somehow seemed fitting under the circumstances. Henry unbuckled the leather straps, then used his thumb and pressed against the buttons to release the latch, but nothing happened. He tried again, this time using both hands to press harder. The latch suddenly gave way with a loud – POP! – that startled them all.

Henry slowly raised the lid. The interior was relatively free of dust, and the contents were amazingly preserved. A fitted, compartmentalized tray covered the top. They leaned in together to scan the tray's contents: a straight razor, handkerchiefs, socks, a pipe, small animal figures carved from wood, a small mirror with a string on it so it could be hung, and various other items.

Henry and Val carefully removed the tray and set it aside to gain access to the main body of the trunk. Two books and a Bible sat on top, but the trunk was filled mostly with clothing. There were several shirts and pairs of trousers, three pairs of long johns, two folded blankets and a pair of new-looking shoes that Creslein had been apparently saving for a special occasion.

Carroll checked the books, hoping one of them might be Creslein's personal journal, similar to Pascal's that was still missing from the McDowell crime scene. Not finding a journal, Carroll set the books aside.

Henry pointed out that the trunk contained another section. It was not really a secret compartment. Like the top tray, it was just another section to facilitate storage. He lifted it out easily. They were disappointed to find that it contained only more clothing and another blanket. Val was placing the blanket on the table when something fell out of it.

It was a stack of letters, bound together on four sides by string. The top envelope was so yellowed and faded that it was unreadable. She looked at the second letter and saw that it was addressed L.B. Creslein. They all were. The handwriting on the envelopes appeared to be identical, indicating all had been authored by the same person.

Val looked at Carroll. He simply nodded, giving her the go-ahead to open one. He would have loved to open them himself, but he was too excited. His hands were shaking, so he kept them hidden under the table.

"Have you got some surgical gloves, Henry?" she inquired. "These letters are so old that we need to be careful not to damage or smudge them."

"I sure do, in my truck," he said, trotted toward the front door. He returned with his First Responder bag and pulled out enough gloves for all three of them.

Val made sure that hers were snug before she opened the letter on the top of the stack. They knew that Creslein was the recipient, so instead of reading it from the beginning, she flipped straight to the last page.

"Holy sh–" she tried, but her favorite exclamation turned into a wheeze. She simply held the letter up so Carroll and Henry could read the name of the author – John Pascal.

There were a total of twenty-nine letters, all from Pascal to Creslein. The earliest was dated January 10, 1871. The last was dated, May 27, 1895, two days before Pascal died in the logging accident. They put them in chronological order and divided them between them to read.

Carroll instructed Henry and Val to make note of any references to Georgia, the colony, or anything to do with the war, particularly if it referred to Jefferson Davis or the treasury. He also wanted them to look for an explanation of how the two men might be connected.

The only noise in the dining room over the next forty minutes came from the sound of paper as the three readers carefully moved from one delicate page to the next. Carroll finished first even though he had taken the extra letters. He quietly got up and checked on Betty and Aunt Ruth before taking a break. Henry and Val finished soon after and, after taking their breaks, the three reconvened in the dining room.

They compared their notes to see what stood out. One of the things they noted was that several of the letters were obviously written as responses to ones that Pascal had received from Creslein. Several started with In response to your question, or, having received your letter of such and such.

"Is there any chance that the Creslein letters might be preserved somewhere?" Val asked.

Carroll had been wondering the same thing. While the Pascal letters were a fantastic find, reading them was like listening to a one-sided phone conversation. The letters might provide some useful information, but they would never know the entire conversation unless Creslein's letters to Pascal were also found.

"It's possible. After all, we found these," he answered. "But let's be realistic. It would be a miracle."

It was late, but Carroll called Ben to inform him about finding the trunk in the attic.

"You're the luckiest son of a bitch I know," Ben laughed, after hearing the letters were from Creslein, the same name Carroll had asked him to check on earlier.

"I've been through the archives at the library and museum dozens, maybe even hundreds of times," Walden said, "and I don't remember seeing letters from either Creslein or Pascal, but that doesn't mean that they're not there. I'll recheck the library and the museum."

"Perfect," Carroll responded. "Can you get on it the first thing in the morning and let me know what you come up with?"

Walden pointed out that it was almost 1:00 so it was technically already in the morning.

"Would it be okay if I waited until they were open? Or would you prefer that I go ahead and break into both of them now?"

"Wise ass! Call me as soon as you know something, okay?"

"No problem," Ben chuckled.

Carroll returned to the group discussion. It first appeared that Creslein and Pascal were step or half-brothers. They had different last names, but there were several references to our father.

Carroll came up with another theory. He thought they might be referring to Jefferson Davis, the former Rebel president. As much as Val was into the whole treasure hunt thing, she was not so sure about his hypothesis.

"But we don't know that for sure and there's no way to prove that Pascal is talking about Jefferson Davis."

Carroll reminded her that sometimes being a nerd comes in handy. He read a line from the first letter, written in 1871:

"I attended the memorial for the great General Robert E. Lee, where our father gave a most eloquent remembrance."

"Jefferson Davis presided over the memorial service for Robert E. Lee," he informed her.

When she still was not completely convinced, he pointed out two more letters. One, from 1877, informed Creslein, "Our father has moved to Biloxi, Mississippi."

Carroll noted that Davis had indeed moved to Biloxi that year. The other letter left no doubt. It spoke of father's passing in New Orleans on December 6, 1889.

"Go ahead and google to see where Jefferson Davis died and on what date," he told her. "I'll wait."

"There's no need," she consented, flipping him off and sending Henry on a laughing binge.

Henry had a question after he recovered, "But Pascal never once referred to Jefferson Davis by his name. Why not? The war was over and Davis was out of prison and a free man again. I don't get it. What was the big secret?"

Carroll explained that he initially thought they were using the term as a form of deference, similar to how the revolutionaries and even people today still refer to George Washington as the father of our country. He reminded them that in the eyes of Creslein and Pascal, Davis was the father of the Confederacy.

"You said initially," Val noted. "So if it wasn't that, then what else was it?"

"You're right," Carroll admitted. "The war was over so Davis wasn't in any danger, but what if Creslein and Pascal were talking about something so important, so secret, that they had to talk about it in code?"

Val broke into a big grin as visions of being a Goonie returned. She and Carroll filled Henry in on their previous research about the treasury.

"I've heard them stories my whole life," Henry scoffed, shaking his head. "There's nothing to 'em. They're just fairy tales."

"Maybe you're right," said Carroll. "In fact, you probably are, but whoever killed Thomas McDowell and Lenny Sauls still believes otherwise or they wouldn't have killed him for it. So, we're going to follow the clues."

Carroll did not change Henry's mind about the Confederate treasury, but his strategy on finding Thomas McDowell's killer was sound, so Henry concurred with it.

As they continued to reread and scrutinize the letters, it became increasingly clear Creslein and Pascal were talking in code and that they were referencing the 1865 flight of Jefferson Davis from Richmond, Virginia, to the final capture site in Irwinville, Georgia. There were numerous descriptions that matched the months of April and May of 1865, such as "on Father's final trip to Georgia" or, "I stopped at the place where Father was reunited with Mother after their temporary separation."

"Remember, Pascal was with Jefferson Davis almost all the way from Virginia until he was captured in Irwinville just nine miles away from here," Carroll reminded them.

Having done such detailed research on Jefferson Davis's flight and the removal of the Confederate treasury, Carroll thought it was evident that Pascal was using the terms, livestock, cattle, goats and hogs, to refer to the treasury in his coded letters. Val and Henry agreed.

Livestock probably referenced the treasury as a whole, but they could not determine which animal corresponded with which specific part of the treasury. For instance, was the word cattle being used to refer to gold, currency or the chest of silver?

Another point they agreed on was that the letters showed that the overall numbers of "livestock" were depleted as it moved from Richmond to Georgia. There were other specific references that matched historically.

Pascal's mentioning that "some of cattle and hogs were sold in Washington, Georgia," was one of the best examples. He was clearly talking about the payout to the troops on May 4, 1865. Val made another exciting find, a comment about some cattle rustlers near Chennault, Georgia in May. Of course, the letter did not mention that this particular incident occurred not in 1896, but more than 30 years earlier. That would have allowed people to figure out that it was in reference to part of the treasury that was stolen.

Now that it was clear that Creslein was talking about the missing treasury, the pieces began coming together more quickly. Henry pointed out something that he had read.

"A couple of my letters talked about strays from the herd." He said. "That's the first time that Creslein had used that word, strays."

Val and Carroll looked at each other and then toward Henry. It was an astute observation. Henry had one-upped them. In every other letter, Creslein had referred to the livestock as either being sold or rustled. They had decided that sold indicated withdrawals from the treasury, such as payment to troops or purchasing. Rustled obviously referred to outright theft like the robbery that occurred in Chennault, Georgia.

Val had a theory about Pascal's use of the word *stray*:

"Could they be talking about diverting part of the treasury to another location?"

Henry pulled out the letters he was referencing. There were no dates, but the two places referring to where the strays roamed away were when it was moving south, one in North Carolina and one in South Carolina, respectively.

They knew the treasury left Richmond, Virginia, and arrived in Danville on April 2, 1865, and that it was done in such haste that it was not even counted until four days later, on April 6.

"Four days is a long time," said Carroll. "It wouldn't be difficult to imagine how some of it could have been removed before it was counted. And if it was taken during those four days, before it was counted, then it wouldn't be missing, would it?"

He also noted that some of the letters indicated that another shipment of livestock had left Virginia more than a month before the main shipment of livestock. This was one of the most exciting developments. There had been rumors of secret shipments of Confederate gold since the end of the war. It was legendary.

Some stories indicated it was split up to hide it from the Union Army, while others reason that it was for practical purposes, as it was needed in different locations. But the most exciting stories are that it was stolen and that it is still out there somewhere waiting to be discovered. Why, only just a few nights before, Carroll had flipped on the TV to find Clint Eastwood in pursuit of that very same loot in The Good, the Bad and the Ugly.

Carroll's problem with the whole hidden treasure story as it related to Fitzgerald was that it just did not make sense. There was too much of a time discrepancy. Davis was captured in May of 1865. If Pascal and Creslein were writing about the treasury in 1895, then why did they leave it hidden and untouched for thirty years? Carroll found a plausible explanation in the letters.

"Pascal wrote to Creslein, explaining that his two partners had passed away," he said. "There's no mention of how they died but, from his letter, it appears that they died in separate locations – weeks or, more likely, months apart, and, in Creslein's words, leaving me alone to tend to the livestock. Carroll pointed out that that left Pascal as the only person on earth who knew the exact whereabouts of the hidden treasury."

"One of the things that's bugged me is why he left it hidden for 30 years," Carroll continued. "I think I may have the answer. Pascal was wounded on the morning of May 10, 1865 when Jefferson Davis was captured."

He went on to explain that although Pascal survived, he had likely suffered with his injury for years, to the point where he was physically unable to travel. There was also a reference to a bout with smallpox in the letters that could account for additional time.

Henry still did not buy it, saying, "If you combine all that time, then you're talking about what –five years? Maybe ten at most? That means he still left it sitting there for twenty years. No way!"

"I think the recovery time could have been much longer," said Val. "Think about the medical practices in the 1860s. If he got smallpox after his leg was amputated, then he could have been incapacitated for years."

Carroll sat straight up in his chair, "What are you talking about?" he asked. "Why did you say amputated?"

"Duh! That's what you call it when your leg is caught off."

"They amputated his leg?" said Carroll.

"Yeah. He lost his leg after he was shot," she replied matter-of-factly. "You didn't know that? And does it really matter?"

She pulled one of the letters from her stack and read the account where Pascal described how he was shot in the left leg in Irwinville when President Davis was captured. Pascal was taken prisoner and was transported to Macon where he received treatment; however, the leg became infected, necessitating amputation.

Carroll sat there, momentarily stunned, before he turned on his laptop and scrolled through the thumbnails of the photos from the Blue & Gray Museum. He pulled up the photo of Pascal and Lewis Clute.

"Unbelievable! I'm an idiot!" he said, palming his forehead.

"It's not really that unbelievable that you're an idiot," a grinning Val reassured him, "but just what are you referring to?"

He spun the laptop around so that she and Henry could view the photo. It showed the Union veteran, Lewis Clute, standing by John Pascal who appeared to have two healthy legs.

"Could it be a prosthetic?" Henry wondered.

"No. They didn't really have anything like that. Most amputees had peg-legs or actually, just stumps. And, even if they did manage to find something better, take a good look," he said, as he enlarged the photo.

You could clearly see that both of Pascal's legs were intact.

"But, that's not why I'm an idiot. It's not just the legs. Do you notice anything else?" he asked them.

Val and Henry looked at the photo again and shook their heads. Carroll was relieved that they didn't catch it on their first viewing either.

"That's not John Ephraim Pascal," he said.

Val looked at him like he was crazy, "What are you talking about, Uncle Bob? His name is right there under the photo!"

"They left something off," Carroll informed them.

"What?" asked Henry.

"Two letters, J and R," he said. "That's John Ephraim Pascal, Jr.," he added, pointing to the two-legged Pascal in the photo.

None of them had noticed it on their initial viewing, but there was a vast difference in the age between the two men in the photo. Knowing that Clute was born in 1842, Carroll determined that he was at least fifty-three when the photo was taken in 1895. Pascal appeared to be in his late twenties or early thirties at the most. This meant that he was either a baby during the Civil War or was even born after it ended.

"Okay, so we're all idiots," Val acknowledged.

It suddenly made sense. Not two, but all the people who were originally responsible for hiding the treasury assets were dead by 1895. No wonder it sat undiscovered for thirty years.

Carroll connected the final dots;

"We don't know if his father told him about the treasury or if he somehow found the clues on his own, but it was Pascal's son, John Ephraim Pascal Junior who was searching for the treasury in 1895. I believe it was just bad luck or at least bad timing for him. He arrived in the colony too late. By the time he figured out where to look, he found that Robert Solomon, Aunt Ruth's father, had already legally claimed the land."

"So, he gained access to the property the only way that he could," said Henry, now completely on board with Carroll's theory, "by working for my Granddaddy Solomon. That's why he was always around."

"Until he died in the logging accident," Val added.

She also noted that Pascal's last letter, written just two days before his death, encouraged Creslein to come "as soon and as quickly as you are able," she emphasized.

Carroll hypothesized that Creslein arrived only to learn that Pascal had recently died. He had assumed that Pascal owned the land. They scanned through the letters again and confirmed that Pascal never once mentioned that he had failed to acquire rightful ownership.

"It must have been a double blow for Creslein to traverse such a great distance under adverse conditions only to find that his partner was dead, and he couldn't even get onto the land," Carroll sympathized.

The next question became did Creslein know exactly where to look? The answer was probably somewhere in the missing letters. Carroll, Henry and Val were eager to see if Ben could locate them. They continued to compare notes on the letters, but their train was beginning to run out of steam. They temporarily abandoned the letters, focusing their attention on the trunk again. They carefully examined each item, paying more attention to details.

Carroll had initially put the books aside when he determined a journal was not among them. He picked up one of the books and opened it, immediately realizing that he was holding something in his hand that was very rare and, quite likely, valuable.

It was an original first edition of The Picture of Dorian Gray, Oscar Wilde's story of a young man who sells his soul for eternal youth. As he thumbed through the pages, two pieces of paper fluttered to the tabletop.

The first was a recipe for a stew made with venison, deer meat. The second paper was an original certificate issued by the American Tribune Soldier Colony Company showing that Creslein had purchased two shares at ten dollars each. It was signed by the man himself, P.H. Fitzgerald. It was hard for Carroll to believe that he was holding something that Fitzgerald had also held and signed 120 years before.

Being aware of the age of the items and their delicate condition, the three investigators carefully continued with their search of the trunk.

"There's something about checking the pockets of a dead guy that your relative killed that's a bit unnerving," Henry admitted.

Carroll and Val were both laughing at Henry's comment as she picked up a pair of trousers and noticed something in one of the pockets.

"I've got another letter!" she yelled excitedly as she fished it out.

Carroll sat up straight, but he saw Val's face change from a grin to a frown as she inspected the letter more closely.

"Well, it actually looks like just one page of a longer letter," she added dejectedly, "And it's not even the first page."

Val cleared her throat and then proceeded to read the letter using her now-perfected, over exaggerated Southern drawl;

"We decided we oughtta keep the livestock safe foe' the time be'n," she twanged. "It weren't big enough to hold 'em all, so we broke down two wagons and used 'em to sho up the corral."

There was a stifled giggle from over Carroll's left shoulder. He turned around to see that Aunt Ruth had quietly slipped back into the room and had been watching them work. Val's impression was too much for her, and she was having difficulty holding back her laughter. He could relate. Although Val's voice was spot-on, there was something about watching a short Chinese-American-Yankee female imitating a Southern redneck male that made it even funnier.

She continued, "We put extra support along the walls and at the entrance and used the three axles in the corners and one in the center. This would allow us to leave the livestock unattended if needed."

Val stopped reading and shot Carroll a wide-eyed look.

"Is he saying that they buried it in the corral?" she asked. "If so, and if we could figure out where the corral was, then we would know where to dig!"

Carroll didn't immediately respond. He was thinking about the drafts and sketches that he had seen at the Blue and Gray Museum. One sketch especially came to mind. He flipped his own laptop open and pulled up the folder labeled, Photos Fitz.

He scanned the thumbnails of the photos he had taken at the museum and, after finding the thumbnail he was looking for, he opened it and enlarged the photo.

Carroll studied the photo for a couple of minutes before he stood up and walked over to push Aunt Ruth's wheelchair up beside his seat at the table.

"Aunt Ruth, did your folks ever say exactly where the creek ran through your property or how big it was?"

"Didn't have to say," she answered. "I remember it my own self. It was dammed up before I was born, but we used to play in the dry crickbed for years, 'til daddy pushed dirt in it with his first tractor. It weren't no little stream," she added. "The sides was real steep in places."

Carroll brought the photo up to full screen on his laptop. The sketch indicated some landmarks, most notably the community of Swan and Irwinville, as well as creeks. He enlarged the photo even more and pointed to one creek in particular.

"Could this be it?" he asked.

Aunt Ruth adjusted her glasses and leaned forward, studying the sketch closely.

"Which way is north?" she needed to know.

He rotated the photo so that north was the top of the screen and tapped to indicate it. She looked again and nodded.

"Uh-huh. That's about right, then." However she appeared to be confused as she drew her finger along the line that represented the creek. She pointed to the area indicating the corral.

"Daddy never had no pen there far as I know, and this don't look like his write'n. Where did you get it?"

"This was done by John E. Pascal, before your family ever even thought about coming to Georgia."

"The one that got kilt by the logs? That don't make no sense. He didn't get here till after daddy and Uncle Jeb come down."

"No, not him. It was done by his father, John Ephraim Pascal Sr.," Carroll clarified, "about thirty years before that. And, you're right; there never was a corral there."

Henry and Val were now squatting behind Aunt Ruth, viewing the screen over her shoulders. Carroll pointed to a specific corner of the nonexistent corral that overlapped the creek line.

"I know there wasn't a corral there, Aunt Ruth," he said, "but what would have been in this corner right here when you were little?"

"That's where we used to play on the rocks by the well," she answered.

"And was there a place where the water ran back underground before it was dammed up?" he asked, "Did your family ever say?"

"Mama said there was a cave, but daddy said it weren't noth'n but a crack where snakes hid so they covered it with the rocks."

"It's in the well, isn't it!" Val interrupted, no longer able to contain her enthusiasm.

"I'm beginning to think it's still there," Carroll answered.

He could not believe the words actually came from his mouth.

Aunt Ruth shook her head, "Ain't noth'n down there," she insisted. "I been hearing folks talk'n 'bout that miss'n treasure my whole life. Daddy wondered 'bout it too. They dug the well out one time. Went all the way back down to the water and Uncle Jeb even dived down, feeling along the bottom. He 'bout gave Aunt Rita and my mama a heart attack wait'n on 'em to come back up. He finally did and there ain't noth'n down there."

"No there's not," Carroll agreed.

"But, you just said that you think it's still down there," said Henry.

"I really believe it is," Carroll responded.

"Then, it's in the well?" Val asked.

"No."

"Are you feeling better?" she asked, "Because if you are, I'm going to hit you," she threatened him.

"There's not anything down there — at least not on the bottom," he said smiling broadly. "They went too far."

Aunt Ruth looked concerned as she asked, "Bobby, I'm think'n that wreck done rattled your brain!"

"I'm fine, Aunt Ruth. Would I be right if I said that the rock pile was right here by the well?" he said, pointing to the photo.

She nodded in agreement, "Uh huh. That's right."

Carroll closed his laptop and turned to face the group, "It wasn't in the well; it never was."

"You've got to remember, the well wasn't dug until thirty years later," he explained. "They just dug it there because it was already low and it was the best spot. What they obviously didn't know was that, in 1865, three guys had come right through here in a hell of a hurry and found a natural crevice to hide the treasury in. They never built a corral."

Carroll asked Val to retrieve the letter she had found in Creslein's trouser pocket. She promptly pulled it out.

"Read it again," he requested.

She complied, this time reading it seriously and clearly:

"…So we broke down two wagons and used them to shore up the corral. We put extra support along the walls and at the entrance and used the three axles in the corners and one in the center. This would allow us to leave the livestock unattended if needed."

She paused at the same place that she had earlier, but with a new understanding this time. Henry also got it.

"They used the wood from the wagon to reinforce the cave!" Henry exclaimed. "That's why he used the words, shore up! I wondered why they would put an axle in the center of a corral. They didn't. They weren't used as post for a corral, but as columns to brace up the cave. That means that it's probably still–"

Henry's voice trailed off as he looked through the back window out into the dark toward the well. The others could not help but follow his gaze.

"If we're going to do this, then it would be better to do it at night," Carroll cautioned them. "Otherwise, people are going to wonder why we're digging in the backyard."

Henry stood up, "Let's go do it right now!"

It was not exactly what he intended, but Henry was ready. And Val? Val was beyond ready. She was now in full Goonie-mode and probably would have been willing to dig right by herself, with her bare hands, at this point.

"All right," Carroll conceded. "Let's go!"

Henry opened the back door, and they stepped out onto the porch. The temperature was just right, and the waning gibbous moon provided enough natural light for them to work. Henry went to the shed and returned with two shovels and a pickax. Armed with their hand tools and a printout of the sketch, they proceeded to a low spot just a few feet southwest of the well where a few remnants of the rock pile remained.

They first had to remove a massive pecan limb that had broken from a nearby tree and was partially lying on their target area. After they dragged it out of the way, Henry grabbed the pickax and started breaking up the dirt. Carroll and Val took positions on either side of him and began using the shovels, each digging from a different angle. The ground was softer than expected and it went surprisingly quickly – for about twenty minutes. They were down several feet when they started to have difficulty. Val and Henry were beginning to get frustrated, but Carroll saw it as a positive sign.

"That's not the same rock. It's flint rock," he informed them, "the same rock that Aunt Ruth climbed on as a small child and the same that marked the entrance to the crevice."

That was all that he needed to say. Henry and Val redoubled their efforts. They became digging machines. It took them only a few more minutes to locate a possible entrance, but it was very small.

"I can get through it!" Val said.

Henry shook his head, "We need to make it bigger."

"That'll take another thirty minutes to an hour! I can probably get in there now."

"Henry's right," agreed Carroll. "It's too risky."

"Quit treating me like a girl!" she warned them. "It'll be daylight soon, and half the town will be asking why people are digging behind the Jackson House."

She was right, of course. It would likely take another hour to chip away a larger entrance and it would have been noisy, also.

After clearing away more debris and equipping her with Carroll's LED light, they tied a rope around Val and watched as she scurried into the hole like a spider. Carroll and Henry watched her disappear and then, with growing apprehension, listened to the sounds of her crawling and grunting.

"Are you okay?" Carroll called into the hole.

"Yeah, I'm good," she assured him, "but now I know how Saddam Hussein felt!"

Henry and Carroll were still laughing when she spoke again, "It's getting a little wider."

There were a few moments of excruciating silence, followed by more scuffling and grunting, then they heard a painful yell, "Aaaargh!"

Carroll jammed his body into the hole as far as possible, reaching blindly with his arm.

"Val? Val!" he called, as he and Henry began pulling the rope that was tied around her.

"Stop!" she yelled back. "Jesus! Quit pulling the rope! You're banging me into the wall! Are you trying to kill me?"

"What happened," asked Henry.

"I put my leg down on a piece of metal and cut it."

"Metal?" he repeated.

"Yeah, I think it was a spike or something and I can see more. There's no wood left, but I'm guessing that this must be part of the wag—"

She stopped again, then screamed, "Oh, shit! OH, SHIT!"

Believing that she was injured worse than they or she had first thought, Carroll and Henry panicked. They grabbed the pickax and shovel and were desperately trying to enlarge the hole when they heard her scuffling again. Val's hand suddenly popped out of the crevice. Carroll reached down to help pull her out. Instead of grasping his hand, she put something into it.

He looked down to find three coins: two gold and one silver. The silver coin featured an image of Lady Liberty, seated holding a shield in her right hand and a flag in her left, with thirteen stars above her. The opposite side of the coin was embossed with an eagle. The two gold coins were identical. Each featured the head of Lady Liberty on one side and an eagle on the other. They were amazingly heavy. Carroll flipped them over and saw they were twenty dollar gold pieces.

He was still staring at them when Val popped her head out of the hole. The expression on her dirty face was a combination of a grimace of pain and a big grin. She looked like a cross between a gopher and a Chinese chimney sweep. They helped her out and discovered that her leg was injured worse than she had admitted. Henry tore a piece of his shirt off to wrap around it.

"It's there, Uncle Bob!" Val exclaimed, grabbing him by the shoulders. "I don't know how much, because part of it had caved in, but there's more than I thought there would be. No wonder Creslein wouldn't leave! He knew what was in there!"

She was describing what she had seen in the cave, but Carroll's mind was preoccupied. Something had registered upon hearing her mention Creslein's name again. He recalled an entry he had seen in the Roster of the Confederate Soldiers of Georgia.

In her excitement, Val had reverted to the little girl whose words sometimes outran her breath. She had to stop and inhale before continuing.

"And I think there was another chest on the left, but it was covered with dirt. What time is it?" she asked. "Ben should be here for this! We should call him!"

"It's the middle of the night!" Henry chuckled.

"Besides, you know that Granny don't like that boy," he added. "She says L.B. don't stand for Lawrence Benjamin; she says it's for Little Bastard!"

Val and Henry erupted into laughter, but the blood suddenly drained from Carroll's face. He pulled out his cell phone and quickly sent a text.

"Let's get Val inside," he said, looking around cautiously.

Carroll and Henry each grabbed an arm to support Val as she hobbled toward the house. She looked up at him as they arrived at the back steps.

"Okay, Uncle Bob. It's time to 'fess up. What's going on?" she asked. "You should be as excited as we are about this!"

There was no time for a detailed reason, so he just said it: "It's Ben. Ben Walden."

"Yeah, I know," she replied. "I just said we should call him."

"No, I meant Ben Walden killed Thomas McDowell and Lenny Sauls," he answered as they entered the house.

"What?" she exclaimed, thinking she'd heard him incorrectly.

"Yes, Ben Walden. I'm one hundred percent sure this time. He probably knows that I've figured it out by now and, if I'm right, he's not about to just run."

Henry and Val followed as Carroll hurried into the dining room. He stopped abruptly in front of the table. It was empty. There was nothing on it. The laptops, notes and paperwork had all been removed, including the historic letters. Carroll's first thought – and hope – was that Betty must have cleared it, thinking they were finished, but then he saw that his Glock had also been removed.

Carroll's heart sank. He knew Betty would never have touched his gun. He turned and was about to call for her when she wheeled her grandmother into the room.

Carroll knew Ben was there even before he saw him. Betty's face was full of fear, but Ruth Jackson's was stoic. She had dealt with grief and fear for more than a century. She was doing it again now.

"You know, I really feel pretty stupid right now," Walden said, stepping into the dining room behind Betty.

"I've lived here my whole life, and it never even crossed my mind that it was right there in the damn yard!" Ben chuckled.

Walden held his own gun in his right hand and Carroll's Glock in his left.

"Come on, Ben," said Carroll, "You don't want to do this."

"You're right. I don't, but it's not like I have a whole lot of options right now, Bob."

"Sure you do," Carroll reasoned. "You can let everyone else go and keep me."

"Don't try to play me, Bob. I like you. I truly do, but let's be realistic. I've already killed two people and now five people know it. I don't really have a choice here, do I?"

"It was you who killed them?" said Henry angrily, taking a step toward Walden.

"You really need to calm down, Henry," Ben advised him.

He did not shout it. He did not even raise his voice. Ben's tone was more like someone concerned for a distressed friend or loved one. Henry paused and the two men made eye contact.

"Seriously, calm down," Walden warned as he raised his arms and pointed one gun at Betty and the other at her Mrs. Jackson, "or, I'll shoot them right now."

Henry lifted his own empty hands and slowly backed away.

"You'll never get away with it, Ben," Val told him.

"Sure I will. One thing about these old houses is they stand up pretty good; but, if there's ever anything like an electrical short, a chimney fire, or a lightning strike, they can go up like a matchbox. We lose one every decade or so."

Walden returned his main attention to Carroll.

"I've gotta tell you, Bob, I thought you were a good detective," he scoffed. "Pardon the pun, but you've been running around here like a chicken with your head cut off. I'm actually glad to see that you finally figured it out. I truly am! It renews my faith in you!"

"I'm a little slower than others sometimes, but I always get there eventually," Carroll replied. "You're named after your great grandfather, Lawrence Benjamin Creslein."

"So, you did see it," Walden acknowledged. "I didn't even think about it when you asked to borrow a book at the house, because I figured there was no way the name Creslein would ever come up. He was actually my great-great grandfather. My daddy's maternal grandmother was the daughter of Lawrence Benjamin Creslein."

"What book?" Val asked.

"The Roster of the Confederate Soldiers of Georgia," said Carroll. "It lists every known Georgia soldier who fought for the Confederacy. When you mentioned Creslein's name earlier, something kicked in and I realized it was one of the names I'd seen in the book I had borrowed from Ben. And, after that, when Henry said Lawrence Benjamin, it all came together."

Carroll looked back over at Walden.

"I wondered why you only had that one volume of The Roster when there are actually six of them and you're supposedly a history buff," he said. "The truth is the only history you're interested in was anything connected to the missing treasury."

Ben shrugged, "What can I say? You're right. I've heard about it my whole life. My great grandmother used to tell me stories when I was little."

He leaned down and leered at Ruth Jackson, as he added, "She even told me how my great great granddaddy got ran over and killed by a train, but now we know that ain't true, don't we Miss J?"

Carroll had to give Aunt Ruth credit. Even after Ben's jab, she appeared calm. He clearly seemed to know that L.B Creslein had not been killed by the train, but how? The newspaper account had reported it that way, and the only people who knew about it, the Solomons, were all dead – except one. But there was no doubt in Carroll's mind that Ruth Jackson had never uttered a word about it until that night on the porch.

He looked over to find Walden staring at him intently. The smirk on Ben's face morphed into a broad grin. Still pointing the gun in his left hand directly at Ruth Jackson, he reached around with his right and tucked the other weapon in his waist, then removed his cell phone from his back pocket and activated an app. A recording of the elderly Jackson's voice began to play. It was a recording of her describing the events surrounding L.B. Creslein's death. The others appeared dumbfounded, but it was suddenly clear to Carroll. Ben had been using Carroll's own cell phone to eavesdrop on his conversations.

"I've been listening since your first trip," Ben giggled. "You always have your cell phone close, no matter where you are – whether it's here or in Indianapolis or California, and I heard it all, Bob!"

Walden continued, "At first, I couldn't figure out what the hell was going on at that meeting in Tifton at the Lamplighter Pub. I'm glad I was sitting down when I heard you and Val being introduced to Agent Pafford. I thought Billy Bob was the perfect fall-guy for me, but he turned out to be a cop! And, not just a damn cop, but an FBI agent! Holy Hell! I sure didn't see that one coming!"

"And then, when you jumped on Tony as a suspect? I thought it was just too good to be true!" Ben cackled. "I'll give you that one, though. I mean, you seeing him at the Ridgeway around the same time in the morning, and Tony being first to show up at my office, and when Lenny got run over, and then, again, at my house. Man! That was all just icing on the cake!"

"But, your little girl here," he chuckled, looking at Val, "she busted that bubble, too. Of course, I knew Tony was seeing Sheila, and that you would eliminate him as a suspect sooner or later, but I didn't think you two would figure that out for a while and it'd give me some breathing room."

"How did it feel, banging your own head on a dumpster in the alley?" Val asked, letting Ben know she was not afraid of him.

"Pretty damn strange, Val! It was mighty surreal," he laughed. "I actually did too good of a damn job. Hell, I don't even remember dialing 9-1-1, but I did. They said I could've died!"

"Perish the thought," Ruth Jackson murmured.

"You obviously have Pascal's journal," said Carroll. "And I'm betting that you also have the letters from Creslein to Pascal. Something had to keep you motivated to search after so many others tried and failed. How did you get them?"

"I can't say for sure," replied Ben, confirming Carroll's assumption. "They've always been in the family. I think some idiot found them among Pascal's possessions when he died – the son, not the father, and probably glanced through them and saw they were to our relative so they just gave them back."

Walden chuckled, "Pretty ironic really, because old Pascal wasn't quite as good at sticking to their secret code. Everybody back then knew about the rumors of the stolen treasury. The clues were clearly there. If whoever found the letters had paid attention it might have been found then. As for my family, most of them didn't know about the letters or didn't care. It's really a shame that more people don't appreciate history like you do, Bob."

"I've already called for help," Carroll informed Walden.

"Nice try," Ben chuckled, "but I get a notification every time you make a call and you haven't made one since you called me last night."

Carroll knew they were quickly running out of time. Ben would not wait for daylight. The smoke would be seen and the fire department, most likely would still be able to save it – or, at least enough of it for investigators to find evidence. A fire, in a house like this, started during the night, however, was another matter entirely. It probably would not be seen and reported until the flames were visible and out of control. It could very well appear to be an accident.

Before they had entered the house, Carroll had sent a text to both Jerry Hall and John White, the GBI agent he had met at the truck stop stake out:
Ben Walden is killer McDowell & Sauls Jackson home on Lincoln

Because Walden had not mentioned the text, Carroll assumed that he either did not receive notifications about texts, or, it was not an audible notification. If so, he had to keep Ben distracted so that he would not check his phone. Carroll could only hope that his text had been received and help was on the way.

He assessed the situation. He was on Walden's left while Val and Henry were on his right. Ben was still standing behind Betty, and he had pulled the other gun back out so he had weapons in both hands. There was no way they could get to him before he could fire one or both guns.

Carroll was about to speak, but Ruth Jackson beat him to it.

"Well, since you plan on kill'n me anyway I don't spect you'd mind if'n I do some kill'n myself," she said. "Ain't no reason to be leav'n what's left in that bottle of Jefferson's."

Not waiting on a reply, she added, "Bobby, go get us them crystal whiskey glasses out the china cabinet."

Carroll took half a step toward the dining room.

"Wait just a damn minute, Bob!" shouted Ben. "I'm not stupid! You stay right there in that chair! Betty, you go get the damn glasses! And don't try anything or your granny will be the first one to go!"

"I won't do anything," Betty promised. "Please don't hurt Granny."

Walden backed into the corner, so he could watch the others in the room without someone being able to sneak around behind him.

Betty returned with the glasses, but Ben instructed her to leave the others on the tray.

"Just use one and share it," he ordered.

Betty poured a glass and handed it to her grandmother, who took the glass and looked around the room.

"Well, if we was all allowed to have a glass, then we could have a proper toast," she said, shooting a look at Walden, "but since some folks don't have good manners, I guess I'll just have to make do."

"To my family," she said, holding up the glass and making eye contact with each of them, including her recent adoptees.

There was something hidden in the look Aunt Ruth gave Carroll. She was up to something, and it made him nervous. Val apparently caught it, too, as she shifted in her seat uncomfortably. Ruth Jackson concluded her toast, took a sip of the Jefferson's Select and then offered the glass to Carroll. Ben leveled Carroll's own gun toward him as he reached for the glass and pointed the other at Mrs. Jackson.

"You can have a drink, Bob, but I'll shoot you and her both if you try anything."

Carroll did not respond verbally, but he nodded, indicating that he understood. He raised his right hand and held it there as he slowly took the glass with his left. He finished the bourbon in one gulp and handed the glass back to Aunt Ruth.

"Y'all wanna tell me some more about why you expected me to be nice to this boy?" she asked, as she emptied the last of Jefferson's Select from the bottle. Looking straight at Ben, she added, "'cause he ain't noth'n but a little shit."

"You never have liked me have you, Miss J?" Walden noted.

"Naw, I ain't – and quit calling me that. I ain't no old maid. My husband mighta died, but I'm still married. And you can drop that "J," too, 'cause I ain't no rapper neither. My last name is Jackson, not J. Me and yo mama might be friends, but you ain't noth'n like her."

"No, I'm not. I guess I'm more like my great great granddaddy, the man that your uncle killed," he shot back menacingly.

Carroll sat up as the tension increased, thinking What the hell was Aunt Ruth up to?

"I 'bout had enough of your mouth," Aunt Ruth told him.

"You won't have to worry about that much longer, so why don't you just suck on that empty bottle."

"Keep disrespect'n me in my own house and I'll give you something to worry about!" she warned him.

"I told you to SHUT UP you stupid old bitch!" Ben yelled, as he turned toward Ruth Jackson.

Several things happened at that exact moment: Unbeknownst to Walden, a tiny red dot suddenly appeared on his chest just as he heard a faint, strange sound coming from the front of the house, and Betty screamed.

Walden spun back around toward Betty as Aunt Ruth leapt from her wheelchair with her arm already coming from over her shoulder to hurl the whiskey glass in his direction.

The distinct sound of the stretching spring on the front screen door and its recoil snatching the door closed with a loud pop was immediately drowned out by an incredibly loud BANG from the back door and thundering boots and yells of "POLICE! FBI! Everybody down! Now!" coming from every conceivable direction.

Ben Walden raised his arms and fired as Carroll, Val and Henry all simultaneously lunged toward him.

Epilogue

Robert Carroll pulled into the driveway of the Jackson residence and parked, but he could not bring himself to get out of the vehicle immediately. He looked at the front porch. It was hard to believe how much he had come to love this old house and the family that lived in it.

And now, here he was again.

He used a cane to walk as he favored his left leg. Luckily, the bullet had gone clean through, but it was still painful when he put pressure on it..

A black wreath hung on the screen door, but the main interior door stood open as usual. He tried the screen door and found that it was unlatched.

"Hello? Betty? Henry?" he called out as he entered.

"Come on in, Bobby" they answered simultaneously from different parts of the house.

He headed toward the kitchen where he found Betty taking something out of the oven.

"You look nice, Bobby," she complimented. "That's not the same suit you wore to Lenny's funeral, is it?"

"Thanks. No, it's not the same one," he acknowledged. "I flew back to Indy Tuesday. I wanted to tell Thomas McDowell's grandparents that the case was solved in person, and I went home and got it afterward. I don't wear suits much anymore, except when I go to court, weddings or —" Carroll did not finish his sentence.

Henry walked in, also wearing a suit. The two men spoke and shook hands.

"Could I get you a cup of coffee, Bobby?" Betty offered as she automatically poured one for Henry.

"No, thanks," said Carroll, "One more cup and I'll be bouncing off the walls."

The three of them sat down at the small table in the kitchen. Carroll realized that it was the first time that he had sat there. They usually had meals in the dining room.

They tried to make small talk – mumbling about the weather, how it looked like it was going to be a hot summer followed by some trivial nonsense. But they quickly lapsed into an uncomfortable silence.

The quiet made the high-pitched whirring noise from the main hallway and subsequent loud crash sound like a semi-truck had smashed into the house. They rushed into the hallway to find a broken knickknack table on the floor, surrounded by broken ceramics and glass.

"Granny! Are you all right?" Henry asked, as Betty brushed pieces of broken glass from her lap.

"I don't know how y'all spect me to drive this damn thing with one working arm!" she complained, partially lifting her right arm in a sling.

Like a one-person crew on a NASCAR track, Betty hurried to the kitchen and returned just as quickly with a broom, dustpan and small trashcan to clear the scene of the accident.

"Granny, I've already told you, you've got to slow down," Henry cautioned, "You've never had a motorized wheelchair before, so you're going to have to get used to it."

"If'n I wanted to go slow, I woulda stayed in my old chair," she half-shouted. "Ain't no use to have'n this if'n I don't use it."

Val emerged from Aunt Ruth's bedroom, shaking her head, "I told her to wait for me, but, no! Granny's too damn impatient!"

"And you're too damn slow," Aunt Ruth fired back. "I'm the one who's 'posed to be old, but you take longer than me to get ready. Beats all I ever seen!"

"That's because you're already perfect," Val reasoned. "I'm still a work in a progress. Besides," she added, "you've only been shot once. This is the second time around for me."

Betty dropped the broken pieces of knickknacks into the trash, saying, "Granny, you ain't got no business being out this soon after just getting out of hospital. Why in the world would you want to go to Ben Walden's funeral anyway?"

"Well, now – first, don't you go sass'n off at me! Even if I wasn't yo' granny, I'm get'n ready to be 111 years old, so ain't no damn body fix'n to tell me what to do! And the second thang is, me and Ben Walden's mama been friends since before any of y'all was born, so I'm going out of respect for her."

"Yes, ma'am," Betty replied as she, Val and Henry finished picking the broken items up from the floor.

"Bobby, did you talk to that real estate man like I asked you?"

"Yes, ma'am, I did. It's all done. You'll have the paperwork by the end of the day, deeding the house to the McDowells. That was a very generous thing that you did, Aunt Ruth."

"Weren't noth'n 'bout being generous," she replied. "It was only the right thing to do, 'specially after you told me you found out that that McDowell boy was only gonna ask me for enough to buy his grandparents a house and move 'em down here."

She pulled a tissue from tha table and wiped her eyes, adding, "I wouldn't have it if it weren't for him. And look at the price he paid for it."

"Well, it was still a nice thing," Carroll insisted.

Aunt Ruth swished her hand toward him like he was a gnat.

"You talk'n 'bout me like I'm Oprah," she scoffed. "First, I can't believe they gonna let me keep it all. It ain't like it was mine to start with."

"It was on your land," Carroll reminded her, "and although there's still some legalities to go through, it looks like it's all yours."

"Oh, you can be sure they'll get their share in taxes!" said Val.

"You got that right!" Henry chimed in.

"It's still hard to believe," Betty said. "Granny was already comfortable financially, and she's never cared about being rich or anything."

"Well, that ain't entirely true," Ruth Jackson admitted, "I had me a dream one time – that I won the lottery. It was so good that it woke me up. I wrote the numbers down and played 'em the next day and the rest of the week. Didn't win a damn thang though!" she added disgustedly, causing them to erupt into laughter.

"Other thang is, I got my family set, so they gonna be taken care of. What am I gonna do, go to Las Vegas? Besides, that place next door's been empty for go'in on a year and I like that I get to pick my neighbors my own self."

Carroll opened the screen door.

"Are you sure that you want to go to the funeral?" he asked her.

"Now, you just heard what I told Betty about his mama being my friend, so don't be asking no more," she chided.

Henry was carefully guiding the wheelchair down the ramp toward the sidewalk when Aunt Ruth added, "And I wanna make sure that little bastard is really dead."

"Granny!" Betty exclaimed, shaking her head.

"Oh hell! A few minutes ago you were wondering why I was going to the funeral and now you're feel'n sorry for the little son of a bitch? He tried to kill me!"

"Well, you turned out to be more deadly with an empty whiskey glass than he was with two guns," said Henry.

"I told him not to disrespect me in my own house," she reminded them. "Besides calling me names, he didn't give us enough time to enjoy finishing off that bottle of Jefferson's proper."

"It's still hard to believe that it was the blow to the head by the whiskey glass that did it and not the hit he took from the SWAT sniper," Val said, as she reached down and picked a speck of something from her granny's dress.

"That comes from her days as a ballplayer," Betty informed them.

"You played ball, Granny?" asked Val.

"I sure did – played in the Negro League with Toni Stone, Mamie "Peanuts" Johnson and Connie Morgan. Peanuts always told folks that I was the only pitcher that she was afraid of."

"I'm going to have to hear that story for sure," said Carroll.

He stepped to the rear passenger door, opened it and moved aside as Henry guided the chair toward the vehicle.

"I'm guess'n you opened that door for Betty," Aunt Ruth quipped, "– 'cause I'm riding in the front!"

Betty giggled, "I'll sit there, Bobby," she said as she climbed into the back of the car.

Henry and Val were loading Aunt Ruth's chair into the back as Carroll helped her onto the front passenger seat.

"Bobby?" she said.

"Yes, ma'am?" he answered as he made sure her dress was clear of the car door.

"You plan'n to come back for my birthday party next month?"

"Wild horses couldn't keep me away, Aunt Ruth."

She reached over and patted his hand, "Well I 'spect you know what to get me for my present then, don't you?" she asked, smacking her lips.

He pulled the strap snug and clicked her seatbelt.

"Yes ma'am. I 'spect I do."

ABOUT THE AUTHOR

Chet Powell retired from his law enforcement career in spring of 2010. After spending the remainder of that year rescuing wildlife throughout the Gulf of Mexico following the Deepwater Horizon oil spill disaster, he founded the Georgia Wildlife Rescue Association, which has since merged with WREN, the *Wildlife Resource and Education Network*. He also formed KOLORS; a youth program that teaches leadership and tolerance. His collection of nonfiction short stories entitled, *C.J.'s Boy*, will be released in Fall of 2016.